FROM THE BESTSELLING AUTHOR
WHO SHOCKED MILLIONS WITH . . .
SUFFER THE CHILDREN
CRY FOR THE STRANGERS
COMES THE BLIND FURY
PUNISH THE SINNERS
WHEN THE WIND BLOWS
NOW, COMES THE ULTIMATE
NIGHTMARE . . .

JOHN SAUL'S
THE GOD PROJECT

"Of his six books, *The God Project* is by far the best written, the best plotted, and certainly the most entertaining."
—*New York Daily News*

"Every paranoid twinge . . . is expertly, shockingly exploited in Saul's nightmare tale."
—*Cosmopolitan*

"Each chapter leaves you breathless for more . . . if you're a patsy for a fast, enjoyable book, you'll like *The God Project*. The characters are well defined and carry the action forward at a fast clip. And the ending has a few wonderful twists."
—*San Diego Tribune*

Saul is "a writer with the touch for raising gooseflesh."
—*Detroit News*

"Here is the kind of book you can sail through . . . going faster and faster . . . tantalizing."
—*The San Francisco Chronicle*

"Saul's fans will gobble it up and ask for more."
—*Kirkus Reviews*

"A chilling tale."

—*Publishers Weekly*

"If you want perfect summer reading, try *The God Project*."
—*Fort Worth Star-Telegram*

The
GOD
PROJECT
John Saul

BANTAM BOOKS
Toronto · New York · London · Sydney

THE GOD PROJECT
A Bantam Book

Bantam Hardcover edition / September 1982
Bantam rack-size edition / June 1983

Library of Congress Catalogue Card No.: 82-90289

ISBN 0-553-23336-X

Published simultaneously in the United States and Canada

PRINTED IN THE UNITED STATES OF AMERICA

H   0 9 8 7 6 5 4 3 2 1

For Sarita,
and the memory of Leon

The
GOD
PROJECT

Chapter 1

SALLY MONTGOMERY LEANED DOWN and kissed her daughter, then tucked the pink crocheted blanket that her mother had made in honor of Julie's birth—and which Sally hated—around the baby's shoulders. Julie, six months old, squirmed sleepily, half-opened her eyes, and gurgled.

"Are you my little angel?" Sally murmured, touching the baby's tiny nose. Again Julie gurgled, and Sally wiped a speck of saliva from her chin, kissed her once more, then left the bedroom. She had never quite gotten around to converting it into a nursery.

It wasn't that she hadn't intended to. Indeed, the room had been planned as a nursery ever since Jason had been born eight years earlier. She and Steve had made elaborate plans, even gone as far as picking out wallpaper and ordering curtains. But Sally Montgomery simply wasn't the decorating type. Besides, though she had never admitted it to anyone but Steve, the idea of redoing an entire room just for the enjoyment of an infant had always struck her as silly. All it meant was that you had to keep redoing it as the baby grew up.

In the gloom of the night-light, Sally glanced around the room and decided she had been right. The curtains, though they were blue, were still bright and clean, and

1

the walls, still the same white they had been when she and Steve had bought the house nine years ago, were covered with an array of prints and pictures that any self-respecting baby should enjoy—Mickey Mouse on one wall and Donald Duck opposite him, with a batch of Pooh characters filling up the empty spaces. Even the mobile that turned slowly above Julie's crib had been chosen as much for the quality of its construction as for its design, though Sally had, almost reluctantly, come to appreciate the abstract forms which the saleslady had assured her would "do wonders for Baby's imagination." When they were grown, and had children of their own, she would pull the pictures and the mobile out of the attic and split them between Jason and Julie, who by then would have come to a new appreciation of them.

Chuckling at what she knew was an overdeveloped sense of practicality, Sally quietly closed the door to the baby's room and went downstairs. As she passed the door to the master bedroom she paused, listening to Steve's snoring, and was tempted to forget the report she was working on and crawl into bed with him. But again, the practical side of her came to the fore, and she pulled that door, too, closed and went downstairs.

She glanced at the papers covering the desk. Better to get the report done tonight, and have the papers cleared off before Steve came down in the morning and demanded to know why "his" desk was cluttered with "her" things. Years ago she had given up trying to convince him that the desk was "theirs." Steve had certain territorial ideas. The kitchen, for instance, was hers, even though he was a better cook than she was. The bathrooms were hers, too, while the family room, which by all rights should definitely have been theirs, was his. On the other hand, their bedroom, which they both loved, was hers, while the garage, which neither of them particularly wanted, was his.

The yard, being apart from the house, had somehow managed to wind up being "theirs," which meant that whoever complained about it had to do something about it. All in all, Sally decided as she wandered into "her"

2

kitchen and began making a pot of tea, the division of the house and yard had worked out very well, like everything else in their marriage. She stared at the pan of water on the stove and idly wondered if it was true that as long as she watched it, it wouldn't boil. Then, for her own amusement, she picked up a pencil and began jotting figures on the scratch pad beside the telephone. Figuring the resistance of the metal in the electrical coils, the power of the current, and the volume of water, she came to the conclusion that the water should start boiling in eight minutes, give or take fifteen seconds, whether she watched it or not.

And that, she thought as the water began bubbling right on time, is the pleasure of having a mathematical mind. She poured the water over the tea bags and carried the pot and a cup back to the desk.

Much of the clutter was made up of computer printouts, and it was Sally's job to analyze the program of which the printouts were the results. Somewhere in the program there was a bug, and the college admissions office, which had dreamed up the program in the first place, had asked Sally to find it. The program, designed to review the records of hopeful high school seniors, had disqualified every applicant for the fall semester. When Sally had suggested that perhaps the program was perfect and the applicants simply weren't qualified, the dean of admissions had been less than amused. Soberly, he had handed Sally the program and the output, and asked her to find the problem by Monday morning.

And find it she would, for Sally Montgomery, as well as being beautiful, was brainy. Too brainy for her own good, her mother had always told her. Now, as she began analyzing the program in comparison to the printout it had produced, she could almost hear her mother's voice telling her she shouldn't be down here working in the middle of the night; she should be upstairs "loving her husband."

"You'll lose him," Phyllis Paine had told Sally over and over again. "A woman's place is in the home, loving her husband and her children. It's not normal for a woman your age to work."

"Then why did I go to college?" Sally had countered back in the days before she had given up arguing with her mother.

"Well, it wasn't to major in mathematics! I'd always hoped you'd do something with your music. Music is good for a woman, particularly the piano. In my day, all women played the piano."

It had gone on for years. Sally had finally stopped trying to explain to her mother that times had changed. She and Steve had agreed from the start that her career was every bit as important as his own. Her mother simply couldn't understand, and never missed an opportunity to let Sally know that in her opinion—the only one that counted, of course—a woman's place was in the home. "Maybe it's all right for women to work down in New York, but in Eastbury, Massachusetts, it just doesn't look right!"

And maybe, Sally reflected as she spotted the error in the program and began rewriting the flawed area, she's right. Maybe we should have gone out to Phoenix last year, and gotten out of this stuffy little town. I could have found a job out there, probably a better one than I have here. But they hadn't gone. They had agreed that since Sally was happy at the college, and Steve saw a glowing future for both of them in Eastbury's burgeoning electronics industry, they should stay right where they were, and where they'd always been.

Until the last few years, Eastbury had been one of those towns in which the older people talked about how good things used to be, and the younger people wondered how they could get out. But then, five years ago, the great change had begun. A change in the tax structure had encouraged fledgling businesses to come to Eastbury. And it had worked. Buildings which had once housed shoe factories and textile mills, then lain empty and crumbling for decades, were bustling once again. People were working—no longer at slave wages on killing shifts, but with flexible hours and premium salaries,

4

creating the electronic miracles that were changing the face of the country.

Eastbury itself, of course, had not changed much. It was still a small town, its plain façade cheered only by a new civic center which was a clumsy attempt at using new money to create old buildings. What had resulted was a city hall that looked like a bank posing as a colonial mansion, and an elaborately landscaped "town square" entirely fenced in with wrought iron fancywork. Still, Eastbury was a safe place, small enough so the Montgomerys knew almost everyone in town, yet large enough to support the college that employed Sally.

The tea was cold, and Sally glanced at the clock, only slightly surprised to see that she'd been working for more than an hour. But the program was done, and Sally was sure that tomorrow morning it would produce the desired printouts. Eastbury College would have a freshman class next year after all.

She meticulously straightened up the desk, readying it for the onslaught of telephone calls that greeted Steve every morning. Using his talents as a salesman in tandem with the contacts he had made growing up in Eastbury, Steve had turned the town into what he liked to refer to as his "private gold mine." Mornings he often worked at home, and afternoons he spent either in his office or at the athletic club he had helped found, not out of any great interest in sports, but because he knew the executives of the new companies liked to work in what they called casual surroundings. Steve believed in giving people what they wanted. In turn, they usually gave him what he wanted, which was invariably a small piece of whatever action was about to take place. When asked what he did, Steve usually defined himself as an entrepreneur. In truth, he was a salesman who specialized in putting people together to the benefit of all concerned. Over the years, it had paid handsomely, not only for the Montgomerys, but for the whole town. It had been Steve who had convinced Inter-Technics to donate a main-frame computer to Eastbury that would tie all

5

the town's small computers together, though Sally had never been convinced that it was one of his better ideas.

But now Steve was beginning to get bored. During the last few months he had begun to talk about the two of them going into business for themselves. Sally would become an independent consultant, and Steve would sell her services.

And mother will call him a pimp, Sally thought. She closed the roll-top desk and went into the kitchen. She was about to pour the untouched tea down the drain when she changed her mind and began reheating it. She wasn't tired, and her work was done, and the children were asleep, and there were no distractions. Tonight would be a good time for her to think over Steve's idea.

In many ways, it was appealing. The two of them would be working together—an idea she liked—but it also meant they would be together almost all the time. She wasn't sure she liked that.

Was there such a thing as too much togetherness? She had a good marriage, and didn't want to disturb it. Deep inside, she had a feeling that one of the reasons their marriage was so good was that both of them had interests beyond the marriage. Working together would end that. Suddenly their entire lives would be bound up in their marriage. That could be bad.

Sally poured herself a cup of the tea, still thinking about the possibilities. And then, in her head, she heard Steve's voice, and saw his blue eyes smiling at her. "You'll never know till you try, will you?" he was asking. Alone in the kitchen, Sally laughed softly and made up her mind. No, she said to herself, I won't. And if it doesn't work, we can always do something else. She finished the tea, put the cup in the sink, and went upstairs.

She was about to go into the bedroom when she paused, listening.

The house was silent, as it always was at that time of night. She listened for a moment, then went on into the bedroom and began undressing. The near-total darkness was broken only by the faint glow of a streetlight half a block away.

She slipped into bed next to Steve, and his arms came out to hold her. She snuggled in, resting her head on his shoulder, her fingers twining in the mat of blond hair that covered his chest.

She pressed herself closer to Steve and felt his arm tighten around her. She closed her eyes, ready to drift off to sleep, content in the knowledge that everything was as close to perfect as she could ever have wanted it, despite what her mother might think. It was, after all, her life, and not her mother's.

And then she was wide-awake again, her eyes open, her body suddenly rigid.

Had she heard something?

Maybe she should wake Steve.

No. Why wake Steve when she was already awake?

She slipped out of his arms and put on a robe. In the hall she stood still, listening carefully, trying to remember if she had locked the doors earlier.

She had.

She could remember it clearly. Right after Steve had gone up to bed, she had gone around the house, throwing the bolts, a habit she had developed during Steve's time on the road, when she had been alone with Jason for so many nights. The habit had never been broken.

The silence gathered around her, and she could hear her heart beating in the darkness.

What was it?

If there was nothing, what was she afraid of?

She told herself she was being silly, and turned back to the bedroom.

Still, the feeling would not go away.

I'll look in on the children, she decided.

She moved down the hall to Jason's room and opened the door. He was in his bed, the covers twisted around his feet, one arm thrown over the teddy bear he still occasionally slept with. Sally gently freed the covers and tucked her son in. Jason moved in his sleep and turned over. In the dim glow from the window, he looked like a miniature version of his father, his blond hair tangled, his little jaw square, with the same dimple in his chin that Sally had always thought made Steve look sexy. How many hearts are you going to break when you grow up? Sally wondered. She leaned over, and kissed Jason gently.

"Aw, Mom," the little boy said.

Sally pretended to scowl at her son. "You were supposed to be asleep."

"I was playin' possum," Jason replied. "Is something wrong?"

"Can't a mother say good night anymore?" Sally asked.

"You're always kissin' me," Jason complained.

Sally leaned down and kissed him again. "Be glad someone does. Not every kid is so lucky." She straightened up and started out of the room. "And don't kick the covers off. You'll catch pneumonia." She left Jason's room, knowing he'd kick the covers off again in five minutes, and that he wouldn't catch pneumonia. If Julie grew up as healthily as Jason had, she would be twice blessed. As she approached Julie's room, she began trying to calculate the odds of raising two children without having to cope with any sicknesses. The odds, she decided, were too narrow to be worth thinking about.

She let herself into the room, and suddenly her sense of apprehension flooded back to her.

She crossed to the crib and looked down at Julie. The baby was as different from her brother as she was from Steve. Julie had Sally's own almost-black hair, dark eyes, and even in her infancy the same delicate bone structure. She's like a doll, Sally thought. A tiny little doll. In the dim light the baby's skin was pale, nearly white, and Sally thought she looked cold, though the pink blanket was still tucked around her shoulders as Sally had left it earlier.

Sally frowned.

Julie was an active baby, never lying still for very long.

Apparently she hadn't moved for more than an hour.

Sally reached down, and touched Julie's face.

It was as cold as it looked.

As she picked up her tiny daughter, Sally Montgomery felt her life falling apart around her.

It wasn't true.

It couldn't be true.

There was nothing wrong with Julie.

She was cold. That's all, just cold. All she had to do was cuddle the baby, and warm her, and everything would be all right again.

Sally Montgomery began screaming—a high, thin, piercing wail that shattered the night.

Steve Montgomery stood in the doorway staring at his wife. "Sally? Sally, what's wrong?" He moved forward tentatively, watching her as she stood near the window, rocking back and forth, muttering in a strangled voice to the tiny form in her arms. Then he was beside her, trying to take the baby out of her arms. Sally's hold on the child tightened, and her eyes, wide and beseeching, found his.

"Call the hospital," she whispered, her voice desperate. "Call now. She's sick. Oh, Steve, she's sick!"

Steve touched Julie's icy flesh and his mind reeled. No! No, she can't be. She just can't be. He turned away and started out of the room, only to be stopped by Jason, who was standing just inside the door, his eyes wide and curious.

"What's wrong?" the little boy asked, looking up at his father. Then he looked past Steve, toward his mother. "Did something happen to Julie?"

"She's—she's sick," Steve said, desperately wanting to believe it. "She's sick, and we have to call the doctor. Come on."

Pulling Jason with him, Steve went into the next room and picked up the phone on the bedside table, dialing frantically. While he waited for someone to answer, he reached out and pulled his son to him, but Jason wriggled out of his father's arms.

"Is she dead?" he asked. "Is Julie dead?"

Steve nodded mutely, and then the operator at Eastbury Community Hospital came on the line. While he was ordering an ambulance for his daughter, he kept his eyes on his son, but after a moment Jason, his face impassive, turned and left the room.

Chapter 2

EASTBURY COMMUNITY HOSPITAL, despite its name, was truly neither a hospital, nor a community service. It was, in actuality, a privately owned clinic. It had started, thirty years earlier, as the office of Dr. Arthur Wiseman. As his practice grew, Wiseman had begun to take on partners. Ten years before, with five other doctors, he had formed Eastbury Community Hospital, Inc., and built the clinic. Now there were seven doctors, all of them specialists, but none of them so specialized they could not function as general practitioners. In addition to the clinic, there was a tiny emergency room, an operating room, a ward, and a few private rooms. For Eastbury, the system worked well: each of the patients at Eastbury Community felt that he had several doctors, and each of the doctors always had six consultants on call. It was the hope of everyone that someday in the not-too-distant future, Eastbury Community would grow into a true hospital, though for the moment it was still a miniature.

In the operating room, Dr. Mark Malone—who, at the age of forty-two, was still not reconciled to the fact that he would forever be known as Young Dr. Malone— smiled down at the unconscious ten-year-old child on the table. A routine, if emergency, appendectomy. He

11

winked at the nurse who had assisted him, then expertly snipped a sample of tissue from the excised organ, and gave it to an aide.

"The usual tests," he said. He glanced at the anesthetist, who nodded to him to indicate that everything was all right, then left the operating room and began washing up. He was staring disconsolately at the clock and wondering why so many appendixes chose to go bad in the wee hours of the morning, when he heard his name on the page.

"Dr. Malone, please. Dr. Malone."

Wiping his hands, he picked up the phone. "Malone."

"You're wanted in the emergency room, Dr. Malone," the voice of the operator informed him.

"Oh, Christ." Malone wracked his brain, trying to remember who was supposed to be on call that night.

The operator answered his unasked question. "It's—it's one of your patients, Doctor."

Malone's frown deepened, but he only grunted into the phone and hung up. He slipped off his surgical gown, put on a white jacket, then started for the emergency room, already sure of what had happened.

The duty man would have handled the emergency. The call to him meant that one of his patients had died, and, since he was in the clinic, someone had decided he should break the news to the parents. He braced himself, preparing for the worst part of his job.

He found the nurse, shaken and pale, just outside the emergency room. "What's happened?" he asked.

"It's a baby," the nurse replied, her voice quaking. She nodded toward the door. "She's in there with her mother. It's Julie Montgomery, and Sally won't let go of her. She just keeps insisting that she has to make the baby warm." Her voice faltered, then she went on. "I—I called Dr. Wiseman."

Malone nodded. Though Julie Montgomery was his patient, the child's mother was Art Wiseman's. "Is he coming?"

"He should be here any minute," the nurse promised. Even as she spoke, the distinguished gray-haired figure of Arthur Wiseman strode purposefully through the door from the parking lot.

The older doctor sized the situation up at once.

Sally Montgomery was sitting on a chair, with Julie cradled in her arms. She looked up at Wiseman, and her eyes were wide and empty.

Shock, Wiseman thought. She's in shock. He moved toward her and tried to take Julie from her arms. Sally drew back and turned away slightly.

"She's cold," Sally said, her voice no more than a whisper. "She's cold, and I have to make her warm."

"I know, Sally," Wiseman said softly. "But why don't you let us do it? Isn't that why you brought her here?"

Sally stared at him for a moment, then nodded her head. "Yes . . . I—I guess so. She's not sick, Dr. Wiseman. I know she's not sick. She's—she's just cold. So cold . . ." Her voice trailed off, and she surrendered the tiny body to the doctor. Then she covered her face with her hands and began to cry. Wiseman gave Julie to Mark Malone.

"See what you can do," he said softly.

Leaving Sally Montgomery under Wiseman's care, Malone took Julie Montgomery's body into a treatment cubicle. For the child, he knew already, there was no hope of resuscitation. But even knowing it was already far too late, he began trying to revive her. A few minutes later, holding Julie as if his will alone could bring her back to life, he felt a presence in the room and glanced up. It was Wiseman.

"Is she gone?" he asked.

Malone nodded. "There's nothing I can do," he said. "She's been dead at least an hour."

Wiseman sighed. "Any idea what happened?"

"I can't be sure yet, but it looks like SIDS."

Wiseman's eyes closed, and he ran his hand through his hair, brushing it back from his forehead. Damn, he swore to himself. Why does it happen? Why? Then he heard Malone's voice again.

"Is Steve here?"

"He was calling someone. His mother-in-law, I think. I ordered Valium for Sally."

"Good. Do you want me to talk to Steve?"

Wiseman, his eyes fixed on Julie Montgomery's tiny body, didn't answer for a moment. When he did, his voice was hollow. "I'll do it," he said. "I know Steve almost as well as I know Sally." He paused, then spoke again. "Will you do an autopsy?"

"Of course," Malone replied, "but I don't think we'll find anything. Julie Montgomery was one of the healthiest babies I've ever seen. And I saw her two days ago. Nothing wrong. Nothing at all. Shit!"

Malone looked down into the tiny face cradled in his arms. Julie Montgomery, to look at her, seemed to be asleep. Except for the deadly pallor and the coldness of her flesh. No injuries, no signs of sickness.

Only death.

"I'll take her downstairs," Malone said. He turned away, and Wiseman watched him until he disappeared around a corner. Only then did he return to the waiting room, where Steve Montgomery was now sitting by his wife, holding her hand. He looked up at the doctor, his eyes questioning. Wiseman shook his head.

"There was nothing that could be done," he said, touching Steve on the shoulder. "Nothing at all."

"But what happened?" Steve asked. "She was fine. There wasn't anything wrong with her. Nothing!"

"We don't know yet," Wiseman replied. "We'll do an autopsy, but I don't think we'll find anything."

"Not find anything?" Sally asked. The emptiness was gone from her eyes now, but her face was filled with a pain that Wiseman found almost more worrisome than the shock had been. She'll get over it, he told himself. It'll be hard, but she'll get over it.

"Why don't you two go home?" he suggested. "There's no reason to stay here. And we'll talk in the morning. All right?"

Sally got to her feet and leaned against Steve. "What happened?" she asked. "Babies don't just die, do they?"

Wiseman watched her, trying to judge her condition. Had it been anyone but Sally Montgomery, he would have waited until morning, but he'd known Sally for years, and he knew she was strong. The Valium had calmed her down and would keep her calm.

"Sometimes they do," he said softly. "It's called sudden infant death syndrome. That's what Mark Malone thinks happened to Julie."

"Oh, God," Steve Montgomery said. He saw Julie's face, her dancing eyes and smiling mouth, her tiny hands reaching for him, grasping his finger with all her own, laughing and gurgling.

And then nothing.

Tears began running down his face. He did nothing to wipe them away.

As the spring dawn crept over Eastbury, Steve Montgomery stood up and went to the window. He and Sally were in the living room, where they'd been all the long night, neither of them wanting to go to bed, neither of them willing to face whatever thoughts might come in the darkness. But now the darkness was gone, and Steve wandered around the room, turning off the lamps.

"Don't," Sally whispered. "Please don't."

Understanding her, Steve turned the lights back on, then went back to sit beside her once more, holding her close against him, neither of them speaking, but drawing strength from each other's presence. After a while there was a sound from upstairs, and then footsteps coming down the stairs. A moment later Sally's mother was in the room. She paused, then came to the sofa and drew Sally into her arms.

"My poor baby," she said softly, her voice soothing. "Oh, my poor baby. What happened? Sally, what happened?"

Her mother's voice seemed to trigger something in Sally, and her tears, the tears that should have been drained from her hours earlier, began to flow once more. She leaned against her mother, her body heaving with her sobs. Over her daughter's head, Phyllis Paine's eyes met her son-in-law's.

"What happened, Steve?" she asked. "What happened to my granddaughter?"

I have to control myself, Steve thought. For Sally, I have to be strong. I have to tell people what happened, and I have to make arrangements, and I have to take care of my wife and my son. Then another thought came to him: I'll never be able to do it. I'll come apart, and my insides will fall out. Oh, God, why did you have to take Julie? Why not me? She was only a baby! Just a little baby.

He wanted to cry too, wanted to bury his head in his wife's bosom, and let go of his pain, and yet he knew he couldn't. Not now, perhaps not ever. He met his mother-in-law's steady gaze.

"Nothing happened to her," he said, forcing himself to keep his voice steady. "She just died. It's called sudden infant death syndrome."

Phyllis's eyes hardened. "A lot of nonsense," she said. "All it means is that the doctors don't know what happened. But something happened to that child. I want to know what."

Her words penetrated Sally's grief. She pulled herself from her mother's embrace and faced her. "What do you mean?" she asked, her voice strident. "What are you saying?"

Phyllis stood up, searching for the right words. She knew where the blame lay, knew very well, but she wouldn't say it. Not yet. Later, when Sally had recovered from the shock, they would have a talk. For now, she would take care of her daughter ... as her daughter should have taken care of Julie.

"I'm not saying anything," she maintained. "All I'm saying is that doctors like to cover for themselves. Babies don't just die, Sally. There's always a reason. But if the doctors are too lazy to find the reason, or don't know enough, they call it crib death. But there *is* always a reason," she repeated. Her eyes moved from Sally to Steve, then back to Sally. When she spoke again, her voice was gentler. "I'm going to stay here for a few days—I'll take care of Jason and the house. Don't either of you worry about anything."

"Thanks, Phyl," Steve said quietly. "Thanks."

"Isn't that what mothers are for?" Phyllis asked. "To take care of their children?" Her eyes settled once more on Sally, then she turned and went back up the stairs. A moment later they heard her talking to Jason, and Jason's own voice, piping loud as he pummeled his grandmother with questions. Sally was silent for a long time, then she spoke to Steve without looking at him.

"She thinks I did something to Julie," she said dully. "Or didn't do something. She thinks it was my fault."

Inwardly, Steve groaned at the hopelessness in his wife's voice, and reached out to hold her. "No, honey, she doesn't think that at all. It's just—it's just Phyllis. You know how she is."

Sally nodded. I know how she is, she thought. But does she know how I am? Does she know me? Her train of thought was broken as Jason came pounding down the stairs. He stood in the middle of the floor, his pajamas falling down, his hands on his hips.

"What happened to Julie?" he asked.

Steve bit his lip. How could he explain it? How could he explain death to an eight-year-old, when he didn't even understand it himself? "Julie died," he said. "We don't know why. She . . . she just died."

Jason was silent, his eyes thoughtful. And then he nodded, and frowned slightly. "Do I have to go to school today?" he asked.

Too tired, too shocked, too drained to recognize the innocence of her son's words, Sally only heard their naive callousness. "Of course you have to go to school today," she screamed. "Do you think I can take care of you? Do you think I can do everything? Do you think . . ." Her voice failed her, and she collapsed, sobbing, back onto the sofa as her mother hurried down the stairs. Jason, his face pale with bafflement and hurt, stared at his mother, then at his father.

"It's all right," Phyllis told him, scooping him into her arms. "Of course you don't have to go to school today. You go upstairs and get dressed, then I'll fix your breakfast. Okay?" She kissed the boy on the cheek and put him back on the floor.

"Okay, Grandma," Jason said softly. Then, with another curious glance at his parents, he ran up the stairs.

When he was gone, Steve put his arms around his wife. "Go to bed, sweetheart," he begged. "You're worn out, and Phyllis can handle everything. We'll take care of you, and everything will be all right. Please?"

Too exhausted to protest, Sally let herself be led upstairs, let Steve undress her and put her to bed, let him tuck her in. But when he had kissed her and left her alone, she didn't sleep.

Instead, she remembered her mother's words. "Isn't that what mothers are for? To take care of their children?" It was an accusation, and Sally knew it. And she knew, deep in her heart, that she had no answer for the accusation. Perhaps she had done something—or not done something—that had caused Julie to die.

Hadn't she considered aborting Julie? Hadn't she and Steve talked about it for a long time, trying to decide whether they really wanted another child? Hadn't they, finally, talked until it was too late?

But they had loved Julie once she was born. Loved her as much as Jason, maybe even more.

Or had they?

Maybe they had only pretended to love her because they knew it was their duty: You have to love your children.

Maybe she hadn't loved Julie enough.

Maybe, deep inside, she still hadn't wanted Julie.

As she drifted slowly into a restless sleep, Sally could still hear her mother's voice, see her mother's eyes, accusing her.

And her daughter was dead, and she had no way of proving that it hadn't been her fault.

She couldn't prove it to her mother; she couldn't prove it to herself.

As she slept, a germ of guilt entered Sally Montgomery's soul, a guilt as deadly for her soul as a cancer might be for her body.

In one night, Sally Montgomery's life had changed.

Chapter 3

Randy Corliss poked aimlessly at the bowl of soggy cereal. He had already made up his mind not to eat it.

Five more minutes, and his mother would be gone.

Then he could throw the cereal into the garbage, swipe a Twinkie, and be on his way. He stared intently at the minute hand on the clock, not quite sure if he could actually see it moving. He wished his mother would buy a clock like the ones at school, where you could really see the hands jump forward every minute, but he knew she wouldn't. Maybe if he asked his father next weekend . . .

He mulled the idea over in his nine-year-old mind, only half-listening as his mother gave her usual speech about coming right home after school, not answering the door unless he knew who was outside, and reporting his arrival to Mrs.-Willis-next-door. At last she leaned over, kissed him on the cheek, and disappeared into the garage adjoining the kitchen. Only when he heard her start the car, and knew she was really gone, did Randy get up and dump the loathsome cereal.

At five minutes after eight, Randy Corliss went out into the bright spring morning and began the long walk that would take him first to Jason Montgomery's house, and then to school. All around him children his own age were drifting from their homes onto the sidewalks, forming groups of twos and threes, whispering and giggling among themselves. All of them, it seemed, had plenty of friends.

All of them except Randy Corliss.

Randy didn't understand exactly why he had so few friends. In fact, a long time ago, when he was six, he'd had lots of friends. But in the last three years, most of them had drifted away.

It wasn't as if he was the only one whose parents were divorced. Lots of the kids lived with only their mothers, and some of them even lived with just their fathers. Those were the kids Randy envied—the ones who lived with their fathers. He decided to talk about that with his father this weekend too. Maybe this time he could convince him. He'd been trying for almost a year now—ever since the time last summer when he'd run away.

Last summer hadn't been much fun at all. Nobody would play with him, and he'd spent the first month of the summer watching the other kids, waiting for them to ask him to play ball, or go for a hike, or go swimming, or do any of the other things they were doing.

But they hadn't, and when he finally broke down and asked Billy Semple what was wrong, Billy, who had been his last friend, only looked at him for a long time, then stared at the cast on his leg, shrugged, and said nothing.

Randy had known what that was all about. He and Billy had been out playing in the Semples' backyard one day, and Randy had decided it might be fun to jump off the roof. First they had tried the garage roof, and it had been easy. Randy had jumped first, landing in the Semples' compost heap, and Billy had followed.

Then Randy had suggested they try the house roof, and Billy had looked fearfully up at the steep pitch. But in the end, not wanting to appear cowardly, Billy had gone along with it. The two of them had gotten a ladder and climbed to the eaves, where they had perched for a couple of minutes, staring down. Randy had been the first to jump.

He had hit the ground, and for a second had felt a flash of pain in his ankles. But then he had rolled, and by the time he had gotten to his feet, the pain was gone. He'd grinned up at Billy.

"Come on!" he'd yelled. "It's easy." When Billy still hesitated, Randy had begun taunting him, and finally, just as Billy made up his mind, Mrs. Semple had come out to the backyard to see what was going on. She'd appeared just in time to see her son hurtle down from the roof and break his right leg. Furious, she'd ordered Randy out of the yard, and later that afternoon she'd called Randy's mother to tell her that Randy was no longer welcome in her home.

Enough, she'd said, was enough. She'd hoped that it wouldn't come to this, but after today she had to join the rest of the mothers in the neighborhood, and forbid her son to play with Randy Corliss anymore.

The fact that it had been an accident had made no difference. Randy was a daredevil, a bad influence.

And so the summer had dragged on. Randy, getting lonelier every day, had begun going off by himself, roaming in the woods, prowling around the town, wishing he knew what had gone wrong.

Then he had met Jason Montgomery, and even though Jason was a year younger than he was, he'd liked Jason right away. Jason, he'd decided, wasn't like the rest of the kids. The rest of them were all cowards, but not Jason. They'd become best friends the day after they met, and all this year Randy had stopped by Jason's house every day on his way to school.

Today he arrived at the Montgomerys' house, and went around to the back, as he always did.

"Jason! Jaaaason!" he called. The back door opened, and he recognized Jason's grandmother. "Isn't Jason here?" he asked.

"He's not going to school today," Jason's grandmother told him. She was starting to close the door, when Jason suddenly appeared, scooting out from behind his grandmother and slipping through the door.

"Hi," Jason said.

Randy stared at his friend curiously. "You sick?" he asked.

"Naw," Jason replied. Then he looked directly at Randy. "My little sister died last night, so I don't have to go to school today."

Randy absorbed the information and wondered what he was supposed to say. He'd only seen Jason's baby sister once, and to him she hadn't seemed like anything special. All she'd done was cry, and Jason had told him she peed all the time. "What happened to her?" he asked at last.

Jason hesitated, then frowned. "I dunno. Dad says she just died. Anyway, I get to stay home from school."

"That's neat," Randy said. Then he frowned at Jason. "Did you do something to her?"

"Why would I do that?" Jason countered.

Randy shifted uncomfortably. "I don't know. I just—I just wondered. Billy Semple's mother thought—" He broke off, unsure how to say what he was thinking. Billy Semple's mother had thought he was trying to hurt Billy, even though she never said it out loud.

"Did you push Billy off the roof?" Jason asked.

"No."

"And I didn't do anything to Julie," Jason said. "At least, I don't think I did."

Then, before Jason could say anything else, his grandmother opened the back door and told him to come back into the house. Randy watched as his friend disappeared inside, then started once more on his way to school.

He didn't really want to go today. Without Jason there, it wouldn't be any fun at all. It would be like it had been last summer, before he had met Jason, while he was waiting for his friends to come back.

Waiting, though, is much easier for an adult than for a nine-year-old, and while he was waiting, Randy had begun entertaining himself by getting into mischief.

He'd started swiping things from the dime store. Nothing big, just a few little things.

Then one day Mr. Higgins, who owned the dime store, had caught him.

Randy would never forget that day. He'd almost been out of the store when he'd felt a hand on his arm and turned to see Mr. Higgins glowering down at him, demanding that he empty his pockets.

The yo-yo didn't have a price tag on it, but Randy didn't even try to pretend he hadn't stolen it. His face pale, his eyes brimming with tears, he'd stammered out an apology and promised never to do it again.

But Mr. Higgins hadn't let the matter go. He'd called the Eastbury police and explained that while he didn't want to press charges, he thought it would be a good idea if someone put the fear of God into Randy Corliss. "A good scare," Randy had heard him say into the phone. "That'll straighten him out." Randy had been taken to the police station, and shown a cell, and told that he might have to spend the night there. Then they'd fingerprinted him and taken his picture, and warned him that if he ever tried to steal anything again, he'd be sent to prison.

When they let him go, Randy was shaking. That night, he began to think about running away.

Nobody liked him, and his mother never seemed to have any time for him. The only person who cared about him, he decided, was his father. He'd called his father, and begged him to come and get him, but Jim Corliss had told him that he couldn't, not yet. Then his father had asked to speak to his mother, and Randy had listened to his mother arguing with his father, telling him that she'd never let Randy go, and that his father better not try to take him. Finally, when the fight was over, he'd talked to his father again.

"I'll see what I can do," Jim had promised. "But there are laws, Randy, and if I just came and got you, I'd be breaking them. Can you understand that?"

Randy tried, but he couldn't. The only thing he could understand was that he hated Eastbury, and he hated his mother, and he hated his friends-who-weren't-his-friends-anymore, and he wanted to go live with his father. Then he got the idea. Maybe his father couldn't come and get him, but what if he went to his father?

Two days later he had made up his mind. When he was sure his mother was asleep, he dressed and sneaked out of the house. He knew where his father lived—it was only five miles away, if you didn't stay on the roads. And he knew the woods; he'd been wandering in them all his life. He figured it would take him an hour or two to get to his father's.

What he hadn't figured was how different the woods would look at night. For a while he walked rapidly along, lighting his way with the flashlight he'd taken from the kitchen drawer, enjoying the adventure. But when the path forked, he began to get confused.

In the daylight, it would have been easy. Everything would have been familiar—the trees, the rocks, the stream that wound its way through the woods toward Langston, where his father lived. But in the darkness, with shadows dancing everywhere, he wasn't sure which way to go. Finally, he made up his mind and told himself everything was fine, even though he didn't believe it.

A little while later he came to another fork in the path. This time he had no idea at all which way was the right way. He stood still for a long time, listening to the sounds of the night—birds murmuring in their sleep, the rustlings of racoons foraging in the underbrush—and finally decided that maybe going through the woods hadn't been a good idea after all. He turned back and started toward home.

Another fork in the path.

Now Randy was getting worried. He didn't remember this fork at all. Had he really passed it before?

The sounds around him were suddenly becoming ominous. Was there something in the darkness, just beyond the beam of the flashlight, watching him?

He spun around, sweeping the woods with the light, and flashes of light came back to him.

There *were* eyes in the night—glowing yellow eyes—and now Randy was frightened. He began running down the path, no longer thinking about where he was going or which path he was on. All he wanted was to get out of the woods.

And then, ahead of him, he saw a light moving in the darkness. Then another, and another. He hurled himself toward the lights, but they disappeared.

They came back, flashing across the trees, then disappearing again.

He stopped short, knowing at last what it was. He was at the edge of the forest, near a road. But which one? He had no idea.

He stayed where he was for a while, wondering what to do next. He really wanted to go home, but he wasn't sure which way home was. He tried to remember what roads went by the woods, but couldn't. Finally, as the night grew colder, he decided he had to do something. He stepped out of the forest and started walking along the road, the flashlight clutched in his right hand.

A car pulled up beside him. An Eastbury police car.

"Goin' somewhere, son?" the policeman asked him.

"H-home," Randy stammered.

"Eastbury?" the cop asked.

"Uh-huh."

"Well, you're goin' the wrong way." The policeman leaned over and opened the door. "Hop in."

Terrified, visions of jail cells dancing in his head, Randy did as he was told. "Are you arresting me?" he asked, his voice even smaller than he felt.

The policeman glanced over at him, a tiny smile playing around the corners of his mouth. "You a big-time crook?"

"Me?" Randy's eyes opened wide. He shook his head. "I—I was going to visit my father."

"Thought you said you were going home."

Randy squirmed in the seat. "Well—my dad's house is home. Isn't it?"

"Not if you live with your mother. You running away?"

Randy stared glumly out the window, sure that he was going to jail. "I—I guess so."

"Things that bad?"

Randy looked up at the cop, who was smiling at him. Could it be possible the cop wasn't mad at him? He nodded shyly.

The cop scowled at him then, but Randy was suddenly no longer scared, and when the man spoke, his worries vanished completely. "I'm Sergeant Bronski," the policeman told him. "Want to have a Coke and talk things over?"

"Where?" Randy countered.

"There's a little place I know." Bronski turned the patrol car around and started back toward Eastbury. "You want me to call your mother?"

"No!"

"How about your dad?"

"Could you call him?"

"Sure." Bronski pulled into an all-night diner, and took Randy inside. He ordered a Coke for Randy and a cup of coffee for himself. Slowly, the story came out, ending with the fight the Corlisses had had on the phone. When Randy was through talking, the policeman looked him squarely in the eye.

"I think we better call your mother, Randy," he said.

"Why?"

"Because that's who you live with. If we call your father, he'll have to call your mother, and she might think he planned all this. Then she might not let you see him at all. Understand?"

"I—I guess so," Randy said uncertainly. The call had been made, and then Sergeant Bronski had taken him home and turned him over to his mother.

His mother had been furious with him, telling him she had enough to worry about just trying to raise him, without having to worry about him running away too. Finally she had sent him back to bed, and Randy had lain awake all night, wondering what to do next.

Ever since that night, he had been wondering what to do. He had begged his father to take him away, and his father, never really saying no but never quite saying yes, had told him to wait, that things would get better.

But months had gone by and not much had changed.

He'd finally met Jason, but his mother still had no time for him. And every time he approached his father, his father told him to wait, told him that he was "working on it." Now spring was here, and soon it would be summer. Would it be another summer to spend by himself, wandering in the woods and prowling around town, looking for something to do? It probably would. If something had happened to Jason's sister, Jason probably wouldn't be allowed to play with him anymore. Once again, he would be all alone.

A horn honked, pulling Randy out of his reverie, and he realized he was alone on the block. He looked at the watch his father had given him for his ninth birthday. It was nearly eight thirty. If he didn't hurry, he was going to be late for school. Then he heard a voice calling to him.

"Randy! Randy Corliss!"

A blue car, a car he didn't recognize, was standing by the curb. A woman was smiling at him from the driver's seat. He approached the car hesitantly, clutching his lunch box.

"Hi, Randy," the woman said.

"Who are you?" Randy stood back from the car, remembering his mother's warnings about never talking to strangers.

"My name's Miss Bowen. Louise Bowen. I came to get you."

"Get me?" Randy asked. "Why?"

"For your father," the woman said. Randy's heart beat faster. His father? His father had sent this woman? Was it really going to happen, finally? "He wanted me to pick you up at home," he heard the woman say, "but I was late. I'm sorry."

"That's all right," Randy said. He moved closer to the car. "Are you taking me to Daddy's house?"

The woman reached across and pushed the passenger door open. "In a little while," she promised. "Get in."

Randy knew he shouldn't get in the car, knew he should turn around and run to the nearest house, looking for help. It was things like this—strangers offering to give you a ride—that his mother had talked to him about ever since he was a little boy.

But this was different. This was a friend of his father's. She had to be, because she seemed to know all about his plans to go live with his father, and his father's plans to take him away from his mother. Besides, it was always men his mother warned him about, never women. He looked at the woman once more. Her brown eyes were twinkling at him, and her smile made him feel like she was sharing an adventure with him. He made up his mind and got into the car, pulling the door closed behind him. The car moved away from the curb.

"Where are we going?" Randy asked.

Louise Bowen glanced over at the boy sitting expectantly on the seat beside her. He was every bit as attractive as the pictures she had been shown, his eyes almost green, with dark, wavy hair framing his pugnacious, snub-nosed face. His body was sturdy, and though she was a stranger to him, he didn't seem to be the least bit frightened of her. Instinctively, Louise liked Randy Corliss.

"We're going to your new school."

Randy frowned. New school? If he was going to a new school, why wasn't his father taking him? The woman seemed to hear him, even though he hadn't spoken out loud.

"You'll see your father very soon. But for a few days, until he gets everything worked out with your mother, you'll be staying at the school. You'll like it there," she promised. "It's a special school, just for little boys like you, and you'll have lots of new friends. Doesn't that sound exciting?"

Randy nodded uncertainly, no longer sure he should have gotten in the car. Still, when he thought about it, it made sense. His father had told him there would be lots of problems when the time came for him to move away from his mother's. And his father had told him he would be going to a new school. And today was the day.

Randy settled down in the seat and glanced out the window. They were heading out of Eastbury on the road toward Langston. That was where his father lived, so everything was all right.

Except that it didn't quite *feel* all right. Deep inside, Randy had a strange sense of something being very wrong.

Chapter 4

I T HAD NOT BEEN ONE of Lucy Corliss's better days. She had spent the morning making the rounds of new listings coming onto the market. Houses that she privately thought weren't worth the land they were built on were being priced at well over a hundred thousand dollars. Between the prices and the mortgage rates, she didn't see how anyone was going to be able to afford to buy. That meant her commissions were going to be off. While pretending to be interested in the houses, she had privately begun reviewing her financial position, and making plans for cuts in her budget. For the moment, the situation wasn't perilous—she had three closings coming up over the next couple of months, and those commissions, if she was careful, would see her through a year. Then what?

Over lunch, she discussed the matter with Bob Owen, who was not only her employer, but her friend. She'd known Bob since childhood, and he'd seen her through a lot.

When her marriage had begun to sour, Bob had been there, listening to her complaints with a sympathetic ear, finally telling her that at some point she was going to have to stop complaining and take some action. When the crunch had at last come, she'd gone to Bob for advice.

The problem, at the time, had been twofold. She was pregnant, and her husband had walked out on her. In fact, she'd admitted to Bob, Jim Corliss had walked out on her *because* she was pregnant, accusing her of trying to tie him down with a baby.

"Did you?" Bob had asked. It had taken Lucy a long time to come up with an answer. At last she had admitted that perhaps, subconsciously, she had. Perhaps she had thought that the responsibilities of fatherhood would calm Jim down, make him see that there was more to life than fast cars and dreams of quick money.

Bob—practical Bob—had advised her to file for a divorce and prepare to go to work. It had even been his idea for her to learn real estate while she was pregnant, so that after the baby was born she would have a way to earn a living. For nine years she had worked out of Bob's office, and she was good at her job. At first she had hired a sitter to come in and look after Randy, but last year she had decided that Randy was old enough to stay by himself for the two hours between the end of the school day and the end of her work day. Margaret Willis, who lived next door, had agreed to keep an eye on Randy. So far it had worked out. Except that today she had a vague sense of unease.

"What's the matter with my girl?" Bob asked, pushing the menu aside and making up his mind to settle for a salad. He looked enviously at Lucy, who ate enormous lunches and dinners and never gained an ounce.

"Your girl—and I don't think your wife would like to hear you call me that, even though she knows it isn't true—is feeling worried today," Lucy replied. She put the menu aside.

"Anything in particular, or everything in general?"

"Well, the market isn't doing a lot for my mood. I can't see who's going to buy the overpriced dogs we saw this morning."

"Someone will," Bob said complacently. "People have

to buy houses. We'll just have to think up new ways to finance them."

"But the houses aren't worth it," Lucy complained.

Now Bob frowned, his bushy eyebrows plunging toward the bridge of his nose. "With an attitude like that, you're certainly not going to be selling any of them."

Lucy smiled wanly and brushed a strand of her pale blond hair out of her eyes. "I'm not sure I want to. Lately, every time I sell someone a house, I feel like I'm making him an indentured servant for the next thirty years."

"Then maybe you'd better do something else."

"Forget it. Besides, it's not really the market that's bothering me—it's Randy."

"Randy? Is something wrong with him?"

"Nothing new. It's just that he seems so unhappy. He doesn't seem to have many friends anymore, and he hates school and home and me and everything else. Sometimes I think maybe I should let Jim take him, for a while at least. Except I don't trust him."

"You don't even know him anymore," Bob pointed out. There were times, every now and then, when Lucy suspected that Bob was trying to get her back together with Jim. Lately, he seemed to be pushing her to see her ex-husband more often than she had to. So far, she had resisted him. "Hasn't it occurred to you that he might have changed?" Bob asked now. "It's been almost ten years. People grow up."

"Even Jim Corliss?" Lucy scoffed. "Do you know how many jobs he's had since he left me? Seven! Seven jobs in nine years, Bob. You call that mature?"

"But only one in the last four years, Lucy. And he's good with Randy."

"Who he never wanted in the first place," Lucy shot back, her voice bitter. "To Jim, Randy's nothing more than a part-time hobby he can deal with over a weekend now and then. But all the time? Come on, Bob, you know damned well Jim would send him back in a week. And what would that do to Randy? He's miserable enough already—having his father reject him could destroy him. I won't do it." She wondered if she should tell Bob that Jim had mentioned the possibility of going to court over Randy, and decided against it. Bob—reasonable Bob—would only suggest that it might not be best for anyone to have a court fight over Randy, and that perhaps she should consider at least sharing the boy with Jim. And that, she knew, was something she wasn't prepared to do.

"I'm sorry," she said as their food arrived. "I don't know why I always wind up crying on your shoulder. Let's talk about something else, okay? Like when you and Elaine can come over for some of my famous burnt steaks? The weather's getting nice, and I feel in the mood for a barbecue. How about this weekend?"

And so the afternoon passed, and Lucy kept her mind off her problems. Or, more exactly, she *tried* to keep her mind off her problems. But by five o'clock, when she left the office, Randy was once more looming at the forefront of her mind.

As she pulled into the driveway of the small house she had bought five years before, her feeling of unease increased. Usually, Randy was there, standing at the living-room window, watching for her.

She went inside and called out to him. There was no answer. Quickly, she went through the house, but nowhere was there any sign of Randy. His room was as it had been this morning, and his school clothes, which he usually left in a heap on the floor, were nowhere to be seen. Satisfied that Randy was not in the house, Lucy went next door to talk to Margaret Willis.

"But why didn't you call me?" Lucy asked when the elderly widow told her that Randy had not been seen at all that afternoon.

Mrs. Willis's hands fluttered nervously. "Why, I simply assumed he'd gone to play with friends," she said, then flushed a deep red as she realized her error. Even on the days when Randy didn't come home immediately after school, he was always home long before his mother was expected. But today, the afternoon had slipped away, and she hadn't seen Randy.

Margaret Willis's ample chin began to quiver. "Oh, dear, I've made a terrible mistake, haven't I? But surely you don't think anything's happened to him? Why, it's not even five thirty yet. Why don't you let me fix you a nice cup of tea?" She tried to draw Lucy into her house, but Lucy pulled away.

"No, no, thank you, Mrs. Willis. I'd better try to find out what's happened to him." Lucy tried to keep her voice calm, but her eyes revealed the fear that was beginning to grip her. Margaret Willis reached out and touched her arm.

"Now, what could have happened to him?" she asked gently. "It's not as if this was Boston, dear. Why, nothing ever happens in Eastbury, you know that. I'll tell you what—I'll make some tea and bring it over to your house."

Tea, Lucy thought. Why is it that half the people in the world think that a nice cup of tea will fix everything? But she was too upset to argue. "All right," she agreed. "I'll leave the front door open."

She hurried down the steps of Mrs. Willis's front porch and cut across the lawn that separated the large Willis house from her own. Inside, the silence pushed her unreasonably close to the edge of panic. She went to the kitchen and made herself sit down at the table that was still littered with breakfast dishes. Consciously, she forced the panic back, telling herself that Margaret Willis was undoubtedly right, that Randy was fine, and would show up any minute. Her fears were silly; she was overreacting to a commonplace situation. Small boys often took off without telling anyone where they were going.

Her intuition told her otherwise. She went to the phone and began searching through her address book, looking for the names of people whose children had once been Randy's friends. She was on her third phone call when Margaret Willis appeared at the back door, carrying a steaming teapot. Lucy stretched the phone cord and reached the knob, feeling irritated that the woman hadn't used the front door. But in Eastbury, neighbors, except for herself, always used back doors. As Mrs. Willis came into the kitchen, she looked inquiringly at Lucy, who only shrugged, then began speaking as Emily Harris came back on the line.

"Geordie says Randy wasn't at school today, Lucy."

"Wasn't there at all?" Lucy asked, her voice hollow.

"That's what Geordie says," Mrs. Harris told her. "And he should know—he's in Randy's class."

"I—I see," Lucy said. There was a silence as each of the women wondered what to say next. It was Emily Harris who finally spoke.

"Lucy, have you talked to Sally Montgomery?"

Lucy groaned to herself. Sally Montgomery should have been the first call she made. If Randy was anywhere, he'd be with Jason. "Oh, God, Emily, I feel like such a fool," she said.

"It's tragic," she heard Emily Harris saying. "I mean, what do you say when something like that happens?"

Lucy felt her stomach tighten. "What are you talking about?" she asked. "What happened?"

Again there was a silence, and when Emily eventually spoke, her voice had dropped to the conspiratorial level that signaled the sort of bad news she loved best. "You mean you haven't heard? Their little girl died last night. They *say* it was crib death . . ." She let the words hang, clearly indicating that she was sure there was more to the story than that. Then her voice brightened, and Lucy suddenly realized why she had never really liked Emily Harris. "But I'm sure nothing's wrong," Emily said. "Jason wasn't at school today, of course, and Randy probably decided to play hookey with him. Geordie's done it more than once," she lied. "All boys do it, especially in spring. I'll bet he'll be home in time for dinner."

"I suppose so," Lucy said without conviction. She decided she had had quite enough of Emily Harris. "Thanks, Emily. Sorry to bother you."

"No bother at all," Emily Harris replied. "Let me

know when you find him, all right? Otherwise I'll worry."

Sure you will, Lucy thought angrily. And you'll be on the phone all night, spreading the latest news too. She hung up, then sipped the tea that Margaret Willis had placed in front of her, and told the older woman what she had just heard.

"Oh, dear," Margaret murmured. "Well, I suppose you'd better call Mrs. Montgomery, hadn't you?"

"I don't know," Lucy replied unhappily. "Oh, I know I should, but what good would it do? Randy couldn't possibly be there, not today. And what would I say to her? Do I tell her I'm sorry her daughter died, but has she happened to see my son? Margaret, I can't! I just can't!"

"Then I will," Margaret said, reaching for the phone book. But before she had found the Montgomerys' number, Lucy suddenly hit the table with her fist.

"His father!" she exclaimed. "Damn it, that's what happened. Jim took Randy!" Once more she picked up the phone, and began dialing furiously, her eyes, filled with worry only a moment ago, now glittering with anger. "That bastard," she rasped through clenched teeth as she listened to her ex-husband's telephone ring on with that strange, impossible tone that seems to occur only when no one is going to answer. Finally, she pressed the button to disconnect the call and dialed the emergency number that was taped to the phone. "I want to report a kidnaping," she said, her voice level.

Ten minutes later she sank back in her chair and tiredly closed her eyes. She could feel Margaret Willis's burning curiosity permeating the kitchen. Even though she knew it would be all over the neighborhood by this evening, she had to talk.

"They said they can't do anything," she began, her voice reflecting the frustration she was feeling. "They said they can't even list him as missing yet, and they said if his father took him, it's a civil matter, and I should talk to a lawyer instead of the police."

"But what do they expect you to do?"

"Wait. They told me to wait, and try to get hold of

Jim. Then, if Randy isn't back by morning, and I can't get hold of Jim, I should call them back." She shook her head helplessly. "How can I do that, Margaret? How can I just sit here and wait?"

"We'll do it together," Margaret Willis said firmly, standing up and beginning to clear the breakfast dishes off the table. "We'll clean up the kitchen and fix supper, and then we'll start cleaning the house."

"But it's clean—" Lucy started to protest, but the elderly woman waved a gentle finger at her.

"Then it will be cleaner. No such thing as too clean, Lucy, and I've always found that cleaning house makes the time pass faster. So we'll clean all night if we have to." Then she smiled affectionately. "But I bet we won't have to," she added. "I'll bet the little rascal will show up in an hour or two, tired, hungry, and dirty. Then we'll feed him and send him to bed. How's that sound?"

To Lucy it sounded horrible, but she knew she would give in to Margaret Willis. It was either that or sit alone, watching the clock tick off the endless minutes while improbable fantasies transformed themselves into frightening realities in the far reaches of her imagination. She would, she knew, go mad with worry if she had to wait alone. Better to fill the time and the emptiness with Margaret's relentless cheerfulness than to try to cope with the hysteria that was building inside her. Morosely, she began cleaning her house.

It was nearly midnight, and the house was spotless, when Jim Corliss finally answered his phone.

"Jim? It's Lucy. I want him back, do you hear? I want you to bring him back right now, or I'm going to call my lawyer."

Jim Corliss knew by the hysteria in her voice that something was wrong. She never called him, except to demand support payments or argue with him about Randy. Suddenly, he became worried. Did she think Randy was with him? But he wasn't scheduled to see his son for another week. "Are you talking about Randy?" he asked cautiously.

37

"Of course I'm talking about Randy," Lucy exploded. "Who do you think I'm talking about? How dare you!"

"How dare I what? Isn't Randy there?"

There was a silence, then Lucy spoke again, her voice suddenly breaking. "You don't have him? You didn't pick him up this morning?"

"Oh, my God," Jim said, his heart pounding as he realized the implications of what his ex-wife was saying. "Lucy, what's happened? Tell me what's happened."

"He's gone, Jim."

"What do you mean, gone? Gone where?"

"I—I don't know," Lucy stammered, her rage dissipating, only to be replaced by the fear she had felt earlier. She explained what had happened that afternoon. "I—I thought you must have picked him up," she finished. "I know how he's been after you to take him away from me. I thought you'd done it."

"I wouldn't, Lucy. I wouldn't do that to you."

"Wouldn't you?" Lucy asked, her voice brittle with suspicion. "I wonder . . ."

"I'm coming over," Jim said suddenly. "I'll be there in twenty minutes."

"No," Lucy protested. "Please, Jim—"

"He's my son too," Jim said firmly. He hung up the phone. Within minutes he was on his way to Eastbury.

There was an awkwardness when Jim and Lucy Corliss faced each other across the threshold of Lucy's house, the kind of uncomfortable silence that comes over two people who have once been close but are no longer sure what to say to each other. For years Lucy had done her best to avoid Jim when he came to pick up Randy, restricting her conversations to a few stilted sentences conveying nothing more than what she deemed to be vital information. Now, as Lucy examined her ex-husband's face, she had an impression of age, but then, noting that Jim's face was as unlined as ever, and his hair the same thick, wavy thatch that it had always been, she decided that it wasn't age that had come to Jim, but something else. The word that came to mind was maturity, but she tried to reject it. If Jim had, indeed, matured over the years, she would have to see more evidence of it than a look in his eyes.

"May I come in?"

Lucy stepped back nervously, stumbled, then quickly recovered herself. "I'm sorry," she said. "Of course." She held the door open as Jim came in and Mrs. Willis, hands fluttering, mumbled a series of greetings, apologies, sympathies, and good-byes. Then she was gone, and a nervous silence settled over the Corlisses.

Jim glanced around the little living room, then offered a tentative smile. "Did I ever tell you I like this room? It's nice—looks just like you. Pretty, warm, and tidy."

Lucy returned Jim's smile stiffly and settled herself into a chair that would, by its placement in the room, separate her from him. The thought that Jim was still very attractive came into her mind, but she put it determinedly aside and began telling him what had happened, ending up with her fear that Randy had been kidnaped.

"But he ran away last summer," Jim pointed out when she had finished.

"This is different," Lucy insisted. "Last summer he ran away in the middle of the night, after that problem with the Semple boy. But nothing's happened recently—there's no reason for him to have run away this morning. And I'd have known—I'd have sensed something at breakfast. But he was just like he always is." She paused, then met Jim's eyes. "He's been kidnaped, Jim. Don't ask me how I know, but I know Randy didn't just run away. Someone took him." Her eyes narrowed. "And I'm still not entirely convinced it wasn't you."

"Oh, God . . ." Jim groaned.

"It's just the kind of thing you'd do, Jim. And I swear, if you've taken him and hidden him somewhere—"

"I haven't," Jim said vehemently. "Lucy, I wouldn't do something like that. I—well, I just wouldn't. Look. Let's call the police again. It seems to me that he's been gone long enough so they should at least be willing to take a report."

"They told me they couldn't do anything for twenty-four hours."

"Twenty-four hours!" Jim exploded. "My God, he's not an adult—he's only nine years old! He could be lost—or hurt." Jim stood up and stormed into the kitchen. A moment later Lucy heard him talking to someone, then shouting. His voice dropped again, and she could no longer make out what he was saying. At last he rejoined her.

"They're sending someone out," he said. But as Lucy looked at him hopefully, he had to tell her what the police had told him. "They'll take a report, but they said the odds are that he's a runaway." He fell silent, and Lucy prodded him.

"Which means what?"

Jim avoided her eyes. "I'm not sure. It could mean anything. Kids are—well, they're running away from home younger every year. They said if he was a little older, we'd probably only see him again if he wants to see us."

Lucy frowned. "What does that mean?"

"Just that with the young ones—the real young ones, like Randy—sometimes they don't know what to do, and after a night or two, they turn themselves in."

"And if he doesn't?" Lucy asked quietly.

"I—I'm not sure. They said something about a search, but they said searches usually don't do much good either. If something's happened to Randy, it's more likely that someone will ... well, that someone will find him by accident."

"You mean if he's dead." Lucy's voice was flat, and her eyes cold, and Jim found himself unable to make any reply other than a nod of his head.

"But he's not dead," Lucy said softly. "I know he's not dead."

Jim swallowed. There was one more possibility the police had mentioned. "They said he might have gone to Boston ..." he began, but then let his words trail off. Better to let the police try to explain to Lucy what could happen to a small boy in Boston.

Chapter 5

AT THE SAME TIME Jim and Lucy Corliss were trying to deal with the loss of their son, Steve and Sally Montgomery were trying to deal with the loss of their daughter.

All afternoon, and into the evening, ever since they had returned from the hospital and their talk with Dr. Malone, Sally had been strangely silent. Several times Steve tried to talk to her, but she seemed not to hear him.

Steve had spent several hours with Jason, trying to explain to him what had happened to Julie, and Jason had listened quietly, his head cocked curiously, his brows furrowed into a thoughtful frown. He seemed, to Steve, to accept the death of his sister as simply one more fact in his young life.

It was, indeed, not so much the fact of Julie's death that worried Jason, but the reason for her death. Over and over, he'd kept coming back to the same question.

"But if there wasn't anything wrong with her, why did she die?"

His eyes, larger and darker than his mother's, looked up at Steve, pleading for an answer Steve couldn't give. Still, he had to try once more.

"We don't know why Julie died," he repeated for at

least the sixth time. "All we know is that it happens sometimes."

"But why did it happen to Julie? Was she a bad girl?"

"No, she was a very good girl."

Jason's brows knit as he puzzled over the dilemma. "But if she was a good girl, why did God kill her?"

"I don't know, son," Steve replied through the sudden constriction in his throat. "I just don't know."

"Is God going to kill me too?"

Steve pulled his son to him and hugged him close. "No, of course not. It didn't have anything to do with us, and it isn't going to happen to you."

"How do you know?" Jason challenged, wriggling loose from his father's embrace. Steve wearily stood up and began tucking Jason in.

"I just know," he said. "Now I want you to go to sleep, okay?"

"Okay," Jason agreed. Then his eyes wandered over to the far corner of his room where a black-and-white guinea pig named Fred lived in a small cage. "Can Fred come sleep by me tonight?" he asked.

Steve smiled. "Sure." He brought the cage over and set it down next to Jason's bed. Inside the cage, Fred began patrolling the perimeter, examining his environment from the new perspective. Then, satisfied, he curled up and buried his nose in his own fur. "Now that's what I want you to do," Steve said. "Bury your nose and go to sleep." He bent down and kissed Jason's cheek, snapped out the light, and left the room.

A moment later, as he came downstairs, his mother-in-law drew him into the den, and the two of them talked for a long time. At last Phyllis shook her head slowly.

"I just don't understand it," she said. "It seems so strange that a perfect child like Julie could just—what? Stop living? Terrible. Terrible! There must have been a reason, Steve. There must have been."

But Steve Montgomery knew there was no reason, at least no reason that the doctors understood. That, he was coming to realize, was the most difficult part of the sudden infant death syndrome: there was nothing to blame, no germ or virus, no abnormal condition—nothing. Simply the fact of unreasonable death and the lingering feeling of failure. Already it was beginning to gnaw at him, but there was nothing he could do about it. He would simply have to live with it and try to put it out of his mind. Even if it meant putting Julie out of his mind too.

"Life is for the living."

The words had sounded reasonable when Malone had spoken them, and Steve knew they were true. Then why did he feel dead inside? Why did he feel as though he might as well bury himself tomorrow along with his daughter? He couldn't feel that way, couldn't *let* himself feel that way. For Sally, and for Jason, he would have to go on, have to function. And yet, would he be able to do any better for them than he had for his daughter?

He shut the thought out of his mind. From now on, he decided, there would have to be places in his mind that were closed off, sealed forever away from his conscious existence. It was either that or go crazy.

Now he sat with Sally, tiredness weakening every fiber in his body, his mind numb, his grief pervading him. Sally was looking at him, and he saw something in her eyes that chilled his soul.

Her eyes, the sparkling brown eyes that had first attracted him to her, had changed. The sparkle had been replaced by a strange intensity that seemed to glow from deep within her.

"She didn't just die," Sally said softly. Steve started to speak to her, but was suddenly unsure whether she was talking to him or to herself. "Babies don't do that. They don't just die." Now her eyes met his. "We must have done something, Steve. We must have."

Steve flinched slightly. Hadn't the same thoughts gone through his own mind? But he couldn't give in to them, and he couldn't let Sally give in to them either. "That's not true, Sally. We loved Julie. We did everything we could—"

"Did we?" Sally asked, her voice suddenly bitter. "I

wonder. I wonder, Steve! Let's face it. We didn't want Julie—neither of us did! One child was all we were going to have, remember? Just one! And we had Jason. A little sooner than we'd planned, but we agreed that he was the only child we wanted. But it didn't happen that way, did it? Something went wrong, and we had Julie, even though we didn't want her. And she died!"

Steve stared at his wife, his face pale and his hands shaking. "What are you saying, Sally?" he asked, his voice so quiet it was almost inaudible. "Are you saying we killed Julie?"

Tears suddenly overflowing, Sally buried her face in her hands. "I don't know, Steve," she sobbed. "I don't know what I'm saying, or what I'm thinking, or anything. I only know that babies don't just die—"

"But they *do*," Steve interrupted. "Dr. Malone said—"

"I don't care what Dr. Malone said!" Sally burst out. "Babies don't just die!"

She ran from the room. Steve listened to her heavy step as she went upstairs.

A little later he followed her and found her already in bed. He undressed silently, slipped into bed beside her, and turned out the light. He could hear her crying and reached out to take her in his arms.

For the first time in all the years of their marriage, Sally drew away from him.

Jason lay in his bed, listening to the silence of the house and wondering when things would get back to the way they used to be.

He didn't like the way his mother had been crying all the time. Up until last night, in fact, he'd never seen her cry at all.

It had frightened him at first, seeing her standing in Julie's room, holding Julie just like she always did, except for the tears running down her face. Usually, when she held Julie, she laughed.

His first thought when he saw her was that she had found out about what he'd done to Julie and was going to be mad at him. But that hadn't been it at all—she was crying because Julie was dead.

Julie hadn't been dead when he'd gone in earlier to look at her.

She'd only been sleeping.

He knew she was sleeping, because he could hear her snuffling softly, like his mother did when she had a cold. So he'd wiped her nose with a corner of the sheet.

That couldn't have hurt her.

But it did wake her up and she'd started crying.

And that was when he'd put the blanket over her face, so no one would hear her crying.

But he hadn't left it there long enough for her to smother. It couldn't have been that long; as soon as she'd stopped crying, he'd taken the blanket off her face and tucked it back around her just the way it had been when he went in to look at her.

But had she still been breathing?

He tried to remember.

He was sure she had. He could almost hear her now, in the silence of the house, even though she was dead.

He listened hard and was sure he heard, very faintly, the sounds of tiny breaths.

And then he remembered: Fred was sleeping next to his bed.

He slid out of bed and knelt next to the guinea pig's cage. The sounds Fred were making were just like the sounds Julie had made after she stopped crying.

Very quiet, but there.

He opened the cage, and Fred, hearing the slight rattle, woke up, opened his eyes and stared at Jason through the gloom. Jason reached in, gently picked up the guinea pig, and took it into bed with him. Soon Fred fell asleep again, this time curled up in the crook of Jason's arm.

Jason listened to the guinea pig breathe, sure that he had heard the same sounds in Julie's room last night just before he had left it. So he hadn't done anything to Julie, not really.

Still, tomorrow or the next day he'd talk to Randy

about it. It was, he realized, sort of like what had happened to Randy after Billy Semple jumped off the roof. Even though Randy hadn't really done anything to Billy, he'd still gotten blamed for Billy's broken leg.

As he fell into a fitful sleep, Jason wondered if the same thing would happen to him, and he'd get blamed for Julie's dying.

Maybe the next time Randy came over they'd do the same thing to Fred that he'd done to Julie and see if Fred died.

At least then he'd know for sure. . . .

Chapter 6

RANDY CORLISS SCRUNCHED UNDER the covers, trying to avoid opening his eyes to the morning light. He was cold, and all night long his sleep had been broken by nightmares. But now the sun was warming his room, and he wanted to drift back to sleep, wanted to forget the loneliness that had overcome him the previous afternoon when he realized his father was not coming for him, at least not that day.

"But it's going to be all right, Randy," Miss Bowen had explained. "Your father is very busy, and for the moment he wants us to take care of you."

"Why?" Randy had asked. Since he'd seen the fence around the Academy, he'd wondered why his father had had him brought here. It didn't, to Randy's eyes, look quite like a school. For one thing, you couldn't even see it from the road. There was just a long driveway and then a gate without a sign. And there weren't any of the kind of school buildings he was used to, only a huge house that looked almost like a castle, with the windows of the second floor covered with bars. He'd seen a couple of boys who looked like they were about the same age he was, but hadn't been able to talk to them. Instead, he'd been taken into an office, where Miss Bowen had told him why he was there.

"It's a special school, for special boys," she assured him. "Boys like you, who've had problems in regular school."

"I haven't had any problems," Randy said.

"I mean problems making friends." Miss Bowen smiled at him, and a little of Randy's apprehension dissipated. "Lots of boys your age have that kind of trouble, you know. Boys who are special, like you."

"I'm special?"

"All the boys here are special. Most of them come from families just like yours."

"You mean where their parents are divorced?"

"Exactly. And most of the boys here didn't want to live with their mothers anymore and didn't like the schools they were going to. So their fathers sent them here, just like your father sent you."

"But where is he?" Randy's face darkened belligerently, and as he watched her, he could see that she wasn't going to answer him. That was the trouble with grown-ups, even his father. When they didn't want to answer your questions, they never even explained why not. They just said you weren't old enough to know. Or sometimes they just pretended they hadn't heard the question, which was what Randy thought Miss Bowen was about to do.

"Wouldn't you like to meet the other boys?" she asked, confirming his suspicions.

"I want to talk to my father," Randy replied, his voice turning stubborn. He was sitting uncomfortably on a high-backed wooden chair, but he folded his arms, and his eyes sparked angrily. "Why can't I call him? I know his number at work."

"But he's out of town. That's why he sent me to pick you up. He *couldn't* come for you. But he'll be back in a few days."

"How many days?" Randy demanded. He was beginning to squirm in his chair now, and his face was flushing. The woman opened her desk drawer and took out a small bottle filled with white tablets. "What's that?" Randy demanded.

"It's some medicine. I want you to take one of these."

"I'm not sick, and I don't ever take pills."

"It's just to calm you down. I know all this is very strange, and I know you're frightened. This pill will help."

"What'll it do to me?" Randy stared at the pill suspiciously. "Will it make me go to sleep?"

"Of course not. But you won't be frightened anymore, or worried."

"I won't take it, and you can't make me." Randy's mouth clamped shut, and his body stiffened. His eyes began darting around the room as he searched for a way out. There was none. The woman was between him and the door, and there were no windows in the office.

"Then you're going to sit there until you change your mind," she told him. "You can make up your own mind. Take the pill, and come with me to meet the other boys, or sit there all day. It's up to you." She set the pill in the center of the blotter on her desk and picked up a file folder. Five minutes passed.

"It won't make me go to sleep?" he asked, coming to the desk and picking up the pill, studying it as if it were an insect.

"It won't make you go to sleep." She got up to go to the water cooler, keeping her eyes on Randy in case he tried to bolt out the door. He didn't.

She handed him a cup of water, still watching closely to be sure he really swallowed the pill. Ten minutes later, when he began to relax, she took him outside and introduced him to his schoolmates.

There were five of them, and they eyed Randy with all the suspicion of preadolescence, silently daring him to pick a fight. He watched them, trying to decide which of them to challenge, but none of them stepped forward, nor did any of them back away. Only when Miss Bowen left them alone with the newcomer did any of them speak.

"Did she give you the pill?" one of them finally asked. His name was Peter Williams, and when he spoke, his voice was neither friendly nor belligerent.

"Uh-huh," Randy replied. "What is it?"

"I think it's Valium," another of the boys said. "My mom used to take it when she was nervous."

"Do you have to take it every day?"

"Nah. Only the first day. Then they don't make you take anything. How come you're here?"

Randy thought about it before he answered, and when he finally spoke, he avoided the others' eyes. "My dad sent me. Mostly to get me away from my mom, I guess."

There was a silence as the other boys exchanged glances and shrugs. "Yeah," Peter said at last. "That's why we're all here, except Billy." He gestured toward the skinny brown-haired boy who stood slightly behind him. Billy stared at his shoes, as Peter explained importantly. "*His* mom sent him here to get him away from his dad. But who cares? It's better than being at home."

That had been yesterday, and this morning Randy was still not convinced that Peter was right. He felt terribly alone, and when he went to look out the window, and saw nothing except forest beyond the fence that surrounded the Academy, a slight chill rippled over him. But then there was a tap at the door, and Adam Rogers stuck his head in.

"You better get dressed. If we aren't down for breakfast in five minutes, we won't get any." Adam came into the room and perched himself on the bed while Randy pulled his clothes on. "You from around here?"

"Eastbury." Randy sized Adam up as he tied his shoelaces. He looked younger than Randy, and was smaller, but his body was wiry and he looked like he was fast. "Where you from?"

"Georgia. That's down south."

"I know where it is. I'm not stupid."

"Nobody said you were," Adam said by way of apology, "but lots of people don't know where anyplace is. Come on." He hopped off the bed and led Randy out of the bedroom and down the stairs into a large dining room. There were two tables in the room, around one of which the other four boys were seated. At another, smaller table sat Louise Bowen. "She thinks she's a den mother or something," Adam whispered as the two of them slid into the two vacant chairs at the big table with the other boys. "But she never talks to us in the morning. Just watches us."

"Why?"

"Search me. But that's one of the neat things about this place—they watch you all the time, but they practically never tell you what to do."

"Yeah," Peter Williams agreed, grinning happily. "Not like at home. My mom was always telling me I was going to hurt myself, or get in trouble, or kill someone, or something. And then I ran away one day, and the cops picked me up, and ever since then she was always on my case."

The other boys began chiming in. As Randy listened, he began to think maybe he'd been wrong to be so suspicious yesterday. All the stories sounded familiar. Most of the boys had been lonely before they came to the Academy, and some of them bragged about how much trouble they'd caused in the schools they'd gone to before.

"But what do you do here?" Randy asked.

"Go to class and play," Peter replied. "It's neat, because we don't have as many classes as regular school. But we play lots of games. They teach us boxing—and wrestling and some other stuff, but a lot of the time they just let us do what we want."

"Anything?" Randy asked.

Peter looked at the other boys questioningly, and when they nodded, so did he. "I guess so. At least, they never told any of us *not* to do anything." He paused, as if turning something over in his mind, then went on, his voice more thoughtful. "But they always watch us. It's funny. There's always someone around, like they want to know what we're doing, but they never tell us much about what to do. Except in class. That's just like regular school."

"How come there's only six of us?" Randy suddenly asked. It seemed to him that the house was big enough for a much larger group than they made up, and he'd always thought private schools had hundreds of students.

Adam Rogers glanced toward Louise Bowen, then leaned close to Randy and whispered. "There used to be more," he said. "When I got here, there were ten of us."

"What happened to the others?" Randy asked.

Peter frowned at Adam. "They left."

"You mean their dads came for them, or they went to another school?"

Across from Randy, a red-headed boy with a sprinkle of freckles across his nose shook his head. "No. They—"

"Shut up, Eric," Peter broke in. "We're not supposed to talk about that."

"Talk about what?" Randy demanded.

"Nothing," Peter told him.

Randy turned his attention back to Eric. "Talk about what, Eric?" he asked again, his eyes locking onto the other boy's. Eric started to open his mouth, then closed it and looked away. "Tell me," Randy insisted.

Eric glanced uneasily toward Louise Bowen. She appeared not to be listening to them. Still, when he spoke, his voice dropped to a whisper, and Randy had to strain to hear him.

"Sometimes kids just—well, they just disappear. We think they die."

"Die?" Randy breathed.

"We don't know," Peter said. "We don't know what happens to them."

"Yes, we do," Eric whispered miserably. "Nobody's been here more than a few months, and everyone who's gone died. That's what happens. You come here, and you die."

"Shut up, Eric," Peter said once again. "We don't know what happened to David and Kevin. Maybe their fathers came for them."

"I hope so," Adam Rogers said, and when Randy looked at him, he saw that Adam's face was pale. "I've been here almost six months. Longer than any of you. I—I hope . . ."

His voice trailed off. The six boys finished their breakfast in silence.

Lucy Corliss sat at her kitchen table and tried to decide what to do. All night she had lain awake, hoping to hear the front door opening signaling Randy's return, or the sound of the telephone notifying her that the police had found him. That was the one thing Sergeant Bronski had promised her last night—that he would put together a search party and comb the woods in which Randy had gotten lost a year ago. He hadn't promised anything; indeed, he had reluctantly told Lucy that the odds of finding Randy in the darkness were almost nil.

But all night long her house had been filled with an eerie silence. Finally, as the eastern sky had begun brightening into dawn, she had made one more call to the police, only to be told that no trace of Randy had yet been found; then she drifted into a fitful sleep, from which she had awakened an hour later. Since then she had been sitting in the kitchen, waiting, resisting the constant impulse to call the police yet again, knowing that if there was anything to report, they would call her.

When the phone suddenly came to life just before nine, its jangling sound nearly made Lucy drop her coffee cup. She grabbed for the receiver, her heart pounding.

"Hello? Hello?"

"It's Jim, Lucy." There was a hopelessness in his voice that told her instantly that the search party had found nothing, but she had to confirm it. "You didn't find him, did you?"

"No."

"Oh, God, Jim, what am I going to do? I just feel so helpless, and—and—" Her voice broke off as she fought to control the tears that threatened to engulf her.

"Take it easy, Lucy," she heard Jim say. "It's not over yet." There was a short silence, then he added, "Are you going to work?"

"Work?" Lucy echoed. She felt a tentacle of panic at the edge of her consciousness, and her voice pitched higher. "How can I go to work? My God, it's my *son* that's missing. I've got to *do* something about it." The panic was beginning to grow, and Lucy lit a cigarette, drawing deeply. As she exhaled the stream of smoke, a little of her tension eased.

"I didn't mean it that way," she heard Jim saying. "I just meant that there's nothing you can do right now. It won't do you or Randy any good for you to sit around the house going out of your mind."

"You're a fine one to say that," Lucy shot back. "How would you know what's going to do me or Randy any good? You can't just come waltzing back into my life after nine years and start telling me what's good for me and what's not. Was it good for me to have you walk out and leave me to bring our son up by myself?"

If he was stung by her words, he showed no sign. "Tell you what," he said. "You do what you think is best, and I'll keep at it with the police. It's all we can do. Okay?"

Lucy took another puff on her cigarette and nodded, even though there was no one to see her. "Okay. But call me if you find anything. Anything at all!"

"Sure." There was a long silence, and then Jim's voice came over the line once again. "Lucy? Are you going to be all right? Do you want me to come over?"

"No. I mean, yes, I'm all right, and no, I don't want you to come over."

"Gotcha," Jim said, and the word almost made Lucy smile. It was a word he had used throughout their marriage on those rare occasions when he understood exactly why she was angry with him and was trying to apologize for having gone too far with whatever excess he was currently involved in. Now, as the word echoed in her mind, she could almost feel the warmth she knew must be in his eyes. "If you need anything," he went on, "you know where to find me."

The line went dead. Lucy held the receiver in her hand for a moment before hanging it up. As she poured herself another cup of coffee, she suddenly made up her mind.

Jim was right—she couldn't hang around the house all day. She quickly drained the coffee cup, then began dressing for work.

For Sally Montgomery, there was a chill to the morning that even the spring sun couldn't penetrate. She stared at herself in the mirror for a long time, studying the strange, haggard image that confronted her—slender arms wrapped protectively around a body she barely recognized as her own, hair limply framing a face etched with lines of exhaustion that even careful makeup hadn't been able to erase—and wondered how she was going to get through this day.

The sounds of morning drifted up the stairs, unfamiliar, for it should have been herself rattling around the kitchen, murmuring to Steve, urging Jason to hurry up. Instead it was her mother's voice she heard, and even the sounds of the coffeepot being put back on the stove and the frying pan clunking softly as it was placed in the sink bore the unmistakably purposeful tenor of her mother's efficiency. She moved to the closet and tried to decide what to wear.

She owned nothing black, never had. Navy blue? Her hands, shaking slightly, plucked a suit from a hanger. Something caught, and instead of stopping to disentangle the unseen snarl, Sally simply yanked at it. The rasping sound of a seam giving way raked across her nerves, and she knew she was going to cry.

I won't, she told herself. Not now. Not over a torn seam. Later. Later, I'll cry. She glanced at the tear in the lining of her suit jacket and felt that she'd won a small victory.

She went to her dresser next, and as she was about to open the second drawer where all her blouses lay neatly folded in tissue paper, her eyes fell on a picture of Julie. The tiny face, screwed into an expression somewhere between laughter and fury, seemed to mock her and reproach her at the same time. Now the tears did come. Sally backed away from the picture, sank to her bed, and buried her face in her hands.

That was how Steve found her a few moments later. He paused at the door, watching his wife, his heart aching not only for her, but for his own inability to comfort her, then crossed the room to sit beside her. With gentle hands he lifted her face and kissed her. "Honey? Is there anything ..." He left the sentence unfinished, knowing there was no real way to complete it.

". . . anything wrong?" Sally finished for him. "Anything you can do for me? I don't know. Oh, Steve, I—I just looked at her picture, and it all came apart. It was like she was staring at me. Like she wanted to know what happened, wanted to know if it was a joke, or if I was mad at her, or—oh, God, I don't know."

Steve held her for a moment, sharing the pain of the moment but knowing there was nothing he could do to ease it. Then Sally pulled away from him and stood up.

"I'll be all right," she said, more to herself than to her husband. "I'll get dressed, and I'll come downstairs, and I'll eat breakfast. I'll take each moment as it comes, and I'll get through." She took a deep breath, then went once more to her dresser. This time she kept her eyes carefully averted from the picture of Julie as she opened the drawer and took out a soft silk blouse. Then, taking her pantyhose with her, she disappeared into the bathroom.

Steve stayed on in the bedroom for a while, his eyes fixed on the picture of his daughter, then suddenly he turned the picture face down on the dresser top. A moment later he was gone, back to the kitchen where his son was waiting for him.

Chapter 7

THE CAR MOVED SLOWLY through the streets of Eastbury, and Sally found herself looking out at the town and its people with a strange detachment she had only felt a few times before. The last time had been when her father had died, and she had been driven through these same streets toward the same cemetery. On that day, as their car passed through the center of town, where the charm of old New England had still been carefully preserved, the people of Eastbury had nodded respectfully toward Sally and her mother. They had understood the death of Jeremiah Paine and been able to express their sympathy toward his family.

But today, Eastbury looked different. People seemed to turn away from the car. What Sally had always perceived as Yankee reserve, today seemed like icy aloofness. Even the town had changed, Sally realized. It had begun to take on a look of coldness, as if along with the new technology had come a new indifference. Where once the town and its inhabitants had seemed to fit each other comfortably, now the people Sally saw moving indifferently through Eastbury's picturesque streets were mostly newcomers who looked as if they had been cut from a mold, then assigned to live in Eastbury. Cookie-cutter people, Sally thought, who could have lived anywhere, and nothing in their lives would change. The new breed, she reflected sadly. It seemed to her that there was some vital force lacking in them, and as the car moved into the parking lot next to the First Presbyterian Church and its adjoining cemetery, she wondered if she, too, had become infected by the malaise that seemed to have chilled the town.

A few minutes later, as she stood in the cemetery where her father was buried, and where, she supposed, she herself would someday lie, Sally Montgomery still felt the chill, though she knew the day was unseasonably warm. There were few people gathered around the grave. Apparently most of Sally's friends were feeling the same way she was feeling: numb and unable to cope. Funerals were to pay final respects to old people and to comfort the living for the loss of someone who had been part of their lives for years. What did you say when an infant died?

Suddenly all the soft murmurings sounded hollow.

"Perhaps it was a blessing . . ." for someone who has been sick for years.

"At least it happened quickly . . ." for someone who had never been sick a day in her life.

"I know how you'll miss her . . ." for a mother or a sister or an aunt.

"I don't know what I'll do without her . . ." to share the burden of loss.

But for a six-month-old baby? Nothing. Nothing to be said, nothing to be offered. And so they stayed away, and Sally understood.

She watched the tiny coffin being lowered into the ground, listened as the minister uttered the final words consigning Julie Montgomery to the care of the Lord, moved woodenly toward the grave to deposit the first clod of the earth that would soon hide her daughter from the sight of the living, then started toward the car, intent only on getting home, getting away from the ceremony that, far from easing her pain, was only intensifying it.

From a few yards away, Arthur Wiseman watched

Sally's forlorn figure and wondered once again why he had come to Julie Montgomery's funeral. He rarely attended funerals at all, and particularly avoided the funerals of his patients. To him, a funeral was little more than a painful reminder of his own failure.

But this one was different. Julie Montgomery had not been his patient, not since the day he'd delivered her. No, this time his patient was still alive. But he had delivered Sally herself, as well as her two children, and she had been on his roster for as long as she had needed the services of an obstetrician-gynecologist. Over the years he had come to regard her with an almost paternal affection. One of his special girls, as he thought of them.

So he had come today, even though he hated funerals, and now, as the service drew to a close, he was beginning to wish he'd stayed away after all. He was going to have to speak to Sally, and he knew the words of condolence would not come easy to him. In the familiar surroundings of his office, the right words always came easily. But here, faced with a patient whose problem was beyond his medical expertise, he was at a loss. And yet, something had to be said. He started toward Sally.

She had nearly reached the car when she felt a hand on her arm. She turned and found herself looking into the troubled eyes of Arthur Wiseman.

"Sally—" he began.

"It was good of you to come, Dr. Wiseman," Sally said, her voice barely audible.

"I know how difficult this must be for you ..." Wiseman said. Then his voice faltered, and he fell silent.

Sally stared at him for a moment, waiting for him to continue. "Do you?" she asked at last. Suddenly, with no forewarning at all, she found her entire being flooded with anger. Why couldn't he find the right words to comfort her? He was a doctor, wasn't he? *Her* doctor? Wasn't it his *job* to know what to say at a time like this? She glared at him, her face a mask of pain and anger. "Do you know how difficult it is for me?" she demanded. "Do you know what it feels like to lose your baby and not even know why?"

Stung, Arthur Wiseman glanced around the cemetery as if he were looking for a means of escape. "No, of course I can't feel what you're feeling," he muttered at last as Sally's gaze remained fixed upon him. "But I hope I can understand it." He could see that she was no longer listening to him as she searched the cemetery for—what? Her husband, probably. Wiseman kept talking, hoping Steve would appear. "I do know how hard it is, Sally. Even for doctors who see death all the time, it's still hard. Especially in cases like Julie's—"

"Julie?" Sally repeated. At mention of her daughter's name, her attention shifted back to the doctor. "What about Julie?"

Wiseman paused, looking deeply into Sally's eyes. There was something in them—a sort of flickering glow—that told him Sally was on the edge of losing control. He searched his mind for something to say, anything that might ease her pain. "But we're learning, Sally. Every year we're learning a little more. I know it's no help to you, but someday we'll know what causes SIDS—"

"It wasn't SIDS," Sally interrupted. "Something happened to Julie." Her voice rose and took on a shrillness that Wiseman immediately recognized as the beginnings of hysteria. "I don't know what it was," Sally plunged on, "but I'm going to find out. It wasn't SIDS—it was something else. Julie was fine. She was just fine!"

Wiseman listened helplessly as Sally's hysteria soared, certain that he'd been wrong to come to the funeral, wrong to speak to Sally Montgomery right now. Here, today, he could see the true depths of her grief. When the time came for her to begin dealing with the reality of her loss, would he be able to help her? He was glad when Steve Montgomery, accompanied by Sally's mother and Jason, appeared beside her.

"Sally?" Steve asked. Sally's gaze shifted over to him, and Steve, too, saw the strange light in her eyes. "Are you all right?"

"I want to go home," Sally whispered, the last of her energy drained by her outburst. "I want to go home, and get away from here. Please? Take me home." She moved once more toward the nearby car, Steve by her side, Jason trailing along behind them. Only Phyllis Paine stayed behind to speak to Wiseman, and there was an anger in her voice that he had rarely heard in the long years of their friendship.

"Arthur, what did you say to her?" she demanded. "What did you say to my daughter?"

"Nothing, Phyllis," Wiseman replied tiredly. "Only that maybe someday we'll have some idea of what causes SIDS."

"At the funeral?" Phyllis asked, her voice reflecting her outrage. "You came to the funeral to talk about what killed Julie?"

Wiseman groaned inwardly, but was careful to maintain a calm façade. "That's hardly what I was doing, Phyllis, and when you think about it, I know you'll realize I would never do something like that. But it's important that Sally understand what happened, and I wanted to let her know that if there's anything I can do, either as her doctor or her friend, I'll do it."

As Wiseman spoke, Steven Montgomery came back to escort his mother-in-law to the waiting car. "There *is* something you can do, Dr. Wiseman," he said. "Just try to let us forget about it. It's over, and nothing can be done. We have to try to forget."

He led Phyllis to the car, helped her in, then turned back to face the doctor once again. "You understand, don't you?" he asked with a bleakness in his voice that Wiseman had rarely heard before. "There's nothing we can do now. Nothing at all." Then Steve, too, got into the car, and Wiseman watched as the Montgomerys drove away. When they were gone, the agony of Sally's eyes and Steve's words remained.

As he left the cemetery, Wiseman pondered the true depth of the tragedy that had befallen the Montgomerys.

For Julie, the tragedy was over.

For her parents, it had just begun.

❖ ❖ ❖

Jason Montgomery jammed the shovel into the ground, jumped on it, then pulled on the handle until the clod of earth came loose. He repeated the process again and again, then stopped to inspect his work.

There was a square, four feet on a side, from which he'd stripped the topsoil. He'd been working for almost an hour—ever since he'd gotten home from his sister's funeral. So far, no one had come out to tell him to stop.

Maybe today, no one would.

If it happened that way—and Jason thought the chances were pretty good—then he would have his fort done by suppertime. It would be four feet deep and covered over with some planks he'd found behind the garage last week. His father had said they were going to be used for a chicken coop, but Jason had decided that since they had no chickens, he might as well use them for the roof of his fort. Besides, all he had to do was lay them on the ground side by side. They wouldn't even have to be nailed. The work was all in the digging. He wished Randy Corliss were there to help him, but he hadn't even been allowed to call Randy today, so now he had to build the fort all by himself.

He picked up the shovel once more and plunged it deep into the softer earth that lay beneath the surface. He felt the shovel hit something and pushed harder. It gave a little, then a lot. Putting the shovel aside, he knelt down in the dirt and began digging at the loose soil with his bare hands.

A moment later he hit the broken bottle.

It had been whole when the shovel struck it, but now its sharp edges slashed at him, cutting deep into the index finger on his left hand. Reflexively, Jason jerked his hand out of the dirt and stuck the finger in his mouth. He sucked hard, tasting the sweet saltiness of the blood, then spat onto the ground.

He inspected his finger carefully. Blood was oozing thickly from the cut, running down his hand, then dripping slowly onto the pile of loose dirt. He squeezed the finger, remembering someone once telling him that you had to make a cut bleed a lot to keep it from getting infected.

When the bleeding slowed a minute later, he inspected the cut. It was about a half-inch long and looked deep. He decided he'd better go wash his hand.

He slipped through the kitchen and dining room, avoiding the living room where he knew his parents were sitting. Even though he didn't really miss his little sister, he knew they were very upset, and he didn't want to bother them. He could take care of the cut himself, or, if he decided he couldn't, he could get his grandmother to help him.

He went upstairs to the bathroom and began washing his hands. The dirt and already-clotting blood swirled down the drain. Once more Jason squeezed at the finger.

This time it didn't bleed.

Puzzled, Jason held his hand up to the light and inspected it.

He couldn't find the cut.

He stared at his finger, and in a moment found the faintest tracing of a scar where the injury had been.

His brow furrowed into a curious scowl as he tried to figure out what had happened.

It had bled a lot.

Now there was nothing.

Did cuts heal that fast? In the past when he'd skinned his knee or something, the Band-Aid always had to stay on for a couple of days.

Of course, who knew what happened *under* the Band-Aid? His mother had never let him look.

Maybe all cuts healed this fast.

Or maybe the cut hadn't been as bad as he'd thought.

He tried to remember how much it had hurt and couldn't remember it having hurt much at all. Not like when he skinned his knees or his elbows, when it stung for a couple of seconds. With the cut, he'd hardly felt anything. In fact, if it hadn't been for the blood, he probably wouldn't even have noticed it.

He turned off the water, dried his hands, then went

back downstairs and outside. He looked at the ground where all the blood had dripped. There didn't seem to be much left. And then, from next door, he heard a voice calling him, and looked up to see Joey Connors waving to him.

"Hey, Jason," Joey was saying, "you wanna come over and see my puppies?"

"Puppies?" Jason repeated, his eyes widening with eagerness, the cut finger forgotten. "You got puppies?"

Joey nodded. "Daisy had 'em day before yesterday, but my mom wouldn't let me call you."

"How come?" Jason asked as he climbed over the fence and dropped into the Connors' yard.

" 'Cause of your sister. Did you go to the funeral?"

"Uh-huh."

"What was it like?"

Jason stopped a minute, thinking. "Like a funeral, I guess," he said. Then, "Can I have one of the puppies?"

To an adult, Jason Montgomery's reaction to the death of his sister might have seemed callous. To him, her death was as unreal as she had been, and in his life, not much had changed. In fact, for Jason, the most notable event of the day was probably the finger that healed in ten minutes flat.

In her daughter's guest room, Phyllis Paine packed the last of her belongings into her suitcase and snapped it shut. Her eyes scanned the room absently. She was sure she had left nothing out. In her own mind she was already at home, taking up the myriad details of which life, for her, was composed. Phyllis was not a cold woman. When Julie died, Phyllis had experienced one of those private moments of unutterable grief, and then, taking herself in hand, had risen to the occasion. For two days she had run her daughter's home as she ran her own—efficiently, quietly, and with a sense of purpose. She had done her best to give Sally room in which to mourn. Now Sally had to begin putting her life back together again. All Phyllis's instincts told her to stay on, and "do" for Sally. She knew the pain Sally was feeling; she had felt it herself so long ago when her own first child had been stillborn. But no one had "done" for her. She had been forced to deal with her feelings, cope with the turns life can take, and persevere. And so she had buried her little boy, as Sally had just buried her little girl, and then gone on with life.

She picked up her suitcase and carried it downstairs. Sally and Steve were in the living room, sitting on a sofa, a distance between them that seemed greater than the few inches that separated them.

"Steve, would you call a taxi for me, please?"

Sally's head swung slowly around, and her eyes, clouded by tears that still threatened to overflow at any moment, seemed puzzled. "A taxi?" she repeated vacantly. "Where are you going?"

"Home, dear," Phyllis said gently. She forced herself to remain impassive to the barely perceptible shudder that passed over her daughter. Her gaze shifted to her son-in-law and she nodded slightly; Steve left her alone with Sally. Only then did she move to the sofa and sit by her daughter, taking Sally's hand in her own.

There was a long silence between the two women, and for a moment Phyllis wasn't sure how to bridge it. Finally she squeezed Sally's hand reassuringly.

"I was wrong yesterday, dear," she said, "and I want to apologize."

Sally's eyes, full of fright and dazed, met her mother's. "Wrong? About what?"

"About Julie," Phyllis said. "About how she died. I don't know why I said what I did before—about babies not just dying. It was stupid of me."

Sally's expression cleared slightly. "I don't know what you mean."

"I mean I was wrong to insinuate that something must have happened to Julie. I know now that nothing did. She simply died, and we have to accept that."

"Like you accepted what happened to my brother?" Though her voice was level, there was a coldness in her tone that shocked Phyllis even more than the words.

"How did you know about that?"

"Daddy told me. A long time ago."

"He had no right—" Phyllis began.

"He had every right, Mother," Sally replied. "He was trying to explain to me why—well, why you're the way you are."

"I see," Phyllis replied, sinking back into the depths of the sofa. It was the first time her son had been mentioned in Phyllis's presence since the day he had been born. "And did it explain anything?" she heard herself asking.

"No, not really," Sally replied, her voice distant, as if she were thinking of something else.

"Then let me try," Phyllis said, choosing her words carefully, afraid that even talking of that time nearly thirty years in the past might destroy the careful structure she had built for herself. "I blamed myself for the fact that your brother was born dead, even though the doctors told me it wasn't my fault. Just as you might be blaming yourself for what happened to Julie. In the months afterward, I wanted to die myself. I almost did. I—well, I almost killed myself. But then something changed my mind. Don't ask what—I don't even remember. But I suddenly realized that no matter how I felt about the son I never knew, I had responsibilities. To your father, and, a few years later, to you. And so I took each day as it came, and I got through. And I'm still getting through, Sally, just as you must. One day at a time. Don't think about what Julie might have been. Don't even think about what she was. Just take each day as it comes, and do what you must do. Life is for the living, Sally, and no matter how you're feeling now, you're still alive."

There was a silence as Sally tried to absorb her mother's words. They sounded so cold, so uncaring. And in her mind, Sally kept seeing her daughter, asleep in her crib, but not asleep.

Dying.

Dying from what?

For how long?

She swallowed, trying by the gesture to drive the image from her mind, but knowing it was useless. And then she saw Steve standing a few feet away, watching her. How long had he been there? Had he been listening?

"She's right, you know," he said. He *had* been listening. For some reason Sally felt betrayed. "We have to put our lives together again, darling, and we have to do it by ourselves."

"But I need—"

"You need Jason, and you need me," Steve went on, his voice firm. "You need to pick up the threads of your life. And you can't do that as long as Phyllis is here. Don't you see that?"

Sally shifted on the couch, drawing herself away from her mother. "You want me to forget about Julie, don't you?" she said. "You want me to do what Mother did and pretend she didn't exist at all. Well, I can't do that. I won't do that. She was my daughter, Steve. She was my little girl, and something killed her. I have to find out what! I have to, and I will!"

"Sally—" Steve started toward his wife, but the sudden jangling of the telephone stopped him. His eyes, beseeching, stayed on Sally for a moment. "Oh, Jesus," he muttered. He disappeared into the kitchen to answer the phone while Sally and her mother sat in tense silence in the living room. And then Steve was back.

"Sally, someone wants to talk to you."

"Not now," Sally said, her voice dull.

"I think you'd better take it. I think it's important."

Sally started to protest once more, but the expression in her husband's eyes changed her mind. Stiffly, her body aching with exhaustion, she got to her feet and went to the kitchen.

"Hello?"

"Mrs. Montgomery? My name is Lois Petropoulous. You don't know me, but—"

"My husband said you have something to say to me," Sally broke in. "This isn't a good time for me—"

"I know. I'm terribly sorry about your daughter. I know what you're going through. The same thing happened to me six months ago."

"I beg your pardon?"

"There's a group of us, Mrs. Montgomery. Six couples. We meet once a week, trying to deal with the deaths of our children."

Sally frowned. What was the woman talking about? A group for the parents of dead children? "I'm sorry," she said, "but I don't—"

"Don't hang up, Mrs. Montgomery, please? It's the SIDS Foundation. They set up these groups so we can try to help each other understand what happened. We meet on Tuesdays, and I hope you and your husband might come tonight."

Sally fought to hold her temper. They weren't going to leave her alone. None of them. Not her husband, not her mother. And now the strangers were going to start on her, meddling in her life, trying to tell her what was good for her. Well, she would have none of it. She'd deal with her problems in her own way. "Thank you for calling," she said politely, "but Julie did not die of SIDS, so there would be no point in my coming to your meeting, would there?" Without waiting for a reply, she hung up the phone and returned to the living room. Through the window she could see a cab pulling up in front of the house. Her mother was standing up, looking at her expectantly. Sally composed herself, intent on hiding the resentment she was feeling for both Phyllis and Steve.

"Shall I walk you to the cab?"

Phyllis ignored the question. "Who was on the phone? Was it something to do with Julie?"

"No, Mother. It was nothing." She began guiding her mother toward the door. "I'm sorry for what I said. I'm just terribly tired right now. But you're right—life *is* for the living. I'll be all right." She gave her mother a quick hug, and kissed her on the cheek. "Really I will."

The two of them paused at the front door, but there

was nothing left to say. And then Phyllis was gone, and Sally returned to her husband.

"We're going to that meeting," Steve said as soon as Sally had returned to the living room.

Sally looked at him, her eyes clear. "But why? It's a meeting for SIDS parents, and that's not us."

"It *is* us, Sally," Steve said quietly. "I'm going to that meeting, and you're going with me, and that's that. Do you understand?"

The hardness of his voice hit Sally like a blow. She searched his face, trying to see what had changed. He had never spoken to her that way before, never as long as she had known him. And yet his voice had left no room for doubt—he had given her an order and expected to be obeyed. Her eyes narrowed, and when she spoke, there was a hardness in her own voice that was foreign to her. "Then we'll go," she said. "But I still see no purpose to it."

A few minutes later she went into the room where Julie had lived to begin the process of clearing out all the things she would never need again. She stripped the bedding from Julie's crib, then folded up the crib itself. She went through the chest of drawers, pausing over each tiny dress or blouse—so many of them had never been worn, and now never would be. Finally, she took down the mobile that had been drifting over Julie's crib since the very beginning, stared at it sadly for a moment, then reluctantly dropped it into the wastebasket.

Everything was changed.

Her family was changed.

Her husband was changed.

She herself was changed.

From now on everything was going to be different.

Oh, she would do her best to be like her mother. She would accept her responsibilities. She would live for the living.

And yet, deep inside, a part of her was convinced that there was a reason for Julie's death, and even as she put away Julie's things, she knew that sooner or later she would have to discover that reason. And so, when she eventually left that room for the last time, she knew that she would never be like her mother at all.

In two days Sally Montgomery had changed in ways that the people close to her had not even begun to understand.

Chapter 8

Eastbury elementary school, its whitewashed exterior turning gray and its grounds unkempt, sat defensively huddled in the midst of a small grove of maples as if it was trying to hide. As Lucy Corliss approached it, she found herself feeling oddly sorry for the bedraggled building—it was almost as if the school itself was aware of the fact that it was on the edge of ruin, and was hoping that if no one noticed it was there, someone would forget to tear it down. As Lucy passed through the front door, she could sense that the depressing appearance of the school's façade had permeated throughout. There was a feeling of gloom that the dim lights in the corridor did nothing to dispel. It was nearly four o'clock on Tuesday afternoon, and the silence of the place made her wonder if anyone was still there. She walked purposefully toward Randy's classroom, her heels clicking hollowly on the wood floor.

Harriet Grady, nearing sixty but carrying the strain of her thirty-five years of teaching as gracefully as anyone could, was preparing to leave for the day when Lucy appeared in her classroom. She recognized Lucy immediately and rose to her feet. "Mrs. Corliss," she said warmly. "Please come in. Is there any news about Randy?"

71

Lucy glanced around the room. It, too, needed a coat of paint, and there were several cracked panes in the large casement windows that broke the west wall. She walked to one of the windows and stared out, not seeing anything really, but trying to decide where to begin. Now that she was here, she was no longer sure why she had come. "Do you think Randy ran away?" she asked at last. A moment later she felt the teacher's hand touching her arm.

"I don't know," Harriet replied. "It's so hard to know the children these days. They all seem—what? Older than their years, I suppose. So many of the children just don't seem like children anymore. It's almost as if there are things in their minds they don't want you to know."

Lucy nodded. "Randy's been that way since he was a baby. I always have the feeling I don't quite know him. I suppose it's because I don't get to spend as much time with him as I should."

"Children need their parents," Harriet commented, and Lucy sensed a trace of condemnation in her tone.

"Unfortunately, marriages don't always work out."

"Or people don't work them out," the teacher countered.

Lucy's eyes narrowed angrily. "Miss Grady, I didn't come here to talk about my marriage. I came here to talk about my son."

The two women's eyes met and Harriet Grady's expression softened. "I'm sorry," she said. "I suppose I'm getting to be a crotchety old lady. I can't get used to the fact that most of my children have only one parent. It seems such a pity, and I always wonder if it isn't one of the reasons so many of the children have problems."

"Like Randy?" Lucy asked.

"Randy, and a lot of others." Harriet Grady appraised Lucy Corliss carefully and decided there was no point in mincing words. "But of course you know that Randy's been more of a problem than most."

"How?"

Harriet moved back to her desk, sat down, and pulled

a file folder from the top drawer. She began glancing through it.

"Discipline problems. Except it's not quite that easy."

"I'm not sure I understand," Lucy said. She reached out to take the file, but Harriet Grady held on to it.

"I'm sorry," she apologized. "I'm afraid I'm not supposed to let you see these."

Lucy stared at the teacher, trying to grasp what she was saying. "Not let me see them? My God, Miss Grady, my son is missing! And if there's information about him in that file that I need to know about, you have no right to keep it from me. I'm his mother, Miss Grady, I have a right to know everything about my son."

"Well, I really just don't know," Harriet Grady fretted. "You have to understand, Mrs. Corliss—files on students contain all kinds of information, much of it quite objective, but some of it purely subjective. And we just don't like anyone to see the subjective portions. Anyone at all."

"Except the teachers," Lucy interjected, her voice grating with anger.

"Except the teachers," Harriet agreed. She leaned back in her chair and brushed a strand of hair from her eyes. "Mrs. Corliss," she went on, "I know how you must feel and I wish I could tell you something to make you feel better. But what can I say? Randy has tried to run away before."

"He was going to see his father," Lucy protested. "And he was only gone a few hours."

"But he still ran," the teacher insisted. "There's something about Randy—something odd. He doesn't always seem to have good judgment."

"Good judgment?" Lucy echoed. "He's only nine years old. What on earth are you talking about?"

Harriet Grady sighed and fingered the file for a moment. "I wish I could tell you. It's something I can't quite put my finger on. It's as if Randy thinks he can do anything any time he wants. He doesn't seem to be afraid of anything, and it gets him into trouble."

Lucy frowned. "What kind of trouble?"

"Nothing serious," Harriet assured her. "At least not yet. But we're always afraid that someday he's going to hurt himself."

"Hurt himself? How?"

Harriet Grady searched her mind, trying to think of a way to illustrate what she was trying to say. Finally, she gave up, and reluctantly handed Lucy the file. "Look at the top page," she said. "And I suppose, if you insist, you might as well look at the rest of the file too. It's all more or less the same."

Lucy took the file, opened it, and quickly read the first page. Her skin began to crawl, but she forced herself to finish reading the report, then glanced through the other pages. As Miss Grady had said, it was all the same. Her hands trembling, she returned the folder to the teacher.

"Tell me what happened," she whispered. "Tell me about that day."

Harriet Grady cleared her throat, then began. "It was last September. One of the children brought a black widow spider into class. It was in a jar, but I kept it on my desk, and let the children come up to look at it. I warned them that it was poisonous, and they were all very careful. Most of them wouldn't even pick up the jar. Randy not only picked it up; he opened it and put his hand inside."

"Good Lord," Lucy whispered. "What happened?"

"He started poking at it, and the spider tried to get away from him. But it finally attacked. I tried to take the jar away from him, but he wouldn't let me. He didn't seem frightened—he seemed fascinated."

"Even when the spider bit him?"

"Fortunately, it didn't. I finally knocked the jar out of his hands, and smashed the spider. Then I took him to the nurse and had her look at the hand. There were no bites."

"It didn't bite him at all?"

"Apparently not. And even when the nurse explained to him what a black widow bite can do, he didn't seem worried. He just said he'd played with them before, and nothing had happened."

Nausea rose to Lucy's throat as she began to realize what might have happened to Randy. "Why didn't you tell me?" she asked. "Why didn't someone—"

Harriet Grady's mouth twisted into a frosty smile. "Do what, Mrs. Corliss? Send a note home with Randy saying 'Dear Mrs. Corliss, today Randy didn't get bitten by a spider?' You'd have thought I was crazy."

Lucy closed her eyes and nodded. "I probably would." She thought for a moment, trying to decide what significance the teacher's information might have for her. But there was nothing. Nothing but a history of dangerous stunts and pranks, any of which might have seriously injured or even killed Randy, but none of which, so far, had apparently harmed him. When she opened her eyes, Harriet Grady was looking at her with an expression that told Lucy the teacher was sharing her thoughts.

"I suppose it's possible that Randy could have gone off on some kind of an adventure and it went wrong," the teacher offered. Then she stood up and began leading Lucy to the door. "I wish I could tell you more, Mrs. Corliss, but I never knew what Randy was going to do next. Now I don't know what to think." She squeezed Lucy's arm reassuringly. "He *will* be found, Mrs. Corliss. And knowing Randy, whatever's happened, he'll come out all right. He always has so far."

But when Lucy left her classroom, Harriet Grady went back to her desk and scanned Randy Corliss's file once again. To her, Randy was a hopeless case. If there ever was a boy who was going to get himself in trouble, it was Randy. She closed the file, put it back in the desk, and locked the drawer.

Lucy was almost out of the building when she noticed the small sign identifying the nurse's office. She hesitated, then tapped on the frosted glass panel.

"Come in," a voice called out. Lucy opened the door and stepped inside. A woman only slightly older than herself, dressed in a white uniform, was sitting at a desk reading a paperback novel. She glanced up and grinned.

"If you're an irate taxpayer, I'm technically off duty. I just hang around most afternoons in case one of the kids hurts himself on the playground. Everyone says I'm dedicated."

Lucy laughed in spite of herself. The nurse had an open expression that was in sharp contrast to the stern visage of Randy's teacher.

"I'm not an irate taxpayer," Lucy told her. "I'm a worried mother."

Immediately the grin faded from the nurse's face, and she stood up.

"Are you Mrs. Corliss?" she asked. "We're all so worried about Randy. Is there anything I can do?"

"I don't know," Lucy admitted. "I was on my way out, and I happened to see the sign. And Miss Grady was just telling me about something that happened last fall—"

"The black widow," the nurse interrupted. "Your boy was very lucky there."

"That's what Miss Grady said. She—she thinks Randy ran away. Everybody does."

"Everybody except you, right?" The nurse gestured toward a chair. "Sit down. I'm Annie Oliphant, and I've heard all the possible jokes having to do with orphans and elephants." Once more her expression turned serious. "I'm afraid there's not much I can do for you. Randy was one boy I hardly ever saw." She went to a filing cabinet, pulled out a thin folder, and glanced quickly through it.

"May I see that?" Lucy asked, her tone deliberately sarcastic. "Or is it confidential?"

Annie Oliphant handed her the file. "Nothing in there that's a deep, dark secret. And I'll bet there's nothing in any of Randy's other files that's going to shake national security either. I think secrets just make everyone around here feel important."

Lucy flipped through the pages of Randy's medical file. The information was sparse and mostly meaningless to her. "I don't suppose any of this could relate to Randy's disappearance, could it?" she asked.

"I don't see how," the nurse agreed. "The only thing interesting about that file is that it describes a disgustingly healthy kid. If they were all like Randy, I wouldn't have a job. Look at this." She took the file out of Lucy's hands and started from the beginning. "No major illnesses. No minor illnesses. No injuries, major or minor. Tonsils intact and healthy. Appendix in place. Even his *teeth*, for heaven's sake! The lower ones are at least crooked, but not enough to bother with braces, and there isn't a cavity in his head. What did you do, raise him in a box?"

Again, Lucy couldn't help laughing. "Hardly. I guess we've just been lucky. Up till now." She paused, and when she spoke again, her voice was lower. "Do you know Randy very well?"

The nurse shook her head. "All I ever did was look him over once a year. He wasn't one for getting sick in the cafeteria or banging himself up. I'm afraid the only kids I really know are the sickly ones, and as you can see, Randy can hardly be called sickly."

Lucy flipped through the file once more. "Could I have a copy of this?" she asked.

"Sure." Lucy followed her down the hall, and watched from the doorway as the nurse began duplicating the file.

"I can't imagine what good this will be," Annie said uncertainly as she gave the copies to Lucy.

"I can't either," Lucy replied, her voice suddenly quavering. "I suppose it just makes me feel as though I've *done* something. You don't know what it's like, having your child missing. I feel so helpless. I don't even know where to begin. I thought maybe someone here might know something, or have noticed something— anything." Lucy could hear her desperation in her trembling voice and was afraid for a moment that she was going to cry. She fell silent, fighting the tears.

"I'm so sorry, Mrs. Corliss." The nurse's voice was gentle as she guided Lucy toward the main doors of the school. "It just seems to be the times we live in. Things happen to children when they're younger now. First the teen-agers started running away, and now it seems like the preteens are starting to do it. And they're drinking and using drugs too. I wish I knew why."

Lucy's tearfulness gave way to anger. "Randy doesn't drink, and he doesn't use drugs! And he didn't run away!" Her voice rose dangerously. "Something happened to him, and I'm going to find out what!"

She ran through the doors and down the steps, then hurried toward her car. She could feel the nurse's eyes on her as she started the engine, but she didn't glance back as she jammed the car into gear, pressed the accelerator, and sped away.

"Anything?"

"Nothing."

Jim and Lucy Corliss stood facing each other. After a long moment Lucy stepped back to let him come into her house. He glanced around the dimness of the living room, then went to the window and opened the drapes. Evening sunlight seemed to wash some of the strain from his ex-wife's face.

"You can't live in darkness, Lucy. That won't help you or Randy."

Lucy sighed heavily, and sank into a chair. "I know. The truth is, I didn't even realize they were closed. I guess I never opened them at all this morning."

"You've got to—"

"Don't lecture me, Jim. I don't think I can stand it. Isn't there any trace of him at all?"

Jim shook his head. "Nothing. They're doing everything they can, Lucy, believe me. I was with them all day. We searched the woods he got lost in last year, and talked to practically everyone on his route to school. No one saw him; no one knows anything. They'll keep searching tomorrow, but after that—" He shrugged despondently.

"You mean they'll stop looking?" Lucy demanded.

"But he's only a little boy, Jim. They *can't* stop looking for him, can they?"

Jim moved to the sideboard and helped himself to a drink, and Lucy, even in the midst of her anguish, found herself gauging its strength. Surprisingly, it appeared to her to be fairly weak. "Fix me one?" she asked.

"Sure." He poured a second highball and crossed to her, handed her the drink, then retreated to a chair a few feet away. "You have to understand, Lucy. It isn't that they don't want to look for him. They *are* looking, and they say they'll keep on. But they simply can't keep doing it full-time. Eventually, unless there're signs of violence, or a ransom note, they're going to have to assume he ran away."

"But he didn't," Lucy insisted. "I know he didn't. And please, Jim, don't ask me how I know. I just do."

"I wasn't going to ask you that," Jim said gently. "I was going to ask you if you've had dinner."

Lucy looked at him sharply. Did he expect her to cook for him now? He seemed to read her mind.

"I'd like to take you out, Lucy." He saw her body stiffen and her eyes become guarded. "Don't," he said. "I know what you're thinking. You're wondering what I'm after. Well, I'm not after anything, Lucy. It's just that— well, we've lost our son, and for some reason right now I'm finding it very difficult to relate to anyone but you. And I'm worried about you."

"About me?" Lucy asked, her skepticism clear in her voice.

"I know. I know, I know, I know! I was a thoughtless inconsiderate selfish bastard, and I deserved to be thrown out. In fact, I probably should have been drawn and quartered, then strung up for the vultures to feed on. Perhaps even keelhauled"—her lips were beginning to twitch just slightly—"or marooned on a desert island . . ."

"I'd draw the line at the keelhauling," Lucy burst out. "You never could hold your breath for more than a few seconds." She fell silent, examining him carefully, looking for a clue as to what was going on in his mind. She

79

wanted to believe him, to believe that he wanted nothing more from her than company for dinner and the companionship that, right now, only she could give him.

She made up her mind.

"Do you remember the Speckled Hen?" she asked. It was a little place, a few miles out of Eastbury. When they were first married, it had been their favorite place, but she hadn't been there for nearly ten years.

"Is it still there?" Jim asked.

"It was last week," Lucy said. "I had a listing out there, and I almost went in for lunch."

"Why didn't you?"

This time there was something in his eyes that made Lucy keep her own counsel. "I just changed my mind," she said. She finished her drink and stood up. "Let's go. I don't promise to be great company, but you're right. I need to eat, and I need to be with someone this evening."

"Even me?"

"Even you. Maybe, tonight, only you."

As they drove to the restaurant, Lucy tried to analyze what it was about Jim that had changed. Several times she caught herself watching him out of the corner of her eye. The profile was still perfect, though his jaw seemed even stronger than it had been twelve years ago.

No, the changes weren't in his physical being; they were somewhere else.

His manner had changed. He seemed, to Lucy, to be more aware of things beyond himself. Also, there was a stability to him, and a hint of humor that was unfamiliar to her. Oh, he'd always been funny, but it had always been at the expense of someone else, usually her.

"What changed you?" she suddenly heard herself asking. If the question surprised him, he gave no sign.

"Life," he said. "I guess I got tired of landing on my ass. It was either change my ways or pad my butt, and I decided wearing a pillow wouldn't work. Maybe your throwing me out was the best thing that ever happened to me. For the first time, I didn't have anyone to fall on, so I decided to stop falling."

There was a long silence then, and Lucy didn't speak again until they were in the parking lot of the restaurant.

"Jim?"

He turned to face her, and once more it was as if he'd read her mind.

"Don't worry," he said. "For a while, at least, I can take care of both of us. If you want to fall apart, you go ahead. You may not think I'm good for much, but right now I'm all you've got. And you can depend on me, Lucy. Okay?"

Her tears brimmed over, and she sat still, letting them flow. Jim sat quietly beside her, holding her hand in his own.

The Speckled Hen was very much as they remembered it, and for the next few hours they talked of things other than their son.

They talked of times past, when things had been good, and times past, when things had been bad.

Mostly, they were silent. No one watching them would have known they'd been divorced for nearly ten years. To an outsider they would have appeared very much married, with much on their minds, but little need to talk.

By the time he took her home, Jim and Lucy Corliss were becoming friends again.

Chapter 9

THE NIGHT WAS WARM and humid, a precursor of the summer that was soon to come, and Steve Montgomery left his window rolled down as he searched for the right house. "It should be in this block," he said, slowing the car and peering through the darkness for the numbers which seemed to him to be deliberately hidden from anyone who might be looking for them.

"I still don't see why you insisted on coming." Sally's voice was cold. She sat stiffly upright on the seat next to him, her arms folded across her breast, the fingers of her right hand kneading the flesh of her left arm. Steve brought the car to a halt, switched off the ignition, and turned to face his wife.

"It can't hurt, and it might help," he said. He reached out to touch his wife, but she drew away from him. He sighed, and when he spoke again, he was careful to keep his growing impatience out of his voice. "Look, honey, how can it possibly hurt? You don't have to say a word if you don't want to. But all these people have been through the same thing we've been through. If anyone can help us come to grips with this thing, they can."

He searched Sally's face, hoping for a sign that perhaps she was willing to face the reality of what had happened to Julie. But her face remained unchanged, her eyes brooding, her expression one of puzzled detachment.

Steve knew what was happening. She was sifting through her mind, trying to find a clue that would unlock the mystery of Julie's death for her. It had begun that afternoon, when instead of beginning to put her life back together, as Steve was trying to do with himself, she had sat straight up on the sofa, a medical book in her lap, reading intently page after page of material that Steve was nearly certain she didn't understand. But he understood very well what she was doing.

She was looking for what he had already come to think of as The Real Reason for Julie's death.

It had begun the night before. As Steve lay trying to fall asleep, and thinking about the funeral to be faced the next morning, Sally had left their bed and begun wandering through the house as though she were looking for something. Steve heard her footsteps in the hall, heard the soft click of a door opening and closing, and knew that she had gone to Jason's room to reassure herself that her son was still alive. Twice he had gone downstairs to talk to her, only to find her hunched up on the sofa, a book open on her lap, reading.

And refusing to talk to him, except to doggedly repeat the litany: Babies don't just die. But tonight, he hoped, Sally might begin to accept that theirs had. He got out of the car and went around to open the door for Sally.

Holding her arm, he guided her up the steps of the large frame house, then pressed the bell. A moment later the door was opened, and a friendly-looking woman about the same age as Sally smiled at them.

"You must be the Montgomerys," she said. "I'm so glad you could come. I'm Lois Petropoulous." She guided them into the living room and introduced them to the twelve people who were gathered there. There was a disparity to the group that Steve found startling at first. There was a black couple, and an Oriental man with his Caucasian wife. Two of the women had no husbands, and one couple stood out only for the apparent poverty of their lives. The woman's face, like her husband's, was gaunt, and there was a hopelessness in her eyes that was reflected in the shabbiness of her dress. Steve scanned the group, searching for a common bond among them, but there was none. Apparently all that had brought them together was the fact that each of them had lost a child to sudden infant death syndrome.

Two places had been held for them on a large sofa. Steve lowered himself gratefully into its soft comfort. Sally, next to him, remained rigidly erect, her hands clasped together in her lap.

"We don't really have a leader in the group," Lois Petropoulous explained. "In fact, we don't really have a regular meeting place either. The group keeps changing, and we keep moving from house to house, as people come and go."

"How long do people stay in the group?" Steve asked.

"As long as they need to, or as long as they feel needed," the gaunt-looking woman, whose name was Irene, said. "Kevin and I have been part of it for over a year now."

Another woman—Steve thought her name was Muriel—suddenly grinned. "We think Irene and Kevin stick around because we're cheap entertainment." Steve felt himself flushing and was surprised to hear several people, including Irene and Kevin, chuckling.

"Don't be surprised at anything you might hear," Lois said, smiling kindly. "We all have to deal with SIDS in our own way, and sometimes humor is the only way. But we also shed a lot of tears, and sometimes we get pretty loud. You have no idea how much anger builds up after you lose a child the way we all have. One of the reasons we're here is to vent that anger. In this group there are no rules. Say what you feel, or what you think, and be assured that someone else here has felt and thought exactly the same thing. What's most important is to realize that you're not alone. Everyone here has gone through what you're going through." She glanced around the room. "Well," she said, her voice suddenly nervous, "I suppose we've already begun, but I'm going to make my big announcement anyway, even though I'd planned to start the meeting with it. I'm pregnant."

All the eyes in the room suddenly fastened on Lois, and she squirmed self-consciously. "And the first person who says 'after what happened?' gets the award for bad taste for tonight."

"After what happened?" five voices immediately asked. When the laughter died, Muriel Flannery spoke out of the silence.

"But aren't you scared, Lois? I mean, really?"

"Of course I'm scared," Lois replied. "I'm terrified. And you can believe I don't expect to get much sleep the first couple of years. I'll be watching this baby like a hawk, even with the alarm."

"I'm not sure I could do that to a baby," another voice said. "I mean, wire it up like that. It seems so—so cruel. Almost like a lab experiment, or something."

"But without it, I'd be afraid to let the baby sleep."

Steve Montgomery stared from one face to another. What were they talking about? An alarm for children? He'd never heard of such a thing. Seeing his expression, Kevin tried to explain. "We're talking about an infant monitor. You attach it to the baby when its sleeping, and it goes off if the baby stops breathing. Except that no one knows if it really works for SIDS. There's something else, called apnea, where the baby just seems to forget to breathe."

"But I thought that's what SIDS was," Steve said.

"I wish it were," another of the men put in. "But it seems there's more to SIDS than that. With SIDS, there's a constriction of the throat, so even if the baby tries to breathe, it can't. And for that, the alarm doesn't seem to do any good at all."

The conversation went on, moving from subject to subject. Steve found himself listening intently. These people, he began to realize, were just like himself—ordinary people who had become the victims of something they had always assumed could only happen to someone else. Each of them was dealing with it in a different way. There was grief and puzzlement in the room and a lot of anger. But for all of them, there was understanding.

Beside her husband, Sally Montgomery listened to the voices droning on and wondered why Steve had insisted they come to this meeting. There was nothing here for her, and she had a distinct feeling that she was wasting her time. She should be at home, looking after Jason, and studying her books, searching for the answer that kept eluding her as to what had happened to her daughter.

Suddenly, she heard a voice addressing her. It was Alex Petropoulous, and his intelligent eyes were fixed on her, his expression quizzical.

"You don't seem to be paying much attention, Mrs. Montgomery," he said. "Is there something on your mind?"

She made herself relax and sink back onto the couch, her hands smoothing the soft linen of her dress. "I'm afraid I've got a lot on my mind," she explained. "You see, my baby didn't die of SIDS. It was something else."

Across the room, a woman who had been quiet all evening suddenly spoke.

"I'm Jan Ransom, Mrs. Montgomery," she said. "Would you mind telling us what happened to your baby?"

"I—I don't know yet," Sally admitted. "But I'll find out."

"Of course you will," Jan agreed. "Just like I did. I spent nearly a year trying to find out what happened to my daughter, and I finally did."

Sally looked at the woman sharply. "What was it?" she asked.

"SIDS," Jan said, shrugging her shoulders. "You know, one of the hardest things to accept is the simple fact that with SIDS no one can tell you what happened. For me, the idea that the doctors—the people who are always supposed to know what happened and why it happened—didn't have the slightest idea why my baby died was absolutely unacceptable. So I started reading and studying and talking to everyone I could think of. And no one knew. Of course, what I was really doing was burying my head in the sand. Deep down, I was afraid that if there was no reasonable explanation for my baby's dying, I must have made it happen myself."

"No one would want to kill her own baby," Muriel Flannery said softly.

"No?" Jan Ransom replied bitterly. "People kill their own babies every day. And I never wanted a baby in the first place."

For the first time, Sally Montgomery began listening.

"I had my life all planned," Jan went on. "I was going to finish my master's—I'm in communications—then go to New York and get a job in advertising. When I was in my thirties, I'd get married, and my husband would be as career-minded as I am. No children. They only get in the way, and besides, what kind of world is this to bring up children in? Energy shortages, overpopulation, all the usual things. And then one day I turned up pregnant."

"Why didn't you have an abortion?" someone asked.

Jan Ransom smiled bitterly. "Did I forget to tell you? I was raised a Catholic. I thought I'd gotten over that, but it turned out I hadn't. Oh, I went for the birth control—that didn't bother me at all. But when it came right down to having an abortion, I just couldn't do it. And then, when the baby came, I couldn't put it up for adoption either. Maybe I should have."

"It wouldn't have made any difference," Lois Petropoulous told her. "SIDS doesn't have anything to do with who's raising the baby."

"Doesn't it?" Jan shot back. "Who says? And how do they know? If they don't know what SIDS is, how can they say it doesn't have anything to do with the parents? Maybe," she added, her voice trembling, "the baby senses that its mother doesn't want it and just decides to die."

Sally felt her fingers digging into her thighs as she listened to Jan Ransom. Right here, in front of all these people, the woman was voicing all the dark suspicions with which Sally had tormented herself in the small hours of the night. Now she could feel Jan Ransom's eyes on her. When she looked up, the young woman was smiling at her gently.

"I don't think I killed my baby anymore, Mrs. Montgomery," she said softly. "And I'm sure you didn't kill yours either. I don't know exactly why you're so sure that SIDS didn't kill your baby, but I do know that if the doctors say that's what happened, it's best to believe them. You can't spend the rest of your life searching for answers that don't exist. You have to go on with your life and accept what happened."

"I'm not sure I can do that," Sally said, suddenly standing up. "But I know that I have nothing in common with you people. Steve?" Without waiting for a reply, Sally started toward the door. Steve, his face flushing with embarrassment, tried to apologize for his wife.

"It's all right," Lois Petropoulous told him. "This isn't the first time this has happened, and it won't be the last. When she needs us, we'll still be here. If not us, then there will be others. Take care of her, Steve. She needs you very badly right now."

She stood by the door and watched Steve and Sally Montgomery disappear into the night. As she returned to the living room, she wondered if Sally Montgomery would come back and get the help she needed, or if she would insist on bearing her problems alone until the day came, as it inevitably would, when those problems would close in on her, and destroy her.

Jason Montgomery sat on the floor of his room, watching as his guinea pig happily darted from corner to corner, enjoying its respite from the confines of its cage. From downstairs Jason could hear the sound of the television droning on as the sitter dozed in front of it. He'd gone down a few minutes ago, but when he'd found her asleep, he'd decided not to wake her up. She wasn't like some of the sitters he'd had, who were always baking cookies or willing to play games. She was too old, he'd decided long ago, and all she wanted was to be left alone. And if she wasn't, sometimes she got crabby. So Jason had stood at the door for a minute, watching her, then gone back upstairs to play with Fred.

His parents, he knew, had gone to some meeting, but he wasn't sure what it was about. Something to do with his sister and getting used to the fact that she was dead. But Jason didn't understand why his parents had to go to a meeting. Hadn't there already been a funeral? He'd thought that's what the funeral was for, but now he guessed he'd been wrong.

He decided it was one more thing he'd talk to Randy Corliss about the next time he saw him.

Except that this afternoon Joey Connors had told him that Randy had run away, and most of the kids thought that even if he came back, he'd probably be sent to Juvenile Hall, where he'd be punished.

Fred moved across the floor, his tiny nose snuffling at the carpet, then crept into Jason's lap to be petted. Jason began scratching the rodent behind the ears and talking quietly to it.

"Is that what'll happen to me?" he asked. "But I didn't really do anything to Julie. All I did was put the blanket on her face for a minute." He stared down at the guinea pig, wondering for the hundredth time if he could really have hurt Julie by putting the blanket over her head. He was almost sure he hadn't.

Almost.

But what if he had? How would he ever know?

He picked up the guinea pig, pulled his extra blanket off his bed, then knelt down on the floor once again.

"Now, you pretend like you're Julie," he said. He put Fred on the floor, and rolled him over on his back. The guinea pig struggled for a moment, then, as Jason began tickling its stomach, lay still.

"There," Jason said. "Doesn't that feel good?" Then he stopped tickling his pet and waited. The tiny animal lay still, waiting for the petting to resume.

Carefully, Jason wrapped the blanket around the guinea pig and held it firm. He began counting.

Fred wriggled and squirmed in the woolen folds, and Jason could feel him trying to bite, but it was no use.

By the time Jason had counted to one hundred, there was no more movement within the blanket.

He tried to remember—had Julie stopped struggling? He thought she hadn't, and he was almost sure he'd held the blanket over her face for much longer than he'd kept Fred wrapped in it.

Almost sure.

Carefully, he lifted the blanket, sure that Fred, suddenly freed, would scurry under the bed.

The guinea pig lay still. Even when Jason prodded it with his finger, it didn't move.

Maybe, he decided, he *had* done something to Julie. But if he had, he hadn't meant to. No more than he'd meant to kill Fred.

He picked the guinea pig's body up and cradled it in his hands for a minute, wondering what to do.

Maybe, he decided, guinea pigs were like babies.

Maybe they just died sometimes.

He put Fred back in his cage, then went to bed, and by the time his parents came home, he was fast asleep.

It was Sally who found the guinea pig.

While Steve drove the baby-sitter home, she slipped into Jason's room to make sure he was all right. She bent over him, listened to him breathe for a moment, then gently kissed him on the forehead. She was about to leave his room, when she realized something was wrong.

The scuffling noises that Fred made whenever his sleep was disturbed were missing. Sally switched on the lamp next to Jason's bed and went to the cage in the corner. Fred, looking strangely unnatural, was sprawled on the bottom of the cage. She knelt, opened the cage, and picked him up. As she realized he was dead, an involuntary sound escaped her lips.

"What's wrong?" she heard Jason asking from behind her. She turned to see her son sitting up in bed, sleepily rubbing his eyes. "Is something wrong with Fred?"

"He's dead," Sally breathed, fighting off the terrible emotions that were welling up inside her. It's only a guinea pig, she told herself. It's not Jason, it's not Julie, it's only a damned guinea pig.

But still, it was too familiar. Bursting into tears, she dropped the dead animal and fled from the room. Behind her, she heard Jason's voice.

"What happened to him, Mommy? Did the same thing happen to Fred that happened to Julie?"

Chapter 10

SALLY MONTGOMERY SAT IN her living room, a small spool of light flooding the book she was trying to read.

The words on the pages made no sense to her. They kept drifting away, slipping off the pages, and over and over again she realized that she had read a paragraph but had no memory of it.

When Steve had come back from taking the sitter home, and Sally had told him about the guinea pig, all he had done was tell her to forget about it, then gone upstairs, brought the dead rodent down, and taken it outside to bury it in the backyard. By morning, he assured her, both she and Jason would have forgotten about it.

But would she?

She kept hearing Jason's words echoing in her head.

"Did the same thing happen to Fred that happened to Julie?"

What had happened to Julie?

Involuntarily, images of her son began to flit through her mind.

Jason, standing at the door of the nursery, staring at her as she held Julie's body.

Jason at the funeral, watching as his sister's coffin was

lowered into the ground, his eyes dry, his expression one of—what?

It had been, she admitted to herself now, an expression of disinterest.

As the long night wore on, she had twice gone upstairs to check on Jason. Each time she had found him sleeping peacefully, his breathing deep and strong, one arm thrown across his chest, the other dangling over the side of the bed. If either the loss of his sister or the loss of his pet was bothering him, it wasn't keeping him awake. Twice she had stood at the foot of his bed for long minutes, trying to drive horrible thoughts from the edges of her mind. And both times she had at last forced herself to leave his room without waking him just to prove to herself that he was all right.

Or to ask him questions she wasn't at all sure she wanted to voice.

Now, as she tried once more to concentrate on the book of childhood diseases that lay in her lap, she found herself once more thinking of Jan Ransom's words.

"Never wanted a baby in the first place . . ."

"Maybe the baby senses that the mother doesn't want it . . ."

Finally, heedless of the time, she picked up the phone book and flipped through it.

There it was:

RANSOM, JANELLE 504 ALDER ESTBY 555-3624

The phone rang seven times before a sleepy voice answered.

"Miss Ransom? This—this is Sally Montgomery. I was at the meeting tonight?"

Instantly the sleepiness was gone from the voice at the other end of the line. "Sally! Of course. You know, I had the strangest feeling you might call tonight. I—well, I had the feeling I hit a nerve."

Sally wasn't sure what to say, and as she was trying to decide how to proceed, she suddenly felt as if she was being watched. Turning, she saw Steve standing in the doorway. She swallowed hard, and when she spoke into the phone, her voice sounded unnaturally high.

"I—I thought perhaps we could have lunch next week."

"Of course," Jan Ransom replied immediately. "Any particular day?"

"Whatever's good for you."

"Then let's not wait for next week," Jan suggested. "Let's say Friday at noon. Do you know the Speckled Hen?"

They made the date, and Sally slowly put the phone back on its cradle, still not sure why she wanted to talk further to Jan Ransom. All she knew was that she did.

Steve came into the room and sat down beside her. "Can I ask whom you were talking to?"

"I wish you wouldn't," Sally said uncertainly.

Steve hesitated, then, seeing clearly the strain and exhaustion in Sally's whole being, decided not to press the issue. He stood up and switched off the light. "Come on, honey. Let's go to bed."

Sally let herself be led upstairs and helped into bed, and she didn't resist when Steve drew her close. But when he spoke again, her body went rigid.

"Maybe we should have another baby," she heard him saying. "Maybe we should start one right away."

Silently, Sally moved away from him, and as the hours of the night wore on, she felt the gulf between herself and her husband slowly widening.

Chapter 11

LUCY CORLISS GLANCED at the clock. It was nearly eleven, and another day, the third since Randy had disappeared, was nearly over. "Here's to tomorrow," she said bitterly, raising her empty cup. "Want some more coffee?"

Jim shook his head and watched as Lucy moved to the stove. They'd been sitting at the kitchen table all evening, Jim doing his best to keep Lucy calm. It had begun six hours ago, when he'd shown up at her door, his face pale. "What is it?" she'd asked. "Did you hear something?"

Jim had shaken his head. "Not really. Could I come in?"

Puzzled, Lucy had let him into the house and taken him to the kitchen. To Jim, it had seemed a sign of acceptance; when he was growing up, his mother had entertained her friends only in the kitchen—the living room was for the minister.

"I just came from the police station," he told her after she'd poured him the first of the endless pots of coffee the two of them had consumed during the evening. "I talked to Sergeant Bronski."

"And?" Lucy prompted when Jim seemed reluctant to go on.

"And he started talking about statistics."

"What sort of statistics?"

"About cases like ours," Jim replied, his eyes meeting hers. "Cases like Randy."

"I see," Lucy said softly. Her mind wandered back over the day she had just spent talking to people, knocking on every door along Randy's route to school, pleading with people, begging them to try to remember anything they'd seen that day, anything that might give her a hint as to what had happened to her son. Always the answer had been the same.

People were sorry, but they had seen nothing, heard nothing, noticed nothing. And all of them, both before and after the search of the forest, had been interviewed by the police.

"Lucy," she heard Jim saying, "they told me we have to prepare ourselves for the fact that when Randy is found—if he's found . . ." His voice trailed off, and he felt tears brimming in his eyes. He looked away from Lucy.

". . . he'll be dead?" Lucy asked, her voice devoid of emotion. "I know that, Jim. Anyway, I've been told that. I don't believe it. I just have a feeling—"

"Lucy," Jim groaned. "Lucy, I know what you think, I know how you feel. But you have to be ready. Bronski told me that if there were anything—a note, or a phone call, or even some sign of a struggle somewhere, it would be one thing. But with nothing, no clues, all they can think is that Randy either ran away, or—or whoever took him wasn't interested in ransom."

"You mean some pervert picking him up for sex?" Lucy asked, her voice uncannily level. "Raping him, and then killing him?"

"Something like that—" Jim faltered.

"That didn't happen," Lucy stated. "If that had happened, I'd know it. Deep in my heart, I'd know it. He's not dead, Jim, and he didn't run away."

"Then where is he? Why haven't we heard *something*?"

But Lucy had only shaken her head. "Jim, I've talked to everyone I can think of, asked questions, looked for

God-knows-what, and all I can think of is that in a book, or in a movie, it's always different. The mother goes out looking for her child and she finds him. But it's not that easy. I haven't found anything. Not one damned thing. All I've got after three days is this."

She had picked up the file that the school nurse had given her and tossed it across the table to her ex-husband, who flipped through it, then put it aside. It still lay on the table, where it had lain all through the evening as they ate dinner, talked, sipped at their coffee, tried to figure out what to do next, talked of other things, and always, inexorably, returned to the subject of their son.

Now, as Lucy refilled her cup and came back to the table again, Jim picked up the report once more. He looked through it.

The only thing about it that made it unique was the picture it painted of a remarkably healthy little boy.

Too healthy?

Jim began studying the file again, searching it for all the things that should have been there.

The absences from school.

The upset stomachs after lunch.

The skinned knees from inevitable falls.

The sore throats and colds that no child escapes.

None of it was there.

Jim went over the report yet again, searching for anything he might have missed. Finally, he closed the folder and faced his wife. "Lucy, did you notice anything odd about Randy's file?"

She looked at him pensively. "Odd? How do you mean?"

"According to this, Randy's never been sick a day in his life, never had a cavity in his mouth, never even so much as skinned his knee."

"So?"

Jim frowned. "Well, I don't know about you, but I've never heard of such a thing before." He reopened the report and began quoting it to Lucy. All of it was clear—

all except for a small notation at the bottom of the first page:

CHILD #0263

"What's this mean? Do they assign each of the kids a number now?"

Lucy shook her head. "It's a survey code. I wondered about it, too, so I called the school nurse this morning. CHILD stands for Children's Health Institute for Latent Diseases, and oh-two-six-three was the number assigned to Randy."

"Assigned to him for what?" Jim asked.

"Some sort of survey. Miss Oliphant said they've been tracking Randy for a long time."

"Tracking him? You mean watching him?"

"Not exactly. Every few months the school forwards Randy's health records to the Institute, that's all."

"How many of the kids are they tracking?"

Lucy frowned. "What do you mean?"

"Are they tracking all the kids at the school? All the ones in Randy's class?"

"I don't know," Lucy said. She picked up the file and looked at the notation once again, trying to remember just what Annie Oliphant had told her about the survey. Had she even asked how many of Randy's schoolmates were involved? She couldn't remember. She went to the phone and began dialing.

"Lucy, it's after midnight," Jim reminded her.

"But it might be important." Lucy waved him silent and turned her attention to the phone. "Miss Oliphant? It's Lucy Corliss. I hate to bother you so late, but I keep wondering about this survey Randy was involved in. Was his whole class being studied?"

She listened for a moment, asked a few more questions, then thanked the nurse again, and hung up.

"Well?" Jim asked.

"It's strange," Lucy said. "She told me she doesn't know anything about the survey. There are several children from Eastbury involved, and Randy's the oldest.

Every month she sends copies of the children's records to Boston, to the CHILD headquarters. They supply the envelopes and the postage, but they've never told her what the survey is about or what the results are."

"But who authorized the survey?" Jim asked. "I mean, don't you have to give your permission for Randy's records to be sent out?"

"I don't know," Lucy replied. "I suppose I might have signed some kind of consent form somewhere along the line. You know how it is—kids bring home so many forms, and they never give them to you until breakfast the day they're due."

"Actually," Jim commented, his voice not unkind, "I don't know about such things. I guess there's a lot I don't know much about."

His eyes had taken on a look of such loneliness that Lucy went to him and slipped her arms around him. "Well, don't start worrying about all that now," she told him. "I can guarantee you that if you *had* been around, you wouldn't have read all the forms either."

Jim grinned at her. "You mean you'd have forgiven me for being irresponsible?" Lucy drew away from him, and Jim wished he'd left the mild taunt unsaid. "I'm sorry," he apologized, but Lucy was already studying Randy's medical file again.

"Miss Oliphant said something else. She said that all the subjects of the survey have one thing in common: All their files read like Randy's. It seems they're all in perfect health and always have been."

Now Jim stared at her.

"All of them?" he said.

Lucy nodded.

"But—but how can that be?"

"What do you mean?"

"How long has the survey been going on?"

"At least since they started school."

"And all the kids they're surveying have perfect health?"

"That's what Annie Oliphant said." What was he getting at?

"Lucy, doesn't it strike you as odd that this survey has been going on for some time—we don't really know how long—and all its subjects have perfect health? I mean, it seems to me that it would be reasonable if when Randy was, say, ten years old, someone came along and suggested that *because* he'd been in perfect health all his life, they'd like to start tracking him to see what's going to happen. But apparently this outfit in Boston had some reason to think there was going to be something special about Randy and the others and started tracking them early."

"What are you saying, Jim?" Lucy asked, sure she already knew what was coming.

"I'm saying that it seems to me we might have some kind of clue about Randy after all. I think tomorrow one of us better get in touch with CHILD, and find out just what this survey is about, and how Randy fits in. Apparently there *is* something special about Randy. We'd better find out what it is."

As she went to bed later that night, Lucy wondered what could possibly come of talking to the Children's Health Institute for Latent Diseases. Was Jim just sending her off on another wild-goose chase?

Still, it would be something to do, and anything, right now, was better than nothing.

With nothing to do, she would go crazy, and she couldn't allow herself to do that.

Not until she knew what had happened to her son.

Chapter 12

AFTER ONLY THREE DAYS at the Academy, Randy Corliss had grown accustomed to the routine. For the first time, he felt as though he belonged somewhere. The sense of being alone in the world, of being somehow set apart from the other kids his age, was gone. At the Academy he was like all the other boys.

School at the Academy wasn't like school in Eastbury. Here, all the classes were compressed into the morning, except for physical education, and the things they studied seemed to Randy much more interesting than the things they had been taught at home. Also, at the Academy everyone seemed to care whether or not you learned. It wasn't like the public schools at all. As long as Randy could remember, if he got bored with something and stopped paying attention, no one seemed to care. All his teachers had just gone along at their own pace, never noticing that their students had lost interest.

But here, everything seemed to go faster. Here, they expected you to learn, so you learned. And they spent most of their time on subjects Randy liked. A lot of history, which Randy liked because most of history seemed to be, one way or another, about war, and Randy found war fascinating. There was, to his young mind, something wonderful about men marching into battle. And the way Miss Bowen taught it, war was almost like a game. You obeyed the rules, and did exactly as you were told, and you won. Time after time, in lesson after lesson, Randy learned that battles were lost only because the troops had not done as they'd been told. To him, it all made perfect sense, because as he thought about it, he realized that in all his nine years, the only times he'd really gotten into trouble were the times he'd disobeyed someone.

At the Academy it was the same way. As long as you followed the routine, everything went fine. When you were supposed to do something, you did it. If you failed, you did it again until you got it right. But the main thing was to do as you were told. Otherwise things happened.

The quick hand of retribution had fallen on Randy only once, on the night after he'd arrived at the Academy. It had been dinnertime, and Peter had come to his room to take him down to the dining room. Randy had been reading, and the end of the chapter was only two pages away. He had told Peter he'd be down in a minute and finished the chapter.

By the time he got to the dining room, his place at the table was gone—even his chair—and none of the other boys even looked at him. Miss Bowen got up from the staff table. Dinner was at six o'clock, she said, not five after six; he'd missed it. He was about to protest that the other boys hadn't even started to eat yet, but as he faced her, something in the woman's eyes told him that anything he might say would be useless. He was sent to his room and spent the rest of the evening by himself. No one came to his room, no one even spoke to him, though he left his door open all night. From then on Randy was careful to do exactly as he was told.

Not that it was difficult. Mornings seemed to be the time when discipline was strictest, and in the afternoons, after gym class, they were turned loose, free to do as they pleased. In the afternoons no one ever told them what to do or how to do it. Indeed, though Randy always felt as though someone was watching him, he'd never been able to see the watchers. It was, he'd finally decided, like some kind of test, but he didn't know what the rules were or what was expected of him. Nor did he know what would happen to him if he failed.

For the first few days, of course, Randy had wondered exactly why he was there and why his father hadn't come to see him or at least called him. Then, as he got used to the Academy, he began to stop worrying about it.

Now it was Thursday afternoon, and Randy and Peter had just finished gym. The afternoon stretched before them, and they were wandering in the woods that lay close by the main building of the Academy.

"You wanna play King of the Mountain?" Peter suddenly asked.

Randy looked around. As far as he could tell, the ground the Academy sat on was perfectly flat, except for a shallow pond they used for swimming. "What are we gonna use for a mountain?"

"Come on," Peter replied. He started through the woods, and in a few minutes they came to a path. A few hundred yards farther, there was a clearing in the woods. In the center of the clearing stood a massive granite outcropping, towering thirty feet above the ground.

"What is it?" Randy breathed.

"It's a rock, dummy," Peter said scornfully. "How do I know what it is?"

"Can you climb it?"

"Sure. I've climbed it lots of times. Me and another guy used to play on it all the time."

"Who?"

"Jeff Grey."

Randy had never heard the name before. "Who's he?"

"He used to be here before you came."

"Where is he now?"

"How should I know?" Peter replied, but something in his voice told Randy that he knew more than he was telling. Suddenly Eric's words, half forgotten, came back to him.

"Sometimes kids ... just disappear. We think they die."

Was that what had happened to Jeff Grey? He was about to ask, but Peter was already starting the game. "You wanna play or not?" Peter called. "First one to the top tries to keep the other one from getting up!" Peter charged up the heap of rubble, then began scrambling up the rock, his hands and feet moving instinctively from ledge to ledge. Randy watched for a moment, then began climbing a few feet away from Peter.

For the first ten feet the climb was easy. The rock rose out of the ground at an angle, and over the centuries its surface had been cracked and split by the freezing New England winters. Randy concentrated on moving upward as fast as he could, paying little attention to Peter.

And then, as the rock grew steeper, he felt a hand close on his shoulder, tugging at him. He turned, and there was Peter, right next to him, bracing himself against a ledge, grinning.

"Good-bye!" Peter sang out. He shoved hard, and Randy felt himself lose his balance as his left foot slipped out of place. He grasped at a branch of laurel that was growing out of the rock, then felt it break off in his hand. Suddenly, he was skidding downward, his arms and legs jarring against the stone, but never finding support. He hit the ground and lay on his back, wondering if he'd hurt himself. But it hadn't been a bad fall, and he could feel no pain. Then, from above him, he heard the humiliating sound of Peter's laughter.

As Peter once more began working his way upward, Randy got to his feet and began looking for another place to climb. He circled the crag carefully, knowing there was now no chance of beating his friend to the top. Now he would have to fight his way onto the summit.

He found a spot where the first part of the climb would be the most difficult, but where there seemed to be a fairly wide ledge, high up, on which he could brace himself while he tried to wrestle Peter down.

He began climbing slowly, trying to memorize each

step he made so that in the event he fell again he might be able to catch himself before he tumbled all the way down. He ignored the taunts that floated down to him as Peter proclaimed himself king of the mountain.

Then he was on the ledge, and the flat top of the outcropping was level with his chest. Peter stood above him, grinning maliciously.

"That's as far as you get. Come any farther, and I'll push you off."

Randy put his arms on the summit, but before he could scramble onto it, Peter had pushed him back. "Give up?" Peter demanded.

"Why should I?" Randy shot back. "You cheated."

"I didn't either," Peter told him. "All I said was you had to get to the top. I didn't say you couldn't push the other guy back down."

Once more Randy tried to scramble over the ledge, and once more Peter stopped him, this time stepping on Randy's fingers to make him let go of his handhold. Randy jerked his hand free, then sucked on his injured knuckles for a moment while he tried to decide what to do next. He glanced backward over his shoulder, and there, beyond the trees, he could see the forbidding mass of the Academy. He could almost feel eyes watching him and began to wonder if he was going to get in trouble when he got back.

Then he looked down.

Far below him, the rubble around the base of the crag looked threatening, and Randy realized that if he fell from here, the first part of the fall would be the easy part. If he didn't stop himself in the first ten feet, there would be no way to keep himself from plunging the last twenty. And if that happened . . .

He turned his attention to Peter once more.

"Give up?" Peter asked again.

"No!" Randy shouted. He made a move with his right hand, but pulled it away just as Peter's foot came out to crush his fingers.

He grabbed Peter by the ankle, using both hands even though he knew it was risky.

Peter, surprised, stared at him for a moment, then tried to jerk his leg free.

Randy held on.

Peter tried to kick him with his free foot, but Randy twisted his leg, and Peter lost his balance, and had to use his other foot to keep from falling.

He bent down and picked up a rock.

"Let go of my leg."

"No."

"Let go, or I'll bash your head in!"

"No!"

Randy looked up and suddenly realized Peter wasn't kidding. The rock, large and heavy, was swinging downward.

Instinctively, Randy yanked at Peter's leg, bracing himself carefully on the lower ledge. As he watched, Peter's eyes widened, and the rock fell from his hand.

And then Peter teetered a moment, his balance gone, and began swaying forward. Both boys realized what was happening at the same moment.

"Catch me!" Peter screamed.

It was too late. Randy reached for his friend's leg, but his fingers only brushed against the denim of Peter's jeans. As Randy watched helplessly, Peter plunged head-first into the pile of rubble below.

Louise Bowen knelt next to Peter's limp body and checked for a pulse. Satisfied, she carefully opened one of the little boy's eyes and examined the dilation of the pupil. Next to her, Randy Corliss hovered nervously, tears streaming down his terrified face.

"Is he dead?"

"Of course not," Louise assured him. "He's unconscious, but he's alive."

"I didn't mean to do it," Randy wailed. "Really, Miss Bowen, it wasn't my fault. We were playing King of the—"

"I *know* what happened."

The impatience in her voice made Randy subside into

silence, and as he watched her examine Peter, he wondered what would happen to him now.

When Billy Semple had jumped off the roof and broken his leg, everyone had been furious with him, even though it hadn't been his fault. But what about this? He *had* deliberately tripped Peter, even if it was because Peter was going to hit him with a rock. What if Peter died? Would they take him to jail?

As Randy watched, Louise Bowen carefully turned Peter over, and it was suddenly obvious what had happened.

Peter must have landed on his head, pitching over onto his back. His hair was matted with blood, and the back of his skull was caved in. Fragments of bone were embedded in the bloody scalp.

By rights, Louise Bowen knew, Peter Williams should be dead.

Then, while Randy Corliss vomited into the bushes, Louise Bowen picked Peter up, began making her way toward the huge gothic building that housed the Academy.

His stomach still churning with horror at what had happened to Peter, and his mind whirling with thoughts about what might still happen to him, Randy followed a few minutes later.

Randy listened to the muffled chimes of the clock in the downstairs hall as it struck midnight. As its last note faded away, he listened for other sounds, but there were none. And yet the silence didn't feel right to him. It wasn't the kind of peaceful silence he was used to, but another kind; it made him feel like something was wrong.

And, of course, something was: Peter Williams.

At dinner Peter Williams's place had been removed from the table. If the other boys had noticed—and Randy was sure they must have—none of them said anything. Instead, they quietly ate their dinners, then excused themselves, and disappeared upstairs.

Randy had waited until they were gone, then shyly approached Miss Bowen.

"Is Peter going to be all right?" he'd asked.

Miss Bowen had met his gaze, hesitated, then reached out to touch him on the cheek.

"He's gone," she'd told him. "He's gone, but you mustn't worry about it. We know what happened, and nobody blames you. It was an accident, and nobody is responsible for accidents. Do you understand?"

Randy had nodded his head uncertainly, then he, too, had retreated to the upper reaches of the building. But instead of joining the other boys, he had stayed in his room, trying to figure out what Miss Bowen had meant.

And now, at midnight, he was still trying to figure it out.

"He's gone." That was what Miss Bowen had said. She hadn't said Peter was dead, just that he was gone.

But that didn't make any sense. Where had he gone and when? Randy had been in the building ever since the accident, and no ambulance had come for Peter. No cars had even left the Academy. So where had Peter gone?

The silence and darkness suddenly closed in on Randy, and he got out of bed, put on his robe, and went to the door. He opened it and peered out into the hall. A few yards away, at the head of the main stairs, there was a desk where someone always sat, as if guarding the house.

Tonight there was no one at the desk.

Puzzled, Randy left his room and moved down the hall until he was standing at the top of the stairs. He paused and listened.

All he could hear was the soft ticking of the clock.

He descended the stairs slowly, stopping every few steps, sure that at any moment Miss Bowen would appear in the foyer and send him back to bed. But then he was in the foyer himself and still there was no sound.

From where he stood, he could see that the living and dining rooms were both empty, so he turned and started toward the back of the house, where the offices were. He went past Miss Bowen's office, then past several other closed doors. And then, as he was about to turn back, he heard the sound of muffled voices coming from behind the next door.

He crept closer, and listened. Then, hesitantly, he reached out and turned the doorknob. He waited, sure that someone would call out to him, but no one did.

Finally, he pushed the door open a crack and pressed his eye close so he could see into the room.

It was all white, with a table in the center that was surrounded with what looked to Randy like medical equipment. In fact, the room looked just like the operating rooms of hospitals that he'd seen on television. And around the table, five people were gathered.

They were wearing white gowns and face masks, but Randy was able to recognize Miss Bowen from her eyes and the wisps of curly hair that stuck out from under her cap. He was sure that the man at the end of the table was Mr. Hamlin, who he knew was the director of the Academy.

And then someone moved, and Randy saw who was on the operating table.

It was Peter Williams. His head was locked into a metal frame. His hair had been shaved off and the back of his skull cut away.

Randy froze, his eyes wide, his heart pounding.

So Peter wasn't gone after all, and he wasn't dead. He was still here.

But what were they doing to him? Were Mr. Hamlin and Miss Bowen doctors?

They must be, or they wouldn't be operating on Peter.

And then he heard Miss Bowen speak.

"What are you doing? You'll kill him!"

"I won't kill him," Randy heard Mr. Hamlin reply. "If he was going to die, he already would have."

Randy stood transfixed for a few more minutes, listening to the doctors as they worked, understanding only a few of their words, but knowing with a terrifying clarity that something was very wrong. At last, when he could stand it no longer without screaming, he pulled the door quietly shut, and crept back up to his room.

George Hamlin, who was, indeed, a doctor as well as the director of the Academy, glanced around at the other members of his surgical team and wished their masks were transparent. He would have liked particularly to be able to read Louise Bowen's expression right now. Of all his staff, he knew that only Bowen was likely to object to what he had done. The others, whatever roles they performed for the subjects at the Academy, were all doctors who shared not only his medical skills, but his devotion to research. But Bowen was different. She had never, as long as she had been part of Hamlin's team, been able to develop the proper scientific objectivity. Indeed, had it not been for the importance of keeping the project a secret for the time being, he would have fired her long ago. For the moment, though, he would simply have to tolerate her. "All right," he said softly. "I think that's about it."

The operation had taken nearly three hours. During that time an anesthetist had stood by, ready to move in should Peter Williams have shown signs of regaining consciousness. But Peter had not; throughout his ordeal, he had remained in the coma that had come over him at the time of his fall.

George Hamlin had begun working on Peter at ten o'clock, narrating his findings and his procedures as he went.

"The scalp is healing; all bleeding has stopped. Clear signs of osteoregeneration."

He had carefully picked pieces of bone from Peter's head, dropping them into a jar of saline solution that stood at his elbow. He worked quickly and expertly, and in moments the wound was cleaned.

Beneath the hole in Peter's skull a badly damaged brain had lain exposed.

"Jesus," someone whispered. "It's a mess."

But Hamlin had ignored the interruption and begun cutting at the cortical material, removing the damaged tissue. That, too, had gone into a bottle of saline solution.

"The damage doesn't seem to have gone too deep," Harry Garner, Hamlin's senior assistant had commented. "Are there any signs of regeneration?"

"Not yet." Hamlin's manner, as always, had been curt. He was making up his mind what to do next, and it was at that moment, as he had stared down into the gaping hole filled with living matter, that the part of him that was devoted to pure research took over.

The scalpel flashed downward, slicing deep into the cerebral cortex, cutting inward and downward through the occipital lobe until the cerebellum was exposed. Behind him he heard a gasp and wasn't surprised when Louise Bowen's voice penetrated his concentration with the words that had so terrified Randy Corliss.

"What are you doing? You'll kill him."

"I won't kill him," Hamlin had replied coldly. "If he was going to die, he already would have."

And now, an hour later, the operation completed, Peter Williams lay in a coma, his face placid, his breathing slow and steady, his vital signs strong.

But inside his head, part of his brain was gone. Hamlin had cut a core through the occipital lobe and the cerebellum, penetrating deep into the medulla oblongata.

The wound was still open.

"Do you want us to close for you?" Garner asked.

"I don't want it closed at all. Put him in the lab and watch him twenty-four hours a day."

"He'll never survive twenty-four hours," someone said quietly.

"We won't know that until tomorrow, will we?" Hamlin replied. "I want this subject watched. If there's any sign of regeneration in the brain—and I think you all know I mean unusual regeneration—I want to know about it immediately."

"And if he wakes up?" Louise Bowen asked.

Hamlin faced her. His expression was impassive, but his eyes glinted coldly in the bright lights of the operating room. "If he wakes up," he said, "I trust you'll ask him how he feels. In fact," he added, "it would be interesting to find out if he still feels anything at all." And then George Hamlin was gone, leaving his associates to do whatever was necessary to facilitate the survival of Peter Williams.

For Hamlin himself, Peter Williams as a person had never existed.

He was simply one more subject, Number 0168. And the subject was apparently a failure. Perhaps he would have better results with the new one, Number 0263. What was his name?

Hamlin thought for a moment, and then it came to him.

Corliss. That was it: Randy Corliss.

Starting tomorrow, he must begin watching the new subject more carefully.

Chapter 13

SALLY MONTGOMERY PAUSED just inside the entrance to the Speckled Hen, and wondered if she shouldn't turn around and walk back out again. She glanced at herself in the enormous mirror that dominated the foyer of the restaurant and felt reassured. Nothing in her reflection betrayed her nervousness. To an observer she would look to be exactly what she was—a young professional woman. She was wearing a red suit with navy blue accents, deliberately chosen to draw attention to itself and away from the strain in her face, which she had tried to hide behind a layer of carefully applied makeup.

"I'm Mrs. Montgomery," she told the smiling hostess. "I'm meeting Mrs. Ransom."

"Of course," the hostess replied. "If you'll follow me?" With Sally trailing behind her, the woman threaded her way through the crowded restaurant to a small table tucked away in an alcove near the kitchen. Jan Ransom was sipping a spritzer and said nothing until the hostess had left the table.

"I asked for this table because it's far from prying ears. No sense whispering our secrets to the world, is there?"

Sally let herself relax a little and glanced around, relieved to see that there wasn't a familiar face anywhere in the room. A waiter appeared, and she ordered a glass of wine, then turned her attention to Janelle Ransom.

"I suppose you must have thought I was crazy, calling you in the middle of the night," she began. Jan Ransom made a deprecating gesture.

"Don't be silly. All of us are like that at first. For a while I thought I was going crazy. I was calling people I hardly know and trying to explain what had happened to my little girl. I suppose I was really trying to explain it to myself." She fell silent as the waiter reappeared with Sally's drink. When he was gone again, she held up her glass. "To us," she proposed. "Lord knows, people who've been through what we've been through need to stick together." The two women sipped on their drinks for a moment and scanned the menu.

"Can I ask you something?" Jan asked after the waiter had taken their orders. "Why did you choose me to call? Did I say something the other night?"

Sally nodded. "I don't quite know how to start ..." She faltered. Jan smiled at her encouragingly.

"Start any way you want, and don't worry about my feelings. One thing you learn after you lose a baby to SIDS is that there are times when you have to say everything you're feeling, no matter how awful it sounds, and hear everything people are saying, no matter how much it hurts."

Sally took a deep breath. "You said the other night that you hadn't wanted your baby—"

"Until she was born," Jan broke in. "Once she was born, I fell in love with her." A faraway look came into Jan's eyes and she smiled. "You should have seen her, Sally. She was the most beautiful baby you ever saw, even right after she was born. None of that wizened-monkey look. She was tiny, but I swear she came into the world laughing and never stopped. Until that day ..." She trailed off and the smile disappeared from her face. When she spoke again, there was a hard edge of bitterness to her voice. "I still wonder, you know. I still wonder if it was something I did, or didn't do."

"I know," Sally whispered. "That's what's terrifying me too. I—well, I hadn't planned on having Julie either. Even my son was a couple of years ahead of schedule. Funny, isn't it? Some women want children desperately and can't have them. And then there are women like us, who do our best not to get pregnant, but nothing works."

"Forget the pill?" Jan asked.

Sally shook her head. "I'm allergic. I was using an IUD."

"So much more romantic, right? You know it's there, and nobody has to stop to install equipment. No worrying about whether you remembered to take the pill. Just a little tiny device and all the peace of mind in the world. And then you're pregnant."

"You had a coil too?"

"Uh-huh. It seemed like the best way. You know why? Religion. You want a laugh? I had it all figured out that with the IUD, I'd only be committing one sin, and I thought I could get away with that. The pill was going to be a sin a day, and even though I don't go to church, I knew I'd have a little twinge of guilt every time I took it. So I went into Dr. Wiseman's office one day, got my coil and my guilt, and went home and forgot about it."

Sally frowned. "Dr. Wiseman?" she repeated. "Arthur Wiseman?"

"Do you know him?"

"He's my doctor."

Jan Ransom chuckled hollowly. "Now what do you suppose the odds are on that? Two women, the same doctor, the same device, the same failure, and then SIDS."

Sally Montgomery did not share Jan's amusement. What, she wondered, *were* the odds? She began calculating in her head, but there were too many variables.

" . . . and you have to go on living," she heard Jan saying.

"You sound like my mother."

"And like my own. Sally, it's hard to accept what's happened. No one knows that better than I do. But there's nothing else you can do. Nothing's going to bring Julie back and nothing's going to make you feel better. All you can do is try to let the wounds start to heal."

"But I can't do that," Sally said quietly. "I can't just go on as if nothing happened. Something did happen and I have to know what it was." She held up a hand as Jan started to say something. "And don't tell me it was SIDS. I won't accept that. It just doesn't make any sense."

"But that's just it, Sally. Don't you see? SIDS *doesn't* make sense—that's the awful part of it."

Sally sat silently, her eyes meeting Jan Ransom's. "Do you think I'm going crazy?" she asked at last.

Jan chewed on her lower lip a moment, then shook her head. "No. No more than I went crazy the first few months. Do what you have to do, Sally. In time it will all work out." Then she smiled ruefully. "You know something? I was hoping I might be able to help you today—help you cut some corners. But I can't, can I? All I can do is let you know that I understand what you're going through. You have to go through it yourself." She raised her glass.

"Good luck."

The clinic seemed oddly quiet as Sally walked down the green-walled corridor toward Arthur Wiseman's office, and the sound of her heels clicking on the tile floor echoed with an eerie hollowness. But it's not the clinic that seems empty, she decided as she turned the last corner. It's me. I don't know exactly what I'm doing here, so it seems strange. Strange and scary. Then she stepped into Dr. Wiseman's outer office. His nurse looked up at her, smiling uncertainly.

"Mrs. Montgomery? Did you have an appointment today?" She reached for her book.

"No," Sally reassured her. "I was just hoping maybe I could talk to the doctor for a couple of minutes. Would it be possible?"

The nurse turned her attention to the appointment book, then nodded. "I think we can just shoehorn you

116

in." She grinned and winked conspiratorially. "In fact, it's an easy fit—I had a cancellation an hour ago, and the doctor was counting on an hour to himself. We just won't give it to him." She stood up, then, after tapping briefly on the closed door to the inner office, went in. A moment later she reappeared. "Go right in, Mrs. Montgomery."

Arthur Wiseman was waiting for her, his hand outstretched, his expression cordial. "Sally! What a pleasant surprise." The smile melted from his face to be replaced by a look of concern. "Nothing's wrong, is it?"

"I don't know," Sally said pensively, settling herself into the chair next to his desk. "I just wanted to ask you about a couple of things. I've been talking to some people, including Janelle Ransom."

Wiseman's brows rose a little. "Jan? How did you meet her?"

"The SIDS Foundation. Steve and I went to one of the meetings they sponsor."

"I see. And Jan was there?"

Sally nodded. "We had lunch today, and I discovered something that worries me. We were both using IUDs when we got pregnant."

"And?" Wiseman asked.

"And, well, I suppose it just seemed like too much of a coincidence that we were both using IUDs and both got pregnant and both lost our daughters to SIDS."

Wiseman sighed heavily and leaned back. Here it comes, he thought. When there is no easy explanation for a death, the family turns on the doctor. "Just what is it you think might have happened?"

"I don't know," Sally admitted. "It just occurred to me that perhaps the IUD might have . . . well . . ."

"Injured the fetus?" Wiseman asked. He leaned forward, folding his arms on the desk. "Sally, that's patently impossible. In order for you to have conceived, the IUD would have to have been flushed out of your system. And that, statistically, happens in two out of ten cases. I told you that right from the start, if you remember. Except for the pill, which you can't use, there's no

117

foolproof method of birth control. And with an IUD, you never know when your body rejects it. It happened to you years ago, and you had Jason. Then, for eight years there was no problem. Maybe it was the new device we tried and our mistake was in trying a third kind a couple of years ago. But I'm not sure it would have mattered. You don't feel it when it's in, and you don't feel it when it's gone. But it absolutely couldn't have affected the fetus, that I can assure you. The similarities between your case and Jan Ransom's are simply coincidence. And not much of a coincidence, except for the fact that you both lost your babies to SIDS."

"Don't you think that's enough to make me wonder?" Sally asked.

"Of course it is," Wiseman said, relaxing back into his chair. "And of course you should have come to see me. But I'm not sure what I can do for you."

Sally's eyes moved to the CRT on Wiseman's desk. It was, she knew, a remote terminal of the computer that served most of the needs of the town. "Perhaps you could show me Julie's records," she suggested.

Wiseman hesitated, instinctively searching his mind for a valid excuse to deny Sally's request. There was none. "All right," he agreed at last. "But since she was Mark Malone's patient, I think he should be here too." He picked up the phone, spoke briefly, and then hung up.

"Do you really think we'll find anything in Julie's records?" he asked as they waited.

"I don't know," Sally said truthfully. "In fact, I'm not even sure I'll be able to understand them."

"Well, I can understand them," Wiseman assured her. A moment later the office door opened, and the pediatrician appeared. He greeted Sally, then looked questioningly toward Wiseman, who explained what Sally had proposed.

"Sounds like a good idea," Malone said, after quickly reviewing what he remembered of Julie's records. There was nothing, as far as he knew, that could upset Sally. He switched the computer terminal on and swiftly tapped in some instructions. Then he smiled encouragingly at Sally. "Come around here."

Sally went around the desk to stand close to Malone as the CRT screen began to fill up with the medical record of her daughter. Other than the birth data, there wasn't much: the results of the monthly examinations that Julie had been given, the last just two days before she died, all of which, Wiseman explained, reflected a picture of a remarkably healthy baby. Then there was the final report of her death, with a copy of the death certificate.

"I don't even know what I might be looking for," Sally said as she scanned the screen.

"You'd be looking for something wrong," Wiseman told her. "But according to this Julie wasn't damaged in any way, either before or after the birth." He looked to Mark Malone for confirmation, and the younger doctor nodded his agreement.

Sally pressed one of the cursor keys on the console, and the record began scrolling upward until the screen was filled with a series of letters and numbers that looked, to Sally's untrained eyes, like gibberish. "What's all this?" she asked.

Malone shrugged indifferently. "Test results. Analyses of blood samples, tissue samples, urine samples. All of it very routine and very normal."

"I see," Sally muttered. Then she frowned. As the data continued to roll up the screen, a number, set off by itself, suddenly appeared in the lower right-hand corner. Sally took her finger off the cursor key. "What's that?"

Wiseman stared at the number, frowned slightly, then looked up at Malone. "Do you know what this is?"

"It's just a code number," Malone replied. "It refers to a survey being done by a group in Boston, the Children's Health Institute for Latent Diseases."

"And they were surveying Julie?" Sally asked. "What for?"

Malone shrugged. "I don't really know. In fact, I doubt they're sure themselves."

"I don't understand." Sally moved back to her chair, and faced the two doctors. "This group—"

"It's called CHILD," Malone said.

"CHILD is studying children, but they don't know why?"

"It's what they call a random survey," Malone began. He started to explain it to Sally, but she held up a hand to stop him. She knew very well how such a survey operated. She had, indeed, designed several of them herself.

Basically, it involved the use of a table of random numbers to select a small fraction of a population that would accurately reflect the population as a whole. Sally herself had helped the Health Department design a survey of the population of Eastbury a few years back, to determine the incidence of swine flu in the town. It had boiled down to a matter of choices: either survey the entire town, or use a computer to assign everyone in town a number, then employ a table of random digits, itself devised by the computer, to choose a cross-section that would accurately reflect the whole.

To a layman, Sally knew, it sounded like hocus-pocus, but she also knew it was a statistically correct and absolutely accurate method of surveying a population for practically anything. And the beauty of it was that as the size of the population to be studied grew, the proportion of the population that actually would have to be surveyed grew smaller.

In Eastbury, for instance, only a few hundred people had needed to be surveyed in order to project the exact incidence of swine flu within the town.

"I know how studies like that work," Sally said. "But what's the study about?"

"As far as I know, it's just a general survey," Malone replied. "Apparently their computer constantly scans the records in our little computer—and a lot of others too— and randomly chose Julie for the survey. I think they were planning to track her right through her first twenty-one years."

"And you let them do that?" Sally asked. She was all

too familiar with computers and their ability to pry into people's lives. "You let them simply invade your records? I thought medical records were supposed to be confidential."

"But they are," Wiseman told her as Malone glanced at him helplessly. "I'm sure the Institute assured us when we agreed to the survey that even they wouldn't know the names of the subjects. Otherwise we wouldn't have gone along with it." He glanced down at Julie Montgomery's records once more and smiled at Sally. "All they know about Julie is that child number nine-six-eight-two was a victim of SIDS, plus her medical data. They don't know her name, and they don't care about it. Studies like this go on all the time, Sally. You must know that. And you also must know that the computers make their selections, then are programed to forget the names of the subjects as soon as they've been assigned numbers."

"And you believe this?" Sally asked, her voice suddenly growing bitter. "How do you think they keep track of their subjects? If no one knows who belongs to what number, how are they going to keep up with their subjects? People move, you know. And someone has to put the data into a computer somewhere, along with the numbers, so that your Institute's computer can get it out again. My God, Julie's number—which you yourself just said is supposed to be confidential, is right there on her records for anybody to see!" Wiseman started to interrupt her, but Sally plunged on, her anger growing as she talked. "You're doctors, both of you, and I won't question your knowledge of medicine. But I'm a computer expert. I've been trained to use them, and I know what they can do. Do you? Do you know how easy it is for computers to talk to each other, to go through each other's files? Anybody in this country can find out anything about anybody else if he knows how to use a computer and can get the access codes. And if you're good enough with computers, you can program them to give you the codes that are supposed to hide the secrets." Sally was on her feet now, pacing the room. "Why wasn't I told about this survey?" she demanded. "I'm Julie's mother. If someone was watching my child, I had a right to know about it."

"Sally . . ." Malone began, but she ignored him.

"Maybe there *was* something wrong with Julie. Maybe they knew something was wrong with her!"

Now Wiseman, too, stood up. "Sally," he said firmly, "I want you to sit down and listen to me." Her eyes glazed with indignation, Sally stared at him and he thought she was going to bolt from his office. Then, as he and Malone watched, she forced her anger back and sank once more into the chair next to the desk.

"I'm sorry," she said. "It's just that I can't get over the feeling that something happened to Julie—something terrible."

Wiseman returned to his place behind the desk, but kept his eyes on Sally, searching her face carefully. He could see the signs of stress behind her makeup—the dark circles lurking beneath her eyes, the high color of her cheeks, the strain in the set of her mouth.

"Sally," he began, his baritone voice filling the room with its soothing tones. "I want you to understand something. There was nothing wrong with Julie. Nothing at all." He could see her body stiffen and knew she was resisting his words. He turned to Malone for assistance.

"It's true, Mrs. Montgomery," the pediatrician agreed. "There was nothing wrong with her, and there was nothing in her records—*anywhere*—that could lead anyone else to think anything was wrong with her."

Now Wiseman picked up the thread. "As for CHILD, they're a highly respected institution. They've contributed a great deal of knowledge to the field of medicine, particularly with regard to children. To think that there was anything"—he searched for the right word, and finally found it—"anything *menacing* about the fact that Julie was a subject of one of their surveys is simply beyond reason." Dr. Wiseman's voice dropped, and even through her anger Sally began to feel that he was patronizing her. "Now, what I'm going to do is this," he went on. "I'm going to give you their address, and I want you to go to them and find out for yourself just what the survey was all about, how Julie was selected for it, and what's being done with the data they're collecting. All right?"

Sally smiled at Wiseman, but the smile was cold. "Dr. Wiseman, did you really think I wouldn't do all that on my own?" She rose to her feet, picked up her bag, and went to the door. Then she turned back to face the two doctors. "Something happened to my daughter. I know you both think I'm a hysterical woman, and perhaps you're right. But I'm going to find out what happened to Julie. Believe me, I'm going to find out."

When she was gone, Arthur Wiseman switched off the CRT, then turned to Malone.

"I'm sorry," he said. "I wish none of this had had to happen, but with cases like this, you just can't avoid it."

Malone smiled at the older man. "It's all right, Arthur. Part of the job."

Wiseman nodded and returned to his desk. He picked up a medical journal, a clear signal for Malone to leave the office. But when he was alone, Arthur Wiseman's thoughts stayed on Sally Montgomery. Her adjustment to the loss of her daughter was not proceeding within the parameters that he considered normal. Sally, he was sure, was beginning to exhibit obsessive behavior, and if it continued, something would have to be done.

He turned the matter over in his mind, examining it from every angle. Finally, sighing heavily, he picked up the telephone and began to dial.

Sally moved swiftly down the corridor toward the entrance of the clinic, her emotions roiling. Wiseman's manner—his insufferable calm in the face of her tragedy and his patronizing attitude—infuriated her. It seemed to her that there was an arrogance about the man that she had never seen before.

Never seen, or chosen to ignore?

She emerged from the clinic and paused, letting the spring air flow over her, breathing deeply, as if the warm breeze could clear away the feeling of oppression that had come over her in Wiseman's office. She could still hear his voice, resonating in her mind, as he rambled on about "accepting reality," "going on with life," and all the other platitudes that, she suddenly realized, had been flowing from his lips for the last ten years.

From now on, she decided, she would be on her guard when she talked to Dr. Wiseman.

Chapter 14

S ALLY MONTGOMERY GLANCED at the clock on the dashboard. It was a few minutes past three, and Eastbury Elementary was only a block out of her way. She made a left turn on Maple Street and pulled up in front of the school. Maybe she'd treat Jason to an ice cream cone on the way home. She waited in the car, still trying to calm the anger she was feeling from her talk with the two doctors.

And yet, as she thought about it, she realized that her anger really shouldn't be directed toward them. It was that group in Boston—CHILD—that was doing the snooping. And snooping, Sally was sure, was exactly what it was. That was the trouble with computer technology: It had turned the country into a nation of gossips. Everywhere you turned there was information stored away on tapes and disks and dots, much of it useless, most of it forgotten as soon as it was collected, but all of it stored away somewhere. And why? Sally, over the years, had come to the conclusion that all the data collecting had nothing to do with research. It was just plain old nosiness, and she had always half-resented it.

Only half, because Sally was also well aware that she was part of that snoop-culture, and while she had often questioned the uses to which computers were put, she had always been fascinated by the technology. But today, she realized, the chickens had come home to roost. That incredible ability to invade an individual's privacy had been turned on her own child.

In her head she began to speculate on how CHILD might have been planning to track Julie for twenty-one years. Just through hospital records? But what if Julie had grown up to be as healthy as Jason? There would have been no hospital records.

And then it came to her.

School records.

Sally got out of her car just as the school bell rang and children began to erupt from the building. She spotted Jason in the crowd, waved to him, and waited as he ran over to her.

"I thought I'd pick you up and take you out for an ice cream cone," she said. Jason grinned happily and scrambled into the car. Sally started back around to the driver's side, then changed her mind. "Wait here a minute," she told her son. "I have to talk to someone." Without waiting for Jason to reply, she walked purposefully into the school.

"Miss Oliphant?"

The nurse glanced up, trying to place the face. Not a member of the school staff, therefore a parent. She put on her best welcoming smile and stood up. "Guilty."

"I'm Sally Montgomery. Jason Montgomery's mother?"

"That explains why I didn't place you," Annie Oliphant replied. "I know the mothers only of the sick ones." Then the smile faded from her lips as she remembered what had happened to Jason's sister. "Oh, Mrs. Montgomery, I'm sorry. What a stupid thing for me to say. I can't tell you how sorry all of us were to hear about your baby."

"You know about Julie?" Sally asked, relieved that at least she wouldn't have to try to explain Julie's death to the nurse.

"Everyone in town knows. I wish there was something I could do. In fact, I wondered if I ought to talk to

Jason about it, but then decided that I'd only be meddling. I've been keeping an eye on him though. He seems to be handling it very well. But, of course, he's a remarkable little boy anyway, isn't he?"

Sally nodded distractedly, wondering how to broach the subject she wanted to discuss with the nurse. "He's out in the car waiting for me," she said at last. "And since I was here, I thought I'd ask you a question."

"Anything," Annie said, sinking back down into her chair. "Anything at all."

"Well, it might be a dumb question," Sally went on. "It has to do with an organization in Boston, one that studies children—"

"You mean CHILD?" Annie interrupted, her brows arching in surprise.

"You *do* know of them?"

"Of course. They're surveying some of our students."

"Surveying them? How?" But even as Sally spoke, she answered her own question. "Through a computer, right?"

"You got it. Every few months they request an update. It's some kind of project that involves tracking certain children through a certain age—"

"Twenty-one," Sally interrupted.

"Oh, you know about the project. When I talked to Mrs. Corliss the other day, the whole thing seemed to come as a complete surprise to her. I'd always assumed the parents of the children knew all about the study, but Mrs. Corliss hadn't even known it existed." Then her expression clouded. "It's such a shame about Randy running away, isn't it?"

Sally's mind whirled as she tried to sort out what Annie Oliphant had just told her. She lowered herself onto the chair next to the nurse's desk and reached out to touch the other woman's arm.

"Miss Oliphant—"

"Call me Annie."

"Thank you. Annie, I just found out about this study today." She told the nurse what had happened that afternoon and how she had come to ask the question that had started the conversation. "But what you just said sounded as though I should have known about the survey all along."

Annie Oliphant frowned. "But I thought you *did* know," she said. "Jason's part of the survey too. Jason, and Randy Corliss, and two younger boys."

"I see," Sally breathed. Suddenly she felt numb. What was going on? And what had Annie just said about Randy Corliss?

"He seems to have run away," the nurse answered when Sally repeated her question out loud. "Except that his mother thinks he was kidnaped." She shook her head sympathetically. "I suppose she just can't accept the idea that her own child might have run away from her, and she's trying to find some other reason for the fact that he's gone. Some reason that takes the final responsibility off herself."

"I suppose so," Sally murmured as she rose from the chair. Her mind was still spinning, but at least she knew where to go next. "Thank you for talking to me, Annie. You've been very helpful." Then her gaze fell on the file folder that still contained Jason's health records. "Could I have a copy of that?"

Annie hesitated. She had already broken the rules by giving Lucy Corliss a copy of Randy's file, and she wasn't at all sure she wanted to repeat the offense. Still, the circumstances of the two mothers seemed to her to have certain parallels. She made up her mind and disappeared from the room for a few minutes. Finally she returned and handed Sally the Xerox copies of the file. "I don't see how I've helped you, but if I have, I'm glad," she said. She walked with Sally to the front door and watched as Sally hurried down the steps and went to her car. Then she returned to her office and stared at the file cabinet for a moment. She began straightening up her office, but as she worked, her mind kept going back to CHILD and the survey. How much information did they have? And what were they using it for? She didn't, she realized, have the faintest idea. All she really knew was that slowly, all over the country, banks of information were being built up about everybody. But what did it mean?

For one thing, no one would be able to disappear. No matter who you were, or where you went, anyone who really wanted to could find you. All they'd have to do would be to ask the computers.

Annie wasn't sure that was a good idea.

Sometimes people need to hide, and they should be able to.

For the first time, it occurred to Annie Oliphant that the whole idea of using computers to watch people was very frightening.

If there was a computer watching nine-year-old boys grow up, was there also, somewhere, a computer watching her?

While Jason Montgomery played in the tiny backyard, Sally and Lucy sat in Lucy's kitchen, sipping coffee and talking. The first moments had been difficult, as each of the women tried to apologize for not having offered her sympathy earlier, yet each of them understood the pain of the other.

For the last half-hour they had been discussing the survey their children were involved in.

"But what are they doing?" Sally asked yet again. "What are they looking for?"

Lucy shrugged helplessly. "I wish I could tell you, Sally. Maybe next week I'll be able to. I've got an appointment on Monday, and I won't leave until I know what that study is all about."

"Do you really think it has anything to do with Randy's disappearance?"

Lucy sighed. "I don't know anything anymore. But it's the only really odd thing I can come up with. Extra-healthy boys. They're studying extra-healthy boys; but how could they know which ones are going to be extra-healthy when they're babies? It doesn't make any sense."

"Maybe it does," Sally said thoughtfully. "Maybe they started out with a huge population and began narrowing it down as some of the subjects began showing the traits they were looking for. Maybe by the time the children get to be Randy's and Jason's ages, they've been able to focus on the population they're interested in."

"And maybe the moon is made out of green cheese," Lucy snapped. "Think about it, Sally. Annie Oliphant told you there are only four boys at the school involved in the survey and all of them are younger than Randy. According to your idea, there should be a lot of children being surveyed, at least in kindergarten and the first couple of grades. But there are only four. So there was something special about those four, and the Children's Health Institute for Latent Diseases knew about it."

"And what about Julie?" Sally asked, her voice quivering. "Was there something special about her too?"

Lucy reached across the table and squeezed Sally's hand. "Oh, Sally, I'm sorry. It's just that I'm trying to figure out what might be going on. And—and maybe there was something about Julie that nobody knows about."

"And maybe there wasn't," Sally replied. She stood up and began gathering her things together. "Maybe we're both a little bit crazy, Lucy. Maybe I'd better go home and do what everyone wants me to do—forget about Julie and go on with my life."

"And what about Jason?" Lucy countered. "Julie's dead, and Randy's missing, and Jason's part of that study too! What about him?"

Sally's eyes suddenly blazed. "What about him? What about *all* the other children in the survey? Apparently nothing's wrong with the others, at least not the ones here in Eastbury." And then, as she saw the hurt in Lucy's eyes, it was Sally's turn to apologize for her hasty words. "Lucy, forgive me. I didn't think—I just let loose. Of course I'm worried about Jason. Ever since Julie died, I've been worried sick about Jason. I'm edgy all the time, and I can't work, and half the time I think I'm losing my mind. But I don't know what to do next."

"Then don't do anything," Lucy said. "Don't do anything at all. Wait until Monday. I'll go to Boston, and

I'll talk to the people at the Institute. Then we can decide what to do next. Okay?"

Silently, Sally nodded her head. A few minutes later, as she and Jason were on their way home, Sally found herself glancing over at her son.

Was there something about him that made him special?

Deep in her heart, she hoped not. All she really wanted for her little boy right then was for him to be just like all the other little boys.

Certainly, he *looked* just like other boys.

But was he?

For Steve and Sally Montgomery, the evening was like a play, with each of them trying, as best as possible, to pretend nothing was wrong between them, or within their home.

And yet the house itself seemed not to have recovered from the loss of its youngest occupant, and there was an emptiness to the rooms of which both Steve and Sally were acutely aware.

Steve tried to fill the void with three martinis, but even as he drank them, he knew it was useless. Instead of feeling the euphoria that ordinarily enveloped him with the second drink, he was becoming increasingly depressed. As he fixed the third drink, his back to his wife, he heard himself speaking.

"Aren't you making dinner tonight?" There was a cutting edge to his voice and, as the words floated in the atmosphere, he wished he could retrieve them. He turned to face Sally, an apology on his lips, but the damage had already been done.

"If you're in such a hurry, you might start fixing it yourself."

Jason, sprawled on the floor in front of the television, looked up at his parents, sensing the tension in the room. "Why don't we go out?" he suggested.

"Because money doesn't grow on trees," Steve snapped. As his son's chin began to tremble, he set his drink down, then knelt down to tousle Jason's hair. "I'm sorry, sport. I guess your mom and I are just feeling edgy."

Jason squirmed uncomfortably. "It's okay," he mumbled. A moment later he slipped out of the room and Sally heard him going upstairs. When the sound of his footsteps had disappeared, she turned to Steve.

"They're studying him too, you know," she said. "It wasn't just Julie. They're watching Jason too."

"Oh, Jesus," Steve groaned. He'd listened to Sally's recital of the day's events earlier. As far as he could see, none of it meant anything. It was all nothing more than coincidence. Why wouldn't she drop it? "For Christ's sake, honey, can't you leave it alone?" he demanded, but remorse at his own words immediately flooded over him.

It had been that way ever since the funeral. It was as if, with her burial, Julie had thrown him off balance, had somehow disturbed the symmetry of his life, drained away the joy he used to feel. Now he felt as though a stranger was living in his body, an angry, mournful stranger who had no way of dealing with the equally strange people around him. The only solution, he knew, was to forget about Julie, to forget that she had ever existed, and somehow to go back to the time before she had been conceived, when there had been only Sally and Jason and himself. If he could do that—if *they* could do that—then things would be all right again. They would be a family again.

But every day, every hour, something happened, or something was said, that reminded him of his little girl, and the scabs were ripped from his wounds and he began to hurt all over again.

And then he would lash out.

Lash out at Sally, lash out at Jason, lash out at anything or anyone that was available. The worst of it was that even though he understood what was happening to him, he could do nothing to stop it, nor could he bring himself to try to explain it to Sally.

He no longer knew what to do about Sally. He had thought that time would take care of her wounds, as he hoped time would take care of his own. But then, late this afternoon, he had had that call from Dr. Wiseman.

Wiseman was worried about Sally. His conversation had been filled with words and phrases of which Steve had only a vague understanding.

"Obsessive behavior."

"Paranoid tendencies."

"Neurotic compulsion."

All of it, Steve knew, boiled down to the fact that while he was trying to forget what had happened, his wife was refusing to face it. Instead, she was grasping at straws, looking for plots where there were no plots. And if it continued, according to Wiseman, Sally could wind up with serious mental problems.

Dinner, when it finally was on the table, was an unhappy affair, with Steve at one end of the table, Sally at the other, and Jason caught in the middle, understanding only that something had gone wrong—something connected with his sister's death—and his parents didn't seem to love each other anymore. He ate as fast as he could, then excused himself and went up to his room. When he was gone, Steve carefully folded his napkin and set it next to his plate.

"I think we have to talk," he said.

Sally, her lips still drawn into a tight line that reflected the anger she had been feeling since before dinner, glared at him. "Are you going to apologize for the way you spoke to Jason and me?"

"Yes, I am," Steve replied. He fell silent, trying to decide how to proceed. Finally, as the silence grew uncomfortable, he made himself begin. "Look, Sally, I know both of us are under terrible strain, and I know we both have to handle this in our own way. But I'm worried about you. Dr. Wiseman called today—"

"Did he?" Sally cut in. There was a coldness to her voice that Steve had never heard before. "Somehow, that doesn't surprise me," she said. "Did he tell you he thinks I'm a hysteric? He does, you know."

"Sally." Steve made his voice as soothing as he could. "He didn't say anything of the sort. He's worried about you, and so am I. We can't go on this way. We're tearing ourselves apart. Look at us. Barely speaking to each other, and when we do, it's not very pleasant. And what about Jason? We're hurting him too."

The words stung Sally, for she knew they were true. Yet she couldn't keep from thinking about Julie and what might have happened to her. She had to find out, had to know that whatever had happened to Julie had not been her own fault. If she couldn't do that, how could she go on living, go on being a mother to Jason? How could she ever know a moment's peace if the thought was ever-present in the back of her mind that she might have done something that killed her own baby. And yet, Jason was still there, and Steve, too, and she loved them both very deeply. For tonight, at least, she would put her problems out of her mind and take care of her family.

"You're right," she said out loud. "Steve, I'm sorry." She leaned back in her chair and toyed with her fork. "That sounds hollow, doesn't it? Our world is falling apart, and all I can do is say 'I'm sorry.' But what good does it do?" Without waiting for an answer, she stood up and started toward the stairs. "I'll go try to make up with Jason. Can you take care of the dishes?"

"Sure." As his wife disappeared from the dining room, Steve began clearing the table. At least, he decided, it was a beginning.

As she passed the door to the little room that had been Julie's, Sally steeled herself against the urge to open it, to look inside, knowing that the wish was futile, that it would not all turn out to have been a nightmare, that Julie would not be miraculously returned to her crib, breathing softly and steadily, gurgling in her sleep. She forced herself to walk steadfastly onward until she came to Jason's room. The door was slightly ajar.

There was no sound from within, and for a moment Sally felt an unreasonable sense of panic. Again she steeled herself, and she pushed the door open.

Jason was sitting at his little worktable, his chemistry

set spread out in front of him, his face a study in concentration as he carefully poured a liquid from a plastic bottle into a test tube.

"Hi!" Sally said. "May I come in?"

Startled, Jason jerked his head upward, and the plastic bottle slipped from his hand. He grabbed at it, catching it just before the contents spilled into his lap. Some of the liquid splashed onto his hand, and he screamed in sudden pain.

Sally's eyes widened in fear as she watched her son rise up from his chair and stare at his hand. Already, it was beginning to turn an angry red. Then Sally came to her senses and rushed forward to pick the terrified boy up and carry him to the bathroom.

"What was it?" she asked as she turned the water on full force and held Jason's hand under the faucet.

"Acid," Jason stammered. "Muriatic acid. I was di—"

"Never mind what you were doing with it," Sally told him. "Let's get it off."

Through the rushing water she could see the blistering skin on Jason's hand. On his fingers the acid had already burned into the flesh.

"I've told you never to play with anything dangerous," she said. "Where'd you get muriatic acid?"

"At the pool store," Jason said placidly. The cool water had flushed the pain out of his hand, and he stared at it now with more curiosity than fear. "I was diluting it down. Why'd you have to come in like that?"

"I came in to see what you were doing, and it's a good thing I did." Sally shut off the water and examined the hand. Now, without the water running over the burn, it didn't look so bad. There were blisters, but apparently the skin wasn't broken after all. Still, burns were easily infected. "Come on, let's take this hand down to your father."

Steve, though, was on his way up the stairs. "What's going on? Did one of you scream?"

"It's your son," Sally said, falling back into that odd form of defense whereby the misbehaving child is ascribed solely to the other parent. "He was playing with acid, and it spilled on his hand."

"It was Mom's fault," Jason chimed in. "If she hadn't startled me . . ."

"Never mind that," Sally cut him off. "Steve, take a look at it. I flushed it with cold water, but it's blistered horribly. At first I thought it had gone right through his skin. Maybe we should take him to the hospital—"

But Steve was already examining the injured hand.

There were no blisters.

All he could see was a slight redness to Jason's skin, and even that seemed to be clearing up as he watched. The redness, he decided, was nothing more than a reaction to the cold water. He grinned at Jason encouragingly. "Does it hurt?"

Jason shook his head.

"Not at all?"

Again, Jason shook his head. "It stung a little, but as soon as Mom ran the water on it, it stopped."

Steve shifted his attention to Sally, who was staring at her son's hand. "You really want to take him to the hospital for this? Sally, there's nothing wrong with his hand."

But it was blistered, Sally thought. I *know* it was. Just two minutes ago it had looked horrible.

Or had it? Had she overreacted to the whole thing? Had her eyes and her emotions played tricks on her?

She felt Steve's eyes on her, and when she faced him she could read his thoughts as clearly as if he was speaking to her.

Are you crazy? he seemed to be asking. Is that what's happened? Have you gone crazy?

As she turned away and went up to her bedroom Sally realized that even if Steve had asked the question out loud, she would have had no answer.

Lucy Corliss pulled up to the building in which her ex-husband lived and let the engine idle for a moment before switching it off and getting out of the car.

She walked up the front steps of the building and pressed the buzzer next to Jim's name.

The apartment was on the second floor, in a corner of the building, and Jim was anxiously waiting for her at the door.

"Has something happened? Have you heard something?"

"Not really," Lucy said uncertainly as she stepped into the living room. She stopped just inside the room and stared. "For heaven's sake," she muttered. The room was small, but one side of it was dominated by a fireplace around which were a love seat and two wing chairs covered in the rust-brown material she had nearly selected for her own almost identical furniture. Between the chairs and the couch was a glass and brass coffee table, on which rested a sculpture that Lucy had never seen before, a bronze figure, obviously oriental, one leg raised, and the arms arched into the air.

"It's a Thai dancer," Jim told her. "I couldn't really afford it, but I decided I could live without two years worth of nights on the town, and I bought it."

"It's beautiful," Lucy breathed, moving closer to the statue and lowering herself onto one of the wing chairs.

"And you never thought I'd spend money on something like that?" Jim asked, his voice lilting with a half-taunting humor. "I'm afraid I gave up on Mediterranean furniture and decor by *Playboy* about the same time I moved out of Adultery Acres." He sat down on the sofa opposite her, and his expression turned serious. "Something *did* happen, didn't it?" he asked.

Lucy nodded, then told him about the visit she had had with Sally Montgomery that afternoon.

"And is that why you came over here?" Jim asked when she was done. "To see if I could figure out what's going on?"

"Not really," Lucy replied. "I'm putting all that on hold till Monday. There just isn't anything I can do right now. It seems like both of us have done everything we can, and—" Her voice broke, and she let herself sink into the softness of the chair. "I guess I'm just wearing out,

Jim. And I almost didn't come over here. But I was lonely, and I was driving around, and suddenly the only person I could think of to talk to was you." She glanced at Jim sharply, hoping he wouldn't misunderstand her. "I mean, right now you and I have a lot in common, despite our differences."

"Maybe there aren't so many differences anymore," Jim suggested. Then, before Lucy could answer, he stood up. "Can I fix us some drinks?"

"Do you have any gin?"

"Tanqueray."

"With some tonic." As Jim disappeared into the kitchen, Lucy stood up and wandered around the room. In a bookcase against the wall opposite the fireplace she found several books she had read over the past few years and a series of framed pictures.

Mostly, they were of Randy.

Several of them were of herself, and all but one had been taken before the divorce. One of them, though, was recent.

"I see you found my gallery," Jim observed as he came back into the room.

"Where did you get this?" Lucy asked, picking up the picture. It had been taken two years earlier.

Jim blushed slightly. "I'm afraid I got sneaky. Randy told me you'd had a portrait made for his grandmother, and I called every studio in town till I found it." He paused for a moment. "I'm sorry about your mother. I always liked her, even though she never thought much of me."

Lucy smiled at him. "I think if she knew you now, she might change her mind."

The two of them stood still for a moment, and Lucy had a feeling Jim was going to kiss her. And then, as if he sensed her sudden unease, he moved away from her. "You doing anything for dinner?"

"I hadn't really thought about it," Lucy admitted. All day she'd been dreading the evening alone in the empty house. Then, after Sally had gone, she'd finally gotten into the car and driven aimlessly for nearly two hours, trying to decide where to go, until a little while ago, when she'd found herself a few blocks from Jim's apartment. "You want to go out somewhere?"

"Not really," Jim replied, his easy grin spreading over his face. "I still have to pay for the Thai dancer, and there's Randy's education to think of. So I've learned to cook. Feeling brave? I make a mean Stroganoff."

"Fine," Lucy decided. The idea of spending a quiet evening with Jim was suddenly very appealing. Then she said, "Jim? When you mentioned Randy's education just now, were you ... Do you really think we're going to find him?"

Jim hesitated for a moment, forcing himself to maintain a cheerful façade. "Who knows? I know what Sergeant Bronski thinks, and I know what the statistics are, and I don't have any more of an idea than you do as to what to do next. So, I suppose, we should accept the fact that he's gone. But deep down inside I don't believe he ran away either. I believe in you, Lucy, and if you think someone took him, then someone took him. If you think he's alive, then he's alive. And if you think we'll find him, then we'll find him. So I guess I better not spend his college money yet, had I?"

Lucy felt her eyes tearing, and made no move to wipe the dampness away. Instead, she reached out and tentatively touched Jim's hand.

"Thank you," she whispered.

Their eyes met, and then suddenly Jim winked. "And on Monday, you get down to CHILD and find out what they did with our son. Okay?"

Silently, Lucy nodded.

Chapter 15

THE GLASS-AND-STEEL MONOLITH that housed the offices of CHILD rose up out of the heart of the city like a great impersonal tombstone. The faceless people within it would continue their endless sojourn, year after year, until one day they would finally leave their offices and begin their "golden years," unaware they had spent most of their lives within a spiritual graveyard. As Lucy Corliss approached its expressionless façade on that unusually muggy spring morning, she felt as though she already knew what would happen inside.

Nothing.

The people at CHILD, she was sure, would be reflections of the building in which they worked—efficient, featureless, bland, and, in the end, impenetrable. Still, she had to try.

The elevator rose swiftly and silently to the thirty-second floor, and when its doors slid open, Lucy was confronted with a wide corridor stretching away in both directions. At the end of the hall was a pair of imposing double doors. Behind those doors lay the CHILD offices. Steeling herself, Lucy opened the doors and slipped into a mahogany-paneled reception room containing a small sitting area—empty—and a desk behind which sat a cool blonde who appeared to be cut from the same die as morning talk-show hostesses. Lucy approached the desk, but the receptionist, talking softly on the telephone, held up her hand as if forbidding Lucy to get too close. A moment later she hung up the phone and turned on her smile.

"May I help you?"

"I'd like to see Mr. Randolph. Paul Randolph?"

The receptionist, who neither wore a name badge nor had a nameplate propped helpfully on her desk, looked doubtful.

"I'm afraid Mr. Randolph is very busy."

"I have an appointment," Lucy said firmly.

The receptionist frowned. "With Mr. Randolph?"

"That's right," Lucy replied, her original sense of intimidation turning rapidly to irritation. "My name is Lucy Corliss. If you'll just tell me where his office is—" But the receptionist was already on the phone, talking softly to someone hidden in the depths of the offices. Then she was back to Lucy, smiling brightly.

"If you'll just take a seat, Mrs. Corliss? It'll just be a minute, and I'll be happy to get you some coffee while you wait."

But Lucy didn't want coffee. She simply wanted to sit for a minute and savor her tiny victory over the cool blonde. The blonde, however, saw fit to ignore her.

A moment later a much older woman strode into the reception room and offered Lucy her hand.

"I'm Eva Phillips, Paul Randolph's secretary. We're so sorry to keep you waiting, but you know how things can be."

She ushered Lucy through the offices, chattering amiably all the way, and finally showed her into a large corner office dominated by an enormous desk. Behind the desk sat a man who was obviously Paul Randolph.

He was in his indeterminate forties, his face smooth and handsome in a bland sort of way. His sandy hair was thinning, and, to his credit, he made no attempt to hide that fact. He rose to greet Lucy, and as he came around the end of his desk, he moved with a lithe grace that Lucy had always associated with old money, private schools, and summers on the Cape. When he spoke, his voice was perfectly modulated, his accent pure Brahmin.

"Mrs. Corliss, how nice to meet you. Won't you sit down?" He indicated a sofa that sat at right angles to his desk, and without thinking about it, Lucy seated herself where Randolph intended her to sit. He himself took a chair that was substantially firmer than the sofa, and Lucy, not quite understanding the psychological ploy, suddenly felt that she was somehow at a disadvantage. From his slightly higher position, Paul Randolph smiled cordially down at her. "Would you like coffee?"

"No, thank you," Lucy replied. With a quick gesture, Randolph dismissed Eva Phillips, who silently closed the door as she left the room.

"Now, what can I do for you?" Randolph asked. "May I assume you've become interested in our work?"

My God, Lucy thought, he thinks I want to donate money. "Yes, I have," she said. "You see, I just found out a few days ago that your people have been studying my son."

The smile on Randolph's face stayed firmly in place, but something in his eyes changed, and Lucy immediately realized that the man was suddenly on guard. When he spoke, however, his voice was as mellow as before.

"I see. Of course, we study thousands of children here. And I must say," he added with a touch of a chuckle, "this is the first time one of the children's parents has come to see me."

"Mr. Randolph, my son has been kidnaped."

Finally, the smile faded from the man's lips. "I beg your pardon, Mrs. Corliss?"

"I said my son has been kidnaped. At least that's what I think happened to him. The police ..." She faltered for a moment, then, in a rush, poured out the whole story of the last few days. When she was done, Randolph sat silently, his eyes clouded with concern, his hands clasped together.

"But what brought you here, Mrs. Corliss? Surely you

don't think that we could have had anything to do with your son's disappearance?"

Lucy hesitated. Put so bluntly, in surroundings as eminently respectable as those of CHILD, it sounded unthinkable. And yet, that was exactly what she thought.

"I don't know," Lucy hedged, sure that if she told him the truth he would show her the door. "I don't know what to think. But when I found the notation in Randy's medical files and learned that he'd been part of a project I knew nothing about, well, naturally I began to wonder."

Randolph's head bobbed understandingly. His smile returned. "So you want to know what we're doing, is that it?"

"Exactly."

Randolph rose and began to pace the room. "Well, I'll do my best, but I have to tell you that I'm not even sure I understand it all myself. I'm afraid I'm an administrator, not a scientist."

"Then you'll use language I can understand."

"I'll try. To begin with, the work we're doing here is what you might call passive work, as opposed to active work. We conduct surveys and put together statistics, primarily concerning genetics."

"I'm not sure I do understand."

Randolph lowered himself into the chair behind his desk and leaned back, folding his hands across his stomach. "All right, let's go back to the beginning. Are you aware that almost all babies, at birth or even before, go through a process of genetic screening?"

"Sort of." Lucy was beginning to feel that she was going to get lost right at the start. But Randolph smiled at her encouragingly.

"It's really not terribly complicated. Samples of the baby's tissue are taken, and the chromosomes are analyzed. We can often discover genetic weaknesses that, if left uncorrected, can lead to various problems, the most obvious, but not the least of which, is Down's syndrome."

Lucy held up a protesting hand. "I'm sorry, but you're losing me," she said.

Randolph tried again. "All right. The chromosomes, or genes, act as a pattern for the cells. They dictate what chemicals the cells will produce, and, therefore, determine the cell's shape, function, and purpose. Over the years, we've discovered that certain genetic deficiencies cause chemical imbalances that, in turn, cause certain mental or physical problems later on in life."

"And what, exactly, does CHILD do?"

"It's very simple, really. All we do is track certain children, from the time of birth through adulthood. We keep track of their genetic records and then simply observe them. For instance, let's suppose that there are two children who, at the age of, say, ten or eleven, begin to develop symptoms of mental illness. Say, also, that there are no environmental similarities between the children. But say, even further, that when we go through our records, we discover that both children share a specific genetic abnormality. Bingo! It would appear that the particular disorder displayed by the two children may have its roots in genetics."

Lucy shook her head. "It sounds too simple."

"Yes," Randolph agreed. "But even granted the oversimplification, that's basically what we do. In the long run, of course, the idea is to determine which genetic deficiencies are benign and which ones are going to cause problems to the child later. It's up to other researchers to try to figure out ways of correcting or compensating for the deficiencies and abnormalities."

"And that's all you do?" Lucy asked.

"That's all we do," Randolph assured her.

"Then why wasn't I told you were studying Randy?"

"Perhaps you were and don't remember it," Randolph suggested.

"Where my son is concerned, I wouldn't have forgotten," Lucy shot back. "I would have wanted to know exactly what the study was about, what would be required from Randy, and how he had been chosen."

"But that's just the point, Mrs. Corliss." Randolph's

voice was gentle and soothing. "The study was no more than a survey, it required nothing from Randy, and he was chosen at random. It was purely a matter of chance that Randy was selected for our study."

"Then you won't mind showing me the results of the study, will you?"

"Results? But, Mrs. Corliss, there aren't any results yet. The survey will go on until the children are all grown up."

"But what about the ones who don't grow up?" Lucy asked. "What about the ones who die in infancy, or get sick, or are victims of accidents? Surely you must have *some* results? If you don't, I should think you'd have given the whole thing up by now."

For the first time, Randolph seemed at a loss for words. Lucy decided to press her advantage. "Mr. Randolph, the nurse at Randy's school says that of all the children in the school, Randy and the three others you're studying have the best health records. Randy's never been sick a day in his life, never hurt himself badly, never shown any signs of being slow, or abnormal, or anything else. Now, doesn't it seem reasonable that if I discover someone has been studying him, I might also wonder just *why* they were studying him? And if Randy is remarkable—and he is—doesn't it seem reasonable that I might begin to think the people who are studying him might want a closer look?"

The color had drained from Randolph's face, and his smile had settled into a tight line of anger. "Mrs. Corliss, are you suggesting that CHILD kidnaped your son?"

"I don't know, Mr. Randolph," Lucy replied coldly. "But I know it would do a great deal toward setting my mind at rest if you would show me the study Randy was involved in, together with any results that have come from that study. I don't pretend that I'll understand it, but I'll be able to find someone who will. And although I can't be sure of it right now, I suspect that what you've been doing without my consent, and without Randy's consent, amounts to invasion of privacy."

Randolph sank back into his chair. His right hand

brushed distractedly at his hair. "Mrs. Corliss, I'm not sure what I can do for you," he said at last. "But of course, I'll do my best. It will take a little time to find out exactly which of our surveys Randy was involved in and put together a report for you. Believe me, we'll do it. Nothing like this has ever happened before, and CHILD has been functioning for nearly twenty years. But I can tell you right now that we had nothing to do with the disappearance of your son."

"How long will it take?" Lucy asked.

"A couple of days."

Lucy stood up. "Then I'll expect to hear from you, Mr. Randolph. Day after tomorrow?"

"I'll call you, Mrs. Corliss. If you'll just leave your address with my secretary . . ."

Lucy smiled icily. "I'll do that, Mr. Randolph, but I can't imagine it's necessary. I'm sure that somewhere in your files you already have my address."

She picked up her purse, and without offering Randolph her hand, left his office.

When she was gone, Paul Randolph sat down heavily at his desk. Sweat had broken out on his brow.

What he had always feared was starting to happen.

Randy Corliss was spending the afternoon playing a game he still didn't quite understand. It was sort of like hide-and-seek, and sort of like tag, but there was something else involved, and Randy wasn't quite sure he liked it.

The game had started simply enough.

One of the boys was 'it,' and he had to count to a hundred while the other boys scattered and hid. Then the boy who was 'it' began hunting for his friends. When he spotted one of them, he yelled the boy's name, and began chasing him, trying to tag him. If he succeeded, that boy became 'it.'

The catch was that once the boy who was 'it' had named his prey, the other boys could come out of hiding to help the prey.

Suddenly, whoever was 'it' was transformed from hunter to victim.

Randy had made his first mistake right at the start. When the counting had begun, he had run off by himself while the rest of the pack stuck together. He had found a hiding place deep in the woods, near the creek. He waited, sure that he wouldn't be found, listening for a name to be called out, at which point it would be safe to emerge.

The minutes had passed interminably, and Randy tried to figure out what was going on. Finally, he rose from his hiding place only to find that Adam Rogers, who was 'it,' was standing only a few yards away.

"Randy!" Adam screamed and the chase was on.

And that was when Randy realized his mistake. The other boys, all together, were too far away to help him. Within a few seconds Adam had slammed him to the ground, crowing at having won a victory in the first round.

And now Randy was 'it.'

He counted through to a hundred as fast as he could, then looked up.

No one was in sight.

He moved away from the base point next to the main house and started across the lawn, his eyes searching the woods for a sign of his friends.

Nothing.

He moved into the woods, searching carefully, knowing that he would have to find one of the boys alone if he was going to have a chance at winning.

He caught a glimpse of Adam and started to shout his name, but then saw one of the other boys, Jerry Preston, peeking out from behind a tree only a few feet away. Pretending not to see either of them, Randy moved deeper into the woods.

He stopped every few seconds, listening, sure that all the other boys were following him, yet unable to hear them.

Then, ahead of him, he saw Eric Carter, his red hair giving him away, crouched in a clump of laurel near the fence. He moved closer, trying to pretend he hadn't seen Eric.

He looked around, searching the woods behind him for the others. There was silence.

When he judged he was close enough, he suddenly let out a scream.

"ERIC CARTER!"

He hurtled himself forward as Eric exploded out of the laurel and began to run parallel to the fence. For a second Eric seemed to be outdistancing him, but then Randy began to gain. He had almost caught up with his prey, when three boys suddenly burst out of the forest, one of them slightly ahead of him, one next to him, and the other just behind him.

Once again, Randy had fallen into a trap.

He turned to face Adam, who was the closest to him, but Adam suddenly paused, and Randy felt a blow from behind. He stumbled, then fell to the ground as Billy Mayhew and Jerry piled onto him. In the distance, Eric Carter had stopped running and was now watching the fracas, his face wreathed in a smile.

Randy fought as hard as he could, his arms and legs flailing, but it did no good.

"Throw him into the fence," Jerry suggested. "That'll finish him off."

Suddenly the boys were off him, but Adam was holding him firmly by the shoulders as Billy and Jerry each grabbed one of his legs.

"On three," Adam yelled. The boys began swinging Randy, with Adam counting off the cadence.

On three they let go and hurled Randy into the fence.

There was a shower of sparks, and the air was suddenly filled with the odor of burning flesh.

Randy fell to the ground.

The game was over, and the boys gathered around Randy, staring at him curiously. Adam Rogers glanced at Billy Mayhew.

"Do you suppose we'll get in trouble?"

Billy shrugged. "We didn't last time. Why should we this time?"

Then, chattering among themselves, the boys started back through the woods toward the Academy, leaving Randy lying on the ground next to the electrified fence.

Sally Montgomery had spent much of the weekend in her office at Eastbury College. What she was doing, she knew, was probably illegal. It was definitely unethical, but she had wasted no time at all worrying about that. Instead, she had devoted all her time to discovering the access codes that would allow her to tap into the Eastbury Community Hospital records that were stored in the county's computer. It was, like most programing, a matter of trial and error. For anyone without Sally's background, it would have been nearly impossible; for Sally, it was simply a matter of knowing how the codes were constructed, then having the computer begin trying all the possibilities within the framework. The code, when she finally found it, turned out to be ridiculously obvious:

M-E-D-R-E-A-C-H. *MED*ical *R*ecords, *EA*stbury *C*ommunity *H*ospital? Probably. Indeed, when she finally found the code, it had occurred to her that in an age of acronyms, she ought to have been able to figure it out without the aid of the computer.

Now, on Monday morning, she was tapping into the records, attempting to find out whether or not the children that CHILD was surveying had truly been selected through random sampling.

She began by instructing the computer to search the records and put together certain populations.

Children who were being surveyed by the Children's Health Institute for Latent Diseases.

Children who had been victims of SIDS.

Children whose records reflected no health problems.

She went back twenty years. Without the computer it would have taken months simply to compile the data.

Now, after only two hours of work, Sally had begun to see a pattern emerge.

The computer had constructed the populations Sally had asked for and begun comparing them.

Until ten years ago there had been no discernible differences between the children who were being studied by CHILD and the entire population of juvenile patients for the entire county.

The same percentage of each population had come down, at one time or another, with such diseases as mumps, measles, and chicken pox.

The same proportion of each group had displayed similar incidence of emotional problems.

The same proportion of each group had fallen victim to SIDS.

On and on, it had been the same. As far as Sally could see, the CHILD surveys had involved a genuinely random sampling of all the children born at Eastbury Community Hospital.

And then, ten years ago, things began to change.

The incidence of sudden infant death syndrome seemed to have increased among children in Eastbury, particularly among those born at Eastbury Community Hospital.

In itself, Sally knew that such a fact could be statistically meaningless.

What *was* meaningful was that among the entire population of children in Eastbury, SIDS had increased by four percent.

Among the population being surveyed by CHILD, SIDS had increased by nearly ten percent.

Furthermore, the composition of the group of children struck down by SIDS had changed. For the first ten years, the syndrome had appeared with equal frequency in boys and girls. But ten years ago, the statistics began to skew, and baby girls became more frequent victims of the syndrome than baby boys. And among the population of children being surveyed by CHILD, an even higher ratio of girls to boys had died from SIDS.

Sally printed out the lists of populations, and the strange correlations between the two. Then she turned her attention to the other group she was looking at, the population of children whose medical records were remarkable for the excellent health they reflected. Here, Sally ran into a problem. Over the years, too many children had simply moved away from Eastbury, and their records had come to an abrupt end, to be continued in other areas of the country. Areas to which Sally had no easy access.

Still, she thought there was a pattern. It appeared, even from the sketchy records, that over the last ten years, the proportion of remarkably healthy little boys on the CHILD lists had risen.

Again, Sally Montgomery printed out the statistics.

Toward noon Sally asked the computer to complete one more task.

Given all the data in the records, she requested the computer to come to a determination as to whether or not the subjects of the CHILD surveys had, over the last ten years, been chosen on a truly random basis.

The minutes crept by as the computer began digesting all the material stored away in its data banks. At last the screen on Sally's console came to life.

The computer's answer brought tears to Sally's eyes. Through the blur, she read the computer's final summation one more time.

"Insufficient data to make determination."

Sally switched off her terminal, gathered up all the printouts her morning's work had produced, and left her office.

All her work, according to the computer, meant nothing. And yet she was sure that the computer was wrong. Then, as she thought about it, she came to the slow realization that the computer had not said the CHILD surveys weren't random. It had simply refused to take a stand on the question.

That was the problem with computers. They were too objective. Indeed, they were totally objective.

But CHILD, Sally was convinced, was *not* totally objective. The survey, she was sure, was a cover for something else.

A conspiracy.

But would she be able to prove it?

She didn't know.

All she knew was that the more she learned, the more frightened she became.

Chapter 16

STEVE MONTGOMERY PAUSED on the front porch of his mother-in-law's house, wondering if he'd been right in his decision to share his problems with Phyllis Paine. When the idea of talking to her about Sally had first occurred to him, he'd immediately rejected it. But then, this morning, he'd changed his mind. After all, who knew Sally as well as her own mother?

He pressed the button next to the front door and listened to the soft melody of the chimes. When there was no answer, he pressed the bell again. Then, just as he was about to turn away, the door opened, and Phyllis, her eyes rimmed in red, and her face suddenly showing her years, gazed out at him.

"Steve." Her eyes darted around as she looked for Sally, then her brows furrowed in puzzlement. "Isn't Sally with you?"

"No." Offering no further explanation, Steve asked if he could come in, and Phyllis suddenly stepped back.

"Of course. I'm sorry, Steve. I—well, I'm afraid I haven't been having a very good day."

Steve paused. "Maybe I should come back another time."

"No, no." She closed the door, and led Steve into the parlor. "I was just getting rid of some things." Sighing tiredly, she seated herself on the edge of the sofa. "Some dresses I was making for Julie," she went on. "They were in the sewing room, all cut, and I've been waking up every night, feeling guilty about not having finished them." Her lips twisted into a desolate smile. "You know me—once I start something, I have to finish it. Anyway, I've been waking up in the middle of the night and going to the sewing room to finish the dresses, and it isn't until I start working on them that I remember . . . what happened. So just now I threw them away. I took them out to the garbage can and threw them away."

Her eyes, reflecting an uncertainty that Steve had never seen before, searched his face. "It seemed like a terrible thing to do," she whispered. "And yet, I couldn't think of anything else. It was a symbol, I suppose. A way of forcing myself to face up to what's happened." Suddenly she straightened up and folded her hands in her lap. "But that's not why you're here, is it?" The uncertainty in her eyes disappeared, to be replaced by the penetrating sharpness Steve was used to. "It's Sally, isn't it?"

Steve shifted uncomfortably, then nodded his head.

"Things aren't going well, are they? I mean, even considering the circumstances?"

"No," Steve said quietly. "And I'm beginning to wonder what to do."

Phyllis's brows rose. "About Sally?"

"Dr. Wiseman called me on Friday. He's worried about her—he seems to think she's avoiding facing up to the fact that Julie's death can't be explained by trying to prove that something else happened. Something more reasonable."

"I see," Phyllis said. "And what do you think?"

"I don't know what to think. I barely saw her over the weekend. When she wasn't at her office, she was holed up in the den, and she wouldn't tell me what she was working on. But I'm sure it had something to do with"—he faltered, then plunged on—"with Julie. And she's been talking to Lucy Corliss."

"Lucy Corliss? Why does that name—oh! The mother of that little boy who's missing. What's his name?"

"Randy. He was a friend of Jason's. But that's not what she was talking to Mrs. Corliss about, at least not directly. It seems that Jason and Randy as well as Julie were being studied by some group in Boston."

Phyllis's brows arched skeptically. "What's unusual about that? These days it seems as if someone's studying all of us all the time." Then her expression changed. "Oh, God, she hasn't come up with some sort of conspiracy theory, has she?"

"Well, I wouldn't want to go—"

"*Has* she?"

"I'm afraid so," Steve replied, his shoulders sagging.

Phyllis shook her head sadly. "Have you talked to Arthur about it?" she asked.

"No. I wanted to talk to you first. I guess I was afraid Dr. Wiseman might see what Sally's doing as some sort of—what? Neurotic behavior?" He groaned. "Oh, Christ, Phyllis, I can hardly believe we're having this conversation."

"And yet we are," Phyllis replied firmly. "And since we are, the question is, what are we to do about it? Do you want me to talk to Arthur?"

"Would you?"

Now it was Phyllis's turn to sigh. "I suppose so. I have to talk to him anyway. I'm afraid I was quite rude to him at the funeral, and I had no right to be. I owe him an apology. I'll drop by the clinic this afternoon."

"I'd appreciate it," Steve told her. "I know how you hate getting—"

Phyllis waved his words away. "Don't be silly. You know I try not to interfere, but I'm still Sally's mother, and I still worry, even though I try not to show it." Her expression changed slightly, and her eyes fell appraisingly upon Steve. "What about you? Are you all right? You look terrible."

"I'm holding myself together."

"See that you continue to," Phyllis said. She rose to escort her son-in-law to the door. "You're a man, Steve, and Sally's going to have to count on you." Her voice dropped, as if she were about to impart a secret. "I've never thought Sally was as stable as she appears to be, you know. It's always seemed to me there were tensions in Sally, and under the wrong circumstances—" She suddenly fell silent, and as he left her house, Steve knew she thought she'd said too much.

"Want some more coffee?" Sally asked.

Lucy Corliss shook her head. "What I really want is a drink, but I'll be damned if I'll have one this early in the day." The clock read three twenty, and she had been sitting at Sally's kitchen table for nearly two hours. She fingered the stack of computer printouts, then leaned back and folded her arms across her chest. "So all this might mean something, or it might not," she said. Sally had already explained the meaning of the computer's evaluation of its own work.

"It does," Sally insisted. "I'm sure it does. It's just that the damned computer can't prove it."

"So we're nowhere," Lucy said. "It looks like something is going on, but we can't prove it. And you can bet I'll get nothing out of Randolph. God, how I hate those smooth bastards."

"But he said he'd have *something* for you?"

"Oh, sure. But you can bet that whatever it is, it won't be the truth. If there was no secret about what they're doing, why wouldn't they have let us know they were studying our children? And they didn't," Lucy added bitterly. "I'm one of those people who keeps everything. I even have laundry receipts from Randy's diaper service. They're getting yellow, but I have them. Anyway, I went over everything—everything! There's nothing about a survey, no forms, no requests for permission, nothing! And you know what, Sally? The more I think about it, the angrier I get. Even if it has nothing to do with Randy's disappearing, the whole idea just gets to me. I mean, if they've been watching Randy and Jason, and even Julie, what about us? Are we all being watched? Don't any of us have any privacy anymore? It's scary!"

"It's the new age," Sally said quietly. "I don't think there's anything any of us can do but get used to it. But what about all these?" she asked, gesturing toward the printouts. "We've *got* to do something about this."

Suddenly Lucy had an idea. "Could I have them?" she asked.

Sally frowned. "What for?"

"I want to show them to someone," Lucy replied. Sally started to ask another question, but Lucy held up her hand. "Just trust me," she said. "I might wind up looking like a fool, but there's no reason why you should too."

The back door slammed open, and Jason appeared. "Hi, Mom," he called. "I'm—" Then he saw Lucy, and his words died on his lips. "Hi, Mrs. Corliss," he went on. Suddenly he looked hopeful. "Is Randy back?"

Lucy had to fight to control the tears that came into her eyes at Jason's words, but she made herself smile. "Not yet," she told him, "but I'm sure it won't be long now. Do you miss him?"

Jason nodded solemnly. "He's my best friend. I hope nothing happened to him."

Lucy stood up abruptly, picked up the printouts, and started toward the door. "I'll take good care of these, Sally," she promised. Then, before either Sally or Jason could say anything more, she was gone. Sally, still seated at the kitchen table, held her arms out to her son.

"Come here," she said softly, and Jason, though unsure what his mother wanted, let himself be hugged. "I love you," Sally whispered. "I love you so much."

Jason, wriggling in her arms, suddenly looked up and grinned. "Enough to let me make fudge?" he asked.

For some reason, the devilish look on her son's face broke the tension Sally had been living under for over a week, and she began laughing.

"Sure," she said, releasing Jason and standing up. "In fact, making fudge seems like the best idea I've heard all day!"

Jason watched as Sally mixed together the milk, sugar,

and chocolate, added a dash of salt, and put the pan on the stove.

"Want me to check the thermometer?" he asked.

"You can if you want," Sally said with a shrug. "But it's never been off yet, has it?"

"No," Jason agreed, "but my chemistry book says you should always check your equipment before you start an experiment."

"When you're as old as I am, making fudge isn't an experiment anymore."

Jason filled a pan with water, put the long candy thermometer into it, and set it on a vacant burner. Then he turned the heat on, and while he waited for the water to boil, fished a bottle of pop out of the refrigerator. Sally glared at him.

"Drink that, and you won't get to scrape out the pan," she warned.

Jason glanced at the stove where the fudge was just barely beginning to heat, then at the bottle in his hand, which was all ready to be drunk. "Aw, Mom," he muttered.

"Make up your mind."

Reluctantly, Jason put the pop back in the refrigerator. "Dad would have let me drink it," he complained as he went back to check on his pan of water. It was beginning to simmer, and he climbed up on the kitchen stool to watch the thermometer.

It read 200 degrees, but even as he watched it, he could see the mercury climbing. He shifted his attention to the fudge. It, too, was beginning to boil.

"The thermometer'll be ready in a minute."

Sally was buttering a pan. She glanced up, smiling at the intensity with which Jason watched the thermometer.

"When it gets to two-twelve, let it sit a minute. If it doesn't go up any farther, it's reading right. Then you can move it over to the candy pan. But *don't* stir the candy!"

"I know," Jason said, his voice filled with scorn. "If you stir it, it crystallizes. Anybody knows that."

"You didn't till I taught you," Sally teased. She began chopping up some walnuts, but kept an eye on Jason when, a few moments later, he moved the thermometer from the boiling water into the candy. "Now, don't let the candy go above two-thirty-four."

Jason, his eyes glued to the steadily creeping mercury, ignored her.

He watched as the temperature reached 230 degrees, then 232. He was about to get down from the stool, ready to pick up the pan as soon as it rose two more degrees, when suddenly the temperature seemed to spurt.

As the red column in the thermometer started past 234, he picked up the pan and groped with his left foot for the step that should have been there.

It wasn't.

Startled, he tried to set the pan back on the stove, but it was too late. His balance was gone, and he tumbled to the floor, the pan of boiling fudge still clutched in his right hand. His scream of fright made Sally look up just in time to see the searing liquid gush over Jason's arm and spread out on the floor.

Sally forced back the scream that boiled up from her own throat. She dropped her knife as she scooped Jason up from the floor and instinctively moved him toward the sink. Then she began running cold water while she held his arm under the tap.

As the brown mess washed away, she saw the blistering skin underneath.

Jason, strangely still, stared at his arm.

"Why doesn't it hurt?" he asked. Then, again, "Why doesn't it hurt?"

Pausing only to snatch her car keys from the table and wrap his arm in a towel, Sally rushed Jason out the back door. A moment later she was on her way to the hospital.

Last time, she had been too late, and her daughter had died.

This time she would not be too late.

Jason was her only child now; she would allow nothing to happen to him.

As Jason sat silently beside her, his arm swathed in a kitchen towel, she sped through the streets of Eastbury.

Arthur Wiseman was walking Phyllis Paine out to her car. They had talked for nearly an hour, but reached no conclusions. All that had been decided was that for the next few weeks they would keep a careful eye on Sally. And then, as they passed the emergency room, they heard her voice.

"But I *saw* it, Dr. Malone," she was saying, her voice strident, and her face flushed with anger. "I tell you, I *saw* the blisters. Don't tell me he's all right! He's *not* all right. He's burned! Don't you understand?"

"Who?" Phyllis demanded. Sally whirled around, staring at her mother in surprise. "Who's burned?" Phyllis repeated.

"Mother, what are you doing here?"

"Never mind that," Phyllis replied. "Has something happened to Jason?"

Sally's eyes brimmed with tears and she nodded. "We were making fudge. He—he slipped, and the fudge poured out all over his arm." Suddenly she was sobbing, and Phyllis gathered her into her arms. "Oh, Mother, it was horrible. And it was my fault. I should have been doing it myself."

"Hush, child," Phyllis crooned. Her eyes shifted to Mark Malone, who stood to one side, slowly shaking his head. "How bad is it, Doctor?"

Malone shrugged. "Not that bad at all, Mrs. Paine. In fact, it really doesn't look like anything."

Phyllis Paine's expression hardened, and a scowl formed on her brow. "Now see here, young man. If that pan of fudge was boiling, the boy must have been hurt. Where is he?"

Malone nodded toward a small treatment room. Phyllis helped Sally into a chair, then strode toward the door. Inside the little room she found Jason, stripped to the waist, sitting on a table.

"Hi, Grandma," he said, grinning at her. "Wanna see my arm?"

He offered his right arm for her inspection. Phyllis bent over it, examining it carefully. "Well, it doesn't look like much, does it?"

Jason shook his head. "And it hardly hurt at all," he announced proudly. "But it was real hot, Grandma. The thermometer read two hundred and thirty-four. That's what they call the soft-ball stage. It means that if you drop the fudge in cold water—"

"I know what it means," Phyllis said severely. "And I also know what heat like that does to little boys like you. You stay right where you are, young man." She let go of his arm and returned to the waiting area. Sally, blotting at her eyes with a Kleenex, looked up at her anxiously. "It certainly doesn't look like much," Phyllis said.

Sally's face crumpled. "But it was blistered," she whispered, almost to herself. "I saw it, and it was blistered."

Over Sally's head, Phyllis's eyes met Malone's. "It seems to me there must be some confusion," she said. "Apparently it was my grandson who was watching the thermometer, and he must have misread it. It was probably only *one* hundred and thirty-four."

Slowly, Sally's head came up, and she stared at her mother. "But it wasn't, Mother," she said. "It was boiling, and it burned Jason's arm very badly." She stood up and went to the treatment room. A moment later she returned, holding Jason by the hand. "I'm sorry you don't believe me," she said. She turned to Malone. "Is there any reason for us to stay?"

"Mrs. Montgomery, it *couldn't* have been as bad as you think. You must have been upset—"

"Of course I was upset," Sally shot back. "Anyone would have been. But I saw what I saw. Now please answer my question. Does Jason need to stay here or be bandaged?"

"No—"

"Thank you," Sally said, her voice icy. She turned,

about to speak to her mother, then paused. There was something about the way her mother and Dr. Wiseman were looking at her that made her feel strange, as if she had just been tested, and found wanting. But then, as they became aware she was watching, their expressions changed. Wiseman extended his hand to Phyllis.

"Now, if there's anything else you need, just call me. How about dinner on Wednesday?"

"Fine, Arthur," Phyllis replied. She turned to Sally. "Well, shall we go? I'll follow you home and help you clean up the mess."

"Never mind, Mother." Sally's voice was cold, but Phyllis ignored it.

"No arguments! That's what mothers are for." But as she guided Sally and Jason out into the parking lot, she glanced back at Arthur Wiseman.

He looked as worried as she felt.

Sergeant Carl Bronski stared at the pile of computer printouts, and shrugged helplessly. "I'm sorry, Mrs. Corliss, but I'm afraid I'm just not following you."

Once again Lucy tried to explain what the columns of numbers meant, and once again Bronski listened attentively. When she was done, though, he shook his head sadly.

"But even you admit it doesn't really mean anything."

"It means that CHILD is up to something," Lucy replied. "I don't know what, and I don't know why, but something's going on."

Bronski nodded tiredly. It had been going on for two hours, and though he understood full well how Lucy Corliss was feeling, he didn't see what he could do about it. "But if you won't even tell me where these came from, and if you can't really explain what they mean, what do you expect me to do?"

"I expect you to find out what CHILD was doing with my son," Lucy said. "I expect you to do what you're supposed to do, and investigate this."

"But, Mrs. Corliss, there isn't anything to investigate.

A few pages of numbers that don't really mean anything. It's just not something I can use to justify an investigation of an outfit the size of CHILD."

There was a long silence. Lucy sank back in her chair. "All right," she said, her voice suddenly calm. "How about this? How about if I talk to the person I got this information from, and they agree to talk to you, to explain what all this means? Will you at least listen to h—them?"

Her, Bronski thought. Will I listen to *her*. But who is she? Another hysterical mother? But if that's all she is, where'd she get this stuff? Finally, he said, "Okay. You talk to her, and if she wants to talk to me, I'll listen."

Seeming satisfied, Lucy Corliss gathered her things together and left the Eastbury police department. But long after she was gone, Carl Bronski sat at his desk, thinking.

He remembered Randy Corliss very well, and though he had never admitted it to anybody, he had had his private doubts that the boy would run away.

Yes, he decided, if Lucy Corliss's friend wanted to talk to him, he would listen.

Chapter 17

Randy Corliss lay in bed in a small room at the rear of the main floor of the Academy. His breathing was steady, and all the instruments wired to his small body displayed normal readings. His hands, covered with bandages, rested at his sides. A white-clad figure hovered over him, observing him closely, comparing the readings on the instruments to the evidence displayed by Randy's physical being.

Randy's eyes fluttered slightly, then opened.

He looked up and frowned uncertainly. Above him, the ceiling was unfamiliar. It was the wrong color, and the cracks in the plaster weren't in the right places.

He tried to remember what had happened. He'd been playing a game with his friends, and they'd done something to him, something that had frightened him.

He'd been running, and then they'd caught him, and—and what?

The fence. They'd thrown him against the fence, and he'd felt a burning sensation, and—and—

But there wasn't any more. After that, it was all a blank.

Suddenly, a face loomed above him, and he recognized Dr. Hamlin, who seemed to be smiling at him.

"How are we doing?" he heard Hamlin ask.

"What happened?" Randy countered. He hated it when people acted like however you felt was how they felt too.

"You had a little accident," Dr. Hamlin explained. "Someone left the electricity on in the fence, and you stumbled into it. But you're going to be fine. Just fine." He reached out to touch Randy, but Randy suddenly had a vision of Dr. Hamlin holding a scalpel, and cutting into Peter Williams's brain. He shrank away from the doctor's hands.

"What's going to happen to me?"

"Happen to you? What could happen to you?"

"I—I don't know," Randy faltered. Then, for the first time, he became aware that his hands were bandaged. "Is something wrong with my hands?"

Again, Hamlin smiled. "Well, why don't we just take those bandages off and have a look," he suggested. He seated himself on a chair next to the bed and began unwrapping the gauze from Randy's hands.

The skin, clear and healthy-looking, showed no signs of the severe burns that had been apparent when Randy had been brought in that afternoon.

For the first few minutes, as he had examined the unconscious child, Hamlin had been tempted to order full-scale exploratory surgery, to determine the effects the 240 volts of electricity had had on Randy's body. But then, as he had watched, Randy's vital signs had begun to improve, and he had decided to wait.

Perhaps, finally, he was on the verge of success.

And so he had spent the last several hours observing Randy and watching the monitors attached to the child. Slowly, but miraculously, Randy's pulse and respiration had returned to normal.

His brainwaves, monitored by the electroencephalograph, had evened out, until they once again reflected a normal pattern.

And now, even Randy's skin had healed.

Randy Corliss, who should have been dead, was in perfect physical condition.

"Can I go back to my room?" he heard Randy ask.

"Well, now, I don't really see why not," Hamlin agreed. "But you're a very lucky little boy. Did you know that?"

"If I was lucky, I wouldn't have had the accident, would I?" Randy asked, his voice filled with a suspicion that Hamlin couldn't quite understand. Wasn't the boy even glad he was all right? He decided that he would never understand the mentality of children. "Maybe not," he agreed. "But you have to admit that you were lucky it happened here, where we have lots of doctors. If you'd been somewhere else, you might have died."

Randy looked up at him, his eyes dark and serious. He appeared to Hamlin as if he was seeing something far away, something in his memory. "But I'm going to die anyway, aren't I?"

Hamlin scowled. "What makes you say that?"

Randy twisted at the bed covers, and his eyes roamed the room as if he didn't want to look at Hamlin. "Some of the boys talk. Some of them say that lots of boys die here. But they say we're not supposed to talk about it. Is that true?"

Hamlin sat silently, cursing to himself. That was the trouble with little boys. If you told them not to talk about something, invariably that was the one thing they talked about. And the problem, of course, was that what the boys were saying was true. So far, every one of the boys who had been brought here had died. But could he tell that to the little boy in the bed? Absolutely not. Instead, he reached out to pat Randy reassuringly on the hand.

"A few of our boys have died. But that happens in every school, doesn't it? But I'll bet you won't. I'll bet you'll be the first of my perfect children. And now's the time to find out."

As Randy nervously waited, Hamlin left the room, then returned with a piece of equipment that looked to Randy like nothing more than a box with a dial on it, some cord, and two shiny metal handles.

"What's that?" he asked suspiciously while Hamlin plugged the box into an oversize socket in the wall.

"It's a rheostat," Hamlin explained, carefully keeping the anxiety he was feeling from betraying itself in his voice. "I just want to do one more test, to see if you're really all right. Then you can go back to your room."

"What kind of test?"

Hamlin hesitated. "A sensitivity test," he finally explained. "All you have to do is hold on to these handles, and tell me when you feel something."

Randy scowled at the box. "What kind of something?"

"Anything. Anything at all. Warmth, or cold, or some kind of sensation. Just anything. All right?"

Randy wondered what would happen to him if he refused. Would they strap him down and clamp his head in a vise, like they'd done to Peter? He didn't know, and he decided the best thing he could do was to go along with whatever Dr. Hamlin wanted. He took one of the electrodes in each of his hands.

George Hamlin turned on the power and slowly began turning the rheostat up, his eyes flickering from the dial on the transformer to the instruments monitoring Randy, to Randy himself.

For the first few seconds, as he steadily increased the force of the electrical current that was passing through Randy's body, there was no reaction at all.

Then, as the current reached 200 volts, Randy's eyes widened slightly. "It tickles," he said.

Tickles.

The word thundered in Hamlin's mind. A few hours ago, only a little more voltage than this had knocked the boy unconscious and done severe damage to his heart, his nervous system, and his brain.

And now, all it did was tickle him.

Not only had Randy's regeneration been quick and complete, but he seemed to have built a resistance against the source of the trauma itself.

Impulsively, George Hamlin twisted the rheostat to full power.

Randy Corliss only giggled.

It had worked. At last, it had worked. Hamlin shut off the power and assured himself once more that all

Randy's vital signs were still normal. Then he disconnected the monitoring equipment and squeezed Randy's shoulder.

"You can go back to your room," he said. "It's all over, and there's nothing wrong with you. Nothing at all." Without another word, he left the room.

When Hamlin was gone, Randy lay still for a while, wondering what the doctor had meant. Then he got out of bed, gathered up his clothes, and went to the door. He started down the hall that would take him back to the main section of the Academy, but then he paused outside a closed door. He looked up and down the hall, and, seeing no one, tried the door. It was unlocked, and Randy slipped inside.

In the room, lying in bed, his face expressionless and his body perfectly still, was Peter Williams. Slowly, Randy moved close to Peter's bed.

He could hear Peter breathing, but the sound was shallow and rasping, as if something were stuck in Peter's throat.

So Peter wasn't dead. Peter was still alive, even after everything that had happened to him.

Was that what Dr. Hamlin had meant by being a perfect child? That no matter what happened to you, you wouldn't die?

As he left the infirmary and started walking toward his own room in the dormitory, Randy began to wonder if he wanted to be a perfect child.

He decided he didn't—not if it meant ending up like Peter Williams.

George Hamlin peeled off his horn-rimmed glasses and used two fingers to massage the bridge of his nose. The gesture was more habitual than anything else; his energy level, as always, was high. He was prepared to work through the night.

First, there had been the apparent breakthrough with Randy Corliss.

Then there had been the call from Boston.

Paul Randolph's call had disturbed him more than he

had let on. It was nothing, he was sure, no more than an upset mother clutching at any straw that might lead her to her son. Even so, it had disturbed him that the mother had turned out to be Lucy Corliss. Why today? Why should the security of the project be threatened today, and by the mother of the one subject who offered a promise of success?

But he had put his concerns aside. All it meant, really, was that he would simply have to work faster. He picked up his laboratory analyses once more and began studying them.

The problem, he knew, had always had to do with the restrictive endonuclease-ligase compound—the combination of enzymes that altered the genetic structure of the egg just prior to conception. The process was basically a simple one, once he had developed the tools to accomplish it. It was a matter of cutting out a section of the deoxyribonucleic acid—DNA—then repairing it in an altered form. But it had taken Hamlin years to develop the compounds, all of which had to be tested by trial and error.

They had been years of lonely, unrecognized work that, so far, had led only to a series of total, if unspectacular, failures.

Failures that had not been, and never would be, noticed by the scientific community, but failures, nevertheless.

George Hamlin did not like failures.

He turned back to the first page of the report and began reading it through once more. He flipped through page after page of charts, graphic correlations of causes and effects, chemical analyses of the enzymes they had used, medical histories of every subject since the project had begun.

The key, he was now certain, lay in Randy Corliss. He turned to the page describing the genetic analysis of the boy.

It was the introns that interested him.

The answer, he had always been sure, was locked in the introns that lay like genetic garbage along the double helix of DNA. Ever since he had begun studying them, George Hamlin had disagreed with the prevailing theory that the introns were nothing more than gibberish to be edited out of the genetic codes as the process of converting DNA into RNA, and finally into the messenger RNA that would direct cell development, was carried out.

No, Hamlin had long ago decided that introns were something else, and he had finally come to the conclusion that they were a sort of evolutionary experimentation lab, in which nature put together new combinations of the genetic alphabet, then segregated them off, so they wouldn't be activated except by genetic chance. Thus, only if the experiment proved successful, and the organism lived, would the activated intron, now an exon, be passed on to succeeding generations.

What Hamlin had decided to do was find a way to activate the introns artificially, determine their functions, and then learn to control them and use them.

And slowly, over the years, he had succeeded.

That was when he had begun experimenting on human beings.

That was when the secrecy had begun, and that was when the failures had begun.

And now, locked somewhere within the small, sturdy body of Randy Corliss, the final answer seemed to be emerging.

It was too soon to tell, but it was only a matter of a few months now.

All that had to happen was for Randy Corliss to survive.

The years of secrecy would be over, and George Hamlin would take his place in the ranks of preeminent genetic engineers.

He wished, as he had many times over the years, that he could carry out his experiments entirely in his lab. But that was impossible.

Extrauterine conception was no problem—combining a sperm with an egg outside the womb had been accomplished years ago.

The problem was that there were so many subjects, so many embryos to be brought to maturity, and not nearly enough women who would agree to bear those "test-tube babies," particularly knowing full well that those babies would be far more the children of George Hamlin than the children of themselves and their husbands.

And so he had made the decision.

The DNA in the ovum would be altered *in utero* rather than *in vitro*.

If the experiments failed, the parents would never know exactly what had happened.

If they succeeded, the parents would raise, albeit unknowingly, a group of wonderfully healthy, if not quite human, children.

And success seemed imminent. If Randy Corliss lived.

The four of them sat stiffly in Lucy Corliss's small living room: Lucy and Jim on the love seat, Sally Montgomery and Carl Bronski on the wing chairs.

It had not been easy for Sally to get there. After hearing what had happened that afternoon, both from Sally and her mother, Steve had suggested that Sally was overwrought. Sally, though she thought the word was ridiculous, had let it pass. Then, rather than argue with him, she had quietly agreed that a good night's rest would be the best thing for her. A few minutes later, Lucy had called and asked if she would be willing to explain the computer data to Sergeant Bronski. She had agreed, and that was when the fight had started. And now, along with Steve, she had her mother to contend with. Phyllis had sat impassively at first, trying to ignore the argument. At last she had, in her infuriatingly rational voice, sided with Steve.

Sally, she declared, should not get involved with the problems of strangers. Certainly, she went on, Sally had enough to cope with right now, without taking on the problems of Lucy Corliss.

Finally, Sally had had enough. Barely retaining her civility, she told her husband and her mother where she was going and stormed out of the house.

Now, after explaining to Sergeant Bronski and Jim Corliss what she thought the computer printouts meant, she was beginning to wonder if she'd done the right thing.

All in all, she realized, there wasn't really much of a parallel between Randy Corliss's disappearance, and Julie's death.

The only real link, indeed, seemed to be that both children had been under study by CHILD. And then, as a silence fell over them, Sally suddenly remembered a thought that had crossed her mind while she was working with the computer that morning. A notion that had been tugging at her mind since her lunch with Jan Ransom.

"Lucy," she said, "I know this may sound like a strange question, but—well, did you want Randy? Before he was born, I mean. Did you get pregnant on purpose?"

Before Lucy could answer, Jim Corliss shook his head. "I was the one who didn't want a baby," he said. "In fact, it was Randy who put an end to our marriage. I guess Lucy thought he'd bring us closer together, but that's not the way it happened." His gaze shifted away from Sally, and he began talking directly to Lucy. "I know you meant well, but I ... when you told me you were pregnant, I felt like a prison door was slamming on me. So I bolted."

"But I wasn't trying to get pregnant!" Lucy protested. "Randy wasn't my idea. Just the opposite—I'd had a coil put in because I was pretty sure I knew what would happen if I got pregnant. Unfortunately, I was one of those women who doesn't hold an IUD, but by the time I found that out, it was too late."

Sally sat stunned, trying to sort it all out. Was she being hysterical, or was the whole situation becoming more ominous? There were four of them now, four children, all of them unplanned, all of their mothers "protected" by IUDs when the pregnancies occurred, all of them under study by the Children's Institute for Latent

Diseases. Now two of them were dead and one was missing. Only Jason was left.

"It's horrible," she said, not realizing she was speaking out loud.

"What?" Carl Bronski asked her. "What's horrible?"

Abashed, Sally glanced from one face to another. All of them were looking at her curiously, but all the faces were friendly. "I was just thinking," she began. "Thinking about you, and me, and Jan Ransom, and all the coincidences." She went through them one by one, half-expecting someone—Bronski probably—to tell her she was overreacting, to explain to her that she was seeing a conspiracy where none existed, to suggest that she get some counseling.

No one did.

When she was finished, there was a long silence that was finally broken by Sally herself.

"Lucy," she asked, her voice oddly constricted. "Who was your obstetrician?"

Lucy frowned thoughtfully. "Somebody over at the Community Hospital. After Randy was born, I never saw him again. I'm afraid I'm just not much of a one for doctors. But his name was Weisfield, or something like that."

"Was it Wiseman?" Sally asked, knowing the answer.

Lucy brightened. "That's it! Arthur Wiseman. I hated him, but at the time he was all I could—" She broke off, seeing the twisted expression on Sally's face. "What is it? What did I say?"

"Wiseman is my doctor too," Sally explained. "And Jan Ransom's." Her voice suddenly turned bitter. "He and his bedside manner and his fatherly advice. What the hell was he *doing* to all of us?"

"We don't know that he was doing anything," Carl Bronski said quietly. But privately he decided that it was time for him to devote a great deal more attention to finding out exactly what *had* happened to Randy Corliss.

The house was dark when Sally returned, except for

one light glowing upstairs in the master bedroom. Her mother, apparently, had finally gone home. Sally slipped her key into the lock, let herself into the house, then checked the lower floor to be sure all the windows were closed. As she started upstairs she wondered how she was going to tell Steve that far from withdrawing from Lucy Corliss's problems, she was now going to become even more deeply involved. She knew what his response would be, and she didn't want to hear it. Yet, she wouldn't—couldn't—begin lying to him about what she was doing.

Somehow she would have to make him understand. She knew now that something was happening at Eastbury Community Hospital. Something had happened to her there, and it had happened to Jan Ransom, and it had happened to Lucy Corliss. How many others had it happened to? How many other babies had died, and how many children were missing? She had to know, and Steve had to understand that.

They owed it, if not to themselves or to Julie, to all the women and children to whom, so far, nothing had yet been done.

She reached the top of the stairs and started toward the bedroom, but then changed her mind. She would look in on Jason first, just to reassure herself that everything was all right.

He lay in bed, sound asleep, his right arm dangling over the side of the bed. When she bent down to kiss him, he stirred, and turned over to look up at her.

"Mom? Is that you?" The words were mumbled sleepily, and Jason's eyes, half opened, seemed to be searching for her.

"It's me, honey," she whispered, kneeling by the bed and slipping her arms around him. "How are you? Is everything all right?"

"I'm fine," Jason replied. "Me and Dad spent the whole night playing games with Grandma, and I won." There was a note of accusation in his voice, and Sally half-wished she had been home to enjoy the games. And

174

G...
th...

S...
little...
serio...

An... *she*
How ... *would have*
been ...ently.
been do...

Once ...
him in. S... *guess*
down the... *as I*

He was...
a few min...
to wake hi...
undressed, ...
beside him.

For a long ...
too many visions ...

Julie, lying dead in h...
Jason, his hand ravaged b...
only slightly red a few minutes lat...

Again Jason, his hand covered with ...
blistered and red, then, a few minutes later, ...

And I hadn't meant to have him either, she ...
bitterly to herself.

It had been a little over eight years ago, but still she
remembered how frightened she'd been when she'd gone
to Dr. Wiseman to have that first IUD inserted.

She had been almost as frightened that day as she was
today.

Chapter

STEVE MONTGO...
his desk. Af...
into focus? Pr...
was in the re...
more repor...
ing to be...
executiv...
going ...
been ...
con...
c...

18

...MERY STARED GLUMLY at the report on
...er four readings, would a fifth bring it
...obably not. Besides, he already knew what
...port. It was one more merger proposal, one
...t on a small company that was eagerly wait-
... swallowed up by a larger one with all the
...es of the former taking a profit on the sale, then
...o work for the latter at twice the salaries they had
... earning before. Steve's job was to find the right
...glomerate to make the merger. Under ordinary cir-
...mstances he would have relished the challenge.

Today his concentration was shot. Nothing would
come from wading through the charts and profit projec-
tions one more time. He put the report aside and swiv-
eled his chair around, but even the view of the soft
spring morning beyond the windows did nothing to
change the bleakness of his mood.

Until nine days ago, his life had been nearly perfect.
A wife he loved, children he adored, work he enjoyed.
And now, in a little over a week, his daughter was gone,
his wife had changed, and his son . . .

What about his son?

An image of Jason came into his mind, and for a moment a hint of a smile played around his lips. But then

the smile faded. For just the briefest of moments, he saw the small, still body of the guinea pig that had been his son's pet.

Steve shook himself, banishing from his consciousness the half-formed thought that had flashed through his mind.

The thought, he told himself, had nothing to do with Jason. Rather, it had come from Sally, and her growing obsession that something had been wrong with Julie. That obsession was spreading like a disease to include Jason as well.

It was time, he decided, to have a long talk with Sally's doctor.

Arthur Wiseman grinned at Steve and gestured toward the empty seat in front of his desk. "Is this your first visit to a gynecologist? If it is, let me assure you that you have nothing at all to fear. The examination is painless, and ..." He let the joke trail off as he saw the dark expression in Steve's eyes. "Sit down, Steve," he concluded softly.

The two men watched each other in silence for a moment, Steve wondering if he'd made a mistake in coming to Wiseman, while Wiseman waited patiently for Steve to begin talking. When it became obvious to him that Steve wasn't going to begin, he broke the silence.

"I take it this has something to do with Sally?" he asked, his voice professionally neutral.

Steve nodded. Once more a silence fell over the small office.

Wiseman tried again. "Has something else happened?"

"I'm not really sure," Steve admitted uncomfortably. "I can't really put my finger on anything. It's just that she's—well, she's changed. She's so edgy, and she over-reacts to everything. Like yesterday, when Jason had a little accident in the kitchen."

"I know," Wiseman interrupted. "I was here when she brought Jason in. Sally seemed to think it was a lot worse than it was."

"Exactly! And she's like that with everything. She's

found out about a survey that included both Julie and Randy Corliss, and now she and Randy's mother have cooked up some kind of plot."

Wiseman groaned, remembering his own talk with Sally. "You think she's getting paranoid?" he asked.

The question startled Steve. He hesitated, his brows furrowing deeply. But before he could answer, Wiseman smiled genially.

"It's only a catchword," he said. "Loaded with all kinds of prejudices and connotations. But it does rather get to the heart of the matter, doesn't it?"

"I suppose so," Steve replied, his voice almost inaudible. Then, inhaling deeply, he made himself meet the doctor's eyes. "Do *you* think she's paranoid?"

Wiseman shrugged. "I'm not a psychiatrist, and I don't like to make psychiatric judgments. But," he went on, as relief flooded over Steve Montgomery's face, "that doesn't mean she's not having some severe problems. How could it be otherwise, considering what's happened? The loss of a baby is the worst thing that can happen to a mother, Steve. Most mothers would prefer to die themselves than lose their child. He paused for a moment, drumming his fingers on his desk top. "Would you like me to find someone for Sally to talk to?"

"You mean a psychiatrist?"

"Or some other kind of therapist. I'm not at all sure Sally needs a psychiatrist. If her problems were coming from something physical, that would be one thing. But I think we both know the source of her trouble, and it seems to me that a good psychologist should be able to help."

Steve shook his head slowly. "I don't know," he said at last. "I'm just not sure she'd go. She doesn't think anything's wrong with her."

Wiseman stood up, pointedly glancing at his calendar, and Steve, almost by reflex, echoed the movement.

"No, she'll never do it," Steve said. "I know her, and I just don't think she can be convinced."

"Sometimes," Wiseman replied, "we almost have to force people to do what's best for them."

Before the implications of his words had fully registered on Steve Montgomery, Wiseman showed the young man out of his office, then returned to his desk. He began jotting notes on a pad of paper, then made a list of five psychologists. At the bottom of the sheet he made one final note, reminding himself to check on the status of his malpractice insurance. He tore the sheet off the pad and slid it into the top drawer of his desk just as his nurse opened the door to announce his first patient of the day.

Wiseman rose, smiling warmly, and moved around his desk to greet the young woman who shyly followed the nurse. He took the file the nurse proffered, and waved the woman, Erica Jordan, into the chair so recently occupied by Steve Montgomery. Only when Erica Jordan was settled in the chair and the nurse was gone did Wiseman return to his own seat. He opened the file, glanced over its contents, then smiled at the woman.

"Well, it seems that an IUD is the indicated method," he said.

Erica Jordan paled slightly. "Then I *am* allergic to the pill?"

"Well, I wouldn't go that far," Wiseman replied. "It isn't really a matter of allergies. It's just that the pill has certain side effects, and you seem to be prone to some of them. Migraine headaches for instance. And then there's the cancer in your family."

"I didn't think cancer was hereditary," Erica Jordan protested.

"It isn't, as far as we know. But still, we hesitate to prescribe the pill where there's a history of cancer. Not that there's any direct connection, but it's better to be safe than sorry."

"Damn," Erica said softly. "Why do I have to be allergic to everything? And what if I turn out to be allergic to the IUD too?"

Wiseman shrugged. "It could happen," he admitted. "Maybe you'd better think about a diaphragm again."

Erica screwed up her face and shook her head. "Nope.

I know myself too well for that. Let's go with the coil and hope for the best."

Wiseman picked up the phone and spoke to the nurse, then turned his attention back to Erica Jordan. "If you'll go on into the examining room, Charlene will help you get ready. And I have something that just might help with any possible allergic reaction. It's a salve, and it goes in with the device itself. It's supposed to lessen any irritation and help your body accept the presence of the coil."

"For how long?"

"Quite a while," Wiseman replied. "According to the literature it's effective for up to a month. And of course, I'll want to see you again in a month's time, just to be sure." He smiled encouragement as he guided her to the door. "I'll be with you in a minute."

Half an hour later, with the procedure completed and Erica Jordan on her way back to work, Wiseman slowly and carefully began amending Erica Jordan's medical records to reflect the insertion of an intrauterine contraceptive device into her womb. He was also careful to note that, "in view of the patient's susceptibility to allergic reaction," the application of bicalcioglythemine (BCG) had been both indicated and implemented.

When the record had been updated to his satisfaction, he keyed the proper codes into the computer terminal on his desk and added the new information to the permanent files that were stored in the Shefton County computer.

Paul Randolph sped through the countryside, acutely aware of the budding trees and the warmth of the air. He was, he knew, spending altogether too much time in Boston, cooped up in either his office or his apartment, seldom escaping the city. He shouldn't have left the city today—his desk was piled high with work, and he had been forced to juggle appointments with three possible donors to CHILD. Still, it seemed to him that today he had had no choice. Today, he had a problem.

The long narrow drive ended at the gates of the

Academy. Except that Paul Randolph still thought of it as The Oaks. He rolled down the window and punched a code number into the lock-box that was discreetly concealed in a clump of laurel, and watched the gates swing slowly open. He put the car in gear, drove through then watched in the rearview mirror as the gates closed behind him. Only when he heard the distinctive clunk of the lock did he continue along the winding driveway to the house.

He parked in front of the main entrance, got out, and had already started up the steps when he changed his mind. Turning, he retreated from the house, stepping back to examine it, to *feel* it, much, he imagined, as a prospective buyer might. For himself, he decided, the inspection would end right there. The house, even though it appeared quiet and peaceful, no longer felt right to him. In the months since the project had been relocated to the estate the house seemed to have changed. The warmth it had held during his childhood here was gone, and now it was as if the house itself didn't approve of what was being done within its walls.

And neither, Paul Randolph told himself as he started once more toward the door, do I.

With the authority of familiarity he strode through the entry hall and went directly to the clinic. He recognized Louise Bowen, but when she started to speak to him, he ignored her greeting. "Where's Hamlin?" he demanded.

Her welcoming smile fading from her lips, Louise gestured toward a closed door. "I think he's—" She fell silent as Randolph opened the door, marched through, and closed it behind himself.

Inside the office George Hamlin looked up from his work. He frowned, set his pencil aside, then turned cool eyes on his visitor.

"It really wasn't necessary for you to come out here, Paul," he said. "Your call yesterday was quite sufficient."

Paul Randolph made no immediate reply. Instead, he went to stand at a window, where he stared unseeingly out at the expanse of lawn and woods. When he spoke, he still faced the window, his back to Hamlin. "I've been thinking all night, and what I have to say today is too important to talk about on the telephone."

He waited for Hamlin to speak. Seconds passed by, marked only by the soft ticking of an antique clock on Hamlin's desk. Finally Randolph turned, wondering if, by some incomprehensible chance, Hamlin had actually left the room.

Hamlin hadn't. He was now leaning back in his chair, his feet propped up on his desk, his arms folded across his chest, his features placid. As Randolph turned to face him, he smiled. "It's a good trick, Paul," he said easily. "But I've used it too often myself. If you want to talk to me, face me."

The eyes of the two men locked in a silent struggle for control of the situation. It was Randolph who finally looked away, doing his best to cover his defeat by sinking into a chair and lighting a cigarette. Hamlin watched him wordlessly.

"I've come to a decision, George," Randolph said at last as he slipped his lighter back into his pocket. "I've decided to close the project down."

Hamlin's eyes widened in disbelief, and his feet came off the desk to be planted firmly on the floor. "You can't do that," he said softly. "We're too close to success, and we've got too much time, money, and research invested here."

"And we've also done some things that you and I know are both unethical and illegal," Randolph shot back. "It's no longer a question of money and research. It's now only a question of time, and I'm afraid we've run out of that. We're going to close the project down while we still can."

"What are you talking about?"

"Lucy Corliss," Randolph replied, his voice oozing with deliberate sarcasm. "Have you forgotten already?"

"Of course not," Hamlin replied, carefully ignoring Randolph's baiting. "Randy Corliss's mother. You told me about her yesterday."

"But apparently it bears repeating. It seems she's looking for her son, George, who I assume is still here. She found out that he was being surveyed by CHILD, and she wants to know what the study was all about."

"So you stall her."

"Exactly. I stall her. In fact, I already have. I told her it would take some time to comb the records, and that I'd get back to her."

Hamlin nodded. "Then what's the problem? You have a hundred projects you can give her."

"The problem, George," Randolph replied coldly, "is that you have consistently maintained that there was no way anyone could find out about our surveys, particularly this one. And yet, Lucy Corliss found out that her son was being 'watched,' as she put it. If she found out that we were watching her child, then others will too."

"That doesn't hold, Paul."

"Doesn't it?" Randolph began pacing the room. "I'm afraid I don't have as much faith in what you tell me as I used to, George. Do you remember when we began the project? It would only take a couple of years, you said. That was twelve years ago. It could all be done with lab animals, you said. But that was ten years ago, and you haven't used an animal since. I still don't know how I let you convince me on that point, George—it's going to ruin us all. You also assured me there was no possibility that the integrity of the project could be compromised. But Lucy Corliss has become suspicious. In short, this project is not what it was originally presented to be, it has gone on far too long, and has become a liability to the Institute. I have no other choice than to close it down."

Hamlin leaned forward, resting his clasped hands on the polished surface of the desk. "I'm not closing this project down, Paul," he said in carefully measured tones. As Randolph started to protest, Hamlin cut him off. "I listened to you, and now you can listen to me. All that's happened is that a woman has stumbled across our studies. Statistically, that doesn't surprise me. There's nothing in the world that can be kept a total secret, nothing at all. But what has she found out? Has she actually found out about *this* project? I doubt it."

"So do I," Randolph agreed. "And it's my job to see that she doesn't. It isn't just *this* project, George. CHILD has many other projects going, all of them valuable, and none of them dangerous. But this project could bring down the entire Institute."

Hamlin's eyes narrowed angrily. "It could also make the Institute the most important research center in the world."

Randolph shook his head ruefully. "You just don't understand, do you, George? That's been the problem between you and me since the very beginning. You have no idea of what could be involved here. Sometimes I don't think you even understand exactly what you're doing." He paused, wondering how far he should go. Still, the showdown between them had been coming for years, and now there seemed no point in avoiding it any longer. "I've read your reports, George. All of them. All the euphemisms. 'Nonviable subjects.' 'Failed experiments.' 'Defective organisms.'" Suddenly Randolph's voice dropped, as if he were no longer talking to Hamlin, but to himself. "Do you know how long it was before I let myself admit to what you were doing? Years. For years I read those reports and told myself you were talking about rats or rabbits. Maybe even monkeys. I wouldn't let myself know the truth." He tried to smile, but produced nothing more than a twisted grimace. "I think I'd have made a good Nazi, George, and I think you would have too."

His jaw clenched with fury, Hamlin glowered at Randolph. "I'm a scientist, Paul," he rasped. "There's no room in my world for sentimentality."

"Is that what you call it? Sentimentality?" He shook his head in disbelief. "My God, George, how many children have you killed over the last ten years?"

Hamlin rose, his fury no longer containable, his eyes glowing with unconcealed hatred for the man to whom he had always been forced to answer. "None," he shouted. "God damn it, you fool, it's you who doesn't understand. You've never understood, and you probably never will. These aren't children here, and the women who produced them aren't mothers. They're exactly what I call them in my reports. *Laboratory animals.* Granted, they look human, and they act human, but genetically, I can't *tell* you what they are. It will be up to the courts and the legislatures to decide what they are, but only after I've made them functional. But as long as they keep dying, they're nothing more than failed experiments. But they won't keep dying. God damn it, they won't! I'm on the verge of success, Randolph. I won't be stopped now." Suddenly his rage disappeared, and his eyes took on the look of a hunted animal. "Don't try to stop it, Paul. If you do, I'll bring the Institute down myself. Stay with me, and you can share the glory. Abandon me, and believe me, I'll take you down right along with the project."

And so, at last, it was out in the open. As he watched Hamlin, Randolph realized that he had known it for years: At some point this moment would come. And he had even, deep inside of himself, known what the outcome would be. Hamlin was right. The project was far too extensive and far too close to completion to be abandoned now, unless Hamlin himself agreed to it. And barring the possibility of immediate exposure, and the inevitable end of the project that would follow, nothing would make George Hamlin agree to suspend the project.

So now it was Hamlin who was in control, and as Randolph began trying to adjust himself to his new circumstances, he suddenly remembered the name Hamlin had suggested for the experiments so many years ago.

The God Project.

Now, as it neared completion, Randolph realized that Hamlin himself was playing God.

Chapter 19

RANDY CORLISS GLARED at the instruction book, his face screwed into an expression that combined concentration with disgust. "It's wrong," he said, his eyes moving from the picture to the Lego construction that he and Eric Carter had been working on since lunchtime. The pieces—blue, red, and yellow—were strewn across the floor of Randy's room. "I don't see how they expect us to figure out what's underneath the battle deck."

Eric rocked back, balancing himself on the balls of his feet, and stared at the model. "So what if it's wrong? It doesn't have to be just like the picture. We can make it any way we want to."

"But it should be right," Randy insisted. He pointed to a bright blue plastic gun mount. "That should be farther back, and there's supposed to be something else in front of it. Only I can't figure out what it's supposed to be."

"Lemme see." Eric picked up the book, stared at it for a moment, then made a face. "I can't even figure out what step we're on."

"Fourteen. Right here, after the bridge and the flight deck go on." While Eric studied the diagram, Randy wandered over to the open window and gazed out at the lawn below. The day had warmed up, and there was a dank humidity to the air that made it hard to breathe.

Unconsciously, Randy's right hand moved to the bars over the window. "Did you ever feel like running away?" he suddenly asked.

"I did last year," Eric replied.

"I mean from here. Do you ever want to run away from here?"

"Why should I?"

"I don't know. Just to see if you could, I guess."

"Naa." Eric went back to the diagram, comparing it carefully to the half-finished model on the floor. "I got it!" he exclaimed. "Look!"

Randy glanced once more out the window, then returned to the model. Eric was busy pulling the super-structure apart. When he was finished, he began counting the tiles from the bow of the ship to the stern, then grinned at Randy. "See? We didn't put in enough tiles on the deck. That's why there's no room for the life-boat."

And then, as Randy began examining the model, an odd, choking noise came from Eric. Randy looked up, then frowned.

Something was wrong with Eric. His eyes were opened so wide, they seemed to bulge from his face. His mouth hung slack, and a strange gurgling noise bubbled from his throat.

"What's wrong?"

But Eric made no answer. Instead, as Randy watched, his arms began to flail, and the color drained slowly from his face. In a moment, his flesh had taken on a bluish hue, and he had toppled over onto his side. His legs jerked spasmodically, and then he was still.

"Eric?" Randy's voice suddenly grew into a scream of fear. "Eric!"

Leaving his friend lying on the floor, Randy ran from his room, his terror translating into a scream that echoed through the entire building.

Louise Bowen was sitting moodily in her tiny office, trying to decide what to do. She knew she shouldn't have lingered outside Dr. Hamlin's door, knew she shouldn't have listened to his conversation with Paul Randolph. In fact, she hadn't heard the entire conversation, but when Dr. Hamlin had suddenly raised his voice and begun shouting about the children, she couldn't help but overhear him.

So now, after three years at the Academy, she knew that all her suspicions were true. To Hamlin, the children simply weren't human. And in a way, Louise suspected he might be right. These children were different from other children. Yet they still had names, they still had personalities, they still thought, and felt, and reacted just like all the other children she had ever known.

And deep in her heart, Louise reacted to them as she always had to children. She cared about them, loved them. Every time one of them died, she felt as if she'd lost a baby of her own.

It was time, she reluctantly decided, for her to leave the Academy.

The decision made, Louise pulled a pad from her desk and began composing her letter of resignation. She wrote out the first draft quickly, and was about to begin rewriting it when Randy Corliss's scream rang through the house. Reflexively, she dropped her pen and dashed out of her office into the foyer just as Randy Corliss, his face pale and his eyes wide with fear, charged down the stairs. He looked wildly around; then, seeing Louise, he hurled himself into her arms.

Louise dropped to her knees, holding the boy close. "What is it, Randy?" she asked. "What's happened?"

"It—it's Eric. He's—I think he's dead!" Randy's words dissolved into a choking sob as his body heaved with emotion. And even while part of Louise's mind accepted his words and began to make all the decisions concomitant to yet another death at the Academy, a voice sounded deep within her.

He's human, it said. This little boy is human.

Slowly, she disentangled herself from Randy, and, holding him by the hand, began leading him back upstairs.

"Where is he?"

"In—in my room. He's on the floor, and he's all blue, and—" Randy broke off, his sobs overcoming him once again. Louise said nothing more until they were in Randy's room and she had checked Eric Carter's body for any signs of life. As she had expected, there were none. She pulled the spread from Randy's bed, covered Eric's body, then led Randy out of the room.

Keeping the terrified little boy with her, she moved to the desk at the head of the stairs, picked up the telephone, spoke into it for a moment, then started down to the first floor.

Randy hesitated at the top of the stairs. "Aren't we going to do anything?"

"There's nothing we can do, darling," Louise said quietly. Taking Randy by the hand once more, she led him down the stairs and into her office. She closed the door, then took Randy to a sofa, sat down, and drew him into her lap. Randy, despite his size, made no move to resist. His arms slipped around her neck, and he rested his head against her breast. For a long time, neither of them said anything, and when Randy finally broke the silence, his voice was shaking.

"What happened to Eric?"

Louise wondered how to answer the boy. She knew that she should make up a story. Eric has been sick for a very long time, she would say, and his death wasn't unexpected; what happened to him certainly wasn't going to happen to Randy.

And she knew that she couldn't.

She'd done it so many times before, talked to so many frightened little boys who had lost their friends, told so many lies to so many children.

With Randy she wouldn't lie.

"We don't know what happened to Eric," she said at last.

Randy was silent for a moment, digesting what he'd just been told. Then he asked, "Is that what's going to happen to me? Am I gonna die too?"

It happens to all of you here, Louise thought. But how

could she tell Randy that? She couldn't. She felt Randy tense in her arms and knew her silence must be terrifying to him, but still she couldn't bring herself to lie to him. Not to him, not to any of them, not ever again. And yet, did she have the right to frighten Randy so? She tried to think of something she could say that would ease his terror. "I—I don't think it hurt Eric very much. I think it happened very quickly. I suppose it must have been sort of like fainting. Have you ever fainted?"

"No."

"I have. Just once, but I remember it very well. I was fine one minute, and then all of a sudden I started sweating, and things started going black. And then I woke up, and it was all over. It didn't hurt. It just felt sort of—funny."

"But you woke up," Randy said. "Eric won't."

"No," Louise whispered. "He won't."

And it *does* hurt, Randy added to himself. Miss Bowen hadn't been there and didn't know. But he'd seen Eric's eyes and the expression on his face. He'd heard the awful sounds Eric had made and watched him turn blue. He'd seen Eric's arms waving helplessly in the air and watched him wiggle on the floor.

Deep in his heart, Randy was sure that dying hurt a lot.

He didn't want to die, and he didn't want to hurt. But he didn't know what to do about it. All he knew was that he'd just found out what happened to all the boys who disappeared. They died. And they died because they were at the Academy.

Here. It happened here.

So, if he could get away . . .

But where could he go? He couldn't go to his father. His father had sent him here, so his father must have—

The thought was too horrible, and he made himself stop thinking it.

His mother.

Somehow, he would have to get away from here and find his mother.

He snuggled closer to Louise Bowen, but in his mind

he was nowhere near her. In his mind, he was with his mother.

If he was with his mother, he wouldn't die. . . .

Sitting at his desk in the Eastbury police station, Carl Bronski loosened his necktie, opened the collar of his shirt, and cursed the anachronistic regulation that forbade the wearing of summer uniforms before June twenty-first. But even as he felt the freedom of releasing his neck from the too-tight collar, he realized that it was neither the heat of the day nor the weight of his uniform that was keeping him from concentrating on the file that lay open and unread on his desk.

Rather, it was the conversation he'd had last night with the Corlisses and Sally Montgomery. It had been on his mind all morning, and now, in mid-afternoon, it kept picking at him, niggling at him, demanding his attention when he should be thinking about other things. At last he stood up, retrieved the Corliss file from the cabinet, and took it to the chief's office.

Orville Cantrell, whose florid face and close-cropped white hair had never quite seemed to fit with the warmth of his personality, waved Bronski into a chair, and brought his telephone conversation to a close. Dropping the receiver back on the hook, he rolled his eyes toward the ceiling. "Wanna go out and bust Harrison's peacock again? Old Mrs. Wharton still swears she hears a baby crying in his barn." When Bronski failed to respond, Cantrell held out his hand for the report his sergeant obviously wanted him to see. He glanced at it, dropped it on his desk, and shrugged. "Runaway. I've already seen it."

"Except I'm not so sure it's a runaway."

"Aw, come on, Carl, they're taking off younger every year. And this one's got a previous."

"Still, I don't believe it."

"I've got a couple of minutes—explain."

As carefully as he could, Bronski tried to explain what Lucy Corliss and Sally Montgomery had discovered, leaving nothing out, including Sally's suspicions about

Dr. Wiseman. But even as he unfolded the tale, he suspected that Cantrell was only half-listening, and when he was finished, the chief confirmed it.

"You find out anything about that burglary down at the A&P?"

"I thought we were talking about Randy Corliss."

"Carl, *you* were talking about Randy Corliss. *I* was thinking about the A&P. Charlie Hyer's giving me a lot of trouble about that—thinks we should have solved it by now."

"And Lucy Corliss thinks we should have found her son by now," Carl Bronski said doggedly. "Now I ask you, Orv, which is more important—a couple of thousand dollars, or a nine-year-old boy?"

"To Charlie? The couple thousand."

Carl groaned. "Come on."

Cantrell leaned back and folded his hands behind his head. "Carl, I'm gonna tell you something. When I was your age, which I grant you was quite a ways back, I thought I could spend all my time trying to solve the cases I thought were important. But you know what? I found out that every case is important to the people involved. I know it sounds lousy, but to Charlie Hyer, his couple of thousand are just as important as Lucy Corliss's little boy."

"I'm afraid I don't agree."

"Which is why you're a sergeant and I'm the chief." Cantrell glanced at the clock. "Now, you've got half an hour of duty left, and I want you to spend it on that A&P file. As far as we're concerned, Randy Corliss is a runaway—"

"Didn't you even listen to me?"

"I heard you, and it sounds to me like you got suckered in by a couple of hysterical women who don't want to face reality. What have they got? A bunch of crap out of a computer that probably doesn't even mean anything to the people who put it in! Know what I read? I read that ninety-some percent of everything that goes into computers is never even looked at again. It's just stowed away and forgotten. Hell, as far as I can tell, nobody even knows *what's* in the damn computers anymore. So I don't want you wasting your time trying to figure out what those numbers you were talking about mean." As Bronski started to protest, Cantrell held up a restraining hand. "Carl, I'm sorry about Randy Corliss running away, and I'm sorry that other woman's baby died. Hell, I'm sorry about a lot. But when you talk about Arthur Wiseman maybe 'doing' something to his patients, I've got to think something's wrong. Are you starting to get the picture?"

Bronski stood up. "I get it. No more duty time on Randy Corliss, right?"

"Very right."

Bronski started out of the chief's office. He had the door half-open when Cantrell spoke again, this time in the soft tones his men referred to as his "off-duty" voice.

"'Course, I can't really be held responsible for what you do on your own time, can I? And you might want to keep in mind that even when you're not here, the lights are on, the telex works, and nobody really gives a damn about what facilities are used for what case during what hours."

Bronski turned back. "Did you say something?"

The off-duty voice disappeared as fast as it had come. "I didn't say a damn thing, Sergeant. Now get back to work."

Bronski pulled Cantrell's door shut as he left the office and started back toward his own desk. In the far corner, the telex suddenly began chattering, and Bronski changed course to go over and watch as the tape spewed out of the machine.

There was the usual lot of APBs, mixed with some idle chatter among operators who had become equally idle acquaintances over the years. One item caught Bronski's eye. It was from Atlanta, Georgia, a request for any information about a boy who was assumed to be a runaway. His name was Adam Rogers, and he was nine years old. The message was being sent to Eastbury because the boy's father had once lived there, and the mother thought the child might be looking for him. The name of the father and his last known address followed the body of the communiqué.

Carl Bronski frowned, then reread the message. The thing that struck him as odd was that the last name of the father was not Rogers. It was Kramer, Phillip J. Kramer.

Bronski was suddenly uneasy. "Anybody on this?" he asked the desk sergeant.

The sergeant didn't even look up. "Since it just came in, it doesn't seem likely, does it?"

"Then I'll take it myself." He tore the strip of paper out of the machine and took it back to his desk. After rereading the message one more time, he picked up the Eastbury phone book and flipped to the K's.

No Phillip Kramer was listed.

Turning to the city directory, he looked up the address. The current occupants were Mr. and Mrs. Roland P. Strassman.

Bronski picked up the phone, dialed their number, and a moment later was talking to Mrs. Roland P., whose name turned out to be Mary.

She and her husband had bought the house from Phillip Kramer eight years ago.

No, Mr. Kramer had not been married. Yes, she was sure. In all the papers she and Rolly had signed, Mr. Kramer had always been referred to as "a single man," which had struck her as funny, even though Rolly had told her it was the proper way to talk about someone in legal papers. So she was sure Mr. Kramer hadn't been married.

Bronski thanked her for the information, then sat at his desk, thinking.

His mind kept coming back to the telex.

First the chief had mentioned it, and if Bronski knew Cantrell as well as he thought he did, there was a reason. And then this message, which seemed totally irrelevant, yet made him uneasy.

Nine-year-old boy. Father's name different from son's.
Unwanted child?
Possibly born in Eastbury?

Bronski looked at the clock once more, then at the closed door of Orville Cantrell's office. Making up his mind, he buttoned his collar and slipped into his coat. As he started out of the building, the desk sergeant grinned at him. "Hot case, or cold beer?"

Bronski returned the grin, though he didn't feel amused. "Maybe a little of both. But if the chief asks, tell him I'm working on the A&P thing, okay?"

"Sure."

As he headed toward Lucy Corliss's house, Bronski made a special point of driving down Brockton Street, past Charlie Hyer's A&P. And just as he passed it, he noted with a certain amount of pleasure, it turned four o'clock.

He was off duty.

Chapter 20

JASON MONTGOMERY WRIGGLED uncomfortably in his chair and began counting the raisins in his cereal. Usually it was no more than a game. First he'd try to guess the number, then see if he was right. But this morning it was more: He was concentrating on his cereal in a vain attempt to shut out the sound of his parents' voices.

It seemed to Jason as if the fighting was getting worse. Last week, when he had first become aware that his mother and father were mad at each other, they'd at least waited until he'd gone to bed before they started arguing.

This morning they didn't even seem to know he was there. It was as if he were invisible. He looked up at his parents, who were sitting at either end of the dining-room table. Neither of them seemed aware of him. They were staring at each other, his mother's face stony and his father's red with anger.

"All I want you to do is go see Wiseman this afternoon," he heard his father say. "Is that going to be so horrible? For God's sake, he's been your doctor for years. How can it hurt to go see him?"

"I already saw him," Sally replied. "And I don't trust him anymore."

"But you do trust a woman you hardly know who's not exactly in good shape herself?"

Sally's eyes narrowed as she glared down the length of the table. "And just what is that supposed to mean?"

Steve sighed. Even though it was only 7:30, he already felt exhausted. "It just means that maybe Lucy Corliss could use some counseling herself."

"How would you know?" Sally flared, the pitch of her voice rising dangerously. "You've never even talked to Lucy! How could you know what her mental condition is? Sometimes you talk like a damned fool!"

Putting down his spoon, Jason slid off his chair and left the dining room. But as he went upstairs to get his schoolbooks, his parents' voices drifted after him, fighting about things he didn't understand.

Was something wrong with Randy's mother?

And why did his father want his mother to talk to Dr. Wiseman. Was something wrong with *her*?

He gathered up his books, stuffed them into his green bookbag, then went back downstairs. He looked through the living room into the dining room, and though he couldn't see his father, he could see the tears on his mother's cheeks.

Should he go in and kiss her good-bye? But if he did, and she didn't stop crying, he'd probably start crying himself.

He hated to cry.

Silently, speaking to neither his father nor his mother, Jason slipped out the front door into the warmth of the spring morning. The sounds of his parents' fight faded away as he started along the sidewalk toward school.

Half a block ahead, he saw Joey Connors. Even though he and Joey had never been best friends, Jason decided to catch up with him. He broke into a trot, and in a few seconds was right behind the other boy.

"Hi," he said, falling into step with Joey.

Joey looked at him, made a face, and said nothing.

"What's wrong with you?"

"Nothing. What do *you* want?"

Jason shrugged. "Nothing." What was wrong with

Joey? Was he mad too? The two boys walked along in silence for a few minutes, then Joey spoke again.

"Why don't you walk by yourself?"

"Why should I?" Jason demanded. He hadn't done anything to Joey. Besides, what was he supposed to do, just stand there while Joey walked ahead of him? What if someone was watching? He'd look stupid.

"My mom doesn't want me to hang around with you," Joey replied, facing Jason for the first time.

Now Jason stopped, and Joey did too.

"Why not? What did I ever do to you?"

Joey stared at the sidewalk. "My mom says there's something wrong with your mom, and I shouldn't hang around with you."

Anger welled up in Jason. "You take that back."

"Why should I? Ever since your sister died, your mom's been acting funny, and besides, my mom says something must have happened to your sister."

"What's that supposed to mean?" But even as he asked the question, Jason wondered if Joey's mother knew what he'd done to Julie that night. "She just died."

"Bull!" Joey grinned maliciously. "I bet you did something to her. I bet you and Randy Corliss did something to her, and that's why he ran away."

Suddenly all the tension and confusion that had been churning in Jason fused together. His right hand clenched into a fist, and almost before he realized what he was doing, he swung at Joey.

Joey, too surprised to duck, stood gaping while Jason's fist crashed into his stomach, knocking the wind out of him. He gasped, then hurled himself on Jason. Jason buckled under Joey's weight, falling to the ground with the other boy on top of him. He struggled under Joey, ignoring the fists that were punching at his sides, but when Joey began beating him in the face, he screamed, and heaved himself over, rolling Joey under him. He sat astride Joey, returning the pounding he had just taken, while Joey thrashed on the ground, kicking out and flailing at Jason with his fists.

Suddenly Jason heard sounds, and looked up to see

two other children running toward them. Joey used the distraction to wriggle free, but he was bleeding from the mouth, and his left eye was already swelling. He was crying, partly from pain and partly from anger, and as Jason lay on the ground, Joey began kicking at him. Jason grabbed at Joey's foot, caught it, and jerked the other boy off balance.

Again, they became a tangle of churning arms and legs, but suddenly Joey, realizing he was getting the worst of it despite his larger size, sank his teeth into Jason's arm.

Jason screamed at the sudden pain, jerked free, and stood up. "You chickenshit!" he yelled. "You bit me!" Then he leaped onto Joey and held a threatening fist over the bigger boy's face. "Give up," he said. "Give up or I'll bust your nose."

Joey stared up at him, his eyes wide as he watched the fist. His arms were pinned to his sides by Jason's legs, and he realized that if he tried to move, Jason's fist would crash down into his face.

"I give," he said. Jason hesitated, then climbed off Joey. He waited while Joey got to his feet, then took a step toward the other boy.

Joey hesitated, tears streaming down his face. "I'm gonna tell," he yelled. "I'm gonna tell my mother, and you're gonna be in trouble." Then he turned and began running back down the street toward his house.

Jason watched him go, then faced the other children who were watching him uneasily. Jason sensed that they, too, had heard things about him.

"Whatcha gonna do?" someone asked.

Jason glared at his questioner. "Well, I'm not gonna run home to Momma like some people," he said. Turning his back on the others, he started down the street. No one tried to follow him.

He walked another block, then stopped, wondering if maybe he should go home after all. His clothes were torn and covered with grass stains, and his face was bloody.

But what if his parents were still fighting? Wouldn't they get mad at him too?

He stood indecisively for a minute, then made up his mind.

He wouldn't go home, but he wouldn't go to school either.

Instead, he'd play hookey for the day, and go off by himself.

At least if he was by himself, no one would be mad at him. . . .

"You've decided I'm crazy, haven't you?" Sally's voice reflected the fear that lay like a caged beast within her. As she spoke, she could feel the beast begin to stir, begin to wake into panic. "The two of you have decided I'm crazy."

"Sally, it's not that at all. We just think you've had too many problems bearing down on you, and you need someone to talk to. It won't even *be* Wiseman. He said himself that he's not qualified, but he thinks he can find someone who can help you."

"Someone who can help me to do what? Help me find out what happened to Julie, or help me try to pretend that nothing happened to her at all?"

Before Steve could answer, there was a loud knock at the back door. Steve threw down his napkin, disappeared into the kitchen, and was back a moment later, followed by a furious Kay Connors clutching her son by her hand. When Sally saw Joey's bruised and swollen face, and the bloodstains on his clothes, she gasped.

"Joey, what hap—"

"Your son happened," Kay interrupted, her eyes blazing with indignation. "Look at him. One eye's black, his cheek is cut, he's bruised all over his body, and his knee is bleeding."

Sally dabbed at her own eyes with her napkin. What was Kay talking about? What did Jason have to do with all this? "But Jason's here," she said. "He hasn't left for school yet." She glanced around, sure that Jason would be standing in the door to the living room.

He wasn't.

Her gaze shifted uncertainly to Steve. "Isn't he here? He must be. He didn't say good-bye."

"He must be upstairs." Steve crossed the living room and went into the foyer to stand at the foot of the stairs. "Jason? Jason!"

Upstairs, the house was silent.

"If he's there, he's in the bathroom cleaning himself up," Kay Connors said angrily.

"Kay, I don't know what you're talking about," Sally protested.

"I'm talking about Jason. He picked a fight with Joey, and then proceeded to do this to him."

Steve came back into the dining room, looking puzzled. "He's not here. I checked his room, and his books are gone. He must have left without saying good-bye."

Sally sat quietly for a moment, digesting what her husband had said. It made a sad kind of sense, really. Why would Jason say good-bye that morning? Neither of them had really spoken to him. They'd been too involved in their own struggle.

And what must he have thought of that? She tried to remember him sitting at the table, listening to them. Had she even seen him?

Not really.

Vaguely, she remembered him leaving the table, but that was all. What must he have been feeling, watching her cry, watching his father's angry face, hearing the bitter words that had flowed so freely. Of course he hadn't said good-bye. He must have wanted nothing more than to be out of the house, away from the anger. Sally tried to speak, but her throat constricted, and as her tears began to flow once more she clutched the damp napkin to her mouth and hurried from the room. Steve watched her go, then turned to face Kay Connors.

"What happened, Kay?"

Kay's fury had been dissipated by Sally's tears. She drew Joey closer. "I don't know, really," she admitted.

"Joey left for school, and about ten minutes later he was back. He said Jason picked a fight with him."

"But you're a lot bigger than Jason," Steve said to Joey.

"He hit me first," Joey replied sullenly.

"But why did he hit you?"

Joey's gaze shifted guiltily away from Steve. "I don't know."

"Come on, Joey. There must have been a reason. I can't believe Jason just walked up to you and hit you."

"Well, that's what he did. I was just walking along, and Jason came up behind me and yelled at me. When I turned around, he slugged me."

"Had they had a fight before?" Steve asked Kay.

"I don't see how they could have," Kay said. "I—well, I've tried to keep Joey away from Jason. First there was that Corliss boy—"

"Randy?"

"Randy, yes. He's always been troublesome. And then the last week or so—well, I know Sally's been . . . upset, and it just seemed to me that Joey should stay away."

"I see," Steve said softly. He could see in Kay's eyes the discomfort she was feeling, and wondered just what she'd said to Joey, and what Joey might have said to Jason. But the long hesitation before she'd said the word *upset* told him all he needed to know. "I'll talk to Jason about this, Kay, and try to find out what happened. And if what Joey says turns out to be true, I can assure you that Jason will be punished."

"He's already been punished," Joey said. "I bet he's got two black eyes, and I bit him."

Kay Connors stared down at her son. "You *what?*"

"I bit him," Joey said. "He was on top of me, hitting me in the face, so I grabbed his arm and bit it. It was bleeding."

"Oh, God, Joey," Kay groaned. "Why didn't you tell me that before?"

"You didn't ask."

Feeling suddenly foolish, Kay wondered what to say. But when she looked at Steve Montgomery, there was a trace of a smile playing around his lips. "Maybe I over-reacted a bit," she said.

"And maybe the fight wasn't quite as one-sided as we thought."

Kay nodded. "And maybe someday I'll learn to understand little boys." She took Joey by the hand. "As for you, young man, the next time you get into a fight, don't come crying to me unless the boy was twice your age and four times your size. Now let's get you cleaned up and off to school."

"Aw, Mom, do I have to?"

"Yes, you do. You're going to be late, but that's going to have to be your problem too. The next time you think about fighting, maybe you'll think twice."

Their voices were suddenly cut off as Kay pulled the back door closed behind her. Steve sank back into his chair and poured himself another cup of coffee. But instead of drinking it, he left it sitting on the table while he went upstairs to Sally.

He found her lying on the bed, staring up at the ceiling. She made no move when he came into the room, nor did she speak to him. He crossed to the bed, sat gingerly on its edge, and took her hand.

"Sally?"

Her eyes, large and pleading, suddenly met his, and what he saw frightened him. There was terror there, and confusion, but most of all, sadness.

"What's happening to us?" she asked in a whisper. "Oh, God, Steve, I'm so frightened. Everything's closing in, and I have the most awful feeling."

Steve gathered her up and cradled her against himself. "It's all right, honey," he crooned. "You'll see, everything's going to be all right. We'll go see Dr. Wiseman together and see what he has to say. You're just worn out. Don't you see? There's nothing wrong except that you're worn out from worrying. You can't do this to yourself, Sally. You have to let go of it."

Sally was too exhausted, and too frightened, to argue further, but even as she agreed to see Arthur Wiseman that afternoon, she made up her mind that no matter what happened, she would remain calm and rational.

After all, she reminded herself, I'm *not* irrational, I'm *not* paranoid. I am *not* insane.

She would give Wiseman no reason to suspect otherwise.

Mark Malone was sipping on his coffee and leafing through a copy of the AMA journal when the intercom on his desk suddenly came to life.

"Dr. Malone, this is Suzy. In the emergency room?"

"Yes."

"We've got a patient coming in, and since it's one of yours, I thought you might want to handle it."

"Who?"

"Tony Phelps."

Tony Phelps was two years old and one of Malone's favorite patients, since all he ever had to do for the boy was agree with his mother's assessment that he was certainly "the world's most perfect child." And even privately, Malone wasn't sure the assessment wasn't too far off the mark.

"Tony? What's happened to him?"

"I'm not sure," Suzy replied. "Mrs. Phelps wasn't really too coherent. You know how she is about Tony—it was all she could do to tell me who she was. She was crying, and all she said was 'my baby . . . my baby . . .' I sent an ambulance. They should be back in about ten minutes."

"Okay." Malone shoved the magazine to one side, and switched on his CRT. When the screen began to glow, he quickly entered his access codes, then tapped out the instructions that would retrieve Tony Phelps's medical records from the computer's memory banks. Except for the usual vaccinations and inoculations, Tony's chart was unremarkable except in its brevity. Malone unconsciously nodded an acknowledgment to the machine, and was about to turn it off again when he noticed the small notation on the chart that identified Tony Phelps as another of the children being studied by CHILD. Malone's brows arched slightly.

Then he heard the faint wailing of a siren in the distance. He shut off the console and started toward the emergency room.

Three minutes later, two paramedics burst into the emergency room. One of them carried a screaming child; the other followed, supporting a trembling Arla Phelps. Her face was pale and tear-streaked, but she seemed calmer than she had been when she'd called a few minutes earlier. She glanced around the room, recognized Malone, and hurried over to him.

"Dr. Malone, he drank some Lysol. I don't know how it happened. I was only out of the kitchen a minute, and when I came back—"

But Mark Malone was already gone, following the medics into a treatment room, snapping out orders to the nurse. Arla Phelps, left suddenly alone, sank onto a sagging plastic-covered sofa, and shakily lit a cigarette.

In the treatment room one of the medics restrained Tony Phelps, who had by now stopped screaming but was doing his best to struggle out of the strong hands that held him. Malone began the unpleasant task of forcing a Levin tube through the child's nose, down his throat, and into his stomach. A moment later, the lavage began.

"Will he be all right?" the nurse asked.

"I don't know," Malone replied, his voice grim. "It depends on how much he drank, how strong it was, and how long ago it happened."

Tony began vomiting, and the nurse tried futilely to catch the orangish mess in a bowl. Malone ignored the fact that most of it wound up on his coat.

"Well, at least he has orange juice in the morning," the nurse said by way of an apology.

"Let's get some more water down there."

They repeated the lavage process until Tony was throwing up nothing more than the clear water they were pumping into him. "Okay," Malone said at last. "Clean him up, and keep an eye on him, while I go talk to his mother." Without waiting for a reply, he strode out to the lobby area, where Arla Phelps was working on her fourth cigarette.

"Is he going to be all right?"

"He's still alive," Malone told her. "Tell me exactly what happened. I need to know exactly what he drank, and how much."

"It was Lysol," Arla told him. "I'm not sure how much, but I think it must have been a lot."

"What do you mean by a lot?"

"Half a bottle," the unhappy woman whispered.

Malone's eyes widened in surprise. "Half a bottle?" It was unbelievable. The first swallow should have been enough to make even a two-year-old choke and start screaming. "That doesn't make any sense."

"I was only out of the kitchen a few minutes. Doctor, he's never done anything like that before—never! But when I came back in, he was sitting on the floor, holding the bottle in his hands, drinking it just like it was pop."

Malone thought furiously. If he was to avert a disaster, he had to act quickly and make no mistakes. "Just a minute," he said. He went back to the treatment room, intent on having the contents of Tony Phelps's stomach analyzed.

But when he got there, the emergency seemed to have passed. Tony Phelps, sitting up on the examining table, was giggling happily while the nurse teased him. Malone stood at the door and stared.

"Suzy?" he said at last.

The nurse turned and grinned at him. "Still the world's most perfect child."

"So I see," Malone said. "Do me a favor, will you? Have the lab check out the contents of his stomach to see if there's anything there besides orange juice. I have a feeling our young Mr. Phelps may be playing a bad joke on all of us."

As the nurse hurried out of the room, bearing the bowl and its contents, Mark Malone picked up the gurgling child and held him high in the air. "Is that what you're doing, Tony? Playing a game on us?"

"Where's Mommy?" the little boy asked.

"Right out here." Malone carried Tony out to the lobby and turned him over to Arla, who looked up at him anxiously as she took her son.

"Is he all right?"

"Apparently. But I'd just as soon you stayed around for a while. I'm having the lab check out just what it was that he swallowed."

Twenty minutes later, a laboratory technician appeared, his face a mask. He signaled to Malone, then went into the treatment room. Malone followed.

"I don't know what's with that kid," the technician said softly. "He must have swallowed at least twelve ounces of straight Lysol. You ask me, he should be dead."

So the crisis wasn't over after all.

For Mark Malone, it promised to be a long day, and a difficult one.

Chapter 21

FOR THE FIRST TIME in five years, Sally Montgomery wished she had a cigarette. The problem, she knew, was her hands. If she only had something to do with them, perhaps she wouldn't feel so nervous.

She was lying to herself, and she knew it.

It was Dr. Wiseman who was making her nervous, with his calm eyes and placid expression, his understanding smile and his low-pitched voice.

She had been listening to him for half an hour while Steve waited outside.

All he really wanted, he kept insisting, was for her to talk to someone—a stranger, someone who had never met her before and knew nothing about her. A stranger who would listen to her objectively and then try to help her sort things out. Perhaps, Wiseman even admitted, this stranger might actually agree with her that something was "going on," and his fears for her would prove groundless.

Or perhaps, Sally thought, your friend will be one more voice hammering at me to stop worrying, face reality, and go on with my life. Isn't that what you all say? That I should bury my head in the sand? Pretend nothing's happening? She felt indignation rising up from the pit of her stomach, flooding through her like a riptide, threatening to tear away the veneer of false serenity in which she had wrapped herself.

"Would you like something?" she heard Wiseman saying.

"No—no, nothing at all," Sally said a little too quickly. She forced a smile. "I'm afraid I was just regressing a bit, wishing I had a cigarette." She bit her lower lip, regretting her words even as she spoke them. "It happens every now and then, but I always resist."

"Just as you're resisting me now?" Wiseman said, lounging back in his chair and smiling genially.

Exactly, Sally thought. Aloud she said, "I didn't know I was resisting you. I didn't think I needed to. Do I?"

"I don't see why." He leaned forward, folding his hands and resting them on his desk. "We've known each other for a long time, Sally. If you can't trust me, and you can't trust Steve, whom can you trust? You seem to have decided that for some reason we've turned against you."

Sally frowned in studied puzzlement. "I do? I'm sorry if I've given you that impression. I've listened to every word you've said."

"And dismissed them," Wiseman replied. "Sally, I'm your doctor. I've known you for ten years, but I'm sitting here talking to a stranger. Don't you *want* me to help you?"

Sally felt her guard slip just a little. Did he really want to help her? "Of course I want you to help me. But I want you to help me with my problem, and you only want to help me with what you *think* is my problem. I'm not crazy, Dr. Wiseman—"

"No one has said you are."

Sally's resolve crumbled around her, and all the feelings she had been struggling to control boiled to the surface. "*Everyone* has said so." The words burst out of Sally, and there was nothing she could do to stop them. "I keep hearing it from everyone—you, Steve, my mother, even the neighbors are starting to look at me strangely. 'Oh, dear, here comes poor Sally—you know, ever since her baby died, she's been a little odd.' By next week, they'll be crossing the street to get away from me. But I'm not crazy, Dr. Wiseman. I'm not crazy, and neither is Lucy Corliss. Do you remember her, Dr. Wiseman? You probably don't, but you did the same thing to her that you did to me, and to Jan Ransom, and to God-only-knows how many other women. We didn't want children, so you gave us IUDs. But we had children anyway—for a while. But mine died, and Jan's died, and Lucy's is gone. Is that your kind of birth control? After the fact?"

She started sobbing in fury and frustration. She was dimly aware of Wiseman getting up and moving from behind his desk to lay a gentle hand on her shoulder.

"Sally," she heard him say, "I tried to explain it to you at the time. IUDs don't always work. Sometimes your body rejects them. There's nothing I can do about that."

Sally shook his hand away and rose to face him. "Isn't there? I wonder, Dr. Wiseman. I wonder if there's nothing you could have done, or if there's something you *did* do. And I'll find out! You can't stop me, Dr. Wiseman. Not you, not Steve, not my mother, none of you!" The last vestiges of her control, the control she had nurtured all day, slipped away from her. She stumbled toward the door, grasping at the knob. It stuck, and for a frightening moment she wondered if she had been locked in. But then it turned in her hand and she pulled it open, lurching into the waiting room. Steve, on his feet, reached out to her, but she brushed him aside. As quickly as it had deserted her, her self-control returned. She glared at her husband. "Leave me alone," she said coldly. "Just leave me alone." And then she was gone.

Sudden silence hung in the air for a moment, and then Steve heard Arthur Wiseman's voice. "You'd better come in, Steve. I think we need to talk."

Numbly, Steve allowed himself to be led into the inner office. Wiseman guided him to the chair that Sally had just vacated, then closed the door. He waited while Steve settled into the chair, speaking only after the young man seemed to have recovered from his wife's outburst.

"You heard?"

"Only Sally, and only at the end. My God, what happened in here?"

"I'm not exactly sure," Wiseman said thoughtfully. "I talked to her, and for the first few minutes I thought she was listening to me. And then I had the strangest feeling she'd just sort of clicked off, shutting me out. It was as if she was only willing to listen to what she wanted to hear." He paused, then went on. "And then at the end, when I asked if she wanted our help—well, you heard her. She lost control."

"Oh, God," Steve groaned. "What am I going to do?"

Wiseman's fingers drummed on the desk top. "I'm not positive, Steve, but it seems to me that Sally's on the edge of a major collapse. I hate to suggest it, but I think it might be wise if she had a good rest. Not for a long time, but for a week or two at least. Get her out of Eastbury, away from everything that might remind her of Julie."

"I suppose I could get away for a while," Steve mused.

"That's not what I meant," Wiseman said quietly. "I think Sally needs to be by herself in an environment that's structured for people with her kind of problem."

Steve reluctantly met Wiseman's steady gaze. "You mean a mental hospital."

"I think it might be best."

Steve shook his head. "She won't agree to go."

Wiseman's fingers stopped drumming, and he picked up a pencil. "It isn't always necessary that—well, that the patient agree."

Steve swallowed hard, trying to dissolve the lump that had formed in his throat. "I—I'm not sure I could do that."

"If it's best for Sally, I'm not sure either of us has a choice," Wiseman countered.

Steve took a deep breath and shifted his weight forward in the chair. Surely, there was a better way. "Do we have to decide now?" he asked at last.

"This minute? No. But it shouldn't be put off too long.

Unless Sally gets some help, I don't know how far she might go with this thing. And I can't tell you what effect it might have on your son either."

It was the mention of Jason, coupled with the memory of the morning, that made up Steve's mind.

"All right," he said, his shoulders sagging with defeat. "Let's go find her."

Sally paused in the corridor and took a deep breath. She had her control back, and no matter what happened, she must not lose it again.

Not in front of Wiseman, and not in front of Steve.

But who was left for her to talk to?

Her world, the world that only two weeks ago had seemed limitless, had suddenly narrowed to three people: Lucy and Jim Corliss, and Carl Bronski.

Three people she barely knew.

But three people who believed in her.

She moved through the corridor quickly, intent only on getting out of the clinic, getting to her friends. She was almost through the lobby when she suddenly heard her name.

"Mrs. Montgomery?" the voice said again. It was a familiar voice, but still Sally had to curb her impulse to run. She turned to face the speaker.

It was Dr. Malone, and his brows were furrowed with worry. He was watching her intently. "Is something wrong?" he asked, his voice solicitous.

Sally glanced at a window and caught a vague reflection of herself. Her hair looked messy and her face drawn. She made herself smile. "I'm fine, Dr. Malone. I was just on my way home."

But Malone shook his head. "You're not fine, Mrs. Montgomery. Something's upsetting you. Won't you tell me what it is?"

"I—" Sally's eyes flickered nervously over the lobby. "I really have a great deal to do—"

"Does it have something to do with what happened on Monday?" Malone pressed.

Monday. Monday. Sally's memory churned, trying to

sort things out. What was he talking about? And then she remembered. Jason's arm. "What about it?" she asked coldly.

Malone moved closer to her and Sally took a step backward. He stopped, sensing that she was on the verge of running. "You still think the burns were worse than they looked, don't you?"

"Yes," Sally admitted. "But nobody else does. Something's going on, Dr. Malone, and I'm going to find out what it is. No one's going to stop me. No one's going to convince me that I'm crazy. So please, just let me go."

Malone stood silently for a moment, wishing he knew Sally Montgomery better. Was she buckling under the strain of losing her baby, or had she really stumbled onto something? He decided he'd better find out.

"I don't think you're crazy," he said at last. "I think things on Monday happened exactly the way you told it. Burns and all," he added, seeing the suspicion in Sally's eyes.

"Thank you," Sally breathed, moving toward the door. "I really have to—"

"I think we ought to talk, Mrs. Montgomery," Malone said quietly. He watched Sally carefully, sure that if he said the wrong thing, she would bolt. "Could we talk in my office? I promise we won't be disturbed. By *anyone*." Sally still hesitated. "There's a door from my office directly into the parking lot. Your car is right next to it. That's how I knew you were here." He moved toward her, and again she backed away. "In fact, why don't we go through the parking lot? Then if you still don't want to come into my office, you can just leave."

Sally was silent for a moment, then nodded her head in agreement. The two of them left the lobby and began walking along the side of the building.

"Something happened today, Mrs. Mont—is it all right if I call you Sally?"

She nodded, but said nothing.

"The same kind of thing happened again today, Sally. A woman brought in her son, and from what she said, the little boy should have been dead. Not just burned—dead. But nothing was wrong with him."

Sally stopped and turned to face Malone. She looked deep into his eyes. Was he telling the truth, or was it some kind of trap? Maybe he was just trying to delay her, trying to keep her here until—what? And yet, there was nothing in his eyes to suggest that he was lying to her. "Was the boy being surveyed by CHILD?"

Malone hesitated for a moment, then nodded.

They were near Sally's car now, and she began fishing in her purse for her keys. "Then if I were you, I'd keep a very careful eye on that boy," she said. "And I'd bet money that his mother hadn't planned to have him, and that Dr. Wiseman was his mother's doctor."

Malone knew it was all true. He reached out and touched Sally's arm. This time she didn't draw away.

"Come in for a minute. Please?" He went to the outside door of his office, unlocked it, and went in. Through the window Sally watched him cross to the other door, turn the bolt, then rattle it to prove to her that it was locked. At last, conquering her fear, she went inside.

Mark Malone talked steadily for ten minutes, and when he was done, Sally sighed heavily. "And there's no mistake? The Lysol should have killed him?"

Malone nodded. "If not, he should have been in so much pain that he would have been unconscious. He wasn't. He was mad as hops about the way he was being treated, but as soon as the lavage was finished, he was fine. And there was no mistake about how much of the stuff he'd drunk. He'd gone through it like root beer, and for the amount of damage it did, it might as well have *been* root beer."

The intercom on Malone's desk suddenly crackled, and the voice of Arthur Wiseman filled the room. "Mark, it's Arthur. Have you happened to see Sally Montgomery anywhere around the hospital?"

Malone glanced quickly at Sally, who shook her head vehemently. "No."

"Damn. Okay. If you see her, talk to her, and keep talking to her until I get to you."

"Why? Is something wrong?"

There was a short silence, then he said, "She's been having some problems, Mark. Her husband and I have decided she needs some help, but she doesn't agree. I'm afraid we're going to have to take the decision out of her hands."

Sally was on her feet and at the door to the parking lot by the time the intercom fell silent.

"Sally?" She paused and turned back to face him. "If I'm going to help you, I have to know where you'll be." She stared at him, and he knew that even now she didn't quite trust him. "Just a name," he said softly. "Don't argue, and don't waste time thinking. Just give me a name and get out of here."

"Lucy Corliss," Sally said.

"I'll be there tonight," Mark promised. "We have a lot to talk about." But by the time he'd finished speaking, Sally was gone. He moved to the window and watched as her car skidded out of the parking lot and disappeared down Prospect Street. Only then did he unlock his office door and hurry down the corridor toward Arthur Wiseman's office.

Louise Bowen paused for a moment on the lawn of the Academy to watch the three boys playing some kind of game with a ball. Although she didn't quite understand the point of the game, she could see that it was rough. The idea seemed to be to retain possession of the ball, but with the odds two against one, the game had the appearance of a constantly shifting wrestling match in which there could be no winner until all but one of the boys dropped in exhaustion.

Only Randy Corliss was not playing, and it was Randy in whom Louise was primarily interested.

She knew that what had happened yesterday afternoon was preying heavily on Randy's mind. He had been quieter than usual at breakfast. Then at lunch, while the rest of the boys wrangled about how to spend the afternoon, he had remained completely silent, his expression blank, as if he were somewhere far away, in a world of his own. And then, after lunch, he had disappeared. Now Louise was looking for him, determined to do what she could to assuage his fears.

Randy was in the woods. After lunch he had ignored his friends' pleas for him to join in their game and gone off by himself.

But it wasn't that he wanted to be alone.

He was looking for a way out.

For an hour he had worked his way along the fence, searching for a tree that had a limb extending beyond the strand of barbed wire that topped the barrier.

There was none.

All along the perimeter of the property the trees had been cleared away. Here and there a remaining tree that might once have had long lower branches showed the scars of some long-ago chain saw. But nowhere was there a place where the fence could be scaled without touching it. And then, when he had only fifty yards to go to the gate, he found it.

It was a stream flowing through a culvert that carried it under the fence. The pipe was small, but Randy was almost sure that if he hunched his shoulders together, he could get through. He scrambled down the bank of the stream and tried to peer through the culvert. At the far end, he thought he could see traces of light.

Should he try it now?

He glanced around, wondering if anybody was watching him.

He wasn't sure. At first, he had always felt the eyes on him, and it had bothered him. But after those first few days, he had grown used to the watching. That odd sixth sense had become dulled, and now that he needed to know if he was truly alone, he had no way of telling.

But one thing he was sure of. If he tried to run now and got caught, he wouldn't have another chance. Reluctantly, he turned away from the stream and started back toward the main building. If he was going to try to escape, he would have to do it at night, and he would have to do it from the house. But the windows were barred, and there was always someone awake, watching.

216

He moved through the woods slowly, trying to figure out what he could do. As he stepped from the forest onto the edge of the lawn, he saw an answer.

On the slope of the roof there seemed to be some kind of trap door. Randy stopped and stared at it for a long time. Was it really a trap door? But what was it for? What if it wasn't a trap door at all? What if it was just a skylight, and wouldn't open.

He frowned, trying to puzzle it out. And then, in his innocence, he decided that it *had* to be a trap door, and it *had* to open. Otherwise there was no way out.

But once he was on the roof, what would he do?

A tree. All he had to do was find a tree that reached to the eaves of the three-story building, and he could climb down it. He was about to begin searching for the right tree when he heard his name being called. He recognized Louise Bowen coming toward him.

"Randy, I've been looking all over for you."

"I was just off in the woods, messing around."

She smiled at him and tousled his hair. "I was worried about you."

Randy's first impulse was to pull away from her, but he thought better of it. If he was really going to try to run away, he couldn't let anyone know he might even be thinking about it. Otherwise they would watch him. He slipped his arms around Louise and hugged her. "I was just thinking about what we talked about last night," he said. His heart began pounding, and he prayed she wouldn't see through the lie he was about to tell her. "And I decided God must have wanted Eric to die, and what happened to him isn't going to happen to me."

Louise patted him on the back. "Well, that seems very sensible," she told him. "What made you decide that?"

Randy looked up at her, trying to hide the fear he was feeling. "I don't know. But I'm not scared anymore."

"Well, that's good," Louise said. But when she looked into his eyes, she saw something that told her he was lying. There was a look in his eyes and something about his smile that rang false.

He's going to do something, she thought. He's going to try to run away.

"Do you think I could build a treehouse here?" Randy suddenly asked.

"A treehouse?" Louise echoed. What was he talking about? One minute he was talking about dying, and the next minute he was talking about treehouses.

"You know," Randy said. "A treehouse. All you need is the right tree and some boards and nails."

Louise frowned, certain that somehow there was a connection. "Where do you think you might put it?"

"I don't know," the little boy conceded. "Over there, maybe?"

He pointed toward a grove of maples near the house, and as her gaze followed his gesture, her eyes wandered to the roof of the house. Clearly visible to her, and obviously to Randy too, was the trap door that allowed access to the roof. Suddenly she understood.

"Why, I don't know," she said. "Why don't we go have a look?"

Pleased that she had fallen so easily into his plans, Randy skipped off toward the trees, with Louise Bowen slowly and thoughtfully following after him.

Half an hour later, amid much planning of an elaborate treehouse, both Randy and Louise knew which tree Randy would use when he tried to escape.

As they returned to the house, Louise Bowen tried to decide what to do. She knew she should report her conversation with Randy, as well as her suspicions, to Dr. Hamlin. And yet she couldn't. She knew perfectly well that to Hamlin, Randy was no more than an animal, and she suspected that he wouldn't hesitate to lock the boy up like an animal. So, for the moment, she would say nothing. Instead, she would simply watch Randy very carefully. Then, when she knew exactly what he was planning, she would decide what to do about it.

As for Randy, he was positive that the woman suspected nothing. Tonight he would run away, and he was childishly sure that he wouldn't be caught.

Chapter 22

THE LONG TWILIGHT of the spring evening was just beginning to fade as Sally steered her car toward Lucy Corliss's house. She had been driving aimlessly all afternoon, intent only on staying away from Eastbury until dark, stopping only once to try to eat supper. Supper, it turned out, had been a salad that had sat untouched before her while she sipped cup after cup of bitter coffee.

Twice she had considered calling Steve; twice she had discarded the idea. What could she say to him? That she was sitting by herself in a diner in another town, wondering if it was safe to come home? It would only confirm what he already believed.

She had considered other alternatives. Her mother? But her mother would only call Steve. What about friends? An image of Kay Connors came into her mind. No, there was only one place to go—the place that she had named while talking to Dr. Malone a few hours before.

And so she pulled up in front of Lucy Corliss's house, set the handbrake, and got out of her car. She started toward the house, then paused, frowning.

There was a strange car in Lucy's driveway, a car with medical plates.

Dr. Malone?

Or Arthur Wiseman?

Perhaps she shouldn't go in. Perhaps they were both there, waiting for her.

She forced the idea out of her mind. Paranoid. It was a paranoid thought, and she wouldn't entertain it. With a confidence she didn't feel, she climbed the three steps up to Lucy's front door and rang the bell. The door opened immediately, and Lucy drew her inside.

"Sally—where have you been? We've been so worried. I was watching for you, and then it looked like you weren't going to come in—my God, you look awful!"

Sally instinctively brushed at her hair, and when she spoke she heard her voice quaver. "It was the car in the driveway. I didn't know whose it was."

"It's Mark Malone's. He got here an hour ago."

Sally started to breathe a sigh of relief, then caught it back. "He came alone?"

"All alone," Lucy reassured her. She led Sally toward the living room. "He told us what happened at the hospital today."

As they walked into the living room, Jim Corliss rose to offer his chair to Sally, but she ignored the gesture, choosing instead to settle on the love seat next to Lucy. "All of it?"

"All of what I saw, and all of what you told me," Mark Malone said. "And after you left, I went into Wiseman's office." A look of alarm came over Sally, and Mark quickly reassured her. "I only wanted to find out what they were doing and give you a little time. I'm afraid they were talking to your mother, explaining that if you showed up at her house, she should try to keep you there and call them."

"Oh, God, what am I going to do?"

"You're going to forget all about it for a while." It was Carl Bronski, and the firmness in his voice puzzled Sally. Forget it? How could she? Bronski continued speaking, almost as if she'd voiced her questions. "They can't just come and get you, Sally. They'd have to get a court order, and that involves a hearing. All that takes time, plus a lot more evidence than they've got right now. Also, don't forget that there are four people sitting right here who don't think you're crazy at all, including a doctor and a cop. So even if they're serious about trying to commit you, it isn't going to happen tomorrow, or the next day either. And by then, if we're lucky, we'll know just exactly what the hell is going on."

"Then something *is* going on? I'm not crazy?"

"If you are, we all are," Jim Corliss said. "It seems there's been another coincidence. Carl called Lucy last night about a little boy who's disappeared from Atlanta. He's the same age as Randy and was born here. His parents weren't married."

Sally's eyes met Jim's, and when she spoke, the calmness of her voice told all of them that she had put her personal fears aside. "Was he being surveyed by CHILD?"

"That's what we don't know," Carl said. "I was hoping you could find out for me. Most of those statistics you pulled out of the computer didn't have any names attached to them. They were just numbers."

"Well, it's easy enough to find out," Sally told them. "All I have to do is go down to my office—" Her heart sank as she pictured the keys to her office dangling from the key rack in the kitchen closet. "We can't go to my office. I don't have my keys."

"Can't a security officer let you in?" Bronski asked.

Sally shook her head. "They can, but they won't. If you don't have your keys, they aren't allowed to open any doors for you."

Mark Malone paced the room, weighing the risks of what he was about to suggest against the idea's possible advantages. He made up his mind. "What about the hospital? Why can't Sally and I go down to the hospital and use the terminal in my office?"

"But they'll be looking for me there, won't they?"

"They won't see you," Malone assured her. "We won't even have to go through the lobby. Then we'll see if you and your computer expertise can figure out exactly what's going on."

They rose, ready to leave, when the phone suddenly began ringing. Lucy hesitated, then went to answer it. A moment later she reappeared. "It's for you," she said to her ex-husband, frowning slightly. "It's a woman." Ignoring her faintly accusatory tone, Jim hurried into the kitchen. Moments later, he, too, reappeared.

"That was a friend of mine in Boston," he said, his eyes on Lucy. "Her name's Joan Winslow, and she works for an ad agency. And I haven't dated her for two years. Anyway," he went on as Lucy's eyes narrowed suspiciously, "I asked her to see if she could find out who funds CHILD."

"Who *funds* them?" Lucy sounded exasperated. "What on earth difference could that make?"

"A lot," Jim told her. "You don't really think all these foundations are as independent as they claim to be, do you? Almost all of them, somehow, are funded by people with one sort of an ax to grind or another."

"And CHILD?" Carl Bronski asked.

Jim looked at him bleakly. "A lot of minor grants from a lot of places. But two big ones. Continuing support from an outfit called PharMax—"

"Which is one of the biggest drug companies in the country," Mark Malone interrupted. "It seems like they'd have a natural interest in a group like CHILD."

"It's the other grant that intrigues me," Jim Corliss said quietly. "It makes all the other funds, including the ones from PharMax, look like peanuts."

"Who is it?" Lucy demanded.

Jim's eyes locked on hers, his puzzlement clear in the frown that knotted his forehead. "The Defense Department," he said slowly. "Now, why would the Defense Department be interested in a group like CHILD?"

Jason Montgomery came home just as the full darkness of night was falling over Eastbury. He walked the last few yards very slowly, knowing very well that he was in a lot of trouble. His father, he was sure, would give him a spanking, and his mother—well, she would just look at him, and he would know from her eyes that he'd disappointed her. That would be even worse than the spanking. Jason had found out years ago that spankings only stung for a split second, no matter how hard his father slapped his bottom. He paused, staring at the house.

How much, he wondered, did they know? Had Joey really told on him? Maybe he hadn't. He could explain his torn clothes by saying that he'd—he'd what? He searched in his mind for a reasonable explanation. Maybe he'd climbed a fence and slipped? That was it. He and somebody else had climbed the fence around the schoolyard, and he'd slipped.

But what if they'd found out he skipped school?

He didn't even want to think about that.

Wondering if the fun of ditching school had been worth whatever was waiting for him inside the house, he slid through the front door. "Mom? I'm home!"

From the kitchen, he heard his father's voice.

"Jason? Is that you?" His father came through the dining room, his face red with anger. "Where have you been?"

"I—I—" Jason stammered. Then, in the face of his father's wrath, words failed him. He stared up at his father, his eyes brimming with tears.

Looking down at his son, Steve felt his anger drain away, to be replaced by relief.

His afternoon had not been easy. He'd left the clinic to find the car—and Sally—gone. He'd started walking home and decided to stop by the school to pick up his son.

But even though he'd waited until the school grounds were deserted, Jason hadn't appeared. Finally he'd gone in, found Jason's room, and talked to his teacher.

Jason hadn't been at school that day.

For the rest of the afternoon Steve had spent his time worrying alternately about his wife and his son, neither of whom came home. He'd called everyone he could think of, including Lucy Corliss, but no one had seen either of them. Several times he'd started to take his car and go looking for them, but he'd always changed his mind, afraid that one or the other might call him, needing help, and he wouldn't be there. So he'd waited, nervously pacing the house, willing the phone to ring, glancing out the window every few minutes in hopes of seeing one of the people he loved best.

And at last his son had come home.

"Where've you been?" he asked again, his voice gentle now. "Why didn't you go to school?"

Jason, sensing that his father was no longer angry at him, sniffled a couple of times.

" 'Cause of the fight," he said.

"The fight with Joey?"

The little boy shook his head.

"Then why didn't you come home?"

" 'Cause of the fight you and Mom were having," Jason explained. Then, as if sensing something wrong, he glanced uneasily around. "Isn't Mom here?"

"Not right now," Steve replied. What could he say to Jason? That his mother had run away, and no one knew where she was? Then, for the first time, he noticed Jason's torn clothes. "That must have been some fight you had with Joey," he commented. "Want to tell me about it?"

Slowly Jason began to unfold the story. "And my eye was swollen," he finished, "and my arm was bleeding, and my clothes were torn, so I didn't go to school. But he started it, Dad."

Steve nodded absently, not really hearing Jason's last words. Instead, he was trying to match Jason's list of wounds with what he saw.

His eye was swollen?

His arm was bleeding?

And the torn leg on his pants. Where had that come from?

"What happened to your jeans?"

Jason scowled. "He pushed me down on the sidewalk, and I skinned my knee."

"Show me."

Obediently, Jason rolled up his pant leg. The skin on his knee was clear and smooth. And yet, when Steve examined the jeans, he could see what looked like blood on the inside.

"And what about your arm? Where did he bite you?"

"Right here." Jason touched a spot just above his wrist. It showed no signs of damage either. Nor was there any blemish on Jason's face.

What the hell was going on? Both boys gave the same account of the fight, and Joey Connors had been a mess this morning. "Come on, son," he said quietly. He led Jason into the kitchen, opened a Coke for the boy, then picked up the phone.

"Kay?" he asked when the connection was made. "This is Steve Montgomery. I was just wondering how Joey's doing."

There was a slight pause, then a sigh. "All right, I guess. He's sore, and his bruises won't go away for a couple of days, but there's no real damage." She paused, then added, "Has Jason come home yet? Or Sally?"

"Jason's here," Steve said.

"Is he okay?"

"I'm not sure," Steve said slowly. "But apparently the fight went just about the way Joey said, except that Jason insists Joey started it."

"Which he did," Kay Connors admitted. "What do you mean, you're not sure if Jason's okay? Is he hurt?"

"No, no—nothing like that." He laughed, but the sound was hollow. "In fact, it seems to me he should be hurt worse than he is. I'm afraid that Joey got by far the worst of it."

"I see," Kay replied, her voice noticeably cooler. In fact, she did not see at all, but privately decided that in the future, Joey would be instructed to have nothing whatever to do with Jason Montgomery. Indeed, from now on, the entire Connors family would avoid the Montgomerys. A moment later she found an excuse to end the conversation and cut the connection.

Steve sat silently, wondering what to do. There was no damage where there should have been damage. Even Jason said he'd been hurt in the fight. But what had happened to the wounds?

And then he remembered the fudge and the muriatic acid. Both times it had been Sally who claimed to have seen the damage, and both times he'd thought she was overreacting. But what about now? This time Joey, and Jason himself, had seen the damage. Were they lying? But there was no reason for them to. He reached for the phone again, glancing at the numbers that were scrawled all over the cover of the directory. A moment later he was talking to Eastbury Community Hospital.

"This is Steve Montgomery. Is Dr. Malone in?"

"No, he isn't, Mr. Montgomery."

"Can he be reached somewhere else?"

"One moment." He was put on hold for what seemed an interminable length of time, but at last the operator came back on the line. Dr. Malone was not at home, nor had he informed his service where he was. Could another doctor help?

"Dr. Wiseman," Steve said. "Can you put me in touch with Dr. Wiseman?"

"Of course, Mr. Montgomery." He was put back on hold, and then, seconds later, a new connection was made.

Arthur Wiseman listened quietly while Steve tried to explain what had happened. When he was finished, there was a short silence. Then Wiseman spoke, his voice low and calm.

"Bring the boy down to the hospital, Steve. It doesn't sound like there's anything to worry about, but it won't hurt to have a look at him." He paused, then he added, "Heard anything from Sally yet?"

"No."

Wiseman's voice turned grim. "We can talk about that too."

Randy Corliss waited until the Academy was silent, then waited some more. The minutes crept by. After what seemed like hours, he slipped out of bed and began dressing. Finally he opened his door a crack and peeped out into the hall. At the far end there was a dim light and a desk. At the moment, no one was sitting at the desk.

Randy edged out into the hall and began moving as quietly as he could toward the narrow set of stairs that led from the rear of the second floor up into the attic. He had almost reached the stairs when he heard footsteps behind him. Someone was coming up from the main floor. He dashed the last few feet, scuttled up to the top of the stairs, and waited. He heard a scraping sound and decided that whoever had come up was now sitting at the desk. Gingerly, he tried the door to the attic.

It was unlocked.

He slipped inside, eased the door closed behind himself, and felt around for a light switch. But even as his hands found one, he changed his mind. What if someone were outside and saw lights in the attic? He'd never even make it out of the house.

He'd have to do it in the dark.

He started across the floor, but his footsteps seemed to echo loudly. He stopped again and took off his sneakers, tied the shoelaces together, then hung the shoes themselves around his neck. Once more he began creeping across the attic floor, testing each step before he put his weight on his foot. He moved slowly, his eyes straining to penetrate the near-total blackness, but after what seemed an eternity he found himself under what he believed to be a skylight.

He stared upward.

It *was* a skylight, but in the dimness he could just make out a folding ladder and a latch. From the ladder, a cord dangled just out of his reach. He stretched upward, and his fingers barely brushed its frayed end.

Should he try to find something to stand on? But how? He could grope around in the dark all night and never find anything.

He decided to risk a jump. He flexed his legs a couple of times, judging the distance carefully, then lofted himself off the floor.

His right hand grasped the rope, and as he dropped

back to the attic floor with a soft thump, the ladder creaked and moved down six inches. The thump and the creak made Randy freeze, listening.

On the floor below, Louise Bowen looked up from the report she was working on. Was it her imagination, or had she heard a faint sound? Frowning, she rose from her chair and began making her way down the hall, checking on each of the boys.

Hearing nothing, Randy slowly pulled the ladder down. Its ancient springs groaned in low protest, but to Randy the sound was like blaring trumpets. At last, the ladder touched the floor and he scurried up it. It took him a moment to figure out how the latch worked, but then with a scatter of flaking rust, it came free. He pushed the skylight upward and crept out onto the roof.

The pitch looked much steeper than it had from below, and the slate of the roof felt slippery under Randy's bare feet. Quickly, he put his sneakers back on, laced them tightly, then stood up and tested the footing. The rubber soles seemed to grip the slate firmly, but he wasn't too sure of his balance. Finally, he spread himself out, until he was almost lying flat against the incline, and began crabbing sideways across the roof.

There was only one more room to check, and Louise Bowen hesitated before opening its door. What if Randy was not inside?

But he had to be. Surely, if he were planning to run tonight, he would wait until much later.

Or would he?

She turned the knob of his door and pushed it open. "Randy?"

There was no answer. She switched the light on. Randy's bed was empty.

Slowly, reluctantly, Louise started toward the main stairs. She would have to report that Randy Corliss was gone.

*　　*　　*

Randy could see the treetop looming twenty feet in front of him. All he had to do was ease himself down to the eave, then climb onto the large branch he had spotted this afternoon. But going down the steep angle of the roof was not as easy as scooting across it. He had to place each foot carefully, bracing himself with both hands as he shifted his weight from one foot to another.

And then it happened. His right foot hit a patch of moss and he slipped. He began sliding down the roof, his hands scrabbling for a grip on the worn slate. He felt himself begin to go over the edge and made a desperate grab at the gutter that rimmed the eave. It screeched at the sudden strain, and pulled away from its supports, but it held. Randy swung in the air for a moment, searching wildly for his branch.

It was only a foot away, and with the strength born of fear, Randy worked his way over and swung onto it. Pausing only a moment to catch his breath, he began scrambling down the tree. In a few seconds he was on the ground, sprinting across the lawn toward the woods. Only when he reached them did he stop to look back.

All over the house lights were coming on.

He turned and plunged into the forest, relying on his memory to guide him to the stream and the culvert that would take him under the fence. A faint glow from the moon lighted his way, and he was able to keep moving at a dead run, dodging this way and that, moving steadily away from the house. His breath was getting short, and he was beginning to think he'd taken a wrong turn, when suddenly he heard the sound of running water. And then he was at the top of the bank, the stream just below him.

From behind, he heard the barking of dogs.

He slid down the bank and waded into the water, ignoring its chill. He started upstream and came to the end of the culvert. Without considering the possible consequences, hearing only the baying of the dogs as they searched for his scent, he dove into the narrow pipe.

It was tight, and his shoulders rubbed against both sides as he crept through the rushing water. But then, as his hands and feet began to grow numb from the cold, he saw a faint glow ahead.

He was almost out.

Urging his small body onward, he squirmed the last few feet.

With his goal only inches away, he discovered his mistake.

Firmly imbedded in the end of the culvert was a wire-mesh grate, its heavy screening blocking the passage of anything but the rushing stream.

Hopelessness flooded over Randy for a moment, then receded. Determinedly, he began backing out of the culvert. It seemed to take forever, but at last he was free of the confining pipe, standing in the water, his body charged with a combination of fear and exhilaration.

The dogs were coming closer now. Randy scrambled back up the bank, his mind whirling, searching for a solution.

The fence.

He would have to climb the fence.

He could see one of the dogs now, a huge shadow charging toward him out of the dimness. Turning, he hurled himself toward the fence, but he was too late.

The doberman was on him, snarling, its jaws clamping onto Randy's left ankle. The dog planted its feet firmly in the ground and began shaking its head. Randy tripped, collapsed, then tried to kick out at the dog. His right foot connected with the animal's head, and it let go for a moment. Randy scrambled to his feet, the fence a foot behind him. The dog hesitated, snarled, then leaped toward him. Randy twisted aside, grabbed the dog in mid-leap, and shoved hard.

With a high-pitched scream, the dog died as the voltage of the fence surged through it. Randy, his hand still clutching the animal's skin, stared at it for a moment.

Dimly, he was aware of an odd sensation in his arm. It was an inner tingling and a slight burning sensation. The last time he had touched the fence, he had been knocked out. Suddenly he remembered the test Dr. Hamlin had given him, and now he knew what it had

230

meant. The electricity hadn't killed him the first time, and now it couldn't hurt him at all.

Very close by, he heard the other dogs. Letting go of the dead animal at his feet, Randy reached out and grasped the fence.

Again, there was the strange tickle, and the sensation of warmth, but nothing more.

So everything he had been told while he was growing up was wrong.

Electricity didn't hurt you at all. In fact, it felt kind of good.

A moment later he dropped to the ground on the other side.

Chapter 23

DARKNESS SHROUDED the parking lot of Eastbury Community Hospital, but still Mark Malone drove around to the back entrance and switched his lights off before he pulled in and parked his car next to his office.

"No sense alerting everyone that we're here," he commented. Sally nodded her agreement as she got out of the car and waited for Malone to unlock his office door. Only when they were inside, with both doors securely bolted and the lights turned on, did Sally speak.

"I feel as though I'm doing something illegal."

"You're not," Malone assured her. "Although you were when you broke the codes to the medical records the first time. But this time, it's perfectly legal. If anyone ever asks any questions, I hired you as a computer operator to compile some statistics for me. Okay?"

"Okay." Sally set her purse on Malone's desk and switched on the computer terminal. Moments later she began tapping in the proper codes. "First things first," she murmured. Her fingers flew over the keyboard, finally coming to rest on the key marked ENTER. Sighing slightly, she leaned back in her chair and smiled wanly at Malone. "It'll take a couple of minutes."

Malone shrugged. "How'd you know what to tell it?"

"It's all one computer," Sally explained. "Even though

I spend most of my time with the college records, the instructions are pretty much the same for anything. Right now it's putting together a list of the names and birth dates of every child ever born in this area that CHILD is studying or has ever studied."

Even as she spoke, the screen was filled with a list of names. Sally pressed the cursor key that would allow her to scroll down the cathode ray tube until the entire list had been exposed.

"My God," she breathed. She glanced up at the information line at the top of the screen. The list stopped at line 153, and there were five names on each line. She glanced at the printer that sat a few feet away. Three lights, one red, one amber, and one white, glowed softly, indicating that the machine was ready for use.

Seeing her intent, Malone moved to the printer and rolled a sheet of paper into its platen. "Okay."

Once again Sally's fingers flew over the keyboard, and a second later the printer began chattering. "It'll take three pages," she said. Malone nodded silently, wishing he'd bought the automatic paper feeder he'd seen last year.

While the printer worked, Sally studied the screen. "I wonder if they're all part of the same study? But they can't be," she went on. "CHILD does all kinds of surveys, doesn't it?"

"As far as I know."

Once again, Sally's fingers moved over the keyboard. "I'm having the computer analyze the code numbers CHILD uses and see if it can find any relationships," she said.

The printer suddenly stopped for the last time, and Malone pulled the final sheet from the platen. "The name Carl Bronski gave us is here," he said. "Adam Rogers." He stapled the three pages together. "What shall we do with these?"

"Keep them," Sally replied. "They may be all we get." But then the screen suddenly came alive again, this time filled with four blocks of numbers.

Malone frowned at the screen. "What's that mean?"

"Apparently CHILD is doing four studies, and they've assigned the code numbers by multiples of certain other numbers." She pointed to the block of numbers in the upper left-hand quadrant of the screen. "Those are all multiples of 13. The others are multiples of 17, 19, and 21."

"I'm not sure I get it," Malone said.

Sally's voice became grim. "It means that Dr. Wiseman is lying. According to him, CHILD uses random numbers to decide whom to survey. But these numbers aren't random—they only appear to be when they're all mixed together. What CHILD is really doing is studying selected children and keeping them grouped together by means of the code numbers. Let's try something else."

For the third time, her hands manipulated the keyboard, and once more the screen went blank for a few seconds. As before, the screen began to fill with numbers, but this time there were names attached to them. As Sally stared at the names, her eyes brimmed with tears.

"I told it to find Julie's case number, then list all the names and numbers of the rest of that group," she explained.

All the names were on the list.

Randy Corliss.

Adam Rogers.

Julie Montgomery.

Eden Ransom.

Jason Montgomery.

In all, there were forty-six names. Sally Montgomery and Mark Malone stared at the list for several seconds, each deep in his own thoughts.

"We'd better print it out," Malone said at last.

Sally nodded silently, and her fingers once more began moving over the keyboard, but slowly this time, as if by committing the list to paper she would somehow seal whatever fates awaited the children whose names appeared on it.

Fifty feet away, Arthur Wiseman sat in his office listening quietly while Steve Montgomery once again described Jason's misadventures.

"And that's it?" he asked when Steve had finished his recital.

"That's it."

Wiseman turned to Jason.

"And what about you, son? Did it happen the way your father told it?"

"I—I guess so," Jason faltered. "I mean, the fight happened, and I was bleeding."

"Well, why don't we just have a look at you and see what we can find, all right?"

Jason frowned. He hated it when Dr. Malone poked and prodded at him, and stuck the ice cream stick in his mouth and made him say *aaahhh*. It wasn't as if he was ever sick, or anything was wrong with him. "I'm okay," he said.

"And who said you weren't?" Wiseman countered with mock severity. "All I want to do is take a peek. I haven't seen you since the day you were born, and it seems to me it's only fair if you let me admire my work."

"Were you the doctor who delivered me?" Jason asked. He'd always thought it was Dr. Malone.

"Sure was. Popped you a good one on the bottom, then handed you over to Dr. Malone. You were a scrappy little critter, as I recall. Nearly tore the roof off this place with the screaming and yelling."

Still talking, Wiseman led Jason into the examining room and boosted him up onto the table.

"What are those?" the little boy asked, staring curiously at the stirrups that rose from one end of the table.

"Just something I use now and then. Why don't you take off your shirt?"

Obediently, Jason stripped to the waist, then waited to see what would happen. A moment later he felt the cold chill of the stethoscope as the doctor listened to his heartbeat and his breathing. Then he looked from side to side while Dr. Wiseman carefully watched his eyes.

"Which one got the fist?"

"This one," Jason replied, holding his hand up to his right eye.

Wiseman compared the boy's eyes carefully, and saw no evidence of a bruise. "Couldn't have been much of a punch."

"I guess it wasn't," Jason admitted. "It only hurt for a second."

"And what about the other day, when you spilled the fudge on your arm. Did that hurt?"

"Not much," Jason said, scratching his head while he tried to remember. "I guess it did at first, but not very long. Like the day I cut my finger."

"Your finger?" Wiseman asked.

Jason nodded. "I was making a fort and I cut myself."

"Badly?"

"Nah. It bled for a minute, and I was going to put a Band-Aid on it, but then it healed up."

Now it was Wiseman who scratched his head. "Healed up? Before you put a Band-Aid on it?"

"Sure."

Wiseman thought for a moment, then spoke again. "How would you like to have your blood tested?" he asked.

"What for?"

"Just to find out something," Wiseman replied.

"Okay."

A moment later, while Jason watched, Wiseman plunged a needle into the boy's arm and drew out five cc's of blood. With a single practiced motion, he drew out the needle, placed an alcohol-soaked wad of cotton on the point where the needle had pierced Jason's skin, then folded the boy's arm so that the cotton was held in place. "Just hold your arm like that for a few minutes," he said. Taking the blood sample with him, he returned to his office and picked up the phone. He issued a series of orders, then, putting the receiver back on the hook, he turned to Steve Montgomery.

"Is something wrong?" Steve asked anxiously.

"I don't know," Wiseman replied. "At the moment it doesn't look like it, but I want some tests run on his blood. Also, it appears that Jason may have an unusual ability, which I'm testing right now." He glanced at his watch. Two minutes had elapsed since he had withdrawn the needle from Jason's arm. "Just sit tight a minute."

He returned to the examining room and smiled at the boy. "All right," he said. "Let's have a look and see if you're bleeding."

Jason unfolded his arm, and Wiseman removed the cotton wad from the small wound.

Except that there was no wound there.

He examined the skin very closely, but nowhere could he find so much as a mark indicating that the skin had recently been punctured.

Chewing his lip thoughtfully, Wiseman led Jason back to the office, then sent him on out to the waiting room. "I want to talk to your father for a few minutes. Okay?"

Jason, glad that the examination was over, grinned happily. "Okay." Then something occurred to him. "I always get a sucker from Dr. Malone."

"Well, I'm afraid I don't have any," Wiseman told him. "But maybe, if you're a good boy, I can go down to Dr. Malone's office in a few minutes and find one. How's that?"

"Okay."

Jason disappeared into the waiting room, and Wiseman closed the door behind him.

"Well?" Steve asked.

"Well," Wiseman said softly, "I just don't know. It appears to me that Jason heals at an abnormally fast rate."

"What does that mean?"

Wiseman shrugged helplessly. "I can't tell you. It would seem to me that it means Jason has some kind of abnormality in his body, and it's manifesting itself in an accelerated regeneration of tissue. But I can't be sure what else it might be doing."

Steve frowned. "I don't follow you."

Wiseman wondered what to say, and finally decided to say as little as possible. His fingers began their habitual drumming on the desk top.

"I think perhaps it might be wise to keep Jason here for a day or two," he began. "Jason seems to have some kind of abnormality, and until we find out just what it is and just what its effects are, I'd like to keep him under observation."

"You mean here?" Steve asked. If nothing was wrong with Jason, why should he stay in the hospital?

"Here," Wiseman agreed. Then, after a slight hesitation, he added, "Or perhaps in a diagnostic clinic." He began carefully explaining to Steve exactly what he had in mind.

As he listened to the older man, Steve began to feel as if he had lost control over his life and the lives of his family. First Julie, then Sally, now Jason. What had happened? What *was* happening? He could understand none of it, and as Wiseman continued talking, it all began to sound more and more unreal. By the time Wiseman had finished, Steve's resistance to the idea of putting an apparently healthy child in the hospital had begun to erode. Perhaps, he had begun to think, Jason *should* be put under observation. At least for a while . . .

Randy Corliss stood uncertainly outside the fence. The howling of the dogs grew louder. He wondered how many of them there were.

He'd never heard them before, or seen them. Had they been there all the time? But where? Maybe they'd been kept locked up in the basement. But what did it mean that they were loose now? Did they already know he had escaped, or were they loose every night, guarding the grounds. And then he saw them—three of them—moving steadily along his trail to the point where he'd gone into the water. They paused there; their baying stopped suddenly while they sniffed curiously around, first at the ground, then at the air. And then they turned and began moving toward him. Randy stood still, fascinated by the huge beasts, his fear eased by the high fence that separated him from them.

As he watched they discovered the fourth dog, lying dead near the fence, and suddenly their snuffling and sniffing gave way to whining. They poked at the corpse, pawing at it almost as if they were uncertain of what it was. And then, as one, they caught Randy's scent. Their dead companion suddenly forgotten, they turned toward the fence, fangs bared, and began snarling. The ugly sound grew until the night was once again filled with their terrifying voices.

Randy fled into the woods.

For the first few minutes he simply ran, but then, as the baying of the dogs faded slightly, he paused. He had to think.

If they knew he was gone, they would turn the dogs loose in the forest. Not only that, but they would find the dead dog and know exactly where to let the live ones hunt. And as soon as they caught his scent, he wouldn't have a chance.

And then an image of the dogs at the edge of the stream came to his mind.

His trail had ended there, and they hadn't known what to do.

He must get back to the stream.

It was off to the right somewhere.

Or was it?

He'd been so frightened, he hadn't paid much attention to where he was going. He thought he'd run in a straight line, at least as straight as he could while still threading his way through the trees, but had he really?

He stood still. The blackness seemed to close in around him, shutting out everything—even the howling dogs—and he felt the first ragged edges of panic reaching out for him. It was like when he was learning to swim, and he'd gotten into deep water for the first time. His mother had been there with him, only a couple of feet away, but still he had begun thrashing at the water, terrified that he was going to die.

And then he'd heard his mother's voice calmly telling him not to panic, to let himself float. And now, as that strange sense of terror began flooding over him, he repeated his mother's words.

"Don't panic," he said out loud. Then, again, "Don't panic."

And it worked. The terror eased. The rushing sound in his head that had momentarily blocked out the sounds of the night disappeared, and once more he could hear the dogs. He turned, so the sound seemed to be coming from behind him. And then, slowly and deliberately, he turned to the right and began walking through the woods. He moved slowly, pausing every few minutes to listen.

Finally, he heard it. Ahead of him was the soft, gurgling sound of running water. He began to run.

He came to the brook and waded in, turning left to begin making his way upstream. The bottom was covered with water-smoothed rocks, and even the rubber soles of his sneakers failed to find a firm purchase on them. Randy found himself slipping and sliding, falling into the water, only to pick himself up and keep going.

He waded on and on, with no idea of the direction in which the stream was leading him or what his goal might be. All he knew was that he had to get away from the Academy, or he would die. And in order to get away, he must stay in the water, where the dogs couldn't follow him.

Suddenly the noise of the water increased. Randy searched the darkness ahead. Vaguely he could see that he was approaching a fork; the brook he had been wading in was only an offshoot of a larger stream. What if it was too deep, or the current was too fast? And yet he knew he had no choice. Doggedly, he made his way into the larger stream, and began battling against the current. The water was over his knees now.

He came to a small waterfall, and his path was suddenly blocked. He stopped, staring at the four-foot cascade, and wondered what to do.

To the left there seemed to be a path.

Should he leave the stream?

But what if the dogs came this way and found his scent on the path?

He stayed in the water and began groping for a handhold that would allow him to pull himself up directly through the torrent. At last his right hand found the slippery surface of a branch that had lodged in the rocks. He clung to it while his feet battled the current to find a toehold. And then, for just a moment, his right foot caught and he hauled himself over the ledge to lie gasping and choking in the stream. He looked up. Just ahead of him a large rock rose out of the water. He heaved himself back to his feet and struggled toward it, not sure he had the strength to get to it, but unwilling to sink back into the cold water.

And then he was there. He sank down onto the rock, his breath coming in a series of heaving gasps. He was soaked through, and cold, and his teeth were chattering.

But, for the moment, he was safe.

He had no way of knowing how long he sat on the rock, but it seemed like hours. And then, finally, his teeth stopped chattering, and his breath came easily and evenly. He listened, straining to hear the baying of the dogs, but if it was there, the rushing water made it indistinguishable from any other sound.

At last he got to his feet and continued wading. The stream leveled out, and the rocky bottom was replaced by sand. The wading became easier, and Randy was no longer even tempted to leave the stream.

Ahead a light flashed.

Randy stopped and stood stock-still, staring into the darkness.

Was someone out there with a light, looking for him?

Once again the light flashed. Suddenly, Randy knew what it was.

Ahead of him there was a road, and the flashes of light were cars. He redoubled his efforts and forged ahead, splashing through the water, his mind filled with the memories of the previous summer, when he had been alone in the dark, then seen lights, and finally come to a road. Maybe it would happen like that again, and someone would find him and take him home.

He came to the bridge that carried the road over the stream. He was about to scramble up the bank to wave at the first car that came along, when he suddenly stopped.

What if Dr. Hamlin was out there in a car looking for him? Or Miss Bowen? Or any of them?

He couldn't just climb out.

But he couldn't just keep wading up the stream either. He listened carefully. Here, where the stream slid quietly over a smooth bottom, the night was silent. No matter how hard he tried, he could hear no dogs barking, no sounds of animals crashing through the forest toward him.

Maybe, if he was very careful, it was safe to leave the stream.

He tried to figure out which way the Academy might be. Behind him, he thought, and to the left.

Reluctantly, Randy left the water and made his way up the right bank, then, staying well back from the road, he began moving through the woods, making sure every few steps that the road was still in sight.

To pass the time he began counting his steps.

He had counted to six hundred and thirty-four, when he suddenly became aware of a light flashing in the distance.

Not the headlight of a car, for it wasn't moving.

No, it was the light of a sign. He began running, and in a few moments he was able to read it.

The sign was for a diner, and its flashing message pulsated through the darkness:

OPEN ALL NIGHT

At last, Randy was safe.

Chapter 24

GEORGE HAMLIN GLANCED UP at the clock on the wall of his office. It was nearly ten, he was tired, and a long night of work stretched ahead of him. It was work he hated to have to do. Nevertheless, it had to be done. Now he faced his staff, and wondered if he looked as bad as they did. The five of them sat nervously in a semicircle around his desk, their faces drawn, their eyes furtive. Louise Bowen, upon whom Hamlin placed full responsibility for what was about to happen, sat with her head down, her fingers twisting at the fringe of a woolen shawl that was draped over her shoulders.

She looks old, Hamlin thought irrelevantly. She looks old and tired. Then he took a deep breath and began speaking.

"You all know what's happened. This evening's unfortunate events leave me no choice. The God Project is going to be suspended."

A low murmuring rippled through the room, and the laboratory technician raised a tentative hand. "Isn't there anything we can do?"

"I wish there were," Hamlin replied. "But Randy Corliss is gone, and we have no way of recovering him. The dogs—the dogs lost his scent when he went into the stream. He's gone, and that's that. We have to assume that he's alive, and that he's going to get home, and that he's going to talk about where he's been."

"But what about the burn-out?" someone asked.

Hamlin responded to the question with a twisted smile. "I suppose a miracle could be happening, and Randy could be lying dead out there somewhere right now. But I don't think we can count on that, can we? We have to assume the worst—that Randy Corliss is alive. And so we are going to close the Academy. Tonight."

Louise Bowen's head came up, and she stared at Hamlin with a dazed look. "Tonight?" she repeated. "But—but what about the—"

Hamlin's eyes fastened on her, their icy blue matching the coldness of his voice. "All the subjects will be destroyed. Please bring them to the lab."

"But—" Louise started to protest.

"Now." The two of them stared at each other for a moment, and then Louise rose and made her way out of the suddenly silent room. When she was gone, Hamlin turned his attention to the others. The four of them had been with the project since the beginning, and no matter what happened, he knew he could count on their loyalty. But what about Louise Bowen? Could he count on hers? Probably not. It was one more thing he would, in the end, have to deal with himself. He sighed and began issuing orders. "We'll pack all the records and as much of the equipment as we can. Paul Randolph is sending three trucks from Boston." A note of sarcasm crept into his voice as he watched his staff exchange doubtful glances. "They'll have to be enough, since they're all we have." He paused for a few seconds, then began speaking again, his voice as bitter as his words. "I told Randolph this was a stupid idea. We should have moved to the desert somewhere or out of the country. Using this place was asking for trouble." His voice rose dangerously. "Ten years of work—ten *years*! And after six months out here it's gone. Gone! It makes me—" Hearing the tone of his own voice, he bit back his words. "Never mind," he said, forcing himself to hold his emotions in check. "Let's get started. It's going to be a long night."

Louise Bowen climbed the stairs slowly. She had made a mistake, and now the price for that mistake was going to have to be paid.

It didn't seem right: the mistake had been so small, and the price was so high.

All she had done, really, was hesitate. She had found Randy's room empty and started for the stairs, intent on telling Hamlin that Randy was gone. But then she had hesitated.

Instead of going downstairs, she had gone up to the attic, certain that she would find Randy there. The attic had been empty, but the ladder, normally folded up against the roof, was down, and the skylight was propped open. She had climbed the ladder and looked out over the roof just in time to see Randy slip, catch himself, and start down the tree.

At that point Louise had hesitated no more. She had hurried downstairs to report what had happened, but it was already too late. Randy was gone, and now the others would have to follow.

Louise opened the door to Adam Rogers's room. Adam, his unruly hair falling over his forehead, was propped up in his bed. He looked at Louise apprehensively. "Did they find Randy?"

"No," Louise admitted. Now came the hardest part. "But since everyone is up, we've decided to have a little party. We're all going down to the dining room, and then we have a surprise for each of you."

Adam's face broke into an eager grin, and he scrambled off the bed. "Shall I get dressed?"

"No," Louise said quietly. "You'll be fine just the way you are."

Then, as Adam scampered down the stairs, Louise continued along the hall, stopping at each room to repeat what she had told Adam to Jerry Preston and Billy Mayhew. And both of them, their eyes glowing with anticipation, had followed Adam down the stairs. Her heart breaking, Louise, too, made her way to the dining room, forced herself to smile at the three boys, then went on through the kitchen and into the lab. George Hamlin turned to look at her.

"Are they ready?"

Louise nodded and tried to swallow the lump that had formed in her throat. "I—I told them we were going to have a party," she said, her voice shaking. "Can I make them some cocoa?"

Hamlin scowled in barely contained fury. "Cocoa? You want to make *cocoa* for them?"

Louise's expression hardened with determination. "They don't have to know what's going to happen," she said. "Can't they at least *think* it's a party? It will only take a minute."

Hamlin glanced at the clock, then back at Louise. Then, realizing it would take as long to argue with her as it would to let her have her way, he shrugged indifferently. "All right," he said. "You have fifteen minutes."

As Louise set about making the cocoa, she used the time to compose herself. Whatever happened, she must not let the children see how upset she was. It would be easier for them if they suspected nothing. Forcing a smile, she carried a tray with the pot and four cups into the dining room.

"Here we are," she said as brightly as she could. The three little boys grinned happily.

"What's the surprise?" Jerry Preston asked.

Louise hesitated only a split second. "It's from Dr. Hamlin. He'll tell you all about it."

She poured the cocoa and passed the cups around. And then, four minutes later, George Hamlin appeared at the door as if on cue.

"Jerry?"

Pleased to be the first selected, Jerry Preston grinned at his friends and got up to follow Hamlin out of the dining room.

Once more Hamlin came back, and then Louise Bowen was alone with Adam.

"How come I'm always last?" the little boy complained.

"Are you?" Louise said, not really listening.

"It must be because I'm youngest," Adam said thoughtfully. "When I'm older, will I get to do things first?"

Louise's eyes brimmed with tears as she looked at the solemn face of the little boy. "I don't know," she whispered.

Adam cocked his head and frowned. "Is something wrong?"

Louise bit her lip and brushed at her eyes, but before she was forced to find a reply to his question, Hamlin appeared once more at the door. "All right, Adam," he said. Then his gaze swung over to Louise. "And you come, too, please, Louise."

Hamlin led them through the kitchen and laboratory to a small room at the rear of the house. Adam stared at the odd machine that stood in the middle of the floor. "Is that the surprise?"

"No," Hamlin explained. "It's for a new test we want to give you. Can you get into it by yourself, or do you need some help?"

"I can do it," Adam replied. The machine looked to him like a huge fat metal cigar with a glass door at one end. "What's it do?"

"It's to test your breathing," Hamlin said. "It only takes a minute, and then you can go back to your friends." He helped Adam climb into the machine. "All set?"

The little boy nodded uncertainly, and Hamlin closed and sealed the heavy glass door. Then he turned to face Louise. "Open the valve," he said.

Louise's eyes widened. "No," she whispered. "No, I can't do it—"

Hamlin's voice hardened. "When the project is a success we will all share the glory. Until then we will all share the responsibility. Turn the valve."

Almost against her will, Louise's hand moved to the

valve that would open the decompression lines. "I can't—"

But Hamlin was inexorable. "You can, and you will!"

Watching Adam Rogers through the glass door, Louise turned the valve. There was a quick *whoosh* as air rushed out of the chamber, and a fleeting look of surprise came into Adam's eyes. Then it was over.

Five minutes later Adam Rogers's body joined the others in the crematory that had long ago been installed in this room, and the fires were started.

Lucy Corliss picked up the telephone on the third ring, expecting to hear either Sally Montgomery or Mark Malone at the other end. Instead, when it was a voice she didn't recognize, her heart skipped a beat.

"Is this Mrs. Corliss?" the voice asked again.

"Yes."

"The mother of Randy Corliss?"

Lucy felt her legs begin to shake and quickly sat down on one of the kitchen chairs. Was this it? Was she finally hearing from the people who had taken Randy?

"Yes," she said into the phone. Then louder. "Yes, it is." She covered the mouthpiece. "Jim? Jim!" As her former husband hurried into the room, she strained to hear what the man on the phone was saying.

"This is Max Birnbaum. I got a diner out on the Langston road."

"Yes?" Lucy asked once more. What was the man talking about?

"Anyway, Mrs. Corliss, about ten minutes ago, a kid comes wandering in, all soaking wet, and asks to call you."

"Randy?" Lucy breathed. "Randy's there?"

"Right here, ma'am."

There was a pause, and then Lucy heard Randy's voice, shaking slightly, but unmistakably Randy's. "Mom?"

"Randy? Oh, Randy, what's happened? Where are you?"

"I ran away, Mom. I got scared, so I ran away. I was afraid I was going to die."

"Die?" Lucy echoed. He ran away from home because he was afraid he was going to die? Where had he ever gotten such an idea? "Oh, Randy, I've been so worried—so frightened."

"Will you come and get me?"

"Yes! Oh, Randy, yes! Where are you? I'll come right now. Right now!"

"I'm at Mr. Birnbaum's diner. It's—I don't know. Mr. Birnbaum can tell you how to get here."

Lucy signaled frantically, but Jim already had a pen and paper ready. She scribbled down the directions, spoke to Randy once more, then hung up.

"He's all right," she cried, the strain of the last week draining from her eyes. "Oh, Jim, he's all right!" She hurled herself into his arms, hugging him tightly. "He's back, Jim. Our son's back." And then, seeing Carl Bronski standing in the doorway, his face sober, she drew away from Jim. "Carl? Is something wrong?"

"I don't know," the policeman said. "I hope not. But it could be a trick."

Her happiness deserting her as fast as it had come, Lucy sank back onto her chair. "A trick?"

"What did he say?"

Lucy repeated Randy's words as closely as she could remember them. When she was done, Bronski nodded. "So he ran away after all," he said softly.

"But he wants to come home now," Lucy replied. "It's not a trick—I know it isn't." She turned to Jim, and her voice suddenly grew shy. "Come with me, Jim. Let's go get him together." She looked from Jim to Bronski, then back at Jim again. "It's over. Oh, God, it's over. I'll get my coat, and my purse, and then—" She ran out of the room, and the two men heard her rummaging in the closet for her coat.

"It isn't over at all," Bronski said softly. Jim Corliss looked puzzled. "It still might all be a trick," Bronski went on. Then, while Jim watched, Bronski picked up the telephone book, flipped through the pages, and finally dialed a number. He spoke briefly, then weighed his options. Finally, he decided to gamble on his instincts. "Okay," he told Jim. "I don't think the call was a fake, so I'll let you two go get Randy by yourselves. I can wait until you get him home to hear his story. But keep something in mind, Jim." His voice dropped so Lucy would not overhear his words. "He said he ran away because he was afraid he was going to die. But he didn't say he ran away from *home*. He—well, he might just as easily have run away from whoever took him."

"*If* anyone took him," Jim countered.

"There's still Adam Rogers, and God knows how many others."

Jim sighed, knowing Bronski was right. "Okay. But don't tell that to Lucy right now, will you? Let her have a few minutes. It's been so rough—"

"I won't," Bronski promised. "Tell you what—I'll stay here and man the phone in case Sally or Malone calls. And see if you can keep Randy from talking until you get him back here, all right? I'd like to hear what he has to say first hand."

As they drove through the night toward Langston and the diner where Randy was waiting, Lucy slowly became aware that Jim was not sharing her happiness. At last she could bear it no longer.

"What's wrong?" she asked. "What did Carl say to you while I was getting my coat?"

"Nothing."

Lucy looked at him carefully. Even in the dim light, she could see the worry in his face.

"Don't lie to me, Jim. Not now. Please?"

Jim forced a smile and patted her hand as it rested on his thigh. "There's nothing, sweetheart. Really."

But Lucy was not convinced. They drove on in silence, and twenty minutes later, in the distance, they saw a flashing neon sign.

"That must be it," Jim said softly.

Lucy leaned anxiously forward in the seat, her excitement growing as they pulled into the parking lot next to the diner. She was out of the car even before Jim had finished parking it, running toward the front door. Then she was inside, and there was Randy, sitting with a heavy set, middle-aged man who wore a greasy chef's hat. Recognizing his mother, Randy leaped off his chair.

"Mom! Oh, Mom, I was so scared!" He was in her arms, burying his face in her breast, the tears he had been holding back all night finally flowing.

"It's all right, sweetheart," Lucy whispered. "I'm here now, and it's all right." She patted him gently and held him, rocking him slowly back and forth until his sobbing subsided. Then, as Jim came through the front door, she whispered to him again. "I have a surprise for you."

He looked up at her through his tears. "A surprise? What?"

"Turn around."

Randy turned around. Lucy expected him to tear himself loose from her arms and run to his father. Instead, she felt him stiffen.

"Dad?" he said uncertainly.

"It's me, son," Jim replied. He held his arms out to Randy, but Randy only shrank closer to his mother.

"Don't make me go back there," he said. "Please don't make me go back there."

As she listened to Randy's words, Lucy felt a chill. So that was why Jim had not shared in her happiness. All along, while he was pretending to help her, pretending to be worried about Randy, it had been a lie. All along, he had been the one. She'd been right. Right from the start, she'd been correct to suspect him. Fury rose in her, and she stood up to face Jim Corliss, but before she could speak, he came over and put his hands on her shoulders.

"Don't say it," he begged. "I know what you're going to say, and I know you'll regret it later. It's not over, Lucy. I don't know any more about it than you, but I know it's not over. That's what Bronski told me in the kitchen. He said we don't know *where* Randy ran away from."

"Randy said he ran away from home because he was afraid he was going to die."

"No, I didn't, Mom," Randy said. His parents looked down at him. "I ran away from the Academy. The one Daddy sent me to."

Jim looked steadily into Lucy's eyes. "I swear I don't know what he's talking about, Lucy."

As they drove home Lucy wondered whether to believe him or not. She wanted to. God, how she wanted to. But could she?

The printer was spewing out the last of the computations Sally had ordered when the knock came at the door opening into the corridor. Mark Malone glanced at Sally, whose eyes filled with sudden fear.

"Who is it?" he called.

"Dr. Malone, is that you?" a woman's uncertain voice answered.

Malone moved toward the door and opened it. "It's me."

The nurse smiled in relief. "Thank God. I saw the light under your door and was afraid someone might have broken in." She glanced into the office, recognizing Sally. "Why, hello, Mrs. Montgomery. Are you looking for Jason?"

"Jason?" Sally asked in surprise.

If the nurse noticed Sally's blankness, she gave no sign. "He's in Dr. Wiseman's office with your husband."

"I—what—?"

But before she could say anything else, Mark Malone held up a warning hand. "Thank you," he said to the nurse. "Mrs. Montgomery and I were just discussing the problem." Then, without waiting for the nurse to reply, he closed the door. He turned to Sally, whose expression of surprise had turned to one of worry.

"Jason and Steve are *here*? But why?"

"I don't know," Malone said. "But I don't think we'd better wait around to find out. Someone's sure to tell Wiseman you're here." He began stuffing his briefcase with the printouts. "Shut that thing off, and let's get out of here."

Sally switched the terminal off, stood up, and began gathering her things together. Malone had already opened the door to the parking lot, waiting for her. And then, as she started across the room, Sally stopped. "I can't go."

Malone stared at her. "Sally, we've got to."

But Sally was shaking her head. "I can't go. Jason's here, and I have to find out why."

"Sally—"

"Mark, you have all the data. Take it and go." She looked up at him imploringly. "Mark, he's my son. If something's wrong, I've got to be with him. Don't you see?"

Malone's mind raced, and he came to a quick decision. "I'll go with you," he said. He closed the outside door and moved toward Sally, who took a step back.

"No. Take those printouts and go back to Lucy's. I'll get there as soon as I can."

"If Wiseman gets his hands on you, you might not get back at all," Malone said, his voice tight. He patted the briefcase. "And right now we need you to lead us through all this. Come on."

Taking her by the arm, he led her out of his office and through the corridors to Arthur Wiseman's waiting room. There, sitting on a chair leafing through a magazine, was Jason. He looked up and grinned.

"Hi, Mom. Hi, Dr. Malone."

Sally dropped to her knees and hugged the boy. "Honey, what are you doing here? Are you all right?"

"I'm okay," Jason said, wriggling free of the embrace.

"Then what are you doing here?"

Jason did his best to explain what had happened. "So Dr. Wiseman told Dad to bring me down, and he took some of my blood, and I think he wants me to go somewhere else."

"Somewhere else?" Sally breathed.

Jason looked guilty. "I put my ear against the door and listened," he admitted. "He wants me to go somewhere for ob—" He frowned, then remembered the word. "Observation."

Sally looked up at Malone. "I don't understand—"

"Don't you? I think maybe I do." He reached down and swung Jason up off the chair. "How'd you like to go for a ride with your mother and me, sport?"

"Where?"

"Over to visit some friends." He started out of the waiting room, speaking to Sally over his shoulder. "Come on."

With an uncertain glance at the closed door leading to Dr. Wiseman's inner office, Sally followed.

Chapter 25

"THEN IT'S SETTLED," Arthur Wiseman said. He stood up, stretched, and came around to lean on the edge of his desk. "CHILD has the best children's diagnostic clinic in the country. If they can't find out what's going on with Jason, nobody can. Now, it seems to me that we might as well keep the boy here tonight and send him to Boston in the morning."

But Steve was still not quite sure. "Can't he stay home tonight? It seems to me—"

"And it seems to *me*," Wiseman interrupted emphatically, "that you have quite enough to worry about tonight."

"But there's nothing really wrong with him."

"So it would appear," Wiseman agreed. "But appearances can be deceiving." His voice dropped slightly. "Don't forget Julie."

At mention of his daughter's name, the last of Steve's resistance crumbled. He rose to his feet and went to the door, opening it. "Jason?"

The waiting room was empty. "Jason?" he repeated, more loudly this time. Then Wiseman was beside him.

"He probably got bored and went to the emergency room," the older man suggested.

But when they got to the emergency room, it, too, was

255

empty, with only the duty nurse sitting placidly at her desk.

"Did Jason Montgomery come through here?" Wiseman asked.

The nurse shook her head. "I haven't seen him. Maybe he's in Dr. Malone's office."

"Malone? Is he here?"

Now the nurse's smile faded into an uncertain frown. "Of course. Didn't you see him? He and Mrs. Montgomery—"

"Mrs. Montgomery!" Wiseman flared. Blood rushed into his face as sudden fury raged through him. "I gave orders that if anybody—*anybody*—saw Mrs. Montgomery, I was to be notified immediately."

The nurse trembled under his wrath. "I—I'm sorry, Dr. Wiseman," she stammered. "I didn't know. No one told me when I came on shift, and—" But she was talking to an empty room. Wiseman, followed by Steve Montgomery, was striding down the hall toward Malone's office.

It, too, was empty.

The two men stood silently for a moment, and it was Steve Montgomery who at last spoke, his voice quiet, defeated. "I don't get it."

"Neither do I," Wiseman replied tightly. "But it seems that Sally must have convinced Malone that there's something to her fantasies."

And suddenly Steve knew exactly where his wife had gone. "Lucy Corliss," he said. "They're with Lucy Corliss." He started through Malone's office. "Come on."

"Wait a minute," Wiseman said. Steve turned to face him. "What are you going to do?"

"I'm going to get my wife and son!"

"And if Sally doesn't want to go with you?"

"She has to—I'm her husband!"

"Think, Steve. She doesn't trust you, and she doesn't trust me. Apparently, she only trusts this Corliss woman, and maybe Mark Malone. Nor does she have to do anything she doesn't want to. You can't barge in there and drag her out, even if you think it's for her own good."

Steve's shoulders slumped; suddenly he felt exhausted—exhausted and frustrated. "But I have to do something," he said at last. "I can't just let her take Jason, let things go. I can't . . ."

"For now," Wiseman said softly, "there isn't anything else you can do. Wait until morning, Steve." He led the unhappy man back to his own office, where he opened his drug cabinet, shook four tablets out of a bottle and into an envelope, and handed it to Steve. "Go home and try to get some sleep. If you need to, take these. And stop worrying—Mark Malone is a good man. He won't let anything happen to either Sally or Jason. Then, tomorrow, if she hasn't come home, we'll take whatever action is necessary to protect her."

Steve Montgomery, his mind whirling with conflicting doubts and emotions, made his way out into the night.

"But *why* did you go with that woman?" Lucy asked for the third time. Once again, Randy repeated his answer.

"She said Daddy sent her. They said Daddy was on a trip, and when he got back, he'd come and visit me."

"But I haven't been anywhere, son," Jim Corliss told the little boy. "Ever since the day you disappeared, I've been right here, trying to help your mother find you."

Randy's expression reflected his uncertainty. He turned to his mother.

"It's true, darling," she assured him. "He hasn't been on a trip at all."

"And I'm not going to die?" Randy asked, his voice quavering.

Lucy gathered him into her arms. "Of course you're not going to die," she whispered. "You're a very healthy little boy, and there's no reason on earth for you to die." And yet, as she recalled the strange story he'd related, she wondered.

Nothing about the Academy sounded right. It didn't sound like a school to her, at least not a school she'd ever heard of.

Had he told the truth?

Once or twice, as Randy had talked, she'd caught a

glimpse of Carl Bronski's face, and she'd seen doubt. She'd seen it in his eyes, in the set of his mouth, in the nearly imperceptible shakings of his head. Bronski, she knew, didn't quite believe what he was hearing.

And then, with the arrival of Sally, Jason, and Malone, her doubts were shunted aside while she explained to Sally what had happened. Finally she turned to Malone. "Could you look at him? We got his clothes off him and bathed him, and he seems to be all right, but after what he told us . . ."

"No problem," Malone replied. He turned to the two boys, who were happily whispering together. "Randy? How'd you like to have me take a look at you?"

"I'm okay," Randy said, but before Randy could protest further, Lucy stepped in.

"You're going with Dr. Malone, and then you're going to bed. It's past midnight."

"And Jason's going with you," Sally added.

Suddenly, with the prospect of his friend sleeping over, Randy grinned. "Okay. Can Jason watch the examination?"

"Sure," Malone agreed. "But it's not going to be very interesting. I'm just going to make sure you're breathing. Come on." He led the boys off to Randy's room, and a sudden silence fell over the group in the living room. It was Sally who finally broke it.

"Lucy, I'm so happy for you—it's like a miracle. But where was he?"

"Better wait for Malone," Bronski said. "No point in going through it all twice. What did you find?"

"A lot," Sally replied. "It's all in Mark's bag, at least as much as we could get. And there's no question that something's going on. Dr. Wiseman lied to me, and CHILD lied to you, Lucy. Those children weren't picked randomly."

"You're sure?" Bronski asked.

"I'm sure," Sally said quietly. "I don't know yet how they were picked for that study or what it's all about, but it's all there. Wait until you see." She opened

Malone's briefcase and began pulling the printouts from its depths.

"My Lord," Lucy whispered as the pile grew. "So much."

"And most of it probably doesn't mean a thing. A lot of this is nothing more than copies of medical records."

"What for?"

"For us to search through. Somewhere there's a common factor that makes all these children special. We're going to have to find it."

"What's all this?" Carl Bronski asked. He was holding several sheets of paper that were stapled together. Sally glanced at them.

"The correlations. On the third page there's a list of names of all the children involved in Group Twenty-one."

Jim Corliss, who was also thumbing through the stacks of documents, looked at Sally curiously. "Group Twenty-one?"

"It's a name Mark and I have been using." Quickly, she explained the system CHILD had used for keeping track of its subjects. "And all of our children are in that group," she finished. "Jason and Randy, and Julie, and Jan Ransom's baby."

Bronski pulled the list of names loose from the rest of the papers. "I'll be back in an hour," he said. Before anyone could protest, he was gone.

A few minutes later Mark Malone rejoined the others.

"Randy's fine," he told them. "Not that I expected anything else. Now tell us what happened to him."

Between them Jim and Lucy did their best to retell Randy's story. "I know it doesn't sound plausible," Lucy finished. "I mean, no one can climb over an electrified fence."

"And no one can spill boiling fudge on himself without getting burned, or drink Lysol without even getting sick," Sally added. "But we *know* those things happened too."

Lucy felt a chill go through her. The happiness she had been clinging to ever since she had heard Randy's voice on the telephone began to slip away. "You mean it could all be true?" she asked, turning to Malone.

"I don't know," Malone replied carefully. "But that's why we're here, isn't it? To see if there's any proof in these records." Sighing heavily, he sat down and picked up the medical charts. "Let's start going through them," he said in a weary tone. "And don't ask what we're looking for, because I don't know. Similarities. Just start reading them and try to spot similarities." He passed them out to Jim and Lucy and Sally.

The room fell silent as the four of them began reading.

The desk sergeant at the Eastbury police station looked up in surprise when Carl Bronski walked in.

"What the hell are you doing here?"

"Got a message to put on the telex."

The sergeant, who was a terrible typist, tossed a few obscenities at Bronski. Only when he was done did Bronski tell him that he planned to do the work himself. The desk sergeant brightened. "In that case, help yourself."

Bronski seated himself at the console, and began typing. He worked steadily for twenty minutes, then transmitted his message. He stood up and stretched.

"What's it all about?" the desk sergeant inquired with an obvious lack of interest.

"Don't know yet," Bronski said. "But if you get an answer to any of those, you call me right away. Okay?" He scribbled Lucy Corliss's number on the desk calendar.

"Those?" the sergeant asked. "I thought you said it was *a* message. Singular."

"It was," Bronski replied. "But I sent it to every police department in the country."

The sergeant stared at him. "Holy shit, Bronski. Do you have any idea what the chief's going to say when he sees the bill?"

Bronski grinned. "Probably just about what you said. But by then, I have a feeling he won't really give a damn. Keep an eye on that machine, will you?" He started out the front door, but the sergeant stopped him.

"Mind telling me what it's all about?"

Bronski paused, scratching his head thoughtfully. "I'm not sure," he said at last, "but I'll tell you one thing. If we get back the replies I think we will, you're going to be part of a bigger case than you ever even dreamed of." Then, leaving the mystified sergeant wondering what had gotten into him, Bronski started back to Lucy Corliss's house. On the way, he bought a lot of coffee in little white plastic containers.

It was going to be a long night, and for some reason coffee in cups never kept him awake. If it was cold, it was even better. He made a mental note to take the lids off all the containers as soon as he got back to Lucy's.

"I don't believe you," Jason whispered in the darkness. He was lying on an air mattress that had been inflated and put on the floor next to Randy's bed, with Randy's bedspread wrapped around him as a makeshift blanket. For an hour he had listened while his friend had bragged about his adventures. But the last thing had been too much.

"Well, it's true," Randy insisted. "I threw the dog against the fence, and he died, and then I climbed the fence, and it didn't hurt at all."

"I bet someone turned it off," Jason argued. "If they didn't, you'd be as dead as the dog."

"Bull!" Randy said as loudly as he dared. If his mother heard them, she'd come in and tell them to go to sleep, and he'd hardly begun telling Jason about all the things that had happened to him. "Besides, one day three of the other guys threw me into the fence. That time I got knocked out, but I still didn't really get hurt. I guess I sort of got used to it."

"Maybe there wasn't much electricity in it," Jason suggested.

"Boy, are you stupid. They either have it all on, or they have it all off. There isn't any partway."

"So you say electricity doesn't hurt you?" There was a note of challenge in Jason's voice.

"That's what I've been telling you, isn't it?"

"Prove it."

"How?"

"Just prove it."

Randy turned on the light by his bed and sat up. He looked around the room, his eyes coming to rest on the radio that sat on one of his bookshelves. "All right, I will." He got out of bed, unplugged the radio, then rummaged in a drawer until he found the Swiss Army knife his father had given him the previous Christmas. Bringing the knife and the radio, he squatted down on the floor next to the air mattress.

"Whatcha gonna do?" Jason asked.

"Watch." Randy opened the knife, and cut the cord off the radio. Then, holding the knife in one hand and the cut end of the cord in the other, he carefully stripped away six inches of insulation. When the wires were bare, he put down the knife and took one of the exposed wires in each hand.

"Plug it in," he said.

Jason stared at him, his eyes wide with a mixture of awe and fear. "No," he whispered. "You'll get hurt."

"I won't either," Randy replied. "Go on—plug it in."

Jason picked up the plug and looked around. There, under Randy's bed table, was a double socket, with only the lamp plugged into it. "Are you going to do it or not?" he heard Randy ask.

Jason tried to make up his mind. Was he being chicken? What if something happened to Randy, as he was sure it would? He remembered Julie, and he remembered his guinea pig. With both of them he'd done something he shouldn't have, and they were both dead.

"I can't," he said finally. "I'll hurt you."

"Then I'll do it myself," Randy announced. He jerked the cord out of Jason's hand and jammed the plug into the empty socket. His eyes fixed on Jason, he took one of the bare wires in his left hand.

"Now watch," he whispered. Slowly, while Jason's eyes followed his movements, he reached out with his right hand for the second bare wire. He smiled as he saw Jason holding his breath.

He grabbed the wire and Jason gasped.

"See?" Randy said, grinning broadly. "Look at that."

"So what?" Jason said, trying to sound as if he wasn't impressed. "Maybe there isn't any current."

"Wanna bet?"

"What do you mean?"

"You try it."

The two boys faced each other, Randy confidently holding the bare ends of the radio cord, his expression clearly telling Jason what he thought of him. Then, as if to confirm it, Randy spoke. "Are you chicken?"

"No."

"Then try it."

Jason's voice suddenly grew belligerent. "Okay, I will. Lemme have the cord."

Silently Randy handed the cord over to Jason. Jason took it gingerly with his right hand, staring fearfully at the gleaming strands of wire. Tentatively, he touched them with his left forefinger.

Nothing.

Encouraged, he closed his left hand around the naked end of one side of the cord, then moved his right hand toward the other bare wire.

As he touched it, a spark jumped, and there was a soft crackling sound.

Reflexively, Jason's hand came away from the wire.

"Chicken," Randy sneered.

Jason barely heard him. He was staring curiously at the cord. It had hurt, but not nearly as much as he had been expecting.

"Try it again," Randy urged.

Once more, Randy touched the bare wire, and this time he was able to overcome his reflexes and feel the electricity surge through him.

It didn't hurt. Not really. At first there was a sort of burning sensation, but that subsided to be replaced by something else.

Something not really unpleasant.

Suddenly confident, he closed his right hand tightly over the live wire.

There was still no pain. As the current flowed through him, there was only a faint tickling sensation. He looked at Randy, and slowly a smile came over his face.

"Hey," he said softly. "That's kind of neat, isn't it?" Then he saw the look of disappointment on Randy's face, and suddenly realized that Randy had been hoping it wouldn't work for him, that he'd get a shock. "Are you mad?" he asked.

Randy stared at him for a moment. "I don't know," he said at last. Then he licked his lips. "Why do you suppose it doesn't hurt us?"

"Lots of things don't hurt me," Jason suddenly blurted. "That's why I had to go to the hospital tonight."

Randy cocked his head. "What kind of things?"

Jason's eyes fell on the knife, and he suddenly remembered the day of his sister's funeral, when he'd been playing outside. "I'll show you," he whispered. He picked up the knife and stared at the blade for a second. Then, closing his eyes tightly, he slashed the blade across his hand.

This time it was Randy who gasped.

Jason opened his eyes and stared at his hand. Blood was welling up from a deep cut on his palm.

"It's going to get all over the floor," Randy said.

"No, it won't," Jason told him. "See? It's not bleeding anymore. Got a Kleenex or something?"

Randy rummaged in a drawer and found a rumpled handkerchief. While he watched, Jason sopped up the blood on his hand. The wound had, indeed, stopped bleeding.

"It's pretty bad," Randy whispered.

"Just wait."

As the two boys watched, the gash in Jason's hand began to heal. Three minutes later, even the skin had mended, and there was not even so much as a trace of a scar to mark where the wound had been.

Now it was Randy who stared at Jason with wonder. "Did it hurt?"

Jason shrugged with studied indifference, pleased that he'd outdone his friend. "Just for a second."

"I'm gonna try it," Randy said, picking up the knife. Without giving himself time to change his mind or even think about it, Randy plunged the knife deep into the palm of his hand. He flinched slightly, then stared at the knife. Blood welled up around it.

"Pull it out," Jason whispered.

Jerking hard, Randy wrenched the blade loose, then began mopping at the wound with the already-bloody handkerchief. When the bleeding stopped, the two boys watched.

As with Jason, Randy's wound disappeared within a few minutes.

"Wow," Randy breathed. Then he grinned at Jason. "Know what?" he asked.

"What?"

"We can do anything we want to now, Jason. We can do anything we want to, because nothing can hurt us."

Chapter 26

A S THE FIRST LIGHT OF DAWN glowed dimly through the east windows of his office, Paul Randolph massaged his temples in a vain effort to ease the tensions that had built up through the long night. The two other men in his office were gazing at him, and he had the feeling he was being judged. Overcoming his exhaustion with an effort of sheer will, he attempted to regain control of the meeting.

"Very well, then. The situation as I see it is this: We have the records of the project—the physical records—locked in the vault, ready to go to Washington this afternoon. The computer banks have been emptied of all data pertaining to the project, and the house has been vacated. What about the staff?"

George Hamlin flicked an imaginary speck from his left pantleg. "I can personally guarantee the security of the project as far as my people are concerned. They've all been with me for years, and each of them has a compelling interest in seeing it through."

"And the boy?" the third man in the room asked. He was a middle-aged man whose hard-muscled body denied the appearance of aging that his close-cropped gray hair suggested. When he had first entered the room an hour earlier, Hamlin had known who he was even before

Paul Randolph introduced them. The man's military bearing had given him away.

"Well?" Lieutenant General Scott Carmody prodded.

"Ah. That *is* the problem, isn't it?" Hamlin replied. A wintry smile molded his lips into an expression that Randolph had long ago come to associate with Hamlin's less humane ideas. This morning was no exception. "It seems to me that that is the very area in which we need your help. What I believe some of your people sometimes call 'wet activities'?"

"Let's call a spade a spade," the general dryly translated. "You mean you want us to kill him."

Paul Randolph rose from his chair. "Now just wait a minute, George. There are some things that I cannot allow this Institute to be a party to."

When he replied, Hamlin's voice clearly conveyed the contempt he felt for Randolph. "Are there? It seems to me that this is rather an inappropriate time for you to begin setting moral standards for yourself. Or for any of the rest of us, for that matter." Randolph tried to interrupt, but Hamlin pressed on. "Besides, I see no moral dilemma in having some of the general's personnel pacify Randy Corliss."

"You mean kill him," Randolph corrected.

"As you will. Kill him. Remove him. Whatever. The point is that as far as we know, he's alive, and if he's alive, he's undoubtedly talking. That makes him, and anyone he's talked to, a threat to all of us."

"But to kill him?"

"In all likelihood he's going to die anyway, Paul. All the others have."

The general frowned. "All of them? I thought you were on the verge of success."

"I am," Hamlin told him. "Indeed, at the point that one of the subjects survives to maturity, I *will* have succeeded, and we're not that far away. In fact, I think Randy Corliss just might be our first success, but unfortunately, circumstances don't allow us to continue working with him. He's become a threat."

"George, he's only a little boy—" Randolph broke in.

"*God* makes little boys, Paul. *I* made Randy Corliss." He leaned forward, gazing intently at Randolph. "You've never really grasped the nature of the project, have you, Paul?"

"You know that isn't true, George."

"Isn't it? You keep referring to my subjects as little boys. But Randy Corliss and the others are not boys at all. They are a new species, which I created through genetic engineering. Someday they will serve a specific function for our country"—he nodded toward General Carmody—"but we must never make the mistake of regarding them as human beings. Granted, they bear a great resemblance to our species, but genetically they are different. So I am not talking about murder, Paul. I am simply talking about plugging what could become a disastrous security leak." He turned his attention fully on the general now. "As far as the world knows, what we are doing is not yet possible. That gives us an advantage. It means that our country will soon be able to match biological form to technological function. We will be able to create the people we need. Except that they won't be people. They will be living robots, designed with specific purposes in mind. It seems to me that we have no choice but to do whatever is necessary to protect the integrity of the project."

General Carmody nodded and turned to Randolph. "The Department has a very large investment in this project, Paul. I—*we* expect you to do everything you can to protect that investment. Is that clear?"

"Very." Paul Randolph sighed. "Do whatever you think is best." In his heart, Randolph knew that he had just agreed to the murder of a nine-year-old boy.

"I don't get it," Mark Malone said. "None of this makes any sense at all." He stood up, stretched, then poured himself yet one more cup of steaming hot coffee. Taking a careful sip, he glared malevolently as Carl Bronski gulped down half a cup of his remaining supply of cold brew. "Did you know that cold coffee causes cancer?" he taunted.

Carl ignored the bait. "What doesn't make sense? It seems to me it's all coming together."

"It is," Malone agreed. "And that's what I don't get. According to Sally, CHILD chose all these kids for their survey practically on the day they were born. They assigned the numbers, and the numbers show they assigned the children to the groups right away. And with three of the groups, there's nothing special. But look at Group Twenty-one."

Jim Corliss repeated what all of them had known for hours. "All the girls are dead. Every one of them, and all before the age of eleven months, and all of SIDS."

"But nobody knows anything about SIDS," Malone said doggedly. "It was only a year or so ago that the University of Maryland correlated hormone T-3 with the syndrome, and they still aren't sure whether the high level of T-3 is a cause or effect. So how did CHILD know those girls were going to die?"

"Maybe they didn't," Lucy offered. "Maybe it's coincidence."

"It's no coincidence," Sally told her. "It can't be. The odds are astronomical. And it's not just the girls," she reminded them. "It's some of the boys too. Particularly in the first few years. And then the boys stopped dying, but the girls didn't."

"And everywhere you look," Lucy replied, "it seems to come back to Dr. Wiseman. He was the obstetrician for all forty-six children in Group Twenty-one."

"About four a year," Sally mused. "I wonder how many babies he actually delivers each year?"

"It was twenty-seven last year," Malone replied. His voice suddenly turned grim. "Twenty-seven new little patients for me, and now this."

A silence fell over the group as, once more, they tried to figure out what it could all mean. Then, as Sally started to speak, the intrusive sound of the telephone interrupted her. Jim Corliss picked it up, spoke for a moment, then handed it to Bronski.

"Bill? Is that you?" Bronski asked.

"Yeah," the desk sergeant said. "Where the hell did you get that list of names?"

"Never mind. Have we gotten any replies?"

"From all over the place," the sergeant replied. "And it's weird. How many names were on that list?"

"Twelve."

"Twelve, huh? Well, eight of 'em are listed as runaways. From towns all over the country."

"Runaways?" Carl echoed. Lucy Corliss unconsciously moved closer to her ex-husband.

"That's right. All those cases are still open, and none of them have turned up in the morgues."

"Give me the names and the dates they disappeared." As the desk sergeant droned out the list, Bronski scribbled names and numbers on a piece of paper. "Got it," he said, handing the paper to Malone, who immediately started annotating the correlation sheets. "Thanks a lot, Bill, and if any—"

"Carl, there's more," the sergeant interrupted. The timbre of his voice had changed. Bronski felt his body tense.

"What is it?"

"The rest of them are dead."

"Dead?" Bronski repeated. "With police reports on them? You mean homicides?"

"Apparently not. I told you it was weird. It seems like your other four boys were found dead in public areas."

Bronski suddenly knew what was coming. "Tell me about them," he said softly.

"I got reports from all over the place—Washington State, Kansas, Texas, and Florida. The bodies were found in parks, playgrounds, vacant lots, that sort of thing."

"And?"

"And nothing. No marks on them, no signs of foul play or violence. Nothing. The coroners ruled the same in all the cases."

" 'Unknown natural causes?' "

There was a short silence, then he said, "What's going

on, Carl? If you know something about all this, you better let the rest of us in on it."

"Just give me the names and dates, Bill," Bronski said, ignoring the other man's question. It would take far too long to begin explaining it now.

Once again, the desk sergeant began reciting names, places, and numbers.

At last Bronski hung up the phone and faced the others. "More pieces," he said. "It seems Randy isn't the only runaway in Group Twenty-one, and we've got some more deaths."

Sally stared bleakly at the list of names the computer had generated. Of the original forty-six, all the girls—twenty-two—were dead. Of the twenty-four boys, the nine oldest, including Randy Corliss, were listed as runaways, and four were dead. The name of the oldest boy on the list who had neither died nor run away was Jason Montgomery. As for the other eleven boys, ranging in age from six months to seven years, nothing was known.

"But that doesn't mean they're okay," Bronski said softly. "I sent out only the names of the oldest ones, the ones who could have disappeared and been considered runaways. If a kid under seven turns up missing, we usually assume foul play."

"Maybe now you'll raise the age limit," Lucy said. Then, seeing the hurt in Bronski's eyes, she quickly apologized: "Carl, I shouldn't have said that. You've been wonderful. I had no right to—well, I'm sorry."

"It's all right, Lucy. And I'm not really blameless, am I? Maybe if I'd believed you right away—"

"Never mind," Jim Corliss broke in. "None of us needs to say any of those things to each other. What we need is a plan. What do we do next?"

Instinctively, they all turned to Bronski.

"It's daylight," he said. "I think we'd better get Randy up and see if he can show us where he was."

"You mean go back there?" Lucy cried. "No! You can't make him do that."

Jim took her hand and held it tightly. "Lucy, it'll be

all right. Carl and I will be with him. And we won't do anything."

"We have to know where he was, Lucy," Bronski added.

Lucy opened her mouth as if to protest further, then shut it again, nodding her head. "All right," she murmured.

She went to the bedroom where the two boys were still sleeping, and, being careful not to disturb Jason, woke Randy. He looked at her sleepily, but let himself be led to the living room. Bronski explained to the little boy what he wanted him to do. "Do you think you can?" he asked.

Randy looked uncertain. "I don't know," he finally admitted. "I was scared, and it was dark, and I don't know how far—" He broke off, as if sensing that perhaps no one really believed the story he had told last night.

"I can find it," he said. "I know I can." He disappeared into his room and dressed, then returned to the living room. Five minutes later, together with his father and Sergeant Bronski, he was on his way back to the Academy.

Sally Montgomery, Lucy Corliss, and Mark Malone silently went back to the stack of reports.

Two hours later Mark Malone began to recognize the answer that was buried deep within the records.

"Damn," he said softly. "God damn it to hell."

Chapter 27

THE CAR MOVED SLOWLY AHEAD, and Randy Corliss, sitting between his father and Sergeant Bronski, fidgeted nervously. It seemed to him that they were wasting time. The bridge, he was sure, was still way ahead. He twisted in his seat and peered out the back window. He could still see the diner.

"It's farther up the road," he said. "I couldn't see the diner at all, so it has to be way up ahead."

"Things seem farther at night," Bronski told him. "Besides, you weren't on the road—you were in the woods, so you wouldn't have been able to see as far."

"I just don't think it was this close."

They came to a bend in the road, and a hundred yards farther was a bridge.

"Is that it?" Jim Corliss asked his son.

As Bronski pulled off the road a few feet from the bridge, Randy looked at it uncertainly. "I guess so," he said at last. The three of them got out of the car, and Randy scrambled down the bank to stand beside the stream. Now he was sure. "This is it," he called up to his father.

"Okay. There's a path up here," Jim replied. Randy climbed back up.

"We have to go downstream," he announced.

"How far?" Bronski asked.

"I don't know," Randy replied. He started down the path, with his father and the policeman following. Every few minutes he glanced down at the stream. This morning, in the bright sunlight, everything looked different. Last night the stream had been swift and deep, and he could remember its roaring in his ears. But now its sound was a murmur, and he could see that it was only a couple of feet deep.

Maybe it was the wrong stream, and the bridge had been the wrong bridge. What if he was lost and couldn't find the Academy? Would they think he'd lied about everything?

As he kept walking, he became increasingly nervous. The two men with him exchanged a glance.

"It seems like an awfully long way," Bronski finally commented.

Randy said nothing. Had it really been this far? He tried to remember how far he'd waded, but there were no landmarks, nothing he recognized.

And then he heard the waterfall. He broke into a run, and the two men had to jog to keep up with him.

"This is it," Randy yelled. "This is the waterfall. See?" He pointed excitedly at the cascading stream and the large rock looming above it. "That's the rock I sat on after I climbed the waterfall." He began recounting the struggle he'd had fighting the current, too afraid of the dogs to leave the stream. "Come on," he finished. "There should be a fork just a little way farther." He dashed ahead, and disappeared around a bend in the trail.

"What do you think?" Jim asked.

Bronski shrugged. "I don't know. He found the bridge, and he found the waterfall." Then they heard Randy's voice floating back to them.

"I found it! I found the fork! We're almost there."

Jim and Carl caught up with Randy at the point where the stream split into two smaller channels. "Which fork do we take?" Jim asked.

"This one," Randy said, no longer uncertain. "Come on!"

The path disappeared, and the three of them began pushing their way through a tangle of laurel, keeping as close to the brook as they could.

"It'd be easier to wade," Randy suggested.

"How much farther is it?"

"I don't know. Not much. I could still hear the dogs barking when I got to the fork."

And then they were there. The brook suddenly disappeared into a metal culvert, the end of which was covered by a heavy wire-mesh grating. A few yards beyond the opening of the culvert they could see a high fence. Randy stared silently at the fence for a moment, then turned to look up at his father. "We're here," he said. "That's the fence around the Academy."

Bronski moved forward. The fence stretched off in either direction, and beyond it he could see nothing but more woods. "Where's the house?" he asked.

"You can't see it from here," Randy told him. "It's off that way." He started walking along the fence, but the sound of Sergeant Bronski's voice stopped him.

"Randy? Didn't you say there was a dead dog right about here?"

Randy nodded. "I threw it against the fence, and it got electrocuted."

"Where is it?"

Randy stared through the fence, trying to remember exactly where he'd climbed it.

He couldn't.

He looked for the body of the dog.

It wasn't there.

Tentatively, he reached out and touched the fence.

There was no current.

"But it was here," he said. "I know it was here." He looked up at the two men, sudden tears brimming in his eyes. "I'm not lying," he said. "The gate's off that way, and from there you can see the house." Determinedly, he began walking along the fence, with the two men once again trailing after him.

They came to the gate, and Randy stood still, staring through the bars. In the distance he could see the massive brick house, its barred windows clearly visible in the bright morning sunlight. Flanking him on either side were his father and Sergeant Bronski. Bronski's eyes swept the house and lawn and came to rest on the rusted chain that was wrapped around the gates, holding them securely together.

"Doesn't look like there's anyone here."

"But there's *got* to be," Randy wailed. And yet, as he looked at the house, he knew the policeman was right. There was just something about it, a stillness, that made him sure that everyone had gone. "We could climb the fence and go in," he suggested.

"No, we can't," Carl Bronski said. "All we can do is try to get a search warrant. Come on."

Randy started to protest. "But—"

"No buts," Jim Corliss told his son. "Sergeant Bronski's right."

"But this is where I was!" Randy insisted. "This is where I ran away from last night!"

Bronski knelt down so his eyes were level with Randy's. "And we're going to find out all about it, Randy. But we're going to do it legally. Do you understand? Otherwise the people who kidnaped you will get off scot-free. So we're going to find out who owns this place, and we're going to get a search warrant. Then we can go in, and you can show us all of it. All right?"

Randy scowled. "I don't see why we can't just go in. If there's nobody here—"

"Because that's the way it is," Jim said, the severity of his voice leaving no more room for argument.

They turned away from the gate and started along the driveway that eventually led them back to the main road, where a second chain blocked the drive against intruding traffic. Next to one of the support posts for the chain stood a mailbox with a number painted on its side. Bronski jotted down the number.

Half an hour later, they were back at Bronski's car. It was nearly nine A.M., and they had been gone from Lucy's for nearly two hours.

○   ○   ○

Steve Montgomery, with Arthur Wiseman sitting next to him, pulled up in front of Lucy Corliss's house. He switched the ignition off and set the emergency brake. "There's Sally's car," he said as he opened the door.

"And Mark Malone's," Wiseman added. "Has he been here all night too?"

Having no answer for the question, and sensing that no answer was required, Steve got out of the car and, with Wiseman following, mounted the steps to Lucy's small front porch. He rang the bell, waited a moment, then rang it again. After a moment, the door opened a crack, and a woman's face looked out suspiciously.

"Mrs. Corliss?" Steve asked.

Lucy frowned, her eyes darting between the two men. The older one looked familiar. And then she recognized him. But before she could speak, the younger one was talking again.

"I'm Steve Montgomery. Sally's husband."

The door shut in his face.

On the other side of the closed door, Lucy hesitated, then hurried into the living room where Sally and Mark were still poring over the computer printouts. "Sally, it's your husband," she said in an urgent whisper. "And he's got Wiseman with him."

Sally's tired eyes took on the look of a hunted animal, and instinctively she turned to Mark Malone for help. Malone was already rising to his feet.

"We might as well let them in," he said. Then, as Sally shrank into the chair on which he had been sitting, he tried to reassure her. "It'll be all right. I'm here, and Lucy's here, and Jim and Carl should be back any minute." He moved past Lucy, stepped into the hall, and opened the door.

The two men on the porch looked at him. It was Steve who finally spoke. "Is Sally here?"

"Yes, she is." Malone stepped back to let the two men enter, and Steve moved directly to the living room.

"Sally—" He fell silent, staring at his wife. Her face was pale and her hair, oily and disheveled, hung limply

277

over her shoulders. "My God," Steve whispered. "Sally, what's happened to you?"

"She's exhausted," Malone said. "We're all exhausted. You would be, too, if you'd been up all night."

But Steve Montgomery wasn't listening to him. He had gone to his wife and knelt by her chair, slipping his arms around her to draw her close.

"Sally . . . oh, Sally, it's going to be all right, baby," he whispered. "We've found a place for you. You'll like it there. You can rest, and relax, and stop worrying about everything. Dr. Wiseman found it for us, and he thinks it'll only take a few weeks—"

Sally shook herself free, the exhaustion in her eyes suddenly replaced with fury. When she spoke, her voice was low and trembling, but still the force of her words shook her husband.

"Dr. Wiseman found a place? Oh, God, I'll *bet* he did. A nice little place, is it? Pretty? Good service? And lots of nice doctors who will spend all their time making me well again? But I'm not sick, Steve."

"Sally—" Steve moved toward her, but she backed away.

"Don't touch me," she whispered. It was all catching up with her now, all the anger, all the hurt, all the boiling emotions she'd been holding in check for so long. "Don't put your arms around me and tell me you love me and that you'll make me well again." Her voice began to rise as her self-control slipped away. "Don't tell me that, Steve. It's a lie. *It's all lies.* Everything that man has told you is a lie!" She wheeled around to face Wiseman, her expression a mask of fury. "What have you done to us?" she shrieked. "What have you done to us and to our children?" She hurled herself on Wiseman, her fists pounding against his chest. "How many of us were there? Five? Ten? A hundred? How many dead babies? How many little boys gone? How many? And why? God damn you! *Why?*"

The last of her energy drained, she collapsed to the floor, her screams giving way to sobs. Lucy Corliss crouched beside her, stroking her gently, but her eyes, as they fastened on Wiseman, reflected a cold fury that seemed to cut through to the old doctor's soul.

"I don't understand—" he began.

"Don't tell us that." Lucy cut him off. "Sally isn't crazy. None of us is. We're tired because we've been up all night trying to figure out what you've been doing. But we're not crazy."

"I?" Wiseman asked, his voice hollow. "What *I've* been doing?"

Before anyone could say anything else, Jason came into the room, rubbing sleep from his eyes. At the sight of his father and Dr. Wiseman, he hesitated a moment, his eyes confused, then made up his mind. "I don't *want* to go to that hospital," he cried. "There's nothing wrong with me, and I don't want to go!" He ran to his mother.

Though she was still huddled on the floor, Sally gathered him into her protective arms. She peered up at Lucy with frightened eyes. "Don't let them take us away, Lucy. Please don't let them take us away."

As he watched his wife and son on the floor Steve felt himself begin to come apart. He sank into a chair, his face pale, his hands working helplessly. There before him were the two people he loved best in the world, and they were terrified of him. His eyes searched the room, looking for help, and finally came to rest on Mark Malone.

"I—I—" His voice faltered, then fell silent.

Arthur Wiseman's eyes, too, turned to Malone. "What's going on, Mark?"

Malone coldly eyed the older doctor. "You don't know?"

Wiseman lowered himself uncertainly into a chair. "All I know is that for ten days I've watched one of my favorite patients change from a normal, level-headed, charming woman, into—" He gestured toward Sally, was silent for a moment, then continued. "And now she accuses me of things I can't even imagine. Dead babies? Missing boys? What is she talking about?"

Malone walked to the coffee table and picked up a sheaf of papers. "Maybe you'd better take a look at these." He offered them to Wiseman, who made no move to take them.

"What are they?"

"Records. Correlations. Data that Sally took out of the computer last night."

Wiseman frowned. "The hospital computer? She had no right—"

"I authorized it," Malone told him. "I'm a doctor, remember? Not that I give a damn right now who had the right to do what. The only thing that matters is what's here and what it means."

When Wiseman still hesitated, Malone's voice grew cold. "We're not crazy, Arthur. And it's not just us. It's Jim Corliss and Carl Bronski too. And unless you have an explanation for what's here, I don't mind telling you that I'll see to it you're barred from practice, stripped of your license, and put in prison for the rest of your life. I don't know if I can prove it, Arthur, but all this looks to me like the closest thing I've ever seen to mass murder. I don't know how you did it, and I don't know why, but I know it's all here."

His hands trembling, Wiseman reached out to take the sheaf of papers from Malone. When he spoke, his voice shook. "I don't know what you're talking about, Mark. Believe me, I don't."

"Then you'd better read those," Malone replied. "If you have any questions, I'll try to help you out. Sally's taken me through them so many times, I think I know the correlations by heart. And frankly, I don't think she's in any condition to start over with you."

Steeling himself, Wiseman began reading the sheets of correlations.

Across the street and a quarter of a block down, two men sat in a gray van. While one of them stared through a pair of binoculars and read off license plate numbers, the other took notes. When he had dictated the letters and numbers of all five cars that were parked in Lucy's driveway and on the street in front of her house, Ernie Morantz put the glasses away. "I don't like it."

"What's not to like?" Victor Kaplan asked in reply. "It's just another job."

"Taking out a nine-year-old kid isn't what I call just another job," Morantz said. His face settled into what Kaplan had long ago come to think of as "the mule face," as in "as stubborn as a . . ."

"Orders are orders," he reminded his partner.

"And I've never disobeyed one yet," Morantz snapped. "But terrorists and traitors are one thing. Even picking up illegal aliens. But what's this kid done? They don't think he's going to leave a bomb at Logan Airport, do they? Or is that the new thing? Foreign governments subverting the schoolboys of America? Come off it."

"It doesn't matter," Kaplan insisted. "We've got our orders."

"But nobody told us we'd be walking into a mob scene. And here come some more." The two men fell silent as they watched a sixth car pull up in front of Lucy Corliss's house. Two men and a boy got out, and Morantz, who was once more using his field glasses, spoke quietly. "That's the kid. Shit, he can't be more than four-and-a-half feet tall, and he looks just like any other kid. Wonder who the two other guys are?"

Kaplan took the glasses and watched until all three had disappeared into the house. "One's a cop," he said softly. "The one who was on the right. The other's probably the kid's dad."

"Yeah," Morantz grunted. He started the engine, slipped the van into gear, and cruised slowly past the house.

"Where we going?" Kaplan asked.

"Coffee. And you're going to call Carmody and tell him this job isn't going to be all that easy. It's one thing to bust in on a woman, all by herself, and grab her kid. I'm not saying I like it, mind you, but at least it's possible. This is different, and I want to know what Carmody wants. You see a Ho-Jo on the way in?"

A few minutes later they slid into an orange Naugahyde booth, ordered, then Morantz adjourned to the men's room while Kaplan made the phone call.

When he returned to the table, Morantz found himself still alone, so he passed the time fiddling with a puzzle that had apparently been left by the management for just such an occasion. At the next table a little boy, no more than six years old, had solved the puzzle and was gleefully explaining it to his sister. Morantz strained to hear what the boy was saying, but by the time Kaplan returned, he still had gotten nowhere. "Well?"

The look on Kaplan's face told most of the story. "It's getting worse. Carmody's running a check on all the cars to find out who's in the house. Then he'll make a decision about beefing up the team. We're to call him back in fifteen minutes, and he'll let us know what's happening."

"Shit," Morantz said softly. He picked up the puzzle, which involved some pegs and a triangular board. "Try this," he said, shoving it across to Kaplan. Kaplan stared at the gadget for a minute, studied the directions, then tentatively began jumping the pegs over each other, removing each one he jumped. When he was done, there were three pegs left, and no legitimate way of getting to them.

"So?" he said.

"So the kid in the next booth just solved it. And I bet that kid we're supposed to grab could do it too."

Kaplan frowned. "I don't get it, Ernie. What's this puzzle got to do with anything?"

Ernie Morantz stretched, then slouched deep into the booth. "I don't know," he said. "But it just seems to me that there's something wrong. Kids these days are brighter than adults. They can do things and understand things that don't make any sense to us at all. So what's this Corliss kid done that's so horrible? Hell, I bet Carmody himself doesn't know. But I ask you, does it make any sense that you and I, who were trained to believe in apple pie, motherhood, and the U.S. of A. are now being asked to grab a little American kid and take him out and drown him? I understand commies, and I understand traitors, and I hate them. But I don't hate kids. I don't understand them, but I don't hate them. In fact, I love them. And I'll tell you, Vic—it rubs me the wrong way to be told to go out and kill a little kid."

"So what does all that mean?" Kaplan asked.

There was a long silence. Ernie Morantz shrugged his shoulders. "I don't know, Vic. I just don't know. I guess it means I'll wait and see what Carmody wants. But I can tell you, if he wants us to go into that house like a SWAT team after the S.L.A., he's got the wrong man. I'm not sure I could do it."

"But you're not sure you couldn't either."

Morantz drained his coffee, then slid out of the booth. As he tossed some change on the table, he shook his head sadly. "No, I guess I'm not. Come on, let's go call Carmody and get the bad news."

The news, when they got it three minutes later, was as bad as either of them had expected.

Chapter 28

Arthur Wiseman, his complexion drained of all color and his hands trembling, silently squared the stack of documents and placed them neatly in the center of Lucy Corliss's coffee table. Finally his eyes began wandering over the room, pausing for a moment on each of the faces that were watching him, pausing almost as if he were seeking refuge, then, seeing none, moving on. At last his eyes came to rest on Sally Montgomery.

"There is no question about these statistics? No possibility of a mistake?"

"None worth talking about," Sally said, composed now.

"I suppose not," Wiseman said almost to himself. "I can remember too much of it all—"

"Then you *did* know," Sally flared.

Wiseman stared at her with eyes that had suddenly aged. "No," he said softly. "I should have, but I didn't. You have to understand—all this happened over so many years. What I remember are incidents. The babies—the ones that died. We don't forget them, you know. We learn to deal with the things that happen to children, we even learn to accept their deaths. But we don't forget." His eyes moved away from Sally, moved to the coffee table where, on the top of the stack, the list of children in Group Twenty-one lay. Once again he scanned the names. "They're my children. All of them."

Sally bit her lip. "Julie wasn't your child. She was my child. Mine and Steve's."

"I didn't mean it that way—"

"What are they doing?" Sally demanded. "What is CHILD doing?"

"Sally, I've known you all your life, and you've known me. Can you really believe that I would know about some sort of conspiracy and remain silent?"

But Sally was implacable. "Then why does it all come back to you?"

Wiseman shook his head helplessly. "I don't know. I haven't the slightest idea." He picked up the medical records and began going through them. Suddenly, he looked up. "What about the chromosome analyses?"

Malone frowned. "What about them?"

Wiseman handed him the medical records of the children in Group Twenty-one, his expression uncertain. "I order a chromosome analysis on a child only if there's reason to suspect a problem. And even then, I have to rely on the specialists to identify a defect in a particular chromosome and analyze it."

"So?"

"So, the records of all those children in Group Twenty-one indicate that a complete chromosome analysis was done, but there were no indications of any abnormalities."

Malone's eyes fixed on the older man. "Then who ordered the analyses? And why?"

"I'm sure I don't know—"

"Don't you?" Malone challenged, his voice icy. He turned to the others. "It's the obstetrician who orders tests like these. They're usually done prenatally, when there's a suspected problem with the fetus. But with all these children, there were no apparent problems, none whatsoever. Until they were born, and began dying." He turned back to Wiseman. "So my question, Arthur, is, who ordered these tests, and what were they looking for?" Without waiting for the old doctor to answer,

Malone plunged on. "I think the first part of the answer is clear: You were the obstetrician for all of these children. But what were you looking for? Is there something genetically abnormal about these children that *isn't* reflected in the chromosome analyses?"

Wiseman seemed to sink deeper into his chair, and the records he was holding fluttered to the floor. "My God," he breathed. "What you're suggesting is monstrous."

"What's happened is monstrous," Malone countered, his voice suddenly level. "I'm sure you never expected anyone to find it. Not you, or anyone at CHILD. But Sally found it, Arthur. And if she could find it, others can too. So it's going to come out. We're going to find out what you did to these children's genes."

"No!" Wiseman protested. "I did *nothing* to these children. Whatever's wrong with them, it had to start with their parents. It had to!" But before he could go on, the front door suddenly flew open and Randy Corliss burst into the room, followed by his father and Carl Bronski.

"I found it," Randy crowed. "I found the house!"

Lucy's eyes went immediately to Jim, who nodded. "We stopped at City Hall," he said. "The place is owned by Paul Randolph."

Wiseman frowned. "Paul Randolph is executive director of CHILD."

"Right," Bronski said. He looked curiously at Wiseman and Steve Montgomery, guessing immediately who they were. "What are you two doing here?"

Malone explained to them what had happened. "We still don't know how it was done," he finished. "For that matter, we don't even know exactly *what* was done to these children's genes. But you can bet that somehow they've been altered."

"Can we find out what they did?" Sally asked.

Malone shrugged. "It depends on you. If the information's in the computer, you're the only one of us that can fish it out."

Sally started to speak, but Bronski took over. "Then that'll be your job, Sally. I want you to go to the hospital with Mark and start working with that computer."

His eyes shifted over to Wiseman. "And I want you to go with them, is that clear?"

Wiseman, his face haggard, made a gesture with a trembling hand. "Of course," he mumbled. "Anything . . ."

"The house," Bronski went on. "I can get a search warrant for it by telephone. We think it's empty, but I want to go in. And I'd like to take Randy with me."

"No!"

"Lucy, there's no other way," Jim said.

"There must be, or you wouldn't have come back here," Lucy snapped. "You'd have just gone ahead and done whatever you thought you had to do."

Now Carl Bronski spoke again. "Lucy, that isn't it at all. We came back here because Jim wouldn't agree to taking Randy in unless you agreed too."

"Which I don't," Lucy said.

Jim Corliss sat on the sofa and drew Lucy down next to him. "Honey, you've got to—" Seeing the stony look in her eyes, he broke off and started over. "Of course, you don't *have* to let Randy go. But without Randy, there's not much point in Carl even going in there. As far as we could tell from outside, the place is empty. Carl's excuse for getting a search warrant is that he needs to verify Randy's story of what's inside that house, and that means Randy has to show him."

Lucy, too exhausted to think it all through, turned to Sally for advice.

"If it was Jason, I'd feel the same way you feel," Sally told her. "But still, if CHILD was using that house for something—"

Lucy took a deep breath and stood up. "You're right," she said. "Of course you're right. We have to know what was going on out there." As Carl Bronski picked up the phone, dialed, then began speaking quietly to the judge at the other end, Lucy turned back to Jim. "You'll be careful?"

"Lucy, you have to believe that I'd never let anything happen to Randy."

"Something's already happened to him," Lucy whispered. She reached out and touched his arm. "But it's not just Randy," she said, her voice suddenly shy. "You be careful, too. I—well, I feel as though I just found you again, and I don't think I could stand to lose you now. I'm going to need help from now on, Jim."

"And you're going to have it," Jim promised.

The small group began to break up. Mark Malone packed the computer printouts into his briefcase, then led an ashen-faced and silent Arthur Wiseman out of the house.

Sally and Steve Montgomery left to take Jason to his grandmother's, where he would stay while his parents went to the hospital to work with Mark Malone.

Carl Bronski, with Jim and Randy Corliss, prepared to return to Paul Randolph's estate.

And then, as they were about to depart, Lucy suddenly stood up. "I'm going with you," she told Jim. "I can't stay here by myself—I'll go crazy."

Jim started to protest, but Lucy touched his arm. "I have to go, Jim," she said softly. "I have to be with Randy, and with you."

Their eyes met, and a gentle smile came over Jim's face. "Wherever I go, you go?" he asked.

Lucy hesitated only a moment, then nodded. "From now on."

The Montgomerys drove slowly through the streets of Eastbury, Steve at the wheel, Sally sitting silently next to him, Jason in the back. Jason, too, was uncharacteristically silent, but his parents were too deeply involved in their own thoughts to notice.

It was Steve who finally broke the silence. "I'm sorry, honey."

Her reverie disturbed, Sally glanced over at him. "Did you say something?"

"I was trying to apologize," Steve said. "I thought— well, you know what I thought. But the whole thing seemed so crazy—" He fell silent, regretting his choice of words.

"It *is* crazy." The calmness in her voice surprised Sally as much as it did Steve; by rights she should be screaming, or sobbing, or pounding her fists on something. Anything but this eerie sense of calm that had come over her. But she knew the calmness was only a temporary reaction, a protective device she had wrapped herself in, a screen to ward off for a little while the despair she knew was bound to overtake her when she came to grips with reality.

For reality was contained in the term that had flashed into her mind when Mark Malone had said the words "genetically altered."

Reality was that Jason was not what she had always thought he was. He was something else, something she was unfamiliar with.

A mutant.

Not an eight-year-old boy, not the innocent and perfect product of the mating between herself and her husband.

A mutant.

Something different, something unfamiliar, something unknown.

What was he?

Suddenly all the words she had heard over the past few years held new and sinister meaning for her.

Recombinant DNA.

She barely knew what DNA was.

Genetic engineering.

She knew about that. That was the new science, the science that was going to offer glorious solutions to age-old problems.

But what else was it going to do? Was it going to create a glorious new world, or was it going to create a world full of altered beings, *mutants*, designed for—for what?

She didn't know. And perhaps she never would. Perhaps whatever had been done to Jason had been done for no specific reason at all. Perhaps he was nothing more than an experiment.

The thought chilled her, and she turned around, gazing at her son, trying to fathom how he might have been changed. She reached back to caress Jason's cheek, but he drew back from her touch, his eyes large and worried.

"Why do I have to stay at Grandma's?" he wanted to know.

"It's only for a little while, sweetheart," Sally managed to tell him through the constriction that had formed in her throat. "Just a few hours."

"Why couldn't I stay with Mrs. Corliss, so I could be there when Randy gets back?"

Randy.

Jason and Randy.

Sally tried to remember how long they had been friends, and how long it had been since Jason had had other friends.

Thoughts flickered through her mind, disconnected thoughts that suddenly fit together.

Mutants.

Was that why Jason and Randy had become friends? Did they know about themselves and each other? Had they recognized each other long ago, sensing that the two of them, different from others, were not different from each other?

Sally sank back into her seat without having answered Jason's question.

He didn't look any different. He looked as he'd always looked: a miniature version of his father, with the same deep blue eyes and unruly blond hair, the same energy and enthusiasm for everything, the same stubbornness.

But he was not his father's child, nor was he his mother's child.

Dear God, what had they done to her child? What had they done to *her*? She reached out and took Steve's hand in her own.

"Steve?"

He glanced over at her, and squeezed her hand.

"Take care of us, Steve," she said. "Take care of all of us."

"I will, darling," he promised. But even as he made the promise, Steve Montgomery wondered whether he could keep it. There were so many questions in his mind, and so few answers.

He still wasn't altogether sure that there was any kind of conspiracy. Wiseman, he was sure, was right. Whatever had gone wrong with the children in Group Twenty-one had started with their parents.

It wasn't a conspiracy. It was simply a genetic weakness passed on to the next generation.

It was, actually, his fault.

His fault, and Sally's.

CHILD, in all likelihood, was doing nothing more than watching the children, trying to isolate the defect and find a means to correct it.

So there was really nothing for him to "take care of." All he had to do was learn to live with the fact that he'd failed his children.

Or, anyway, he'd failed Julie.

But had he failed Jason? After all, Jason had never been sick a day in his life. Maybe with Jason, he hadn't failed at all. Maybe Jason, through some strange combination of his genes—and Sally's—was truly the perfect child they had always thought he was.

Maybe everything was going to be all right after all.

By the time they reached Phyllis Paine's house, he was feeling much better about everything.

Jason was fine. Jason was his son, and Jason was alive, and Jason was perfect. And in a few hours, working with Dr. Malone and the computer, Sally would find out that nothing was wrong, and they, like the Corlisses, could get back to the reality of being a family.

Steve relaxed, sure the end of the nightmare was near.

One by one, Arthur Wiseman retrieved the medical histories of the women who had given birth to the children in Group Twenty-one, sure that somewhere in those records his vindication would be found. The pattern emerged very quickly, both to him and to Mark Malone.

It wasn't just Sally Montgomery, and Lucy Corliss, and Jan Ransom.

It was all of them.

Forty-six women, none of whom had wanted children.

Forty-six women, all of whom he had considered to be poor risks for the pill.

Forty-six women, for whom an intrauterine device had been the indicated method of birth control.

Not an unusual number over the space of more than ten years. Indeed, Arthur Wiseman had inserted far more than forty-six IUDs over those years.

But for these forty-six, there was something else. All of them, at one time or another, had complained of one symptom or another—often a history of allergic reactions—which had suggested that their bodies might reject the intrusion of such an object.

And so he had applied, in the uterus of each of these women, and perhaps a hundred others, bicalcioglythemine.

"But what is it?" Mark Malone asked.

"BCG? It's a salve that helps reduce the likelihood of the uterus rejecting the IUD."

"I've never even heard of it," Malone said. "Who makes it?"

"PharMax."

Malone groaned, and Wiseman looked at him curiously. "What's wrong? I've been using it for ten years."

"Which is just about how long we've had this problem, even though we didn't know about it."

"I don't see what the connection could be—"

"PharMax is the source of CHILD's funds. In fact, PharMax set CHILD up in the first place. And why haven't I ever heard of this—what do you call it?"

"BCG. And there's a simple reason why you've never heard of it—you're not an OB-GYN."

"But I keep up with the literature, and I talk to the reps. And Bob Pender's never mentioned anything about BCG to me."

Wiseman's temper began to slip. "Why the hell would he?" he demanded. "You'd have no use for the stuff. And I can tell you, it's nothing more than an antiseptic and a relaxant."

"Maybe," Malone replied quietly. "But I think we'd better have it analyzed, just to see what's in it."

Wiseman glared at the younger man. "Just what are you suggesting?"

"I'm suggesting we find out what you've been treating these women with. My God. Arthur, we've got forty-six children here, more than half of whom are dead. And if you look at the dates on those charts, every one of them would have been exposed to this BCG stuff exactly at the time of conception. Now, if DNA is going to be tampered with, when is it done?"

"In the embryo—"

"Even before that, Arthur. In the egg. In the nucleus of the egg."

The anger he had been feeling—the anger of affronted pride—suddenly drained out of Wiseman, to be replaced by fear.

Fear, and a memory.

How many women had he treated with BCG? Not only treated, but followed up on, reapplying the salve month after month. But had it done its job, the job it was intended for? No. it hadn't. For even in women he had treated with BCG, the devices had still sometimes been rejected, though the salve itself remained. Remained, to do what?

There had been a drug—how many years ago? Nearly thirty. The drug had been called thalidomide, and it had been a tranquilizer.

And doctors all over the world, unaware or uncaring of the fact that it had never been exhaustively tested, had prescribed it for pregnant women. The results had been a nightmare of congenitally deformed infants.

And there had been DES, where the consequence of the drug's use was not immediately apparent, but rather lay like an invisible time bomb deep within the children—the daughters—waiting to explode into a devastating cancer.

Now BCG. What was it going to do? What had it already done?

"I'll take it to the lab," he said quietly. "But I can't believe—" His voice dropped. "I'll take it to the lab."

Leaving Malone in his office, Arthur Wiseman went into his examining room and opened his medicine cabinet. He scanned the shelves quickly, then again, more carefully this time.

Where he was sure the jar of BCG had been, there was now only an empty space on his shelf.

He picked up the phone and reached his nurse. "Has anyone been in my treatment room this morning?"

"Why, yes, Dr. Wiseman. Bob Pender dropped by, and I let him take an inventory of the PharMax products you use."

Wiseman felt a sudden pain in his chest as his heart began to pound. "I see," he said. "Thank you."

Sensing the strain in his voice, the nurse spoke again. "Wasn't that all right? Bob's been inventorying your drugs for years."

"It's all right, Charlene," Wiseman assured her. "I'm sure it's quite all right." He hung up the phone and slowly made his way back to his office. Mark Malone looked up at him, then, seeing the expression on his face, rose.

"What is it, Arthur?"

"Bob Pender was here," Wiseman said softly. "And the BCG is gone."

"Then we'll order more," Malone said. He picked up the phone and asked the hospital operator to connect him with the PharMax sales desk.

"BCG?" the man at the other end repeated. "I'm not sure I've ever heard of that."

Malone started to explain what it was he wanted, then changed his mind and handed the phone to Wiseman.

"Bicalcioglythemine," Wiseman snapped. "I want a twelve-ounce jar, and I want to pick it up today."

There was a pause. Wiseman could hear pages being turned. Finally the voice at the other end spoke again. "Are you sure you have the right company? This is PharMax."

"PharMax is who I want. I've been getting BCG from you people for ten years."

"And this is Eastbury Community Hospital?"

"That's right."

"One moment."

This time Wiseman was put on hold. Nearly two minutes later the voice came back on the line.

"I'm sorry, sir, but this company does not make a product called bicalcioglythemine, and I've just checked your records on our computer. I see nothing indicating that you've ever ordered such a thing before, nor have we ever shipped it or billed you for it. I'm afraid you must have the wrong company."

"I see," Wiseman whispered. When he faced Malone again, his whole body was trembling.

"I don't think we need to have it analyzed, Mark," he said softly. "I suppose, if I did enough research, I could tell you which enzymes must have been in it. There must have been some kind of restriction endonuclease and a ligase. Maybe even some free nucleotides to zip into the DNA. And, of course, the calcium base. But I don't think I could tell you how they put it together or made the whole process work. As far as I knew, what that compound must have done isn't possible even now, let alone ten years ago. But they must have done it. Recombinant DNA, accomplished within the uterus."

The phone rang on Wiseman's desk and he spoke with the nurse once more. When he hung up the phone, his eyes avoided Mark Malone's. "Sally and Steve are here," he said. "Will you talk to them? I don't think I can face them right now. I think I have to ... well, I have to think this thing through. I have to decide what it all means."

Mark Malone rose and started toward the door. Then he turned back and faced Wiseman. "Arthur," he said, his voice low and deadly, "are you sure you didn't make this compound yourself?"

What little color still remained in the old man's face drained away. "Mark, what are you saying?"

"Only that when the time comes, I doubt that anyone will believe you got that stuff from PharMax. Frankly, I don't believe it myself." Malone turned away, and a moment later Arthur Wiseman was left alone in his office.

Chapter 29

JIM CORLISS CAST DOLEFUL EYES on the chain blocking the driveway to the Randolph estate. "Maybe we'd better just leave the car here and walk."

"Nope. I want it near the house." Bronski opened the trunk of his car and took out a large set of chain cutters. "These should do the trick." A moment later the chain, its end link neatly severed, lay on the asphalt, leaving the drive clear. They proceeded on to the gate, where Bronski cut the second chain, then dismantled the electric opening device so the gates swung freely. "After this, the house should be a cinch," he remarked. He put the chain cutters back into the trunk, slid behind the wheel, and gunned the engine.

They drove around to the back of the house, parking the car where it couldn't be seen from the gates. Then, with Lucy and Randy trailing them, the two men approached the house. They knocked loudly at the back door, waited, then knocked again. When there was still no response, they went around to the front and repeated the procedure.

"There's no one here," Lucy said at last. "They've all gone."

"We still have to try," Bronski replied. "Let's go in." He stepped back from the house and gazed up at the barred windows of the second floor. "Seems as though it would be the lower windows they'd keep bars on."

"It was to keep us in," Randy said. "And they always had someone in the hall too. Except that Miss Bowen didn't always stay there."

"Well, at least that makes it easy for us," Bronski murmured. He led the others around to the side of the house, where French doors opened onto a terrace overlooking the lawn. Using the butt of his gun, he shattered a pane of one of the doors, then reached through and twisted the dead bolt. He winked at Randy. "Just like in the movies." He opened the door and led the way in.

"It's the dining room," Randy explained. "And through there is the kitchen. The other doors lead to a big hall, and in the back everyone had offices." He started eagerly across the room, but Bronski stopped him.

"I'll go first."

"Aw . . . there's no one here."

"I'll still go first," Bronski insisted, even though he agreed with Randy. He led the way through the dining room and stopped in the foyer, staring up the broad staircase. "What's up there?"

"The bedrooms," Randy explained. "Mine was almost at the end of the hall. Wanna see it?"

"Okay."

They moved up the stairs, Bronski still in the lead. At the top, situated so that it had a full view of the wide corridor that ran the length of the hall, was a desk, emptied of its contents. They started down the hall.

"This was Eric's room," Randy said, pausing at a closed door.

Bronski glanced at Lucy. "Eric who?" he asked.

"Carter. I think he was from California."

So there it was. Eric Carter had been reported as a runaway from San Jose. Unless . . .

"Randy, did you look at all that stuff we were reading last night?"

Randy shook his head.

"You're sure?"

Randy shrugged. "It was only a bunch of numbers and stuff like that. Why would I want to read that?"

"Okay. You said this *was* Eric's room. Isn't it anymore?"

"Eric died," Randy said. Lucy gasped, and Randy looked anxiously up at her. "That's why I ran away. After Eric died, I got real scared. So I ran away."

"Of course you did," Jim Corliss said. "Why don't you show us how you got out of the house?"

Randy led them to the end of the hall, then up the narrow stairs to the attic, where the ladder, still extended, led up to the open skylight. "Then I went across the roof, and climbed down a tree," Randy explained. "It was easy."

Bronski nodded. Everything was exactly as Randy had said it would be. "Let's go back downstairs."

Now it was Randy who led the way, explaining to his parents and the sergeant what each of the rooms had been used for. At last they were in the clinic area, and Randy showed them the room where Peter Williams had lain unconscious for several days.

"And what's back there?" Bronski asked, pointing to the only door they had not yet opened. Randy stared at it, his lips pursed, and his brows knit together in puzzlement.

"I don't know," he finally admitted. "I was never back there."

"Then let's have a look." Bronski, followed by the three Corlisses, started toward the door that would lead them into the laboratory.

Morantz and Kaplan moved through the trees, being careful to stay well back in their shadows. The boy, they had been told, was the primary assignment. And so, when the house in Eastbury had suddenly disgorged its occupants an hour before, it was the two men, the woman, and the boy whom they followed. It had been an easy tail, for they had known within minutes exactly where they were going. They had hung back, well out of sight, until their quarry reached its destination. Now they were closing in.

"There's the car," Morantz said. Even though there were no prying ears, he still used his habitual working voice, just above a whisper, which he knew only Kaplan could hear.

"We'll go in from behind the garage," Kaplan replied in the same lowered tone. His grip tightened on the canvas bag he was carrying. "Even if they look out, we shouldn't be visible for more than a second or two."

They worked their way a little farther south, putting the large garage between themselves and the house. Only when they were certain they couldn't be seen did they leave the shelter of the woods and dash across the narrow expanse of lawn to crouch beside the brick wall of the outbuilding. Once there, Kaplan opened the bag and removed its contents.

It was a small device—no larger than a cigar box—and all that was visible on its exterior were several tiny, but very powerful, magnets. Kaplan opened the box, carefully rechecking the receiver, the capacitor, and the firing cap. Satisfied, he made the final attachments that would allow the cap to accomplish its purpose, imbedded it in the mass of gelignite that took up the bulk of the space in the box, and reclosed it.

"See anything?"

Morantz, his binoculars pressed to his eyes, shook his head. "If they're in there, they're still up front. Looks like right now is as good a time as any."

Kaplan crouched and, keeping his head low, darted out of the lee of the garage and moved swiftly across the concrete apron upon which Carl Bronski's car, closed and carefully locked, was parked. He stopped next to the right rear wheel, knelt down, and reached under the car with his left hand. A moment later he had found the spot he was looking for, and heard a distinct *thunk* as the magnets on the exterior of the box clamped themselves firmly to the gas tank of the car.

A few seconds later, both Kaplan and Morantz had faded back into the woods.

For now, all they had to do was get back to their van, and wait.

Lucy Corliss stared at the mess and instinctively touched her son. "But what is this place?" she asked, although she knew the answer even as she spoke.

Even in its disheveled state, it was still obvious that the room was some kind of a laboratory. There was a long counter that took up most of one wall, with various pieces of equipment that neither Jim nor Carl Bronski recognized. On the wall opposite the counter, five filing cabinets stood, most of their drawers open, all of them empty.

"Seems like they took the records and left the hardware," Bronski commented.

"Which fits in with a government operation," Jim Corliss pointed out. "Generate a mass of paper, never lose track of a single piece of it, but let the equipment rust. But what was it all about? If all they were doing was medical research, why the secrecy?"

"Come on, Jim. Let's not kid ourselves," Bronski said. "This wasn't just research. Children were being kidnaped and brought out here, where apparently they died." He glanced toward Randy, who was already disappearing into yet another room. When he spoke again, his voice was grim. "And I'll bet that even after they died, they stayed on the premises. Let's see what's in there." The trio moved toward the door of the lab.

They found Randy standing in the small room behind the laboratory, staring at a large piece of equipment, his face puzzled.

"Is that an iron lung?" he asked.

Carl Bronski shook his head. "Not quite," he said, his voice shaking slightly.

"What is it, then?" Lucy asked.

"It looks like a decompression chamber." He hesitated, his eyes once again flickering toward Randy. Lucy, reading Bronski's expression, gently nudged her son.

"Wait for us in the other room, sweetheart," she said.

Then, when he was gone, she turned her attention back to the sergeant. "What's it for?" she asked.

Bronski swallowed hard. "It's the kind of thing they use in dog pounds," he said at last.

Lucy, still not quite comprehending, turned to Jim.

"They use it for the puppies," he explained. "For the puppies nobody wants."

Lucy paled. "Dear God," she whispered. "You mean they used that thing to—?"

"That's the way it looks," Bronski said, his voice suddenly hard. "But they still had bodies to dispose of. And it looks to me like that's why they had that thing."

Lucy, her face ashen, stared at the firebox. "Isn't it just a furnace?"

"It's not like any furnace I ever saw," Bronski replied. "The only place I've ever seen anything like that is in a crematorium." As the Corlisses numbly looked on, he approached the crematory and touched the door.

It was still warm, but not too warm to prevent him from opening it.

The chamber inside was empty.

"They cleaned it up pretty well, but not quite well enough."

In the corners of the chamber there were a few flecks of grayish matter. Producing a plastic bag from his coat pocket, Bronski scooped up a sample of the stuff, sealed the bag, and replaced it in his pocket.

"Come on," he said. "Let's get out of here. We've seen enough, and it'll take a team of techs to go over this place properly. But offhand, I'd say it ought to be pretty easy to find out who was here. There'll be prints all over the place, and God only knows what else." He chuckled, but there was not even a trace of humor in the sound. "When you clear out as fast as they did, you don't stop to clean up after yourselves. You take what you can and run. And that's what these people did. I'll bet they didn't even waste time looking for Randy. Just packed up everything and took off."

A few minutes later they were back in Bronski's car and heading down the driveway. They stopped to re-close the main gate, but ignored the chain that still lay on the ground where they had left it.

"What now?" Jim asked as they turned back onto the main road.

"As soon as we get into radio range, I'll call headquarters and have a team sent out here. Then I think I ought to have a little talk with Paul Randolph. That's right," he added, seeing in the rearview mirror the look of dismay on Lucy's face. "Just me, and maybe someone else from the department. You're out of it now, Lucy. You, and Jim, and the Montgomerys too. From here on in, it's all got to be official." Then, still watching Lucy's face, he caught a glimpse of something moving in the distance. He slowed the car slightly. Behind them, a van was pulling out of a side road.

"Something wrong?" Jim asked.

Bronski said nothing, his eyes glued to the slow-moving van. Only when it turned in the opposite direction did he relax.

"Nothing," he said. "For a second there, I just thought maybe we were being followed."

And yet, even as he continued driving, he felt uneasy. There was something about the van . . .

As they rounded a bend in the road, and Carl Bronski's car disappeared from their view, Morantz spoke softly to Kaplan.

"About ten more seconds," he said. "Give them that, but no more."

Bronski's brain was working furiously now, trying to remember where he'd seen that van before.

Not long ago.

This morning?

But where? And why was the memory so vague?

And then he knew. Lucy Corliss's block, part way down the street. He'd barely noticed it.

But was it the same van?

If it was, then they were being followed. Except the

van had gone the other way. Instead of following them, it was going to—

But if it *had* followed them, whoever was in it knew where they'd been.

And no longer cared.

"Holy Christ!" he yelled. His foot slammed onto the brake and the car spun into a four-wheel skid. "Get out! Get the hell out of the car!"

As the car skewed off the road, he yanked at the door handle. Maybe, just maybe, there was still time.

With a sudden roar, the gelignite attached to the gas tank exploded, ripping the tank loose from the car, splitting its welded seams and igniting its contents.

What a moment before had been an automobile lurching toward a ditch was now a massive fireball rolling into that ditch, through it, then coming to rest a few yards from the edge of the forest.

Carl Bronski died instantly, crushed by the weight of the car, his body a mangled mass resting grotesquely in the bottom of the ditch.

For Jim Corliss, it was worse. As the car rolled, the roof gave way, pressing him down into the front seat, his legs jammed immobile beneath the twisted dashboard.

Flaming gasoline gushed from the ruptured tank, inundating the car, and soon the choking, acrid smell of burning rubber filled the air. Gasping, Jim tried to twist in the seat to help his wife and son, but it did no good. His one free arm groped through the smoke, finding nothing. And then the flames began to eat at him.

"Randy!" he screamed. And then again, "Randy! Lucy!" He took a deep breath, and superheated air flooded into his lungs, searing their delicate tissue, and ending his last slim hope of survival.

In the back seat, Lucy had instinctively grabbed for her son when the car began to skid, and now, as it lay overturned and burning, her mind suddenly went blank with panic. She was going to die, and Randy was going to die, and it was all going to be for nothing. She clutched Randy closer and began screaming.

Randy himself thrashed wildly in his mother's arms,

trying to wriggle free. "Mom!" he yelled. "Mom, let go of me!"

But Lucy, too terrified to understand, knew only that she somehow had to protect her son from the roaring flames. Her mind, filled with a fog of terror, tried to sort things out, tried to make decisions.

Jim. She needed Jim. "Help us," she cried, her voice already beginning to weaken. "Oh, Jim, help us!" And then, through the fear and the heat and the smoke, she became aware that Randy was no longer in her arms. She reached out and finally grasped him. He was wriggling toward the gap between the two front seats of the car. As her hand closed on his ankle, he looked back at her. His eyes were wide and angry, and Lucy suddenly thought she must be hallucinating.

While the flesh on her hand, the hand that held her son's ankle, was seared and blistered, Randy's flesh seemed uninjured. It glowed red in the strange light of the fire, but it seemed to her that it had not yet been harmed. And then she heard Randy talking to her.

"Let me go," he hissed. "I'm not going to die, Mother. I *won't* die." And then, kicking violently, he escaped Lucy's weakened grasp and slipped away from her.

Lucy, a vision of her son's angry face etched in her mind, slipped into unconsciousness.

Randy scrambled through to the front seat. The smoke burned his eyes, and for a moment he lost his orientation. Then he tried to force his way past a blockage and heard a soft moaning sound.

It was his father.

But suddenly all he knew was that he had to get out, that it was getting too hot to breathe. Then he felt a hint of cooler air and realized that the door on the driver's side was open. He wriggled toward it, his clothes burning now, and caught his foot in the steering wheel. Kicking wildly, he jerked himself free and burst out of the flaming wreckage.

He fell to the ground, then almost instinctively rolled through the pool of burning gasoline that surrounded the car. Getting to his feet, he staggered toward the woods.

Away from the flames, Randy collapsed to the ground, his breath coming in faint gasps, his heart pounding. The last thing he saw before his eyes closed was his father's face, barely visible through the shattered glass of the windshield, unrecognizable in the agony of death.

Then blackness closed in around Randy, and he felt nothing more.

But even as he passed into unconsciousness, George Hamlin's genetic miracle had already been triggered. Randy's clothes were gone, burned completely away, and here and there the smooth skin of his body showed faint signs of blistering. But even now the blisters were beginning to dry up and peel away to reveal healthy skin beneath. The injured tissues of Randy's body were regenerating themselves.

Morantz and Kaplan heard the sound of the explosion just as they turned into the driveway of the Randolph estate. Kaplan nodded with satisfaction. "So much for that part of it. How much time do you think we have?"

"As much as we need," Morantz replied. "No one's going to come around here—all the excitement's going to be back there."

"What you might call a diversion."

Morantz threw his partner a dirty look. "We just killed four American citizens, two of whom were a woman and a child. I don't call that a diversion. I call it ... shit, I don't know what to call it." He was silent for a moment, then he said, "I think when this is over, I'm getting out."

"I've heard you say that before," Kaplan countered. "In fact, I hear you say it in the middle of practically every job." The car drew to a halt in front of the gates, and Kaplan got out of the van to open them, then hopped back in when Morantz had driven through. "You want me to do the next one?"

"Not particularly."

They took the van around to the back of the house,

parking it in the exact place where Bronski's car had been only a few minutes before. "Okay," Morantz said as he set the brake and switched off the engine. "Let's get it set up, then get out of here. It's getting along toward noon."

Working swiftly and efficiently, the two men unloaded their supplies and took them into the house. They surveyed the interior with professional detachment, ignoring everything except the layout of the building. When they had decided on the exact layout of the explosives, Morantz shook his head.

"I don't know how they're going to cover this one up," he said. "I can give them rubble, but I can't hide the fact that it was a professional job. What they want done here can't be made to look like an accident."

"Maybe no one's ever going to see it," Kaplan suggested.

"Don't hold your breath. The explosion alone is going to bring everyone running from miles around. And it won't take long to find out what caused it either. Any fire department worth its salt'll figure this one out in about five minutes."

For thirty minutes the two of them worked. Finally, Morantz made the last connection. He straightened up after hiding the timer under the counter in the laboratory and stretched.

"About five hours?" he asked.

Kaplan frowned. "Why so long? What if somebody comes in here this afternoon?"

"They won't," Morantz promised. "But we might as well let them get that mess with the car cleaned up before they have to start on this one." He glanced at his watch, then set the timing device. "Come on. Let's get out of here."

Without looking back, the two men left the house, climbed into the van, then drove back to the road. Morantz parked the car just beyond the gates, got out of the van, closed the gates, and wrapped them with a chain he produced from the back of the van. Then he returned to the van once more, this time to fetch a large painted metal sign. He took it back to the closed gates, and wired it securely into position. Standing back, he read the sign:

DANGER
THIS PROPERTY UNDER QUARANTINE BY ORDER OF
THE UNITED STATES GOVERNMENT

Beneath the warning there was a carefully written paragraph regarding the penalties involved for ignoring or removing the sign and a telephone number which could be called if further information was required.

Satisfied, Morantz got back into the van and started the engine. "Dumb, isn't it?" he remarked as he drove on and eventually turned into the main road. "We could string up barbed wire and every kid in the area would crawl through it just to find out why it was there. But that sign could sit there for years and no one would ignore it."

And then, ahead, they saw three police cars, a fire truck, and two ambulances gathered around the smoldering wreckage of Carl Bronski's car. As they passed it, threading their way through the fleet of emergency vehicles, Kaplan carefully examined what was left of the demolished automobile.

"Nobody could have survived that," he said, his voice betraying a note of satisfaction. "Nobody in the world."

Chapter 30

ARTHUR WISEMAN MOVED SLOWLY around his office, touching things, examining things, remembering.

His medical diploma, neatly framed, but yellowing with age even under the protective glass, hung discreetly behind his desk, a silent reassurance to his patients that he was qualified to do his job.

Around the diploma, in frames of their own, were all the certificates he had gathered over forty years of practice. An array to be proud of, documenting a life devoted to service. Commendations from the town, the county, even the state. Citations from the medical association. The gavel that had been his the year he had served as its president. All of it suddenly confronted him with an overwhelming sense of guilt.

How many had there been?

How many children over the years whom he had unknowingly sentenced to death? How many men and women whose lives he had unwittingly shaken, if not destroyed?

He knew the statistics. It wasn't simply the children who were the victims. It was the families too. The families like the Montgomerys, for whom the loss of an infant seemed to strike a mortal blow to the basic structure of their lives, leaving them floundering helplessly, unable to cope with their own feelings, or those of their mates, or their surviving children.

Until today he had been able to blame that destruction on sudden infant death syndrome. An unknown killer creeping out of the shadows to claim a victim, then slipping away into the nether regions, its identity cloaked in mystery.

Except that for him the cloak had slipped. Arthur Wiseman had seen the face of the enemy.

It was his own face.

Too busy, he thought.

Always, he had been too busy. Too busy caring for his patients, too busy improving his clinic, too busy raising funds so that Eastbury could have a hospital to be proud of.

Too busy to analyze every medication he used.

Too busy to question each new product that came on the market touted by its manufacturers as the latest "medical miracle."

Too busy to question the motives of the manufacturers, too busy to question the results of their own testing programs, too busy, even, to demand the documentation behind the products.

Instead, he had simply accepted the products and used them to treat the symptoms for which they had been created, grateful that the pharmaceutical companies kept developing new products to help his patients.

Except that this time the product had not helped.

This time the product had done something else, and the children were dying.

But not all of them. No, not all of them. Some of them lived.

Lived as what?

What were they, these altered beings that seemed so normal? Were they really the healthy little boys they seemed to be? Or were they something else, created for some specific purpose?

What could the purpose be?

Arthur Wiseman thought about it, and the puzzle was not too difficult for him to figure out.

Children who healed at an unnaturally rapid rate. On the way back to the hospital Malone had mentioned the Defense Department.

Perfect little soldiers, that's what they were.

Children who could grow up to fight battles, and not be killed.

War, suddenly, could be waged at no cost. Send in the killers who can't be killed.

Who would argue that war was wrong if only the other side died?

Arthur Wiseman, alone in his office, looked into the future and saw the new man, bred for a single purpose. To kill. But there would be others.

He could envision entire classes of people, each of them bred to serve a specific need, to perform a specific function which regular people could not, or would not, perform.

Regular people.

And that, Wiseman knew, was the attitude that soon would prevail. Society, barely learning to function without racial segregation, would turn to genetic segregation. Each person would be assigned to his station in life according to his genetic structure, with the "regular people" at the top. But for how long?

Not long. A few generations, perhaps, before the mutants, human in all respects except for a tiny genetic change that gave them special abilities, rebelled. And then what?

Arthur Wiseman neither wanted to know, nor wanted to be a part of, whatever the future might hold. And yet he was already a part of it.

Nothing more than a pawn, perhaps, but it was enough. Never again would he be able to face a patient, let alone try to administer to a patient's needs.

For Arthur Wiseman, his career, and his life, had just come to an end.

He went into his examining room, unlocked his drug cabinet, and removed a bottle. Then, taking the bottle and a hypodermic syringe, he returned to his office.

For a few minutes he worked with the computer,

deleting all references to BCG from his records. His reputation, at least, would remain intact.

Moments later, he was dead.

Randy Corliss opened his eyes. For a moment he wasn't sure where he was, but then, seeing the branches above his head, he began to remember.

He'd been in the back of Sergeant Bronski's car, with his mother. And then something had happened. Sergeant Bronski had started yelling, and the car had skidded, and then—and then—

He sat bolt upright and looked around. Through the trees he could see the smoldering wreckage. All around it there were people.

People, and ambulances, and a fire truck, and—

He got to his feet and stared down at his body. His skin was all reddish, and he wasn't wearing any clothes. And his head felt cold.

Curiously, he touched his head.

Where there should have been hair, he felt only bare skin.

Fire.

There had been a fire. But where were his parents?

He began stumbling out of the woods. "Mommy? Mommy, where are you? Daddy?" Suddenly, he stopped, as the memory of what had happened flooded back to him. Now he was screaming and running toward the blackened car. "Mommy! Daddy!"

The crowd gathered around the wreck turned to stare at the strange apparition that had appeared out of the woods.

"Where the hell did *he* come from?" one of the medics muttered. Grabbing a blanket, he moved toward the naked child, then tried to wrap the blanket around him. Randy struggled against him.

"Mommy!" he screamed again. "Where's my mommy?"

"Easy, son, take it easy," the medic told him. "Where'd you come from?"

But Randy was beyond hearing. Thrashing in the confines of the blanket, he could only keep shouting for his parents, tears streaming down his face. Finally, exhausted, he fell to the ground, where he lay sobbing helplessly.

"Get him into the truck," a second medic said. "He must have been in the car with them. Let's get him to a hospital. Fast."

They carried Randy to one of the ambulances. A moment later, its siren wailing, the vehicle began racing toward Eastbury Community Hospital. The medic carefully unwrapped the blanket and stared at Randy's skin.

"I don't get it," he said to his partner. "Look at him. His clothes are gone, and his hair is gone. He must have been right in the middle of that fire. He should be dead, just like the others."

And yet, as they examined Randy, neither of the medics could find anything more than what appeared to be a few first-degree burns on what was otherwise baby-smooth skin.

Mark Malone stared somberly across his desk, trying to read Sally Montgomery's eyes.

She had sat silently next to her husband while Malone recited what had happened in Wiseman's office. Twice she had been about to interrupt him, but both times Steve had gently squeezed her hand. Now she was sitting still, her eyes thoughtful. Slowly, she rose from the sofa. "I'm going to see him," she said, her voice coldly furious. "I want to hear it all from him."

"I'm not sure he'll see you," Malone said softly. "When I left him, he said he was all through as a doctor—"

"All through as a *doctor*?" Sally exploded. "He's a *killer*, Mark. He killed Julie. Whether he knew what he was doing or not—and if you ask me, he knew exactly what he was doing—he killed her. And God knows how many others. That's why he wanted to commit me—I was finding out too much." She started toward the office door just as the phone rang.

Malone picked up the receiver and listened for a moment. When he hung up, his hands were trembling. "It's too late, Sally," he said softly. "That was Arthur's nurse. She just found him in his office. He's dead."

"Dead?" Sally repeated. "He's dead?"

"There was a hypodermic on his desk. Apparently he killed himself."

Her fury suddenly deserting her, Sally sank back onto the sofa. "Oh, God," she mumbled. "What next?"

As if in direct response to her question, the phone rang once more. This time, as he listened, Malone closed his eyes and nodded, almost as if he'd been expecting more bad news. When he hung up, he seemed unable to speak.

"What is it?" Steve asked. "Mark, has something else happened?"

Malone nodded. "There—there was an accident. Anyway, they think it was an accident."

Sally lifted her head and her eyes widened. "Where—who—?"

"Carl Bronski," Malone whispered. "He's dead. And Lucy and Jim Corliss too."

"No!" Sally screamed. She was on her feet again. Her eyes wild, she staggered toward Malone. "No! It's a lie—they can't be dead. They can't be." Suddenly her legs buckled beneath her, and she fell, sobbing, to the floor.

Malone rose from his desk and came around to help Steve move her back onto the sofa. "I'll give her a sedative," he said. He went to his drug locker, and a moment later Sally's eyes closed, and her breathing evened out. Only then did the doctor speak again.

"Randy's alive," he said. "They're bringing him here now."

"But what happened?" Steve asked.

"I told you—they don't know. The car went off the road and exploded. If they know why, they didn't tell me."

Steve's mind was reeling. He looked from his sedated wife to the doctor, then back to Sally. "What—oh, Christ, Mark, what the hell's happening?"

"I don't know, Steve," Mark Malone said quietly. "All I know is that right now we have to deal with one thing

314

at a time. Let's get Sally into a bed, and then I'd better get to the emergency room. I want to be there when they bring Randy Corliss in."

Paul Randolph nervously paced his office, wishing he still smoked. But smoking was no longer part of the proper image for anyone even remotely connected with medicine, so no matter how badly he wanted a cigarette, he would not light one. He glanced at the other two men in his office and wondered how they could sit so calmly, as if nothing were happening.

They had been waiting all morning now, and still they had heard nothing from Carmody's team, nothing past that first phone call, when they'd found out who had gathered at Lucy Corliss's house.

Damn the woman. Damn her and her friend Mrs. Montgomery both. And that fool, Dr. Malone. How on earth had they gotten *him* involved in their snooping? And what had they found? Damn them all!

"It isn't really so bad, you know," George Hamlin said softly, breaking the silence that had hung over the room for the last half hour. "We deliberately formulated a base that would be used only on women who didn't want children in the first place. It's not as if our failures were children somebody wanted. Just the opposite is true. These women specifically did not want children! Frankly, I can't see how we've damaged them."

"Apparently, they don't see it that way," Paul Randolph replied, his voice oozing as much sarcasm as he was able to muster. "Apparently, they're under the impression that we've murdered and kidnaped their children. And, damn it, we have done just that, haven't we?"

Lieutenant General Scott Carmody shifted his weight uncomfortably. He wasn't used to waiting, and sitting for any length of time made him stiff. "There's always a price," he said. "The army needs these boys, Randolph, and the sooner this project comes together, the better off this country will be."

"No matter what the cost?"

Carmody's voice grew hard. "We've lost men in every

program we've ever started. Sacrifice is part of the price of progress, and we all know it."

Randolph groaned. "Please," he said. "Spare me the old saw about eggs and omelettes. We're talking about children here."

"That has yet to be determined," Hamlin interrupted. He rose, and, stretching, ambled over to the window where, with his arms clasped behind his back, he gazed out at Logan Airport. With the same pleasure he had taken from the sight since he was a boy, he watched a plane hurtle down the runway, then soar into the sky. "I wonder if *my* boys enjoy that?" he mused more to himself than to the others.

"Pardon?" Randolph asked, but before Hamlin could repeat his question, the phone on Randolph's desk jangled to life. Randolph picked it up, then handed it to Carmody, who listened for a few moments, issued some instructions, then hung up. He turned to face the others, the tension of the long night and morning suddenly gone.

"I think we've got it contained," he said. "Lucy and James Corliss are dead, along with Bronski. And Wiseman is dead too."

"Wiseman?" Randolph asked. "What happened?"

"Killed himself."

"What about Randy Corliss?" Hamlin demanded. "Is he dead?"

"No," Carmody replied. "He's not dead. He survived the explosion, and the fire, and got out of the wreckage. He's at Eastbury Community Hospital."

Randolph turned white. "Then how can you say it's contained? If that boy talks—"

But George Hamlin had already grasped the point. "It doesn't matter anymore. What's he going to talk about? We've washed the computers, and by tonight the Academy will be gone too. There's no evidence of anything anymore."

"Except that Randy Corliss knows the names of everyone on the project."

Carmody shrugged. "Not one of whom will ever be

traceable. If you were to go searching for them right now, Randolph, you would have trouble proving that anyone connected with the God Project ever lived. Up to, and including, Dr. Hamlin here. Computers not only allow us to keep track of people, Randolph. They also allow us to bury them."

Randolph sank into his chair. "Then it's over?"

"No," Hamlin replied. "There are still the Montgomerys to contend with. And that, Paul, is going to be your job."

As he listened to George Hamlin outline what he had in mind, Paul Randolph once again wished he had a cigarette.

An hour later, though, as he drove to Eastbury and thought over Hamlin's plan, it began to make sense to him.

Perhaps it was going to work out after all.

And if it didn't?

Paul Randolph didn't even want to think about that possibility.

Chapter 31

SALLY MONTGOMERY OPENED HER EYES, and the first thing she saw was the ceiling. Acoustical plaster, the kind she had always hated. And the color—that awful shade of pale green that was supposed to be restful but was faintly nauseating. So she was in a hospital bed. She had a moment of panic and struggled to sit up. Then she heard Steve's voice.

"It's all right, honey," he was saying. "There's nothing wrong. You just—well, you sort of came apart a couple of hours ago, so Mark gave you something to put you to sleep for a while."

Sally sank back onto the pillow and gazed silently at her husband for a few moments. Was it a trick? Was it really Mark who had given her the shot, or Wiseman?

Wiseman.

Wiseman was dead. Wiseman, and ... and the Corlisses, and Carl Bronski. Tears welled up in her eyes and brimmed over. Steve reached out and gently brushed them away.

"They're all dead, aren't they?" she asked, her voice hollow.

"All except Randy," Steve replied.

"What happened?"

"Not now," Steve protested. "Why don't you go back to sleep?"

"No. I want to know what happened, Steve. I *have* to know."

"It was an accident. Apparently Bronski lost control of the car—a blowout, maybe. Anyway, it skidded off the road, turned over, and the gas tank ruptured."

"Oh, God," Sally groaned. "It must have been horrible." Her eyes met Steve's. "They . . . burned?"

Steve nodded. "Jim and Lucy did. Carl was thrown out of the car. It rolled on him."

"And Randy?"

"He got out. Somehow, he got out. His clothes burned completely off him, and all his hair . . ."

Sally closed her eyes, as if by the action she could erase the image that had come into her mind. "But how could he have survived? The burns—"

"He did survive. And he's all right, Sally. It's like what happened with Jason."

The door opened and Mark Malone appeared. He closed the door behind him, then stepped to the foot of Sally's bed, glanced at her chart, and forced a smile. "I wish I could say you looked better than you do."

"Steve just told me about . . . about . . ." Her voice faded away as her tears once again began to flow. She groped around her bedside table and found a Kleenex. Wiping away the tears, she pushed herself a little higher up in the bed, then forced herself to meet Malone's eyes. "What does it mean, Mark? What's going on?"

"I wish I could tell you," Malone replied. He hesitated, then spoke again. "You have a visitor. But you don't have to see him."

"A visitor? Who?"

"Paul Randolph."

Sally's eyes widened. "From CHILD? He's here? But—but how? Why?"

"He telephoned about an hour ago. He wanted to know if we'd done something to our computer programs."

Sally felt her heart skip a beat. "The programs?"

Malone nodded. "That's what he said. His story was that their computer tried to do a routine scan of the updates of our records and couldn't."

Steve frowned. "What does that mean?"

"It means all the codes are gone," Malone said. "It means that all our evidence has disappeared."

"But it doesn't matter," Sally said. "We've got the printouts—" Malone's shaking head stopped the flow of her words.

"They're gone, Sally. Before Arthur killed himself he destroyed everything. He altered records in the computer and burned all your printouts. It's all gone, Sally. Everything."

As the full meaning of his words sank in, Sally felt suddenly tired. Tired, and beaten. It was over. The information was gone, all of it. But where? And even as she asked herself the question, she knew the answer. "They did it themselves, didn't they?" she asked. "The people at CHILD dumped the whole thing out of the computer."

"Undoubtedly," Malone agreed. "Although Randolph denies it. That's why he came out here. I told him what's been happening out here, and he wants to hear the whole story from you. He says he also wants to tell you what they know about Group Twenty-one. Except they call it the GT-active group."

"What does that mean?" Steve asked.

"It refers to something called introns," Malone said. "I think Randolph can explain it better than I can, but if you don't want to talk to him," he added, turning his attention back to Sally, "you don't have to."

Sally's eyes grew cold. "I want to," she said. "I want to know what they've been doing to the children, and I want to know why."

Malone hesitated, then turned to Steve as if for confirmation. Steve nodded.

"If Sally wants to see him, bring him in. But don't leave us alone with him."

"I won't," Malone promised grimly. "I want to hear this as much as you do." He left the room, and a moment later returned, followed by Paul Randolph, who immediately moved to the side of the bed and took Sally's hand in his own.

"Mrs. Montgomery," he said, "I can't tell you how sorry I am about what's happened. I'm Paul—"

"I know who you are," Sally said, withdrawing her hand from his grasp and slipping it under the sheet. "What I don't understand is why you want to talk to me."

"I need help," Randolph said. "May I sit down?"

Sally nodded.

"I need to know exactly what you found out about what you've been calling Group Twenty-one. I gather you found evidence that their flaw may have been caused by some external stimulus."

"You know that better than I, Mr. Randolph."

"All I know, Mrs. Montgomery," Randolph said earnestly, "is that a number of years ago our Institute came upon a genetic irregularity which we've recently named the GT-active factor. It's very complicated, but basically what it means is that in certain children there is a normally functionless genetic combination called an intron that for some reason has become functional. It has to do with the enzyme bases that mark the beginning and end of the intron sequences in DNA. For some reason, the guanine-thymine sequence, which normally marks the beginning of an intron, has failed in these children. We've only recently identified which intron it is that has become active."

Sally's eyes narrowed with suspicion. "But you've been tracking these children for years," she pointed out.

"Because of a hormone present in their bodies in higher quantities than is normal," Randolph explained. "Hormones, as you may know, are produced under the direction of DNA, just as are all the other compounds in the body. We suspected a genetic irregularity because of the hormone, but it was only recently that we were able to trace it to the GT-active factor. Our next step will be to determine the source of the factor itself, which, until now, we've assumed was hereditary—a combination of the genetic structures of the parents that produces the GT-active factor. But apparently you've discovered evidence to the contrary."

"Yes," Sally said, "I have." Slowly, she began to repeat the story that had begun the night her daughter had died. She talked steadily for nearly an hour, while Paul Randolph sat listening to her, taking occasional notes, but never interrupting her. When she finished, she sank, exhausted, into the pillows, then stared bitterly at Randolph. "But you knew all about it," she said. "It was all there, and it all pointed directly to CHILD. You killed our children, and you kidnaped them, Mr. Randolph."

Paul Randolph avoided her gaze, rose, and drifted distractedly toward the window. When he finally began speaking, his back was still to the room. "You're partly right, of course. We *did* kidnap some children, Mrs. Montgomery. In fact, the next child we intended to take is your son, Jason."

As Sally gasped, Steve rose to his feet, his hands clenched into white-knuckled fists. But then Randolph turned around, his face slack and his eyes bleak. "I'm sorry to have to tell you this," he said softly, "but your son is dying."

Sally flinched. "No!" she cried. "Jason's not dying. He's fine! He's never been sick a day in—"

"None of them are, Mrs. Montgomery," Randolph said quietly. Though his voice was soft, there was a tone to it that demanded the attention of everyone in the room. "That's what makes the whole thing so incredibly difficult. These children, the children with the GT-active factor, seem healthy. They *are* healthy, incredibly so. The hormone appears to be triggered by trauma. That is, any damage to the tissue of these children from any source whatsoever—germs, viruses, injuries—triggers production of the hormone. And the hormone, in turn, spurs tissue regeneration. These children have a regenerative ability that is nothing short of miraculous. Damaged tissue which should normally take days or weeks to repair itself regenerates in a matter of minutes, sometimes even seconds."

Sally's eyes met Steve's as they each remembered the incidents with Jason—the acid, the boiling fudge, the fight with Joey Connors. The unexplainable was suddenly explained.

Reluctantly, she turned her attention back to Randolph. "But you said Jason was—was dying."

"And he is, Mrs. Montgomery. That's the other side of the coin. Although the hormone makes the children appear abnormally healthy, in the end it kills them. It's as if at some point the hormone has drawn on every bit of energy these children possess, and they die. From what we know, they simply seem to burn out. With the little girls it happens very quickly. So far none of them have survived past the age of one year. With the boys the process is slower. Some of them have lived to be nine. None has lived to see his tenth birthday. And that's why we kidnaped some of them."

"Did it occur to you that kidnaping is a federal crime, Mr. Randolph?" Steve asked, his voice crackling with indignation.

"Of course it did," Randolph snapped. "But in the end, it was the only possible course of action."

Steve stared at the distinguished-looking man with a mixture of revulsion and curiosity. "In the end?"

"When we began to understand what was happening, we tried to explain the situation to some of the parents. We wanted to put the children under twenty-four-hour-a-day observation. Needless to say, the parents refused. And why wouldn't they? There was nothing wrong with their children, nothing at all. It was impossible to make them understand what the problem was."

"So you began *stealing* the children?" Sally asked.

"Not at first. We simply kept track of them. You know how—you discovered our tracking system. But two years ago it became obvious to us that *all* the children were going to die. One way or another, the parents were going to lose them. So we took them, hoping that we could eventually discover how the burn-out phenomenon was triggered. So far, we haven't succeeded. But at least now we seem to know the source of the problem." He paused. "Wiseman."

"No," Sally objected. "It wasn't Dr. Wiseman. It couldn't have been. When he found out what was happening, he killed himself."

"Because he thought he'd been used, or because he knew he'd been caught?" Randolph countered.

"What are you saying?"

"Did you know that Arthur Wiseman was something of an expert in genetics?"

Sally looked puzzled, and Mark Malone frowned. "Even *I* didn't know that," he said.

"I don't see what—" Sally began, but Randolph interrupted her.

"If these children were somehow made the victims of some form of recombinant DNA, and apparently they were, it happened in Arthur Wiseman's office. He told Malone about a salve he used, which he claimed he got from PharMax. PharMax has never heard of it. It seems to me that Wiseman must have devised it himself."

"But why?" Sally flared. "Why would he do it?"

"Science," Randolph told her. "There are people in the world, Mrs. Montgomery, for whom research and experimentation exist for their own sake. They feel no responsibility for whatever they might create. For them, creation and discovery are fulfillment in themselves. Such people have no thoughts about the final results of what they are doing, no concern about any possible moral issues. Knowledge is to be sought, and used. If you *can* do something, you *must* do it. And if Wiseman found a way to alter the human form, the temptation to do so must have been overwhelming. It probably wasn't until this morning that the consequences of what he'd done became clear to him. And so he buried the evidence. There's nothing in the computer anymore, Mrs. Montgomery. No records of which children bear the GT-active factor, no records of which women were treated with Wiseman's compound. Nothing." He sank into a chair and shook his head. "I'm not sure we can ever rebuild those records."

Sally lay still, trying to sort it all out. Was he telling her the truth?

He wasn't. Deep inside, Sally was sure that he was lying to her, or, if not lying, then telling her only a part of the truth. After all, she reflected, he had admitted to having kidnaped Randy Corliss.

Had he also, somehow, killed Randy's parents and Carl Bronski?

Again, she wasn't certain. Of one thing, though, she was very sure.

What she had found out, or thought she had found out, had been taken away from her. There was no way she could get it back again. It was all probably still there, buried somewhere in the memory bank of a computer, but so deeply buried and expertly covered that she would never be able to dig it up.

And if she tried, she would very likely be killed.

And I, Sally thought silently to herself, am not going to be killed. I am going to tell this man whatever he wants to hear, and I am going to stay alive and raise my son.

My son.

Jason. Was he dying? Or was that, too, a lie? For that question, only time itself would provide an answer.

Sally pulled herself into a sitting position and carefully smoothed the sheets over her torso. Then she made herself meet Paul Randolph's eyes.

"Thank you," she said softly. "Thank you for coming here and telling me all this. You can't know what it's been like. It's been a nightmare."

"One that's over now, Mrs. Montgomery." He paused. "Except for the children."

"Yes," Sally breathed. "Except for the children. What can we do?"

Randolph made a helpless gesture. "I wish I could tell you. Watch them. Love them. Try to make their lives as happy as you can. And hope."

"Hope?" Sally asked. "Hope for what? You said none of them has lived to reach the age of ten."

"And so they haven't, Mrs. Montgomery. But we know practically nothing about this. Maybe some of them will live. Maybe your son, maybe Randy Corliss. All we can do is watch and hope."

"Randy Corliss." Sally repeated the name, then looked to Steve. "What's going to happen to him?"

Steve shrugged. "I don't know. He probably has relatives—"

"I want him."

"Sally—"

"Steve, I want us to take care of him. I—well, I feel as though he almost belongs to us now. The way he is, and Jason. Oh, Steve, we've got to take care of him. We owe it to Lucy and Jim."

"Sally, we've got to think about this—"

"No, Steve. We've got to do it. And if you don't want to, then I'll do it alone." Her voice suddenly dropped to a whisper. "Besides, it's only going to be for a little while."

Steve swallowed hard, knowing he wouldn't refuse Sally's request. And yet, even as he gave in, he began to wonder what was going to happen to him when each of the boys died. Would it be as it had been with Julie?

He had to talk to Sally about it, and he had to talk to her alone. He glanced up at Mark Malone, and the young doctor, reading the look, signaled to Paul Randolph. "I think we'd better leave these two alone for a while, Mr. Randolph."

Paul Randolph rose. "Of course," he said gently. He moved to offer his hand to Steve, but the gesture was refused. "I'm sorry," he said. "I'm sorry to have had to tell you all this, but sooner or later, it had to come out." Then, with Malone following him, he left the room.

As soon as they were alone, Sally's eyes locked onto Steve's.

"He's lying," she said. "He's lying about everything."

"Sally—"

She ignored his interruption. "It's over, Steve. I've lost. There's nothing I can do except take care of those boys

326

and pretend nothing's wrong. Otherwise they'll kill me. Just like they killed Lucy and Jim and Carl."

"And what about me?" Steve asked.

Sally avoided his eyes. "I don't know, Steve. I don't expect you to believe me. I know what Randolph said sounded reasonable. But I simply do not believe him."

"Then we'll do it your way," Steve said. He sat down on the bed and gathered Sally into his arms. "Whatever happens from here on out, we'll do it your way." He drew her closer and felt her body stiffen. Then suddenly Sally relaxed. Her arms slid around Steve's neck.

"Hold me," she whispered. "Oh, please, just hold me for a minute."

They clung to each other, wondering what pain the future held for them, and how they would cope with it.

Whatever it was, they would face it together.

Mark Malone led Paul Randolph into his office and closed the door behind him.

"They didn't buy it," he said. "At least she didn't."

"No," Randolph replied. "She didn't. But I let her know that she'll never prove a thing, and I gave her Wiseman. There'll be just enough doubt in her mind to keep her quiet."

"Until Jason dies."

For the first time that day, Paul Randolph smiled.

"That's the most beautiful part of it," he said. "Hamlin doesn't think Jason Montgomery or Randy Corliss is going to die. It looks like the project's a success, Mark."

Mark Malone opened the bottom drawer of his desk and pulled out the thick stack of printouts that Sally had gleaned from the computer. He handed them to Randolph, his expression serious.

"You and Hamlin might be interested in seeing just how far Sally'd gotten," he said. "Next time, I think you'd better make sure *no one* can trace you." Then his face brightened, and he reached into the drawer once more, this time bringing out the bottle of Cognac he'd bought on the day the God Project had begun. For ten long years he'd been the project's watchdog. Today he was its savior. He broke the seal and poured them each a generous shot.

"Here's to the future," he said. "And all the wonderful creatures man is about to become."

Epilogue
Three Years Later

SALLY MONTGOMERY FACED HER REFLECTION in the mirror with resignation. Her eyes seemed to have sunk deep within their sockets, and her hair, only three years ago a deep and luxuriant brown, had faded to a lifeless gray. Around her eyes, crow's feet had taken hold and her forehead was creased with worry. And yet, even as she examined the deterioration, she felt no urge to fight it, but only a sense of relief that for her, the pain might soon be over.

It was The Boys who had done it to her.

She no longer thought of Jason as her son, nor of Randy Corliss as her foster son. To her, they had become The Boys. Strange, alien beings she neither knew nor trusted.

It had not been that way at first. At first they had been her children, both of them, with Randy Corliss filling the void in her life that had been left when Julie died. Even now she could remember the flood of emotion that had nearly overwhelmed her when she had gone to see Randy in his room at Eastbury Community Hospital.

He had lain still in bed, his eyes wide, his face expressionless. An image had flashed through her mind of pictures she had seen of children rescued from the concentration camps after World War II, their bodies emaciated, their hair fallen out from starvation, their eyes vacant, bodies and minds numbed by years of unspeakable abuse.

But Randy's skin had been ruddy that day, and the lack of hair had given his head an oddly inhuman appearance. And in his eyes, instead of the look of pain and sorrow that Sally had expected, there had been curiosity, and a certain strange detachment.

"They're dead, aren't they?" he had asked. "Mom and Dad got killed in the fire, didn't they?"

"Yes," she had said, sitting by his bed and taking his hand in hers. "I'm sorry. I'm so sorry, Randy."

"What's going to happen to me?"

At the time, Sally had attributed the question, and the lack of response to his parents' deaths, to shock. She had explained to him that she and Steve were going to take care of him, and that he and Jason would be like brothers now.

Randy had smiled, then gone to sleep.

That had been the beginning.

The next day, she and Steve had taken Randy home and begun the wait. Every moment of every day and night they kept the vigil, waiting for the moment when Jason or Randy would suddenly, with no warning whatever, stop breathing and die.

But it hadn't happened. First the days, then the weeks and months, had slipped by and the boys grew and appeared to thrive. Slowly, imperceptibly, Sally and Steve began to let their guard down. Instead of watching for the boys' deaths, they began planning for their lives. After the end of the first year, when Randy turned eleven, and Jason was just past ten, they took them to Mark Malone for their monthly examination. When he was done with the boys, Dr. Malone spoke to Steve and Sally in his office.

"They're remarkable in every way," he said. "They're both large for their age and unusually well developed. It seems almost as if the GT-active factor, as well as protecting them, allows them to mature more quickly than normal children."

"What does that mean?" Sally asked. "I mean, for them?"

"I'm not sure," Malone admitted. "It could mean nothing, but it could be a first sign of premature aging. It could be that while they'll live very healthy lives, they'll live short lives, even if the burn-out syndrome is never triggered. But that's just speculation," he assured them. "Frankly, with these boys, there's no way of telling what might happen. All we can do is wait and see."

The waiting had gone on for two more years. During those years the boys had grown closer and closer, their personalities taking on each other's traits, until both Sally and Steve had unconsciously fallen into the habit of speaking to them as if they were a single unit. What was told to one would be passed on to the other. The blame for things gone wrong that was assigned to one was assumed by the other. What Randy did, Jason did, and vice versa.

They had no friends, being sufficient unto themselves, but Sally and Steve were never sure whether it was merely that the boys had no need for outside stimulation or whether such stimulation had become unavailable to them.

There had been incidents.

The worst of them had been what Sally had come to think of as The Circus.

It had occurred after the Barnum & Bailey extravaganza had played in Boston, and all the children of the neighborhood had decided to duplicate the show. Most of them, in the end, had decided that being a clown was the better part of valor, but Jason and Randy, though not invited to participate, had provided the thrills.

Their slack-rope act had not bothered Sally, for she had watched them prepare it, worried at first that they might hurt themselves, but impressed in the end that they had had the foresight to learn the trick of balancing on a rope at a low level. Only when they had become confident of themselves had they begun raising the rope, until eventually both of them were able to walk it with ease at a height of ten feet.

She had not watched them rehearse the knife-throwing act, nor had she seen it. But she had heard about it.

The Circus had taken place in the Connors' backyard, and the last act had been Jason and Randy. In turn, each of the boys had stood against the wall of the Connors' garage, while the other threw six steak knives at him. First Jason had stood against the wall, while Randy hurled the evil-looking blades.

One by one, the blades had struck the garage, inches from the target, their handles quivering as their blades dug into the wood siding. When all six knives were surrounding him, Jason had stepped forward, taken a bow, then pulled the knives from the wall.

Then Randy took his place against the wall, his feet spread wide apart, his arms stretched out.

Jason stood ten feet away and aimed the first of the six knives. It whirled through the air and struck the wall between Randy's legs.

The second knife buried itself in the wall next to his left ear.

The third knife struck next to his right ear.

By now the children in the audience were screaming and cheering so loudly that Kay Connors had looked out the window to see what was happening.

She was in time to see the last three knives whirl, in quick succession, through the air.

Two of them struck Randy Corliss's hands, pinning them to the wall.

The third buried itself in Randy's stomach.

The happy cheering turned into terrified screams. Frozen in horror, Mrs. Connors stared woodenly through the window.

She watched Jason calmly go to Randy and yank loose the two knives that were pinning his hands. And then she watched as Randy himself, his face wreathed in happy smiles, pulled the third knife from his own belly.

An hour later, as she listened to Kay Connors relate the story, Sally had tried to remain calm.

"I still don't know how they did it," Kay had said when she was finished telling the tale. Her face was still pale from her fright, and her hands were trembling slightly. "And I don't want to know. But I'll tell you right now, Sally, I don't want those boys at my house again. They scared me nearly to death, and I don't even want to think about how the other children felt. The girls were all crying, and some of the boys too. I know Jason and Randy thought it was a joke, but it wasn't funny."

Sally, of course, had immediately realized that it had not been a trick at all. Jason had simply hurled the knives into his friend, and Randy, far from being seriously injured, had healed within minutes. By the time the screaming children had been sorted out and Kay Connors had gotten to Randy, there hadn't been even so much as a scar left to betray the secret of the "trick."

Four days later, two five-year-old boys had tried to duplicate the trick. One of them had nearly bled to death, but the other one was unhurt, apparently the beneficiary of the flip of the coin that had determined which of the two would be the first target. Sally had suspected differently. Though she could no longer be certain, she thought she remembered the name of the uninjured boy, Tony Phelps, from the list of children in Group Twenty-one.

It was after that incident that Sally had begun to wonder about the boys. They had listened to her quietly while she talked to them, first about the "stunt" they had pulled, which she knew had not been a stunt at all, then about the little boy who had almost died.

"But everybody's going to die," was Randy's only comment.

"Besides," Jason had added, "people who can get hurt shouldn't play our games. They should just do whatever we tell them to do."

"Do what you tell them?" Sally echoed. "Why should people do what you tell them?"

Jason had met her eyes. "Because we're special," he said. "We're special, and that makes us better than other people."

Sally had tried to explain to them that their inability to be hurt, or even to feel pain, did not make them better than other people. If anything, it meant that they had to be particularly careful of other people, because they might accidentally do something that would hurt someone else. The boys had only looked at each other and shrugged.

"We don't do anything by accident," Jason had said.

And so the wondering had begun, and, once more, the watching had begun. And slowly, Sally had come to realize that there was more to The Boys than the GT-active factor. There was a coldness about them, and an ever-increasing sense of their own superiority that was at first disturbing and eventually frightening.

Now Jason was twelve and Randy was thirteen, but they looked five years older.

And they did what they wanted, when they wanted.

Last night, very late, Sally had talked to Steve about them.

"They're not human," she had finished. "They're not human and they're dangerous."

Steve, who had listened quietly for over an hour, had shifted uneasily in his chair, "What do you suggest we do?" he asked.

Sally had swallowed, unsure whether she would be able to voice the idea that had been growing steadily in her mind for several months now. But it had to be voiced. It had to be brought out in the open and discussed. If it wasn't, she would surely lose her mind.

"I think we have to kill them."

Steve Montgomery had stared at his wife. As the import of what she had just said began to register on part of his mind, another part seemed to shift gears, to step back, as if unwilling even to accept the words Sally had uttered.

What's happened to her, that part of his mind had wondered. What's happened to the woman I married?

Sally, over the last three years, had become almost a stranger to him. He had seen the changes in her face, but more than that, he had felt the changes in her spirit. In many ways she seemed more like a hunted animal than anything else.

Hunted, or haunted?

And yet, he had slowly come to realize, what he now saw in his wife was a reflection of what he felt himself. He, too, had come to regard the boys as something apart from himself, something he could only barely comprehend, but was afraid of.

What, he had often wondered, would they grow up to be, if they grew up at all?

At first he had dismissed the question, but then, as time had moved on, and the boys had not died, he had forced himself to face it.

And the only answer he had come up with, time and time again, was that whatever they grew up to be, it would not be human.

And so he, too, had come to feel haunted. Haunted by the feeling that he was raising a new species of man, indistinguishable from other men, but different. Cold, unfeeling, impervious to pain.

Impervious to pain, and therefore impervious to suffering. How many of them were there, and what would they do when the time came, as it inevitably would, when they realized their powers? Steve Montgomery, like his wife, didn't know.

"All right," he had said last night.

Sally had stared at him, momentarily shaken by the ease with which he had apparently accepted her idea. "Is that all you have to say? Just all right?"

Steve had nodded. "Three years ago, when we talked to Paul Randolph, I found out that you'd been right about the children all along. And I made up my mind about something that day. I decided that from that moment on, where the children were concerned, I'd go along with any decision you made. But I've watched those boys too, Sally. Whatever they are, they aren't human. Randy Corliss is not our child, and never has been.

And neither is Jason. I'm not sure what they are, but I know what they're not." Then he repeated the words once again: "They're not human."

And so, earlier today, Sally had gone alone to see Mark Malone, and quietly explained to him what she wanted to do. He had listened to her, and for a long time after she had finished, had sat silently, apparently thinking.

"I need some time, Sally," he'd said at last. "I need some time to think about this."

"How much time?" Sally had asked. "This isn't something I've just made up my mind to, Mark. I've been thinking about it for a long time. The boys are growing up, and I'm afraid of them."

"Have you thought of sending them away to school?"

"Of course I have," Sally replied bitterly. "I've thought of everything, and in the end I always come down to the same thought. They're some kind of monsters, Mark, and they have to be destroyed. It's not myself I'm afraid for—it's everybody. Can't you understand that?"

And Mark, to her relief, had nodded his head. "But I'll still have to think about it," he'd told her. "I'm a doctor. My training is to save lives, not end them."

"I know," Sally whispered unhappily. "Believe me, I wish I could have done this without even talking to you. But I need your help. I—well, I'm afraid I haven't the slightest idea of how to"—she faltered, then made herself finish the sentence—"how to kill them."

Mark had led her to the door. "Let me call you in a couple of hours, Sally. I'll have to think about this thing, and I won't promise you anything. In fact, I wish you hadn't come here today."

And so she had come home. Now she sat in front of her mirror, staring at her strange reflection, recognizing her image, but not understanding the person she had become.

But it didn't matter. Nothing about her own life mattered anymore, not as long as The Boys were alive. Only after they were dead would she worry about herself again. And yet, what if there was no way to kill them? What then?

And then the phone rang.

"It's Mark, Sally. There's something called succinylcholine chloride. If you'll come down to my office, I'll explain it to you."

Late that night, Randy and Jason came downstairs to say good night to Sally and Steve. Sally accepted a kiss from each of them, and then, as they started up the stairs, called to them.

"I almost forgot. Dr. Malone called me today and gave me some medicine for you. He wanted you to have it just before you went to bed."

The boys looked at each other curiously. This was something new. Medicine? Neither of them had ever needed medicine before.

"What's it for?" Randy asked.

"I'm not sure," Sally replied, praying that there would be no trembling in her voice. "It's just some kind of a shot."

"I don't want it," Jason said. His face set into a stubborn expression that both Sally and Steve had come to know too well.

Steve rose from his chair. "You're going to have it, son," he said, keeping his voice carefully under control.

Jason glanced toward Randy, and as Steve moved toward the foot of the stairs, he could feel the boys sizing him up, weighing their combined bulk against his own strength. He started up the stairs. The two boys watched him warily, and Steve braced himself against a possible attack. But then, as he approached the boys, Randy spoke.

"Fuck it, Jason. What the hell can it do to us?"

It can kill you, Steve thought with sudden detachment. Sally had told him about the chemical Mark Malone had given her. It was called succinylcholine chloride, and its effect would be to attack their nervous systems, paralyzing them to the point where they would be unable to breathe. In the few minutes it would take the GT-active factor to overcome the damage, they would be deprived of air and suffocated. Yes, he thought once again, it can kill you.

But the boys had already turned the whole thing into a joke, and while Sally prepared the hypodermic needles, Steve followed them into their room, where they undressed and slid into their beds. Randy grinned at Jason. "You ever had a shot?"

"Not since I was a little kid. But I've had blood tests."

"So have I. That week I was at the Academy, they took tests all the time. You can't even feel it."

"Who's afraid of feeling it?" Jason laughed. "It just pisses me off that Dr. Malone thinks something's wrong with us."

"What does he know?" Randy sneered. And then Sally came in, carrying two needles. Jason looked at them, frowning.

"What is it?"

"Succinylcholine chloride," Sally replied. "Five hundred milligrams for each of you. Which of you wants to be first?"

The boys glanced at each other and shrugged. "I'll go first," Randy offered.

"All right." Sally took his arm and rolled up the left sleeve of his pajama top. The injection, Malone had told her, was to go directly into muscle. The upper arm muscle would be fastest, but any muscle would do. Holding the needle in her right hand, she grasped his arm with her left.

And suddenly she lost her nerve.

Over Randy's head, her eyes met Steve's. "I—I can't do it," she whispered. "I just can't do it."

Steve shook his head. "Don't look at me," he said quietly. "I can't do it either."

And suddenly the boys were laughing at them. "Let me have the needle, Aunt Sally," Randy said. "I'll do it myself. It's no big deal."

"We'll do it together," Jason offered. "On three, we'll each give ourselves a shot in the leg. Okay?"

Silently, feeling as though she were in some kind of a

338

dream, Sally gave each of the boys one of the needles. Then, as she and Steve looked on, they rolled up the legs of their pajamas, and, after Jason had counted to three, jabbed the needles into their legs, and pressed the plungers down. The liquid in the cylinders disappeared into the muscle of their thighs. When it was over, they pulled the needles out of their flesh, and looked at Sally, their eyes filled with contempt.

"Satisfied?" Jason asked.

Sally nodded and took the empty needles from her son. "Now go to bed," she said, her voice choking with all the emotions she had held so carefully in check ever since she had reached her decision. "Go to bed, and go to sleep."

She tucked them in and then did something she hadn't done for a long time. She leaned over and kissed each of them on the forehead. A moment later, leaving the lights on, she and Steve slipped out of the room.

When they were alone, Jason suddenly felt a strange sensation in his body.

"Randy?" he said.

"Hunh?"

There was an odd strangling sound to Randy's voice. Jason tried to sit up to look at his friend.

He couldn't.

All he could do, and even that was a struggle, was roll over and stare across at the other bed. Randy was lying on his back, his eyes wide open, struggling to breathe.

"Wha—what's wrong?" Jason managed to ask. "What—what did they give us?"

"Don't know," Randy gasped. "Can't—can't breathe."

And then, as the full force of the lethal dose of poison struck him, Jason fell back on his pillow, and slipped into unconsciousness.

Downstairs, Sally sat desolately on the sofa, trying to accept what she had just done.

"It was the right thing to do," she said over and over again. "It was the right thing to do and I had to do it."

Her tears overflowed and ran down her cheeks. "But, oh, God, Steve, I'll never be able to live with it. Never."

Steve nodded unhappily. "I keep telling myself they weren't human," he whispered. "But I guess I still don't believe it. Randy, maybe. But Jason? God, Sally, he was our son."

"He wasn't," Sally said, her voice rising. "He wasn't our son. He was something else, and he had to die. He *had* to, Steve. But what's going to happen to us now?"

Steve looked up and Sally felt a sudden calmness emanating from him. "We'll be charged," she heard him say, his voice sounding as if it were coming from a great distance away. "We'll be charged with the murder of our own son and our foster son. And no one will believe it wasn't murder, Sally."

"And they'll be right," Sally cried. Her hands clenched together and she twisted them in her lap as if she were fighting some physical pain that was threatening to overwhelm her. "Oh, God, Steve, they'll be right."

And then, in a moment of silence, they heard a sound from upstairs.

They heard a door open. There were footsteps.

A moment later Jason and Randy came slowly down the stairs and stepped into the living room, where they stood quietly facing Jason's parents.

And, since they were his parents, it was Jason who spoke.

"You can't kill us," he said softly, his eyes sparkling evilly. "Dr. Malone knows that. That's why he gave you that stuff. It was just another experiment. But don't ever try to kill us again, Mother. Because if you do, we will destroy you. Without even thinking about it, we will kill you."

Then, in perfect unison, they turned, and went back up the stairs.

ABOUT THE AUTHOR

JOHN SAUL's first novel, *Suffer the Children*, was published in 1977 to instant bestsellerdom. *Punish the Sinners, Cry for the Strangers, Comes the Blind Fury* and *When the Wind Blows* followed in succeeding years, each a national bestseller. Now, John Saul's trademark setting, a sleepy, isolated town where suddenly no one is safe, forms the background for this master storyteller's most exciting novel yet. John Saul lives in Bellevue, Washington, where he is at work on his next novel.

RELAX!
SIT DOWN
and Catch Up On Your Reading!

DON'T MISS
THESE CURRENT
Bantam Bestsellers

THRILLERS

Gripping suspense . . . explosive action . . . dynamic characters . . . international settings . . . these are the elements that make for great thrillers. And Bantam has the best writers of thrillers today—Robert Ludlum, Frederick Forsyth, Jack Higgins, Clive Cussler—with books guaranteed to keep you riveted to your seat.

Clive Cussler:

☐	22866	PACIFIC VORTEX	$3.95
☐	14641	ICEBERG	$3.95
☐	23328	MEDITERRANEAN CAPER	$3.95
☐	22889	RAISE THE TITANIC!	$3.95
☐	23092	VIXEN 03	$3.95
☐	20663	NIGHT PROBE!	$3.95

Frederick Forsyth:

☐	23105	NO COMEBACKS	$3.50
☐	23535	DAY OF THE JACKAL	$3.95
☐	23159	THE DEVIL'S ALTERNATIVE	$3.95
☐	23273	DOGS OF WAR	$3.95
☐	14757	THE ODESSA FILE	$3.50

Jack Higgins:

☐	23346	DAY OF JUDGMENT	$3.50
☐	23345	THE EAGLE HAS LANDED	$3.95
☐	22787	STORM WARNING	$3.50

Robert Ludlum:

☐	23232	THE ROAD TO GANDOLFO	$3.95
☐	11427	THE SCARLATTI INHERITANCE	$3.95
☐	22986	OSTERMAN WEEKEND	$3.95
☐	22812	THE BOURNE IDENTITY	$3.95
☐	20879	CHANCELLOR MANUSCRIPT	$3.95
☐	20783	HOLCROFT COVENANT	$3.95
☐	20720	THE MATARESE CIRCLE	$3.95

Buy them at your local bookstore or use this handy coupon for ordering:

Bantam Books, Inc., Dept. TH, 414 East Golf Road, Des Plaines, Ill. 60016

Please send me the books I have checked above. I am enclosing $_____ (please add $1.25 to cover postage and handling). Send check or money order —no cash or C.O.D.'s please.

Mr/Mrs/Miss _____

Address_____

City_____ State/Zip_____

TH—8/83

Please allow four to six weeks for delivery. This offer expires 12/83.